Praise for
THE SERPENT & DOVE TRILOGY

"Full of everything I love."
—SARAH J. MAAS, #1 *New York Times* bestselling author
of the A Court of Thorns and Roses series

"Decadent and dangerous."
—RENÉE AHDIEH, *New York Times* bestselling author
of the Wrath & the Dawn series

"A brilliant, unending roller-coaster ride."
—JODI PICOULT, *New York Times* bestselling author
of *Small Great Things* and *A Spark of Light*

THE SCARLET VEIL

SHELBY MAHURIN

HARPER

An Imprint of HarperCollins*Publishers*

Library of Congress Control Number: 2023934143
ISBN 978-0-06-341939-1

Typography by Jessie Gang
24 25 26 27 28   RTLO   10 9 8 7 6 5 4 3 2 1
Special edition, 2024

For Wren, *my sweet little bird*

PART I

Mieux vaut prévenir que guérir.
It is better to prevent than to heal.

PROLOGUE

It is a curious thing, the scent of memory. It takes only a little to send us back in time—a trace of my mother's lavender oil, a hint of my father's pipe smoke. Each reminds me of childhood in its own strange way. My mother applied her oil every morning as she stared at her reflection, counting the new lines on her face. My father smoked his pipe when he received guests. They frightened him, I think, with their hollow eyes and quick hands. They certainly frightened me.

But beeswax—beeswax will always remind me of my sister.

Like clockwork, Filippa would reach for her silver brush when our nursemaid, Evangeline, lit the candles each evening. The wicks would fill the nursery with the soft scent of honey as Filippa undid my braid, as she passed the boar bristles through my hair. As Evangeline settled into her favorite rose-velvet chair and watched us warmly, her eyes crinkling in the misty purple light of dusk.

The wind—crisp on that October night—rustled at the eaves, hesitating, lingering at the promise of a story.

"Mes choux," she murmured, stooping to retrieve her knitting needles from the basket beside her chair. Our family hound, Birdie, curled into an enormous ball at the hearth. "Have I told you the story of Les Éternels?"

As always, Pip spoke first, leaning around my shoulder to

frown at Evangeline. Equal parts suspicious and intrigued. "The Eternal Ones?"

"Yes, dear."

Anticipation fluttered in my belly as I glanced at Pip, our faces mere inches apart. Golden specks still glinted on her cheeks from our portrait lesson that afternoon. They looked like freckles. "Has she?" My voice lacked Evangeline's lyrical grace, Filippa's firm resolve. "I don't think she has."

"She definitely hasn't," Pip confirmed, deadly serious, before turning back to Evangeline. "We should like to hear it, please."

Evangeline arched a brow at her imperious tone. "Is that so?"

"Oh, please tell us, Evangeline!" Forgetting myself entirely, I leapt to my slippered feet and clapped my hands together. Pip— twelve years old to my paltry six—hastily snatched my nightgown, tugging me back to the armoire seat. Her small hands landed on my shoulders.

"Ladies do not shout, Célie. What would Pére say?"

Heat crept into my cheeks as I folded my own hands in my lap, immediately contrite. "*Pretty is as pretty does.*"

"Exactly." She returned her attention to Evangeline, whose lips twitched as she fought a smile. "Please tell us the story, Evangeline. We promise not to interrupt."

"Very good." With practiced ease, Evangeline slid her lithe fingers along the needles, weaving wool into a lovely scarf of petal pink. My favorite color. Pip's scarf—bright white, like freshly fallen snow—already rested in the basket. "Though you still have paint on your face, darling. Be a lamb and wash for me, will you?" She waited until Pippa finished scrubbing her cheeks before continuing. "Right, then. Les Éternels. They're born in the ground—cold as bone, and just as strong—without heart or soul or mind. Only impulse. Only *lust*." She said the word with unexpected relish. "The first one came to our kingdom from a faraway land, living in the shadows, spreading her sickness to the people here. Infecting them with her magic."

Pip resumed brushing my hair. "What kind of magic?"

My nose crinkled as I tilted my head. "What is *lust*?"

Evangeline pretended not to hear me.

"The worst kind of magic, darlings. The absolute *worst* kind." The wind rattled the windows, eager for the story, as Evangeline paused dramatically—except Birdie rolled over with a warbled howl at precisely the same moment, ruining the effect. Evangeline cut the hound an exasperated look. "The kind that requires blood. Requires *death*."

Pippa and I exchanged a covert glance.

"Dames Rouges," I heard her breathe at my ear, nearly indiscernible. "Red Ladies."

Our father had spoken of them once, the strangest and rarest of the occultists who plagued Belterra. He'd thought we hadn't heard him with the funny man in his study, but we had.

"What are you whispering?" Evangeline asked sharply, stabbing her needles in our direction. "Secrets are quite rude, you know."

Pip lifted her chin. She'd forgotten that ladies do not scowl either. "Nothing, Evangeline."

"Yes," I echoed instantly. "Nothing, Evangeline."

Her gaze narrowed. "Plucky little things, aren't you? Well, I should tell you that Les Éternels *love* plucky little girls like you. They think you're the sweetest."

The exhilaration in my chest twisted slightly at her words, and gooseflesh erupted down my neck at the stroke of my sister's brush. I scooted to the edge of my seat, eyes wide. "Do they really?"

"Of course they don't." Pip dropped her brush on the armoire with more force than necessary. With the sternest of expressions, she turned my chin to face her. "Don't listen to her, Célie. She *lies*."

"I most certainly do not," Evangeline said emphatically. "I'll tell you the same as my mother told me—Les Éternels stalk the streets by moonlight, preying on the weak and seducing the immoral. That's why we always sleep at nightfall, darlings, and always say our prayers." When she continued, her lyrical voice rose in cadence, as familiar as the nursery rhyme she hummed every evening. Her needles *click click click*ed in the silence of the room, and even the wind fell still to listen. "Always wear a silver cross, and always walk in pairs. With holy water on your neck and hallowed ground your feet. When in doubt, strike up a match, and burn them with its heat."

I sat up a little straighter. My hands trembled. "I always say my prayers, Evangeline, but I drank all of Filippa's milk at dinner while she wasn't looking. Do you think that made me sweeter than her? Will the bad people want to eat me?"

"Ridiculous." Scoffing, Pippa threaded her fingers through my hair to replait it. Though she was clearly exasperated, her touch remained gentle. She tied the raven strands with a pretty pink bow and draped it over my shoulder. "As if I'd ever let anything happen to you, Célie."

At her words, warmth expanded in my chest, a sparkling surety. Because Filippa never lied. She never snuck treats or played tricks or said things she didn't mean. She never stole my milk.

She would never let anything happen to me.

The wind hovered outside for another second—scratching at the panes once more, impatient for the rest of the story—before passing on unsatisfied. The sun slipped fully beneath the skyline as an autumn moon rose overhead. It bathed the nursery in thin silver light. The beeswax candles seemed to gutter in response, lengthening the shadows between us, and I clasped my sister's hand in the sudden gloom. "I'm sorry I stole your milk," I whispered.

She squeezed my fingers. "I never liked milk anyway."

Evangeline studied us for a long moment, her expression inscrutable as she rose to return her needles and wool to the basket. She patted Birdie on the head before blowing out the tapers on the mantel. "You are good sisters, both of you. Loyal and kind." Striding across the nursery, she kissed our foreheads before helping us into bed, lifting the last candle to our eyes. Hers gleamed with an emotion I didn't understand. "Promise me you'll hold on to each other."

When we nodded, she blew out the candle and made to leave.

Pip wrapped an arm around my shoulders, pulling me close, and I nestled into her pillow. It smelled like her—like summer honey. Like lectures and gentle hands and frowns and snow-white scarves. "I'll never let the witches get you," she said fiercely against my hair. "Never."

"And I'll never let them get *you*."

Evangeline paused at the nursery door and looked back at us with a frown. She tilted her head curiously as the moon slipped behind a cloud, plunging us into total darkness. When a branch clawed at our window, I tensed, but Filippa wrapped her other arm around me firmly.

She didn't know, then.

I didn't know either.

"Silly girls," Evangeline whispered. "Who said anything about witches?"

And then she was gone.

CHAPTER ONE

Empty Cages

I will catch this repugnant little creature if it kills me.

Blowing a limp strand of hair from my forehead, I crouch again and readjust the mechanism on the trap. It took *hours* to fell the willow tree yesterday, to plane the branches and paint the wood and assemble the cages. To collect the wine. It took hours *more* to read every tome in Chasseur Tower about lutins. The goblins prefer willow sap to other varieties—something about its sweet scent—and despite their crude appearance, they appreciate the finer things in life.

Hence the painted cages and bottles of wine.

When I hitched a cart to my horse this morning, loading it full of both, Jean Luc looked at me like I had lost my mind.

Perhaps I *have* lost my mind.

I certainly imagined the life of a huntsman—a hunts*woman*—being somewhat more significant than crouching in a muddy ditch, sweating through an ill-fitting uniform, and luring a crotchety hobgoblin away from a field with alcohol.

Unfortunately, I miscalculated the measurements, and the bottles of wine did not *fit* within the painted cages, forcing me to disassemble each one at the farm. The Chasseurs' laughter still lingers in my ears. They didn't care that I painstakingly learned to use a hammer and nails for this project, *or* that I mutilated my thumb in the process. They didn't care that I bought the gold paint with my own coin either. No, they saw only my mistake. My brilliant work reduced to kindling at our feet. Though Jean Luc hastily tried to help reassemble the cages as best we could—scowling at our brethren's witty commentary—an irate Farmer Marc arrived soon after. As a captain of the Chasseurs, Jean needed to console him.

And I needed to handle the huntsmen alone.

"Tragic." Looming over me, Frederic rolled his brilliant eyes before smirking. The gold in his chestnut hair glinted in the early sun. "Though they are *very* pretty, Mademoiselle Tremblay. Like little dollhouses."

"Please, Frederic," I said through gritted teeth, scrambling to collect the pieces in my skirt. "How many times must I ask you to call me Célie? We are all equals here."

"At least once more, I'm afraid." His grin sharpened to a knifepoint. "You are a lady, after all."

I stalked across the field and down the hill, out of sight—away from him, away from *all* of them—without another word. I knew it was pointless to argue with someone like Frederic.

You are a lady, after all.

Mimicking his asinine voice now, I finish the lock on the last cage and stand to admire my handiwork. Mud coats my boots. It stains six inches of my hem, yet a flicker of triumph still steals through my chest. It won't be long now. The lutins in Farmer Marc's barley will soon smell the willow sap and follow its scent. When they spy the wine, they will react impulsively—the books say lutins are impulsive—and enter the cages. The traps will swing shut, and we will transport the pesky creatures back to La Fôret des Yeux, where they belong.

Simple, really. Like stealing candy from a baby. Not that I'd *actually* steal candy from a baby, of course.

Exhaling a shaky sigh, I plant my hands on my hips and nod a bit more enthusiastically than natural. Yes. The mud and menial labor have most definitely been worth it. The stains will lift from my dress, and better yet—I'll have captured and relocated a whole burrow of lutins without harm. Father Achille, the newly instated Archbishop, will be proud. Perhaps Jean Luc will be too. Yes, this is *good*. Hope continues to swell as I scramble behind the weeds at the edge of the field, watching and waiting. This will be perfect.

This has to be perfect.

A handful of moments pass without movement.

"Come on." Voice low, I scan the rows of barley, trying not to fidget with the Balisarda at my belt. Though months have passed since I took my sacred vow, the sapphire hilt still feels strange and heavy in my hands. Foreign. My foot taps the ground impatiently. The temperatures have grown unseasonably warm for October, and a bead of sweat trickles down my neck. "Come on, come *on*. Where are you?"

The moment stretches onward, followed by another. Or perhaps three. Ten? Over the hill, my brethren hoot and holler at a joke I cannot hear. I don't know how they intend to catch the lutins—none cared to share their plans with me, the first and only woman in their ranks—but I also don't care. I certainly don't need their help, nor do I need an audience after the cage fiasco.

Frederic's condescending expression fills my mind.

And Jean Luc's embarrassed one.

No. I push them both away with a scowl—along with the weeds—climbing to my feet to check the traps once more. *I should never have used wine. What a stupid idea—*

The thought screeches to a halt as a small, wrinkled foot parts the barley. My own feet grow roots. Rapt, I try not to breathe as the brownish-gray creature—hardly the height of my knee—sets his dark, overlarge eyes on the bottle of wine. Indeed, everything about him appears to be a bit too . . . well . . . *too.* His head too large. His features too sharp. His fingers too long.

To be quite frank, he looks like a potato.

Tiptoeing toward the wine, he doesn't seem to notice me—or anything else, for that matter. His gaze remains locked on the dusty bottle, and he smacks his lips eagerly, reaching for it with those spindly fingers. The moment he steps into the cage, it shuts with a decisive *snap*, but the lutin merely clutches the wine to his chest and grins. Two rows of needle-sharp teeth gleam in the sunlight.

I stare at him for a beat, morbidly fascinated.

And then I can no longer help it. I smile too, tilting my head as I approach. He isn't anything like I thought—not repugnant at all, with his knobby knees and round cheeks. When Farmer Marc contacted us yesterday morning, the man raved about *horns* and *claws.*

At last, the lutin's eyes snap to mine, and his smile falters.

"Hello there." Slowly, I kneel before him, placing my hands flat on my lap, where he can see them. "I'm terribly sorry about this"—I motion my chin toward the ornate cage—"but the man who farms this land has requested that you and your family relocate. Do you have a name?"

He stares at me, unblinking, and heat creeps into my cheeks. I glance over my shoulder for any sign of my brethren. I might be wholly and completely ridiculous—and they would crucify me if they found me chatting with a lutin—but it hardly feels right to trap the poor creature without an introduction. "My name is Célie," I add, feeling stupider by the second. Though the books didn't mention language, lutins must communicate *somehow*. I point to myself and repeat, "Célie. *Say-lee.*"

Still he says nothing. If he's even a *he* at all.

Right. Straightening my shoulders, I seize the cage handle because I *am* ridiculous, and I should go check the other cages. But first— "If you twist the cork at the top," I murmur grudgingly, "the bottle will open. I hope you like elderberries."

"Are you talking to the lutin?"

I whirl at Jean Luc's voice, releasing the cage and blushing. "Jean!" His name comes out a squeak. "I—I didn't hear you."

"Clearly." He stands in the weeds where I hid only moments ago. At my guilty expression, he sighs and crosses his arms over his chest. "What are you doing, Célie?"

"Nothing."

"Why don't I believe you?"

"An excellent question. Why *don't* you believe—" But the lutin snakes out a hand before I can finish, snatching my own. With a shriek, I jerk and topple backward—not because of the lutin's *claws* but because of his *voice*. The instant his skin touches mine, the strangest vocalization echoes in my mind: *Larmes Comme Étoiles.*

Jean Luc charges instantly, unsheathing his Balisarda between one stride and the next.

"No, wait!" I fling myself between him and the caged lutin. "*Wait!* He didn't hurt me! He meant no harm!"

"Célie," Jean Luc warns, his voice low and frustrated, "he could be rabid—"

"*Frederic* is rabid. Go wave your knife at him." To the lutin, I smile kindly. "I beg your pardon, sir. What did you say?"

"He didn't *say* anything—"

I shush Jean Luc as the lutin beckons me closer, extending his hand through the bars. It takes several seconds for me to realize he wants to touch me again. "Oh." I swallow hard, not quite relishing the idea. "You—yes, well—"

Jean Luc grips my elbow. "Please tell me you aren't going to touch it. You have no idea where it's *been*."

The lutin gestures more impatiently now, and—before I can change my mind—I stretch out my free hand, brushing his fingertips. His skin there feels rough. Dirty. Like an unearthed root. *My name,* he repeats in an otherworldly trill. *Larmes Comme Étoiles.*

My mouth falls open. "Tears Like Stars?"

With a swift nod, he withdraws his hand to clutch his wine once more, glaring daggers at Jean Luc, who scoffs and tugs me backward. Near light-headed with giddiness, I twirl into his arms. "Did you hear him?" I ask breathlessly. "He said his name means—"

"They don't have names." His arms tighten around me, and he bends to look directly in my eyes. "Lutins don't speak, Célie."

My gaze narrows. "Do you think I'm a liar, then?"

Sighing again—*always* sighing—he sweeps a kiss across my

brow, and I soften slightly. He smells like starch and leather, the linseed oil he uses to polish his Balisarda. Familiar scents. Comforting ones. "I think you have a tender heart," he says, and I know he means it as a compliment. It *should* be a compliment. "I think your cages are brilliant, and I think lutins love elderberries." He pulls back with a smile. "I also think we should go. It's getting late."

"Go?" I blink in confusion, leaning around him to peer up the hill. His biceps tense a little beneath my palms. "But what about the others? The books said a burrow can hold up to twenty lutins. Surely Farmer Marc wants us to take them all." My frown deepens as I realize my brethren's voices have long faded. Indeed, beyond the hill, the entire farm has fallen still and silent, except for a lone rooster's crow. "Where"—something hot like shame cracks open in my belly—"where is everyone, Jean?"

He won't look at me. "I sent them ahead."

"Ahead *where?*"

"To La Fôret des Yeux." He clears his throat and steps backward, sheathing his Balisarda before smiling anew and bending to pick up my cage. After another second, he offers me his free hand. "Are you ready?"

I stare at it as a sickening realization dawns. He would have sent them ahead for only one reason. "They've . . . already trapped the other lutins, haven't they?" When he doesn't answer, I glance up at his face. He gazes back at me carefully, *warily*, as if I'm splintered glass, one touch away from shattering. And perhaps I am. I can no longer count the spider web cracks in my surface, can no longer *know* which crack will break me. Perhaps it'll be this one.

"Jean?" I repeat, insistent.

Another heavy sigh. "Yes," he admits at last. "They've already trapped them."

"*How?*"

Shaking his head, he lifts his hand more determinedly. "It doesn't matter. Your cages were a brilliant idea, and experience will come with time—"

"That isn't an answer." My entire body trembles now, but I cannot stop it. My vision narrows on the cleanly bronze skin of his hand, the brilliant sheen of his close-cropped dark hair. He looks perfectly composed—albeit uncomfortable—while my own strands stick to my neck in disarray and sweat trails down my back. Beneath the mud, my cheeks flush with exertion. With humiliation. "How did they trap an entire *burrow* of lutins in—" Another horrible thought dawns. "Wait, how long did it take them?" My voice rises in accusation, and I point a finger at his nose. "How long have you been waiting for me?"

Tears Like Stars manages to uncork the bottle, downing half the wine in one swallow. He stumbles as Jean Luc gently returns his cage to the ground. "Célie," Jean Luc says, his voice placating. "Don't do this to yourself. Your cage *worked*, and this one—this one even told you his name. That hasn't ever happened before."

"I thought lutins didn't have names," I snap. "And do not condescend to me. How did Frederic and the others trap the lutins? They're too fast to catch by hand, and—and—" At Jean Luc's resigned expression, my face falls. "And they *did* catch them by hand. Oh God." I pinch the bridge of my nose, each breath coming faster, sharper. My chest tightens to the point of pain. "I—I should've helped them, but these traps—" The golden paint leers at me now, tawdry and gauche. "I wasted everyone's time."

You are a lady, after all.

"No." Jean Luc shakes his head fiercely, gripping my filthy hands. "You tried something new, and it worked."

Pressure builds behind my eyes at the lie. All I've done for the last six months is try—try and try and *try*. I lift my chin, sniffing miserably while forcing a smile. "You're right, of course, but we shouldn't leave just yet. There could still be more out there. Perhaps Frederic missed a few—"

"This is the last of them."

"How can you *possibly* know if this is the last—?" I close my eyes as my mind finally catches up. When I speak again, my voice is quiet. Defeated. "Did you send him to me?" He does not answer, and his silence damns us both. My eyes fly open, and I seize his royal-blue coat, shaking it. Shaking *him*. "Did you catch him first, only to—to sneak over here and release him?"

"Don't be ridiculous—"

"*Did* you?"

Averting his gaze, he disentangles himself with firm hands. "I don't have time for this, Célie. I have an urgent council meeting before Mass this evening, and Father Achille has already sent word—he needed me back at the Tower hours ago."

"Why is that?" I try and fail to keep the tremor from my voice. "And what—what urgent council meeting? Has something happened?"

It is an old question. A tired one. For weeks now, Jean Luc has slipped away at odd moments, fervently whispering with Father Achille when he thinks I can't see. He refuses to tell me why they whisper under their breaths, why their faces grow darker each day.

They have a secret, the two of them—an *urgent* one—but whenever I ask about it, Jean Luc's answer remains the same: "It doesn't concern you, Célie. Please don't worry."

He repeats the words like clockwork now, jerking his chin toward our horses. "Come on. I've loaded the cart."

I follow his gaze to the cart in question, where he stacked my cages in neat rows while I chatted with Tears Like Stars. Nineteen in all. The twentieth he carries as he marches around the field without another word. Tears Like Stars—thoroughly drunk now—slumps against the bars, snoring softly in the late afternoon sunshine. To anyone else, the scene might seem charming. Quaint. Perhaps they would nod approvingly at the silver medal on my bodice, the diamond ring on my finger.

You don't need to wield a sword to protect the innocent, Célie. Jean Luc's old words drift back to me on the autumn breeze. *You've proven that more than anyone.*

Time has proven us all liars.

CHAPTER TWO

Pretty Porcelain, Pretty Doll

For the first time in six months, I skip evening Mass. When Jean Luc knocks promptly on my door at half past seven—our chaperone curiously absent—I feign sickness. Also a first. I don't lie as a rule, but tonight, I can't bring myself to care.

"I'm sorry, Jean. I—I think I caught a chill earlier." Coughing against my elbow, I lean into the dim corridor, careful to keep my body concealed. It wouldn't do for him to see me in my nightgown—ivory silk trimmed in lace. One of the many silly, impractical things I brought from my parents' home in West End. Though it doesn't protect me from the icy drafts of Chasseur Tower, it *does* make me feel more like myself.

Besides, Jean Luc insisted on a room with a fireplace when I moved into the dormitories.

My cheeks still heat at the memory. Never mind this is the *only* room with a fireplace in the dormitories.

"Are you all right?" His face twists with concern as he reaches through the gap to check my perfectly normal temperature. "Should I send for a healer?"

"No, no"—I clasp his hand, removing it from my forehead as casually as possible—"peppermint tea and an early night should do the trick. I just turned down the bed."

At the mention of my bed, he withdraws his hand like I've

scalded him. "Ah," he says, straightening and stepping back with an awkward cough. "That— I'm sorry to hear it. I thought maybe you'd want to—but—no, you should most definitely go to sleep." Casting a quick glance over his shoulder, he shakes his head at something I cannot see and clears the rasp from his throat. "If you don't feel better in the morning, just say the word. I'll delegate your responsibilities."

"You shouldn't do that, Jean." I lower my voice, resisting the urge to peer around him into the corridor. Perhaps a chaperone has accompanied him, after all. A heavy sort of disappointment settles over me at the thought, but of *course* he brought a chaperone along—as he should. I would never ask him to risk our reputations or our positions by visiting alone at night. "I can catalog the council library with a cough."

"Just because you *can* doesn't mean you should." He hesitates with a tentative smile. "Not when Frederic is perfectly healthy and knows his alphabet."

Swallowing the lump in my throat, I force myself to return his smile—because my failure with the lutins this morning wasn't his fault, not truly, and a chaperone for the next six months isn't either. Indeed, thanks to Jean Luc and our brethren, the lutins reached La Fôret des Yeux unharmed, and Father Marc will be able to harvest his barley in peace. Everyone wins.

Which means I must've inadvertently won too.

Right.

Throwing caution to the wind, I rest a light hand against his chest, where my engagement ring sparkles between us in the candlelight. "We both know you won't delegate my responsibilities if I stay in bed. You'll do them yourself—and you'll do them *beautifully*—but you can't keep covering for me." When I lean closer instinctively, he does too, his gaze falling to my lips as I whisper, "You aren't just my fiancé, Jean Luc. You're my captain."

He swallows hard, and the motion fills me with a peculiar sort of heat. Before I can act on it—like I'd even know *how* to act on it—his gaze flicks over his shoulder once more, and I imagine our chaperone crossing his arms with a scowl. Instead of a pointed cough, however, an amused voice fills the corridor.

An amused, *familiar* voice.

"Do you want us to leave?" The freckled face of Louise le Blanc—otherwise known as La Dame des Sorcières, or the Lady of the Witches—appears over Jean Luc's shoulder. With an impish grin, she raises her eyebrows at my expression. "You know what they say about . . . six being a crowd."

I blink at her in disbelief. "What do you mean *six*?"

"Nonsense," says another voice from behind her. "Seven is a crowd, not six."

If possible, Lou grins wider. "You speak rather definitively on the subject, Beauregard. Would you like to share with the class?"

"He probably *would* like that." My eyes widen further as Cosette Monvoisin, leader of the Dames Rouges—the smaller, deadlier faction of witches in Belterra—elbows her way past Jean Luc to stand before me. With a grudging sigh, Jean steps aside and flings the door open to reveal Beauregard Lyon, the *king* of all Belterra, and his half brother, Reid Diggory, standing behind him.

Well, Beau's half brother—and my first love.

My mouth nearly falls open at the sight of them. Once upon a time, I would've regarded each with suspicion and fear—*especially* Reid—but the Battle of Cesarine changed all of that. As if reading my thoughts, he lifts his hand in an awkward wave. "I told them we should've sent up a note first."

Of all the group, Reid alone remains without a formal title, but his reputation as the youngest-ever captain of the Chasseurs still precedes him. Of course, that was a long time ago. Before the battle. Before he found his siblings.

Before he discovered his magic.

My smile, however, isn't forced at all now. "Don't be ridiculous. It's *wonderful* to see everyone."

"Likewise." Swooping to kiss my cheek, Coco adds, "As long as you forbid Beau from telling tales of his previous exploits. Trust me, he would be the *only* one who likes them."

"Oh, I don't know." Lou stands on tiptoe to kiss my other cheek, and I cannot help it—instinctively, I engulf them both in a bone-crushing hug. "I quite enjoyed hearing about his rendezvous with the psellismophiliac," she finishes in a muffled voice.

Overwhelming warmth spreads from my chest to my extremities as I release them, as Beau scowls and flicks the back of Lou's head. "I never should've told you about him."

"No." She cackles with glee. "You shouldn't have."

They all turn to me then.

Though arguably four of the most powerful people in the entire kingdom—if not *the* most powerful—they stand in the cramped corridor outside my room as if—as if waiting for me to speak. I stare back at them for several clumsy seconds, unsure what to say. Because they've never visited me *here* before. The Church rarely allows visitors into Chasseur Tower, and Lou, Coco, and Reid—they have better reason than most to never step through our doors again.

Thou shalt not suffer a witch to live.

Though Jean Luc did his best to remove the hateful words after the Battle of Cesarine, their faint imprint still darkens the entrance to the dormitories. My brethren once lived by that scripture.

Lou, Reid, and Coco almost burned for it.

Nonplussed, I finally open my mouth to ask, "Would you like to come in?" just as the bell of Cathédral Saint-Cécile d'Cesarine tolls around us. That warmth in my chest only builds at the sound, and I beam at the four of them in equal measure. No. The *five* of them. Though Jean Luc glares at everyone in silent disapproval, he must've been the one to invite them, even if it meant skipping Mass. When the bell falls silent at last, I ask, "Am I correct in assuming no one plans to attend the service this evening?"

Coco smirks back at me. "We've all caught a chill, it seems."

"And we know just how to treat it." Winking, Lou withdraws a paper bag from her cloak and holds it aloft, shaking its contents with evident pride. PAN'S PATISSERIE gleams in bright golden letters beneath her fingers, and the heady scents of vanilla and cinnamon engulf the corridor. My mouth waters when Lou plucks a sticky bun from the bag and presses it into my hand. "They work rather well for a shitty day too."

"*Language*, Lou." Reid shoots her a sharp look. "We're still in a church."

In his own hands, he holds a pretty bouquet of chrysanthemums and pansies wrapped in pink ribbon. When I catch his gaze, he shakes his head with a small, exasperated smile and offers it to me over Coco's shoulder. Clearing his throat, he says, "You still like pink, right?"

"Who doesn't like pink?" Lou asks at the same time as Coco

pulls a deck of cards from her scarlet cloak.

"Everyone likes pink," she agrees.

"*I* don't like pink." Unwilling to be outdone, Beau presents with a flourish the bottle of wine he held hidden behind his back. "Now, pick your poison, Célie. Will it be the pastries, the cards, or the wine?"

"Why not all three?" Dark eyes sparkling with wicked humor, Coco knocks his bottle away with her cards. "And how do you explain the pillow on your bed if you don't like pink, Your Majesty?"

Undeterred, Beau forces her cards aside with the neck of his bottle. "My little sister embroidered that pillow for me, as you know very well." To me, he adds grudgingly, "And all three *have* been known to cure a soul ache."

A soul ache.

"That," I say ruefully, "is a lovely phrase."

Bristling, Jean Luc steps forward at last to seize both the deck of cards and the bottle of wine before I can choose either one. "Have you all gone mad? I didn't invite you up here to *gamble* and *drink*—"

Coco rolls her eyes. "Are they not drinking wine downstairs at this very moment?"

Jean Luc scowls at her. "It's different, and you know it."

"Keep telling yourself that, Captain," she says in her sweetest voice. Then she turns to me, gestures toward the confiscated cards and wine, and adds, "Consider this a prelude to your birthday festivities, Célie."

"If anyone has earned three days of debauchery, it's you." Though she's still grinning, Lou's expression softens slightly as she continues. "However, if you'd rather be alone tonight, we completely understand. Just say the word, and we'll leave you to it."

With the flick of her wrist and the sharp scent of magic, a cup replaces the sticky bun in my hand, and steam curls in perfect spirals from freshly steeped peppermint tea. With another flick, a glass flagon of honey appears in place of Reid's flowers. "For your throat," she says simply.

I glance down at them in wonder.

Though I've seen magic before, of course—both the good and the bad—it never ceases to amaze me.

"I don't want you to leave." The words spill from me too quickly, too eagerly, but I can't bring myself to pretend otherwise, instead lifting the tea and honey with a helpless shrug. "I mean—er, thank you, but I'm suddenly feeling much better."

An evening of cards and pastries is *exactly* what I need after this wretched day, and I want to kiss Jean Luc square on the lips for offering it—except, of course, that I've just been horribly rude by refusing Lou's gifts. Swiftly, I lift the teacup and swallow an enormous mouthful of the scalding liquid instead.

It blisters my throat on contact, and I nearly choke as the others sweep into the room.

Jean Luc thumps my back in concern. "Are you all right?"

"*Fine.*" Gasping, I thrust the teacup onto my desk, and Lou pulls out a chair and forces me into it. "I just burned my tongue. Nothing to worry about—"

"Don't be ridiculous," she says. "How can you properly enjoy chocolate éclairs with a burnt tongue?"

I eye the patisserie bag hopefully. "You brought chocolate—?"

"Of course I did." Her gaze flicks to Jean Luc, who hovers

behind me with a rather mutinous expression. "I even brought canelé, so *you* can stop scowling at me now. If memory serves, you rather like rum," she adds with a smirk.

Jean shakes his head vehemently. "I do not *like* rum."

"Keep telling yourself that, Captain." With a sharp thumbnail, Coco pricks the tip of her pointer finger, drawing blood, and the scent of magic engulfs us once more. Unlike Lou and her Dames Blanches, who channel their magic from the land, Coco and her kin hold it within their very bodies. "Here." She dabs the blood upon my own finger before pouring a drop of honey atop it. "Lou is right—nothing ruins everything like a burnt tongue."

I don't look at Jean Luc as I lift the blood and honey to my lips. He won't approve, of course. Though the Chasseurs have made leaps and bounds in their ideology—led in no small part by Jean Luc—magic still makes him uncomfortable at the best of times.

The instant Coco's blood touches my tongue, however, the blisters in my mouth heal.

Amazing.

"Better?" Jean Luc asks in a murmur.

Seizing his hand and pulling him away from the others, I smile so hard that my cheeks threaten to burst. "Yes." I drop my voice to a whisper and gesture toward the desk, where Lou begins distributing pastries. Two for her, of course, and one for everyone else. "Thank you, Jean—for all of this. I know it isn't typically how you spend your evenings, but I've *always* wanted to learn how to play tarot." I squeeze his fingers in palpable excitement now. "It really can't be *such* a sin to gamble among friends, can it? Not when Lou brought canelé just for you?" Before he can answer, perhaps *fearing* his answer, I twirl in his arms and rest my head against his chest. "Do you think she knows how to play tarot? Do you think she'll teach us? I've never understood the trick-taking aspect, but between the two of us, surely we can figure it—"

Jean Luc, however, gently disentangles our bodies. "I have no doubt you will."

I blink in confusion—then cross my arms quickly, cheeks warm. In all the excitement, I forgot that I still wear only a night-gown. "What do you mean?"

Sighing, he straightens his coat in an almost subconscious gesture, and my eyes instinctively follow the movement, landing on a peculiar lump in his chest pocket. Small and rectangular in shape, it appears to be some sort of . . . book.

Odd.

Jean Luc rarely visits me in the council library, and I've never considered him to be much of a reader.

Before I can ask, however, his gaze shies away from mine, and he says quietly, "I . . . can't stay, Célie. I'm sorry. I have business to finish for Father Achille."

Business to finish for Father Achille.

It takes a full second for the words to penetrate the haze of my thoughts, but when they do, my heart seems to shrink several sizes in my chest. Because I recognize that cloud of regret in his eyes. Because he won't answer even if I *do* ask, and because I can't bear the thought of one more secret between us. One more rejection.

An awkward silence descends between us instead.

"He expects you to finish this business during Mass?" I ask softly.

Jean Luc rubs the back of his neck in obvious discomfort. "Well, er—no. He thought I'd be attending the service this evening, actually, but he'll understand—"

"So you have at least an hour and a half before he expects you to finish anything." When he still says nothing, I snatch a robe from its hook beside the door, lowering my voice while Lou makes a show of admiring my secondhand jewelry box. Coco agrees with her loudly, and Beau crinkles the patisserie bag before tossing it at Reid's head. "Please . . . can your business not wait until Mass is over?" Then—unable to stand still for a second longer—I catch his hand again, determined to keep the pleading note from my voice. I will not ruin this night with an argument, and I won't let him ruin it either. "I miss you, Jean. I know you're incredibly busy with Father Achille, but I'd . . . like to spend more time together."

He stills in surprise. "You would?"

"Of course I would." I grasp his other hand now too, lifting both to my chest and cradling them there. Right against my heart. "You're my fiancé. I want to share everything with you, including a chocolate éclair and our first game of tarot. Besides," I add weakly, "who else will tell me if Lou tries to cheat?"

He casts another disapproving look in our friends' direction. "We shouldn't be playing tarot at all." With a long-suffering sigh, he brushes a chaste kiss against my knuckles before lacing his fingers through mine. "But I can never tell you no."

The sweet scents of chocolate and cinnamon seem to spoil at the lie, and the honey on my tongue tastes abruptly bitter. I try to ignore both, try to focus on the indecision in Jean Luc's gaze. It means he wants to spend time with me too. I *know* he does. "So your business can wait?" I ask him.

"I *suppose* it can wait."

Straining to smile, I kiss his hands once, twice, three times before releasing him to tighten my robe. "Have I told you today what a *perfect* fiancé you are?"

"No, but feel free to tell me again." Chuckling, he leads me toward the others, plucking the most decadent of the éclairs from the pile and handing it to me. He doesn't take a bite, however. He doesn't claim a canelé either. "You'll be my partner," he says, matter-of-fact.

The éclair feels cold in my hand. "You know how to play tarot?"

"Lou and Beau *might* have taught me on the road. You know"—he clears his throat as if embarrassed, shrugging—"when we shared that bottle of rum."

"Oh."

Lou claps her hands together, startling us both, and I nearly drop my éclair in her lap. "He was complete and utter shit," she says, "so never fear, Célie—we'll have you trouncing him in no time."

As if on cue, faint music rises from the sanctuary below, and the light flickers with a great *boom* of the pipe organ. Jean Luc casts me a quick look when I reach reflexively to steady the nearest candle. A dozen more litter every flat surface of my room. They burn atop my ivory nightstands, my bookshelf, my armoire, competing with the light of the fireplace, where a handful more burn along the mantel. Anyone on the street outside would think they gazed upon a second sun, but not even the sun shines bright enough for me now.

I do not like the dark.

As children, Filippa and I would cling to each other beneath the blanket, giggling and imagining what monsters lived in the darkness of our room. Now I am no longer a child, and I *know* what monster lurks in the darkness—I know the wet feel of it on my skin, the putrid scent of it in my nose. It doesn't matter how often I scrub, how much perfume I wear. The darkness smells of rot.

I take an enormous bite of éclair to calm the sudden spike of my pulse.

Only an hour and a half remains to eat pastries and play tarot with my friends, and nothing, *nothing*, will ruin the evening for me—not Jean Luc's secrets, and certainly not my own. Both will still be waiting for me in the morning.

Our stomachs will be fine, Célie. We'll all be fine.

We'll all be fine.

You should show your scars, Célie. They mean you survived.

They mean you survived.

I survived I survived I survived—

Raising my brows at Lou, I say, "You have to promise not to cheat." Then—on second thought—I turn to Beau as well, pointing the éclair at his nose. "*And* you."

"Me?" He swats it away in mock affront. "When everyone knows *Reid* is the cheater in the family?"

Low laughter rumbles through Reid's chest as he settles on the edge of my bed. "I never cheat. You're just terrible at cards."

"Just because no one ever catches you," Beau says, dragging a chair over from the corner of the room, "doesn't mean you never cheat. There's a difference."

Reid shrugs. "I suppose you'll just have to catch me, then."

"*Some* of us aren't privy to magic—"

"He doesn't use magic, Beau," Lou says without glancing up,

carefully cutting the deck. "We tell him your cards when you aren't looking."

"Excuse me?" Beau's eyes threaten to pop from his head. "You *what?*"

After nodding sagely while removing her boots, Coco perches on the bed next to Reid. "We consider it a win for us all. Célie, you're *my* partner," she adds as Jean Luc slips out of his coat. When he drapes it over the back of Lou's chair, the book in his pocket hangs lower than the rest. I try not to look at it. I try not to think. When Jean opens his mouth to protest, Coco lifts a hand to silence him. "No arguments. After all, the two of you will be partners for the rest of your lives."

Though I force sweet laughter up my throat, I can't help but think how wrong she is.

A partnership implies trust, but Jean Luc will never tell me his business with Father Achille, and I—

I will never tell him what happened in my sister's casket.

The nightmare starts as it always does.

A storm rages outside—the cataclysmic sort of storm that shakes the earth, that overturns houses and uproots trees. The oak in our own backyard splinters in two after a lightning strike. When half of it crashes against our bedroom wall—nearly tearing a hole in the roof—I bolt to Pippa's bed and dive beneath the covers. She welcomes me with open arms.

"Silly little Célie." Crooning, she strokes my hair as lightning flashes all around us, but her voice is not *her* voice at all. It belongs to someone else entirely, and her fingers—they stretch to an unnatural length and contort at the knuckles, seizing my scalp and crackling with energy. Trapping me in her porcelain arms. We're nearly identical, Pip and I, like black-and-white nesting dolls. "Are you frightened, sweeting? Does the magic scare you?" Though I lurch backward, horrified, she tightens her grip, leering with a too-wide smile. It extends beyond her face. "It *should* scare you, yes, because it could kill you if I let it. Would you like that, sweeting? Would you like to die?"

"N-No." The word slips from my lips like a script, like an endless loop I can't escape. The room begins to spin, and I can't see, can't *breathe*. My chest constricts to a pinpoint. "P-P-Please—"

"P-P-*Please*." Sneering derisively, she lifts her hands, but they no longer hold lightning. Marionette strings dangle from each finger instead. They attach to my head, my neck, my shoulders, and when she rises from the bed, I go with her, helpless. A Balisarda appears in my hand. *Worthless* in my hand. She floats to the floor of our nursery, beckoning me closer, drifting to the painted wooden house at the end of my bed. "Come here, sweeting. Such a lovely little doll."

At her words, my feet teeter—*tink, tink, tink*ing with each step— and when I look down, I cannot scream. My mouth is porcelain. My skin is glass. Beneath her emerald gaze, my body begins to contract until I topple over, my cheek cracking against the rug. My Balisarda turns to tin. "Come here," she croons from above me. "Come here, so I may shatter you."

"P-Pippa, I d-d-don't want to p-play anymore—"

With a sinister laugh, she bends in slow motion, and lightning strikes her raven hair so it flashes horrifying white. *Pretty porcelain, pretty doll, your pretty clock doth start. Come rescue her by midnight, or I shall eat her heart.*

With the flick of her finger, I shatter into a thousand pieces, the shards of my eyes soaring into the dollhouse, where there is no lightning, no thunder, no painted faces or porcelain feet.

Here, there is only darkness.

It presses into my nose, my mouth, until I choke on it—on rotting flesh and sickly-sweet honey, on the brittle strands of my sister's hair. They coat my mouth, my tongue, but I can't escape them. My fingers are bloody and raw. Broken. My nails are gone, replaced by splinters of wood. They protrude from my skin as I claw at the lid of her rosewood casket, as I sob her name, as I sob Reid's name, as I scream and scream until my vocal cords fray and snap.

"No one is coming to save us." Pip turns her head toward me slowly, unnaturally, her beautiful face sunken and *wrong*. I shouldn't be able to see in this darkness, but I can—I *can*, and half of it is missing. With a sob, I slam my eyes shut, but she lives beneath my eyelids too. "At least you're here now," she whispers. "At least we didn't die alone."

Mariée . . .

Tears course down my cheeks. They mingle with my blood, with my sick, with *her*. "*Pip*—"

"Our stomachs will be fine, Célie." She touches a skeletal hand to my cheek. "We'll all be fine."

Then she buries that hand in my chest, wrenching out my heart and eating it.

CHAPTER THREE

The Straw Man

The next morning, it feels like I've swallowed glass as I creep through the armory, careful to keep my footsteps light and my coughs quiet—because even Lou's tea cannot heal a night of screams. The sun hasn't yet risen, and my brethren haven't yet descended. With any amount of luck, I'll finish my training session before they arrive for theirs—in and out without an audience.

Jean Luc assured me I wouldn't need training in the traditional sense, but clearly, I can't serve as a huntsman without it.

The other Chasseurs waste no time with books and traps.

I run cold fingers over colder weaponry, almost nicking myself in the darkness. Storm clouds shroud the pale gray light of dawn through the windows. It'll soon rain. Another excellent reason to get on with this. Seizing a lance at random, I nearly wake the dead when it slips from my grip and clatters to the stone floor.

"Christ's bones." I hiss the words, swooping low to retrieve it and struggling to lift the awkward, bulky thing back to the table. How *anyone* can wield such an instrument is beyond me. My eyes dart to the door, to the corridor beyond. If I strain, I can just hear the low voices and gentle sounds of servants in the kitchen, but no one comes to investigate. They don't come at night either—not the servants, not the huntsmen, and not the captain. We all pretend not to hear my screams.

Flustered now—inexplicably agitated—I choose a more sensible staff instead. My Balisarda remains tucked safely away upstairs.

I certainly don't need to *stab* anything today.

With one last glance behind me, I tiptoe to the training yard, where straw men loom along the wrought iron fence, leering at me. Notched wooden posts and archery targets join them, as well as a great stone table in the center. A striped awning shields it from the elements. Jean Luc and Father Achille often stand beneath it, speaking low and furtive about those things they refuse to share.

It doesn't concern you, Célie.

Please don't worry.

Except *nothing* seems to concern me, according to Jean Luc, and I *do* worry—I worry enough to avoid my brethren, to sneak into the training yard at five o'clock in the morning. After my first bout in the yard all those months ago, I quickly realized my skills as a huntsman lay . . . elsewhere.

Like building traps?

Rubbing my eyes, I scowl and sidle up to the first of the straw men.

If my dream last night proved anything, it's that I cannot go home. I cannot go back. I can only go forward.

"Right." I narrow my eyes at the unpleasant effigy, widening my stance as I've seen men do. My skirt—heavy blue wool—blows slightly in the wind. Rolling my neck, I hold the staff out in front of me with both hands. "You can do this, Célie. It's simple." I nod and bounce on the balls of my feet. "Remember what Lou told you. Eyes"—I swipe my stick for good measure—"ears"—I swipe again, harder this time—"nose"—another swipe—"and groin."

Mouth twisting determinedly, I lunge with a vicious jab,

prodding the man in the stomach. The straw doesn't give, however, and my momentum drives the opposite end of the staff into *my* stomach instead, knocking the wind from me. I double over and rub the spot gingerly. Bitterly.

Applause sounds from the armory door. I almost miss it amidst the rumble of thunder overhead, but the laughter—I can't mistake that. It belongs to *him*. Cheeks blazing crimson, I whirl to find Frederic strolling toward me, flanked on either side by a handful of Chasseurs. He smirks and continues to applaud, each clap of his hands slow and emphatic. "Bravo, mademoiselle. That was brilliant." His companions chuckle as he slings an arm across my straw man's shoulders. He doesn't wear his coat this morning, just a thin linen shirt against the chill. "Much better than last time. A marked improvement."

Last time I tripped on my hem and nearly broke my ankle.

Thunder reverberates around us once more. It echoes my black mood. "Frederic." I stoop stiffly to retrieve my staff. Though large in my hand, it looks small and insignificant compared with the longsword in his. "How are you this morning? I trust you slept well?"

"Like a babe." He grins and plucks the staff from me when I move to turn away. "I must admit that I'm curious, though. What are you doing here, Mademoiselle Tremblay? It didn't sound as if you slept well."

So much for pretending.

Gritting my teeth, I struggle to keep my voice even. "I'm here to train, Frederic, same as you. Same as all of you," I add, casting my brethren a pointed look. They don't bother to avert their gazes, to blush or busy themselves elsewhere. And why should they? I'm their greatest source of entertainment.

"*Are* you?" Frederic's grin stretches wider as he examines my staff, rolling it between his calloused fingers. "Well, we hardly train with shoddy old staffs, mademoiselle. This scrap of wood won't debilitate a witch."

"The witches don't *need* to be debilitated." I lift my chin to glare at him. "Not anymore."

"No?" he asks, arching a brow.

"*No.*"

A Chasseur across the yard—a truly unpleasant man by the name of Basile—drops from the top of a notched post. He raps his knuckles against it before calling, "Only two scraps of wood will do that! A stake and a match!" He guffaws as if he's just told an enormously funny joke.

I glare at him, unable to bite my tongue. "Don't let Jean Luc hear you."

Now he does avert his gaze, muttering petulantly, "Take it easy, Célie. I didn't mean anything by it."

"Oh, how silly of me. You're hilarious, of course."

Chuckling, Frederic tosses my staff to the mud. "Don't worry, Basile. Jean Luc isn't here. How could he know unless someone tells him?" He flips his longsword and catches it by the blade before thrusting the handle toward me. "But if you really want to train with us, *Célie*, by all means, I'd like to help." Lightning forks over Saint-Cécile, and he raises his voice to be heard over the thunder. "We all would, wouldn't we?"

Something stirs in his eyes at the question.

Something stirs in the yard.

I take a tentative step backward, glancing at the others, who stalk steadily closer. Two or three have the decency to look uncomfortable now. "That—that won't be necessary," I say, forcing a deep breath. Forcing calm. "I can just spar with the straw man—"

"Oh, no, Célie, that won't do." Frederic shadows my steps until my back presses into another straw man. Panic skitters up my spine.

"Leave her alone, Frederic." One of the others, Charles, shakes his head and steps forward. "Let her train."

"Jean Luc will crucify us if you hurt her," his companion adds. "I'll spar with you instead."

"Jean Luc"—Frederic speaks smoothly, casually, unperturbed except for the hard glint in his eyes—"knows his pretty little fiancée doesn't belong here. What do *you* think, Célie?" He offers me the longsword once more, tilting his head. Still grinning. "Do you belong here?"

I can hear his unspoken question, can *see* it reflected in all their eyes as they watch us.

Are you a huntsman, or are you the captain's pretty little fiancée?

I'm both, I want to snarl at them. But they won't hear me, perhaps *cannot* hear me, so I straighten my shoulders instead, meeting Frederic's gaze and wrapping my fingers around his longsword. "Yes." I bite the word, hoping he hears the snap of my teeth. Hoping they *all* hear it. "I do happen to belong here. Thank you for asking."

With a derisive laugh, he releases the blade.

Unable to bear its weight, I stagger forward, nearly impaling myself as my hem snares my feet, and the sword and I tumble toward the ground. He catches my elbow with a beleaguered sigh, leaning close and lowering his voice. "Just admit it, ma belle. Wouldn't you prefer the library?"

I stiffen at the diminutive.

"No." Wrenching my arm away, I straighten my skirt and smooth my bodice, eyes and cheeks hot. I point to the longsword and struggle to keep my voice steady. "I *would*, however, prefer a different weapon. I can't use that one."

"Obviously."

"Here." Charles, who drifted to my side without notice, offers me a small dagger. The first drop of rain lands upon its needle-thin blade. "Take this."

Before I joined the Chasseurs, I might've lingered on the smile lines around his eyes, the gallantry of such a gesture. The compassion of it. I would've imagined him as a knight in shining armor, incapable of associating with the likes of *Frederic*. I would've imagined the same for myself—or perhaps imagined myself as a maiden locked in a tower. Now I resist the impulse to curtsy, inclining my head instead. "Thank you, Charles."

With another deep breath, I turn toward Frederic, who twirls the longsword between his palms. "Shall we begin?" he asks.

CHAPTER FOUR

Our Girl

When I nod and lift my dagger, he flicks his wrist out casually and knocks my blade to the ground. "First lesson: you cannot use a dagger against a longsword. Even *you* should know that. You certainly spend enough time poring over our old manuscripts—or do you only read fairy stories?"

I snatch my dagger from the mud, firing up instantly. "I cannot *lift* the longsword, you insufferable cretin."

"And how is that my problem?" He circles me now, like a cat with a mouse, while the others settle in for the show. Charles watches us warily. His companion has disappeared. "Have you sought to improve your physical strength? How will you apprehend a rogue loup garou if you cannot even lift a sword? Will you even *want* to apprehend them, I wonder, or will you call them your friends?"

"Don't be ridiculous," I snap. "Of course I will if the situation calls—"

"It calls for it."

"You're living in the past, Frederic." My knuckles whiten around the hilt of my dagger, and I want nothing more than to bash him over the head with it. "The Chasseurs have changed. We no longer need to *debilitate* or *apprehend* those who are different—"

"You're naive if you think your friends saved the world, Célie. Evil still lives here. Perhaps not in the hearts of *all*, but in the hearts of some. Though the Battle of Cesarine changed many things, it did not change that. The world still needs our brotherhood." He plunges his longsword into the chest of the straw man nearest us, where it quivers like a lightning rod. "And so our brotherhood continues. Come. Pretend I'm a werewolf. I've just gorged on a farmer's cattle and feasted on his chickens." Spreading his arms wide with the air of a showman, he says, "Subdue me."

The rain begins to fall in earnest as I stare at him. As I roll up my sleeves to stall for time.

Because I don't know the first thing about subduing a werewolf.

Eyes, ears, nose, and groin. Lou's laughter cuts through the spiraling panic of my thoughts. She visited me in the training yard on the day after my initiation—on the day Jean Luc decided neither of us should ever visit the training yard again. *It doesn't matter who you're up against, Célie—everyone has a groin somewhere. Find it, kick as hard as you can, and get the hell out of there.* I square my shoulders as Basile starts to jeer, widening my stance and lifting my dagger once more.

More Chasseurs have trickled into the yard now. They watch us with unabashed curiosity.

I can do this.

When I lunge for his eyes, however, Frederic catches my wrist easily, twirling me in a sick pirouette and forcing my face into the straw man. Lights pop behind my eyes. He holds me there longer than necessary—with more force than necessary—rubbing my cheeks in the thatch until I nearly scream at the injustice of it all.

Thrashing wildly, I elbow him in the stomach, and he relents with a mocking smile. "Those doe eyes give you away, mademoiselle. They're too expressive."

"You're a *pig*," I snarl.

"Hmm. Emotional too." He sidesteps when I swing wildly for his ear, missing completely and sliding a little in the mud. "Just admit you shouldn't be here, and I will gladly forfeit. You may return to your dresses and your books and your *fireplace* while I return to our cause. That's our girl," he croons as I push soaked hair away from my brow, struggling to see. "Admit you aren't equipped to help us, and we'll send you on your merry way."

"Though I sympathize with your plight, Frederic—truly—I am not *your girl*, and I pity any woman who is."

He knocks me to the ground when I take a flying leap at his nose. I land hard, coughing, trying not to flinch or retch. Those shards in my throat stab deeper, as if they're trying to draw blood. *Silly little Célie*, Morgane still croons. *Such a lovely little doll.*

"Come now." Rolling up his sleeves, Frederic crouches and gestures to my uniform. To my surprise, the black ink of a tattoo marks the skin of his inner forearm. Though I can just see the first two letters—*FR*—the rain renders his shirt nearly translucent, revealing the shape of a name. "Does it not feel like you're playing dress-up?" he asks.

Come here, so I may shatter you.

"As opposed to *what*?" I shove at him, gritting my teeth, but he remains immovable. "Tattooing my name on my arm, so no one forgets who I am?"

Voices erupt from the armory door before he can answer, and we turn in unison—Frederic poised above me, my body supine below—as Jean Luc strides into the training yard, accompanied by three women in powder-blue coats. *Initiates.* Though the rain has thickened to a downpour, Jean's eyes find mine immediately, widening for a fraction of a second. Then his expression darkens. His mouth twists as another bolt of lightning strikes the cathedral, as Charles's companion appears at his shoulder. "What the hell is going on here?" he asks, already stalking toward us.

Frederic doesn't move except for a pleasant smile. "Nothing to report, I'm afraid. Just a little friendly sparring."

Jean Luc unsheathes his Balisarda with thinly veiled menace. "Good. Let's spar, then."

"Of course, Captain." Frederic nods amicably. "As soon as we've finished."

"You *are* finished."

"No, we're not." I pant the words, jerking my head side to side, splattering mud in all directions. Though water fills my ears, a terrible ringing sound remains. My vision narrows on Frederic's smug expression, and my hands curl into fists. "Let me finish this, Jean."

"*Let me finish this, Jean,*" Frederic mimics, too soft for anyone else to catch. Chuckling, he brushes a strand of hair from my eyes. The gesture is too personal, too *private*, and my skin crawls with awareness as Jean Luc shouts something I cannot hear. The ringing sound in my ears intensifies. "Admit that you embarrass him, and I'll let you go."

It doesn't matter who you're up against, Célie—everyone has a groin somewhere.

I react instinctively, *viciously*, kicking the soft flesh between his legs with a satisfying *crunch*.

His eyes fly wide, and perhaps I've miscalculated because he doesn't topple backward—he topples *forward*, and I can't scramble away before he lands on top of me, howling and cursing and wrenching the dagger from my hand. He presses it to my throat in blind fury. "You little *bitch*—"

Jean Luc seizes him by the collar and launches him across the training yard, his eyes as black as the sky overhead. Lightning flashes all around us. "How dare *you* assault one of our own? And Célie Tremblay at that?" He doesn't allow Frederic to slink away, instead charging after him, slamming him into the nearest archery target. Despite Frederic's scowl, despite his *size*, Jean Luc shakes him roughly. "Do you have any idea what she's done for this kingdom? Do you have any idea what she's *sacrificed*?" Dropping Frederic like a sack of potatoes, he appeals to the rest of the training yard now, pointing his Balisarda in my direction. I climb hastily to my feet. "This woman brought down *Morgane le Blanc*— or do you no longer remember our Dame des Sorcières of old? Have you already forgotten her reign of terror in this kingdom? The way she cut down man, woman, and child in her mad quest for vengeance?" He speaks again to Frederic, whose lip curls as he bitterly wipes the mud from his coat. "Well? *Have* you?"

"I haven't forgotten," he snarls.

The Chasseurs stand frozen throughout the yard. They dare not move. They dare not *breathe*.

The initiates still huddle together near the armory, wide-eyed and soaked through. Their faces are unfamiliar. New. I stand taller for them—and also for *me*. Though humiliation still burns in my chest, a tendril of pride unfurls as well. Because Lou and I *did* bring down Morgane le Blanc last year, and we did it together. We did it for good.

"Excellent." Jean Luc sheathes his Balisarda roughly as I creep to his side. He does not look at me. "If I ever see anything like this again," he promises us, his voice lower now, barely discernible, "I'll personally appeal to Father Achille for the perpetrator's immediate dismissal from the Chasseurs. We are better than this."

Frederic spits in disgust as Jean Luc takes my hand, as he leads me past the initiates and into the armory. He doesn't stop there, however. He continues until we reach a broom closet near the kitchen, growing more and more agitated with each step. When he pushes me inside without a word, my stomach sinks.

He leaves the door cracked for propriety's sake.

Then he drops my hand.

"Jean—"

"We agreed," he says tersely, closing his eyes and scrubbing his face. "We agreed you wouldn't train with the others. We agreed not to put ourselves in that position again."

"Put ourselves in *what* position?" That tendril of pride in my chest withers into something ashen and dead, and I wring the water from my hair in a brutal, punishing twist. I cannot keep the tremor from my voice, however. "*My* position? Chasseurs are expected to train, are they not? Preferably together?"

Frowning, he plucks a towel from the shelf and hands it to me. "If you want to train, *I* will train you. I've *told* you this, Célie—"

"You can't keep giving me special treatment! You don't have *time* to train me, Jean, and besides—Frederic has a point. It isn't fair to expect everything from them and nothing from me—"

"I don't expect *nothing* from you—" He stops speaking abruptly, his frown deepening as I wipe the muck from my neck, my collarbone, my throat. His jaw clenches. "You're bleeding."

"What?"

He steps closer, cupping my jaw and tilting my head to examine my throat. "Frederic. That bastard broke your skin. I swear to God, I'll make him muck stables for a *year*—"

"Captain?" An initiate pokes his head into the closet. "Father Achille needs to speak to you. He says there's been a critical development with the—" But he stops short when he sees me, startling at the sight of us alone together. At the sight of us *touching*. Jean Luc sighs and moves away.

"A critical development with *what*?" I snap.

The initiate—several years younger than me, perhaps fourteen—straightens like I've slapped him, his brows furrowing in confusion. He lowers his voice earnestly. "The bodies, mademoiselle."

My eyes narrow in disbelief as I glance between him and Jean. "What *bodies*?"

"That's enough." Jean Luc speaks sharply before the initiate can answer, herding him out the door and shooting a wary glance over his shoulder at me. He doesn't allow me to demand an explanation. He doesn't allow me to fling the towel or seize his coat or scream my frustrations to the heavens. No. He shakes his head curtly, already turning away. "Don't ask, Célie. It doesn't concern you." He hesitates at the door, however, his voice apologetic and his eyes full of regret. "Please don't worry."

CHAPTER FIVE

Crimson Roses

I wait longer than strictly necessary before creeping into the hall, praying the others remain in the yard. I don't want to see them. Indeed, in this moment, I never want to see another blue coat or Balisarda again.

I'm not sulking, of course.

Jean Luc can keep his filthy secrets. Apparently, it doesn't matter *what I've done for this kingdom* or *what I've sacrificed*; it doesn't matter what he spouts in the training yard. Apparently, those are just words—no, *placations* for me and for Frederic and for our dear captain himself. I *am* pretty porcelain, after all. I might shatter at the slightest touch. Brushing furious tears from my cheeks, I storm upstairs, tearing off my ugly coat, my sodden skirt, and flinging both to the corner of my room. Part of me hopes they'll rot there. Part of me hopes they'll putrefy and crumble, so I might never wear them again.

Does it not feel like you're playing dress-up?

My hands curl into fists.

I stopped playing dress-up at fifteen years old—entirely *too* old, as far as Filippa was concerned. She told me as much the first night I caught her sneaking from our nursery. I'd fallen asleep in my tiara—a book about the ice princess Frostine still sprawled across my chest—when her footsteps woke me. I'll never forget the look of scorn on her face, the way she scoffed at my petal-pink nightgown. "Aren't you a little old for pretend?" she asked me.

It was not the last time I cried over my sister.

Silly little Célie.

I stand in my room for another moment—breathing heavily, my chemise dripping—before heaving a sigh and stalking after my uniform. With cold, clumsy fingers, I hang the blue wool by the mantel to dry. Already, a servant has stoked the dying embers of last night's fire, probably at Jean Luc's request. He heard my screams last night. He hears them *every* night. Though Tower rules prevent him from coming to me, from comforting me, he does what he can. Fresh candles arrive at my door twice a week, and flames always roar in my hearth.

I drop my forehead to the mantel, swallowing another hot wave of tears. The emerald ribbon around my wrist—a talisman, of sorts—has nearly come undone from my spat with Frederic, and one tail of the bow trails longer than the other, the pretty loops now limp and pitiful. Just like me. Clenching my teeth, I carefully retie the silk and choose a snow-white gown from the armoire, heedless of the gale outside. By the door, I pluck a bottle-green cloak from its hook and swing the heavy velvet around my shoulders.

Jean Luc is busy.

And I am going to visit my sister.

Father Achille intercepts me in the foyer before I can escape. Striding from the sanctuary—presumably on his way to speak with Jean Luc—he hesitates, frowning, when he sees the look on my face. In his hand, he clutches a small book. "Is something wrong, Célie?"

"Not at all, Your Eminence." Forcing a bright smile—acutely aware of my swollen eyes and red nose—I study the book as discreetly as possible, but I can't discern the faded letters on its cover. It certainly *looks* the same size as the book in Jean Luc's pocket last night. Everything from its yellowed, loose-leaf pages to its battered, leather-covered spine feels ominous, however. And is that dark stain . . . *blood?* When I look closer—nearly squinting now, throwing caution to the wind—he clears his throat and shifts pointedly, hiding the book behind his back. I smile harder. "Apologies for my attire. The rain soaked my uniform while I trained with Frederic this morning."

"Ah. Yes." He shifts again, clearly uncomfortable with the silence that falls between us. As a rather surly, cantankerous old man, Father Achille would rather fall on his Balisarda than address my tears, yet—to the surprise of both of us, I'm sure—he doesn't leave, instead scratching awkwardly at his grizzled beard. Perhaps his newfound position as the Archbishop still hasn't hardened him as it did his predecessor. I hope it never does. "Yes, I heard about Frederic. Are you all right?"

My smile becomes a grimace. "Did Jean Luc not mention that I bested him?"

"Oh?" He clears his throat and keeps scratching, averting his dark eyes to his boots, to the window, to anything and everything except my face. "That part—er, no, it didn't come up, I'm afraid."

I resist the urge to roll my eyes. Sometimes I wonder why God commands us never to lie.

"Right." I lift my fist to my heart, inclining my neck and inching past him. "If you'll excuse me—"

"Célie, wait." He waves me back with a beleaguered sigh. "I have no talent for this, but—well, if you ever need an ear that doesn't belong to your fiancé, I can still hear a little." He hesitates for another painful second—still scratch, scratch, *scratching*—and I pray for the floor to open up and swallow me whole. I suddenly don't want to address my tears either. I just want to *leave*. When he meets my gaze a second time, however, his hand falls, and he nods with resignation. "I was a lot like you once. I didn't know where I fit in here. Didn't know if I *could* fit in here."

I frown at him, startled. "But you're the Archbishop of Belterra."

"I wasn't always." He ushers me toward the grand entrance of Saint-Cécile, and inexplicable affection for him blooms in my chest as he hesitates, unwilling to leave me just yet. Though the rain has stopped, a fine sheen of moisture still douses the steps, the leaves, the cobblestone street below. "You can't live for one moment, Célie."

"What do you mean?"

"When you stabbed that injection into Morgane le Blanc—the strongest and cruelest witch this kingdom has ever known—you did a great thing for Belterra. An admirable thing. But you're more than great and admirable. You're more than that moment. Don't let it define you, and don't let it dictate your future."

My frown deepens, and instinctively, I slip a hand inside my cloak to toy with the emerald ribbon at my wrist. The ends have begun to fray. "I—I'm afraid I still don't understand. I've chosen my future, Your Eminence. I am a Chasseur."

"Hmm." He wraps his robes tighter around his gaunt frame,

scowling at the sky in displeasure. His knees ache when it rains. "And is that what you really want? To be a Chasseur?"

"Of *course* it is. I—I want to serve, to protect, to help make the kingdom a better place. I took a *vow*—"

"Not every choice is a forever one."

"What are you saying?" I take an incredulous step away from him. "Are you saying I shouldn't be here? That I don't *fit*?"

He harrumphs and turns back toward the doors, abruptly disgruntled once more. "I'm saying you fit if you want to fit, but if you *don't* want to fit, well—don't let us steal your future." He glances over his shoulder, limping back into the foyer to escape the chill. "You aren't a fool. Your happiness matters just as much as Jean Luc's."

I expel a harsh breath.

"Oh, and"—he waves a gnarled hand, heedless—"if you're going to the cemetery, stop at le fleuriste first. Helene put together fresh bouquets for the graves of the fallen. Take one to Filippa too."

Dark crimson roses spill from my cart as I arrive at the cemetery beyond Saint-Cécile. An enormous wrought iron gate encircles the property, its black spires piercing heavy clouds. The gates part wide this afternoon, but the effect is far from welcoming. No. It feels like walking into teeth.

A familiar chill sweeps my spine as I coax my horse along the cobblestone path.

When Cosette Monvoisin's Hellfire destroyed the old cemetery last year—and the catacombs of the privileged and wealthy below—the aristocracy had no choice but to erect new headstones for their loved ones here. That included Filippa. Despite my father's vehement protests—imagine, *his* daughter forced to lie beside peasants for eternity—our ancestral tomb burned with all the rest. "She isn't really here," I reminded my mother, who wept for days. "Her soul is gone."

And now, so is her body.

Still, this new land—though hallowed by Florin Cardinal Clément himself—it feels *angry.*

It feels . . . hungry.

"Shhh." I lean forward to comfort my horse, Cabot, who snorts and tosses his great head in agitation. He hates coming here. I hate bringing him. If not for Filippa, I would never step foot among the dead again. "We're almost there."

Near the back of the cemetery, rows upon eerie rows of headstones rise from the earth like fingers. They grasp at my horse's hooves, my cart's wheels, as I swing from the saddle and walk alongside Cabot, placing a bouquet of roses atop each. One grave—and one bouquet—for each person who fell during the Battle of Cesarine. At Father Achille's command, we bring fresh flowers each week. To honor them, he says, but I can't help but feel the real reason is to pacify them.

It's a silly notion, of course. Like Filippa, these people are no longer *here*, and yet . . .

That chill creeps down my spine again.

Like I'm being watched.

"*Mariée . . .*"

The word, spoken so softly I might've imagined it, drifts with the wind, and I lurch to a halt, whipping my head around wildly with a sickening sense of déjà vu. *Please, God, no. Not again.*

I've heard that word before.

Shuddering, I quicken my step and ignore the sudden pressure in my temples. Because I *did* imagine it—of course I did—and this is *precisely* why I avoid cemeteries. These voices in my head aren't real. They've *never* been real, and my mind is playing tricks on me again, just like in Filippa's casket. The voices weren't real then either.

They aren't real.

I repeat the words until I almost believe them, counting each bouquet until I almost forget.

When I finally reach Pippa's grave, I crouch beside it and rest my cheek against the elaborate stone. It feels just as cold as the rest of them, however. Just as damp. Already, moss has crept along its arched edges, obscuring the simple words there: *Filippa Allouette Tremblay, beloved daughter and sister.* I peel the moss away to trace the letters of her name over and over again—because she was so much more than beloved, and now we speak of her in past tense. Now she haunts my nightmares. "I miss you, Pip," I whisper, closing my eyes and shivering. And I want to mean it. I want it *desperately.*

I want to ask her what to do—about Jean Luc, about Frederic, about romance and marriage and crippling disappointment. I want to ask her about her dreams. Did she love the boy she visited at night? Did he love her? Did they envision a life together, the two of them—an illicit life, a *thrilling* one—before Morgane took her?

Did she ever change her mind?

She never told me, and then she was gone, leaving me with a half-drawn picture of herself. Leaving me with half of her smile, half of her secrets. Half of her face.

Gently, I lay the roses at her feet, turning away with deliberate calm. I will not flee. I will not scream. My sister is still my sister, regardless of how Morgane desecrated her, of how Morgane desecrated *me*. I breathe deeply, stroking Cabot's face, and nod to myself—I will return to Chasseur Tower, and I will continue alphabetizing the council library. I will eat a mediocre meal with Jean Luc and our brethren this evening, and I will relish the meat pie and boiled potatoes, the blue wool and heavy Balisarda. "I can carry it," I tell Cabot, placing a kiss on his nose. "I can do this."

I will not play pretend.

Then Cabot rears abruptly with a shriek, tossing his head, and nearly breaks my nose.

"Cabot!" I pitch backward, stunned, but he bolts before I can calm him, before I can do anything but steady myself against my sister's headstone. "What are you—? Come back! *Cabot!* Cabot, come *back!*" Heedless, he only picks up speed—inexplicably terrified—cantering around the bend and out of sight. The wagon ricochets off the cobblestones behind him. Crimson roses soar in each direction. They litter the cemetery like drops of blood, except—

Except—

I press against Filippa's headstone in horror.

Except they wither to black where they touch the ground.

Swallowing hard—my heart pounding a painful beat in my ears—I look to my feet, where Filippa's roses also curl and bleed, their vivid petals shriveling to ash. Putrid rot fills my senses. *This isn't real.* I repeat the frantic words even as I stagger away, as my vision begins to narrow and my throat begins to close. *This isn't real. You're dreaming. It's just a nightmare. It's just—*

I almost don't see the body.

It lies across a grave in the middle of the cemetery, too

pale—nearly *white*, its skin bloodless and ashen—to be anything but dead. "Oh God." My knees lock as I stare at it. At *her*. Because this corpse is clearly feminine, her golden hair snarled with leaves and debris, her full lips still painted scarlet, her scarred hands clasped neatly over her chest, like—like someone *posed* her. I swallow bile, forcing myself to move closer. She wasn't here when I rode through with Cabot earlier, which means— *Oh God, oh God, oh God.*

Her killer could still be here.

My gaze darts to each headstone, each tree, each *leaf*, but despite the storm this morning, all has fallen silent and still. Even the wind has fled this place, as if it too senses the evil here. Head pounding, I creep closer to the body. Closer still. When no one leaps from the shadows, I crouch beside her, and if possible, my stomach sinks further. Because I recognize this woman—*Babette*. Once a courtesan in Madame Helene Labelle's infamous brothel, Babette joined Coco and the other Dames Rouges against Morgane le Blanc in the Battle of Cesarine. She fought with us. She—she helped me hide innocent children from other witches; she *saved* Madame Labelle.

Two neat pinprick wounds decorate her throat where a pulse should be.

"Oh, Babette." With trembling fingers, I brush her hair from her forehead and close her eyes. "Who did this to you?"

Despite her wan color, no blood soils her gown—indeed, she seems to have sustained no injuries beyond the small wounds at her throat. I pry her hands apart to examine her wrists, her nails, and a cross spills from her palms. She clutched it against her heart. I lift it incredulously, the ornate silver bright and brilliant even in overcast light. No blood. Not even a drop.

It makes no *sense*. She still looks as if she's merely sleeping, which means she cannot be long dead—

"*Mariée* . . ."

When the leaves of a birch rustle behind me, I lurch to my feet, spinning wildly, but no one appears except the wind. It returns with a vengeance, whipping at my cheeks, my hair, urging me to move, to leave this place. Though I yearn to heed its call, the initiate spoke of bodies earlier. *Bodies.* As in . . . more than one.

Jean Luc. His name rises like a wall in the maelstrom of my thoughts.

He'll know what to do. He'll know what happened here. I take two hasty steps toward Saint-Cécile before stopping, whirling again, and tearing the cloak from my shoulders. I drape it over Babette. Perhaps it's foolish, but I cannot just leave her here, vulnerable and alone and—

And dead.

Gritting my teeth, I pull the velvet over her beautiful face. "I'll be back soon," I promise her. Then I dash for the wrought iron gate without stopping, without slowing, without looking back. Though the sky descends in a fine mist once more, I ignore it. I ignore the thunder in my ears, the wind in my hair. It tears the heavy locks from my chignon. I push them out of my eyes, skidding around the gate—my sense of purpose plummeting with each step because Babette is dead, *she's dead, she's dead, she's dead*—and collide headlong with the palest man I've ever seen.

CHAPTER SIX

The Coldest Man

He steadies me with broad hands and a skeptical expression, arching a brow at my wild hair and wilder eyes. I look outrageous. I *know* I look outrageous, yet still I seize his leather surcoat—it skims his powerful frame like a second skin, stark black against his pallor—and stare up at him, open-mouthed. Unable to articulate the panic in my chest. It continues to build as my mind catches up with my senses.

This man is paler than Babette.

Colder.

His nostrils flare.

"Are you quite well, mademoiselle?" he murmurs, and his *voice*—deep and rich, it seems to curl around my neck and trap me there. I repress a full-body shiver, inexplicably unnerved. His cheekbones could cut glass. His hair gleams strange and silver.

"A body!" The words burst from me awkwardly, louder and shriller than our proximity demands. He still holds my waist. I still clutch his arms. Indeed, if I wished, I could reach out and touch the shadows beneath his flat black eyes. Those eyes bore into me with cold intensity now. "Th-There's—there's a b-b-body back there." I jerk toward the cemetery gate. "A corpse—"

Slowly, he slants his head to examine the cobblestone path behind me. His voice is scathing. "Several, I imagine."

"No, that's not what I—the roses, they—they withered when they touched the ground, and—"

He blinks. "The roses . . . withered?"

"Yes, they withered and died, and Babette—she died too. She *died* without a drop of spilled blood, just two holes in her neck—"

"Are you sure you're quite well?"

"*No!*" I almost shriek the word now, still clinging to him and proving his point completely. It doesn't matter. I don't have time for reason. My voice climbs steadily higher, and I dig my fingers into his arms as if I can *force* him to understand. Because men value strength. They don't value hysteria; they don't *listen* to hysterical women, and I—I— "I am most certainly *not* quite well! Are you even listening to me? A woman has been *murdered*. Her corpse is currently draped across a grave like some sort of macabre fairy-tale princess, and you—*you*, monsieur"—my terrible unease finally sharpens into suspicion, and I hurl it at him like a blade— "why are you lurking outside a cemetery?"

Rolling his eyes, he breaks my grip with startling ease. My hands fall away from him like broken cobwebs.

"Why are *you* lurking inside one?" His gaze sweeps from my bare shoulders to the mist above us. "In the rain, no less. Do you have a death wish, mademoiselle? Or is it the dead themselves who call to you?"

I recoil from him in disgust.

"The *dead*? Of course they don't—this is—" Exhaling hard through my nose, I force my shoulders back. My chin up. He will not distract me. The rain might soon wash away any clues I've missed, and Jean Luc and the Chasseurs must be notified. "The dead do not *call* to me, monsieur—"

"No?"

"*No*," I repeat firmly, "and to speak as such is rather unusual and suspicious, given the circumstances—"

"But under different circumstances?"

"Actually, I find *you* to be rather unusual and suspicious." I ignore the sardonic twist of his lips and continue with grim determination. "I apologize for this imposition, monsieur, but I—yes, I'm afraid you must come with me. The Chasseurs will want to speak to you, as you're now"—I swallow hard as he cocks his head, studying me—"a p-primary suspect in what is sure to be a murder investigation. Or a witness, at the very least," I add hastily, taking a tentative step backward.

His eyes track the step. The movement, though slight, sends a fresh chill down my spine. "And if I refuse?" he asks.

"Well then, monsieur, I—I will have no choice but to force you."

"How?"

My stomach sinks. "I beg your pardon?"

"How will you force me?" he repeats, intrigued now. And that curiosity—that glint of humor in his black eyes—is somehow worse than his disdain. When he takes another step toward me, I take another step back, and his lips twitch. "Surely you must have some idea, or you wouldn't have threatened it. Go on, pet. Don't stop now. Tell me what you intend to do to me." Those eyes flick briefly down my person—assessing, *amused*—before returning to mine in open challenge. "You don't appear to have a weapon in that gown."

My cheeks burn in open flame as I too glance down at my dress. The rain has rendered it near translucent. Before I can do anything, however—before I can pick up a rock or take off my boot to hurl at him, or perhaps gouge out his eyes—a shout sounds from down the street. We turn in unison, and a lean, familiar figure cuts toward us through the mist. My heart leaps to my throat at the sight of him. "Jean Luc! You're here!"

The humor vanishes from the man's expression.

Thank God.

"Father Achille told me where to find—" Jean Luc's face twists as he draws closer, as he realizes that I'm not alone. That another *man* is here. He quickens his pace. "Who is this? And where is your coat?"

The man in question steps away from us, clasping long, pale fingers behind his back. That tilt of his lips returns—not like before, not quite a smile and not quite a sneer, but something in between. Something unpleasant. Arching a brow at me, he nods curtly toward Jean Luc. "How fortunate for all of us. Tell your little friend about the roses. I'll take my leave."

He moves to turn away.

To even my surprise, my hand snakes out to catch his wrist. His expression darkens at the contact, and slowly, coldly, he looks down at my fingers. I drop them hastily. His bare skin feels like ice. "Captain Toussaint isn't my *little friend*. He's my—my—"

"Fiancé," Jean Luc finishes roughly, seizing my hand and pulling me to his side. "Is this man bothering you?"

"He—" I swallow, shaking my head. "It doesn't matter, Jean. Really. There's something else, something more impor—"

"It matters to *me*."

"But—"

"Is he bothering you?" Jean bites each word with unexpected

venom, and I nearly shriek in frustration, resisting the urge to shake him, to *strangle* him. He still glowers at the man, who now watches us with a strange sort of intensity. It verges on predatory. And his body—it's grown too still. *Unnaturally* still. The hair on my neck lifts as I ignore every instinct and turn my back to him, seizing the lapels of Jean Luc's blue coat.

"Listen to me, Jean. *Listen.*" My hand slips to his belt as I speak, my fingers wrapping around the hilt of his Balisarda. He stiffens at the contact, but he doesn't stop me. His eyes snap to my face, narrowing, and when I nod almost imperceptibly, his own hand replaces mine. He trusts me implicitly. Though I may not be the strongest or fastest or greatest of his Chasseurs, I *am* intuitive, and the man behind us is dangerous. He's also involved in Babette's death somehow. I *know* he is.

"He murdered her," I breathe. "I think he murdered Babette."

That's all it takes.

In a single, fluid motion, Jean Luc spins me behind him and unsheathes his Balisarda, but when he charges forward, the man is already gone. No, not gone—

Vanished.

If not for the withered crimson rose where he once stood, he might've never existed at all.

CHAPTER SEVEN

A Liar, After All

The next hour descends into absolute chaos.

Chasseurs and constabulary alike spill through the streets—searching for the cold man—while another dozen recover Babette's body from the cemetery and inspect the grounds for signs of foul play. I clutch her cross tightly within the pocket of my skirt. I *should* turn it over to Jean Luc, yet my fingers—still ice cold and trembling—refuse to relinquish its ostentatious silver edges. They score my palm as I dart after him, determined to join the proceedings. Determined to *help*. He hardly looks at me, however, instead shouting orders with brutal efficiency, directing Charles to find Babette's next of kin, Basile to alert the morgue of her arrival, Frederic to collect the dead roses as evidence. "Take them to the infirmary," he tells the latter in a low voice, "and send word to La Dame des Sorcières via His Majesty—tell her we need her assistance."

"I can go to Lou!" In stark contrast to his unshakable facade, my voice sounds loud, panicked, even to my own ears. I clear my throat and try again, clenching Babette's cross to the point of pain. "That is, I can contact her directly—"

"No." Jean Luc shakes his head curtly. He still doesn't look at me. "Frederic will go."

"But I can reach her much faster—"

"I said *no*, Célie." His tone brooks no argument. Indeed, his eyes harden as they at last sweep my wet hair, my soiled gown, my sparkling ring, before he turns away to address Father Achille, who arrives with a band of healers. When I don't move, he pauses, glancing back at me over his shoulder. "Go to Chasseur Tower and wait for me in your room. We need to have a discussion."

We need to have a discussion.

The words sink in my stomach like bricks.

"Jean—"

Shouts sound as wide-eyed passersby gather at the cemetery gate, craning to see Babette's body through the tumult. "Go, Célie," he snarls, flicking his hand toward three passing Chasseurs. To them, he says, "Take care of the pedestrians." They reroute their paths instantly, and I glare at him. At *them*. Forcing myself to breathe, I release Babette's cross and hurry after their broad, blue-coated backs. Because I can speak to a crowd just as easily as they can. I can build lutin traps, alphabetize the council library, and *also* assist in a murder investigation. Though I left my coat and Balisarda at home, I am still a Chasseur; I am *more* than Jean Luc's pretty little fiancée, and if he thinks otherwise—if *any* of them think otherwise—I'll prove them wrong here and now.

Mud flecks my hem as I sprint to match their pace, reaching for the slowest's arm. "Please, allow me—"

He jerks away with an impatient shake of his head. "Go home, Célie."

"But I—"

The words die on my tongue as the crowd disbands after a few terse words from his companions.

Not only am I unwanted here, but I am also useless.

My chest feels like it's caving in.

"*Move*," Frederic mutters irritably, brushing me aside when he turns—arms already full of roses—and nearly treads on my foot. His eyes linger on my gown, and his lip curls in distaste. "You've abandoned the pretense, at least. Good riddance." He stalks to my cart without another word, depositing the roses within it.

"Wait!" I race after him through the cemetery gate. I will not cry here. *I will not cry.* "Why don't you collect the roses on the north side? I'll do the ones on the south—"

His scowl only deepens. "I think you've done enough for one day, Mademoiselle Tremblay."

"Don't be ridiculous. I came here on Father Achille's orders—"

"Oh?" Frederic bends to retrieve another rose from the ground. I snatch one near his feet before he can stop me. "Did Father Achille also order you to tamper with the crime scene and fraternize with a person of interest?"

"I—" If possible, my stomach sinks further, and I inhale sharply at the accusations. "Wh-What are you talking about? I couldn't just *leave* her there. She was— I didn't tamper with—I didn't *mean* to tamper with anything."

"What does that matter?" He snatches the rose from my hand, and its thorn nicks my thumb. "You still did."

Clenching my teeth to stop the tremble in my chin, I follow him deeper into the cemetery. Within two steps, however, a familiar hand seizes my own, and Jean Luc spins me to face him with a furious expression. "I don't have time for this, Célie. I told you to return to Chasseur Tower."

I tear my hand away from his, gesturing to the chaos around us. Tears sparkle in my eyes, and I hate that I cannot stop them. I hate that Frederic can see them. I hate that *Jean* can see them—hate that his own gaze begins to soften in response, just as it always does. "*Why?*" I burst out, choking back a sob. *I will not cry.* "All of the other huntsmen are here! They're all here, and they're all helping." When he says nothing, simply stares at me, I force myself to continue, quieter now. Desperate. "Babette was my friend, Jean. You're the captain of the Chasseurs. Let me help too. *Please.*"

At the last, he sighs heavily, shaking his head and closing his eyes as if pained. The huntsmen nearest us pause their tasks to listen as surreptitiously as possible, but I still see them—I still *feel* them—and so does Jean Luc. "If you're truly a Chasseur, you will obey my command. I told you to return to Chasseur Tower," he repeats, and when his eyes snap open, they've hardened once more. His entire body has tensed taut as a bow—one pluck away from snapping—but I clench tighter still. Because when he leans low to meet my gaze, he is no longer Jean Luc, my fiancé and heart. No. He is Captain Toussaint, and I am insubordinate. "That's an order, Célie."

The words should be everything I've ever wanted.

They aren't.

Snickers erupt somewhere to my left, but I ignore them, staring at Jean Luc for a single heartrending beat. It matches the tear trickling down my cheek. I said I wouldn't cry, but I'm a liar too.

"Yes, Captain," I whisper, wiping the tear away and turning on my heel. I don't look at him again. I don't look at Father Achille or Frederic or the dozens of other men who stop to witness my shame. To *pity* it. The ring on my finger feels heavier than usual as I walk back to Chasseur Tower alone. And for the first time in a long time, I wonder if I've made a terrible mistake.

Idle time is my enemy.

Pacing in my dormitory, I lose track of it waiting for Jean Luc to return. With each step, anger sparks and spreads in that aching, empty part of my chest. It's a welcome distraction. Anger is good. Anger is solvable.

We need to have a discussion, Jean Luc told me.

I nearly hiss in frustration at the dying embers of my hearth, picturing his stern face. He had the gall to—to *send me to my room* like I'm not his soldier, not even his *fiancée*, but an unruly child underfoot. All of my candles burn to stubs while I tread an impatient path on the carpet. Some gutter, and some flicker out completely. Though the rain has broken, clouds remain, casting the room in dull gray light. The shadows lengthen.

Go back to Chasseur Tower and wait for me in your room.

Wait for me in your room.

That's an order, Célie.

"That's an order, Célie," I say through gritted teeth, wresting a useless stub from its candlestick and hurling it into the fire. The flames sizzle and snap gleefully, and the sight fills me with such savage delight that I wrench another stub free and fling it after the first. Then another. And another. And another and *another* until my chest heaves and my eyes stream and my head aches with the injustice of it all. How *dare* he order me to do anything after *months* of insisting on special treatment? After months of treating me like porcelain and handling me with kid gloves? How dare he expect me to *obey?*

"You can't have it both ways, Jean." Resolve hardening, I storm to my door and fling it open, relishing the *crash* as it collides with the corridor wall. I wait for one of my brethren to appear, to reprimand me for the noise, but none does. Of course they don't. They're far too busy being huntsmen—true and proper ones, not the kind who disobey their captain's orders. After another second, I sigh and close the door with far gentler hands, muttering, "But they've made it clear I'm not a Chasseur. Not really."

I creep through the empty corridors in search of Jean Luc.

Because he was right. We *do* need to have a discussion, and I won't wait another moment for it.

First, I check his room, knocking on the nondescript door across the Tower with confidence that borders on belligerence, but he doesn't answer. After casting furtive looks down each end of the corridor, I slip the hairpin from my sleeve and pick the lock. An old trick I learned from my sister. The mechanism clicks open with ease, and I peer inside the room for only a moment before realizing he isn't here—his bed remains pristine, untouched, and shutters cover his window, plunging everything in darkness. I retreat quickly.

When the cathedral bell tolls a moment later, signaling five o'clock in the evening, I quicken my step toward the training yard. Surely whatever kept Jean Luc should not have kept him for *three hours*.

After searching the yard to no avail—and the stables, and the infirmary, and Father Achille's study—I move on to the commissary. It *is* dinnertime, after all. Perhaps Jean Luc hasn't eaten today. Perhaps he thought to bring us both supper to defuse the tension. Only a handful of Chasseurs occupy the long wooden tables, however, and Jean Luc doesn't sit among them. "Have you seen Captain Toussaint?" I ask the nearest one. The anxious knot in my stomach rises, lodging in my throat, when the young man refuses to meet my gaze. "Has he returned from the cemetery?"

Has something happened?

He spoons an enormous bite of potato into his mouth, delaying his reply. When he finally speaks, his voice is reluctant. "I don't know."

Though I try not to snap at him, Babette's bloodless corpse rises in my mind's eye—except now the body isn't Babette at all, but Jean Luc. Twin wounds puncture his throat, and that beautiful, cold man looms over his grave, pale fingers clasped and bloody. When he grins at me, his teeth are strangely sharp. I force myself to remain calm. "Do you know where he is? Did he apprehend the suspect? Where is Father Achille?"

The Chasseur shrugs with a grimace and turns away pointedly, resuming conversation with his companion.

Right.

Unease mounting, I set out for the cemetery once more. Perhaps he hasn't returned at all. Perhaps he found a clue—

As I turn the corner into the foyer, however, his voice rises sharply from the stairwell to the dungeon. I pause mid-step, relief crashing through my system. *Of course.* Jean Luc often frequents the council room in times of stress, poring over his notes, his manuscripts, anything to help clarify his thoughts. I dart down the stairs on silent feet, lifting a torch from the stone wall as I go. Another voice soon joins Jean Luc's, however—sharper still, raised as if in anger—and I nearly stumble on the last step.

"And I'm telling *you*, Captain—for the sixth thousandth time—that this is not the work of blood witches."

Lou. Despite the horrendous circumstances, I can't help but exhale in relief. If Lou is here, everything must be fine—or at least, it will be soon. She and Jean Luc often work together in matters of defense; they won't allow Babette's fate to befall anyone else. With both the witches and the huntsmen searching for the cold man, I have no doubt he'll be apprehended soon.

As if in response, a muted thud echoes from the council room—perhaps Jean Luc's fist against the table? "The body was *drained of blood*, Lou. How else do you explain it? How else do you explain *any* of these bodies?"

The words puncture my relief.

"Her name is Babette." Low and strained, a new voice joins the others, and I creep steadily closer, frowning now. Clearly, Lou answered Jean Luc's summons, but Coco? Did he summon her too? "Babette," she repeats, more emphatic now. "Babette Trousset. Stop referring to her as *the body*."

I press a careful ear against the door, ignoring the tendril of unease that unfurls in my chest. *Of course she's here,* I mentally chide myself. *Babette was a blood witch, and Coco is La Princesse Rouge. Of course Jean Luc would contact her.*

"Trousset?" he asks sharply, and the sound of rustling paper fills the room. "We identified her as Babette *Dubuisson*, formerly a courtesan at Madame Helene Labelle's establishment"—more shuffling—"the Bellerose."

Coco's response cuts even sharper. "Babette wasn't the first witch to adopt a pseudonym, and she certainly won't be the last. Your brotherhood ensured that."

"Apologies," Jean Luc mutters, except he doesn't sound apologetic at all. "But you have to admit how this looks. This is the *fifth* body we've found, and—"

"Again with *the bodies*," Lou snaps.

"They *are* bodies," he argues, his patience clearly wearing thin. "Babette might've been a witch, but she's now a key player in a murder investigation."

"I think it's time to call this what it is, Jean," another voice says, quieter and deeper than the others. My chest constricts at the sound of it—not in anticipation this time, but with alarm. Because Reid Diggory should not be in this council room. After the Battle of Cesarine, he made it clear that he had no intention of returning to Chasseur Tower in an official capacity.

Until now.

I press closer to the door as he continues.

"Four of the five victims have been of magical origin—with one human outlier—and all have been found with puncture wounds on their throats and no blood in their bodies. All separate events. All in the last three months." He pauses, and even beyond the door, the silence in the room thickens with apprehension. Though I don't possess the criminal knowledge of Jean Luc or Reid, I know what this means. We all know what this means.

"We're dealing with a serial killer," Reid confirms.

I might forget how to breathe.

"It isn't a blood witch," Coco says stubbornly.

"Do you have any proof of that?" Jean Luc asks, his voice grim. "It looks like blood magic to me."

"Dame Rouges don't murder their own."

"They might to divert suspicion after murdering a human, a Dame Blanche, a loup garou, and a melusine."

"We can't prove it's a serial killer." Another voice—this one *painfully* familiar—joins the fray, and the sheer humiliation of it all pierces my chest like a knife. Frederic is here. *Frederic* has been invited into this room with every person I hold dear, and I have not. Worse still—Jean Luc must have invited him, which means he told Frederic of his secrets and not me. "Serial killers target victims of a similar profile. There's nothing similar between these victims. They aren't even the same species."

Despite the sickening twist of my stomach, I force myself to inhale. To exhale. This is bigger than me, bigger than my own hurt feelings and my friends' bad faith. People have *died*. And furthermore, Jean Luc—he's—he's just doing what he thinks is best. They all are. "Whoever this is might not kill for the thrill," Coco says. "They might kill for a different reason."

"We're missing something," Reid agrees.

"Where is Célie?" Lou asks abruptly.

My heart lurches into my throat at the sound of my name, and I recoil slightly, as if Lou might sense me here, lurking in the corridor to eavesdrop. Perhaps she can. She *is* a witch. When Jean Luc answers her, however—his tone low and reluctant, no, *unwilling*—I can't help but press closer once more, listening like my life depends on it. "I told you before," he mutters. "This doesn't concern Célie."

A beat of silence. Then—

Lou snorts in disbelief. "Like hell it doesn't. Célie is the one who *found* Babette, isn't she?"

"Yes, but—"

"She's still a Chasseur?"

"The most intelligent one, clearly," Coco adds under her breath.

"*Thank* you for that, Cosette." I can practically hear Jean Luc's scowl as he drags a chair from the table, its legs scraping the council room floor, and throws himself in it. "And of course Célie is still a Chasseur. I can hardly discharge her."

I inhale sharply.

"So where is she?" Lou asks.

"Her dormitory." Though I cannot see Lou's and Coco's expressions, Jean Luc can. "Oh, don't look at me like that. This investigation is highly classified, and even if it weren't—we can't fit every Chasseur inside this room."

"You fit *him*." Coco sounds supremely unimpressed, but her words do little to bolster me. My fingers tremble around the torch, and my knees threaten to give way. *I can hardly discharge her.* Jean Luc has never admitted such a thing aloud before—at least not in front of me. "Célie is twice as sharp as the rest of us," Coco says. "She should be here."

"You can't keep this from her forever, Jean," Lou says.

"She found the body." Even Reid's quiet assurance does nothing to steady me. "She's involved now, whether you like it or not."

I think I'm going to be sick.

"You don't understand." Frustration harshens Jean Luc's voice, and that emotion—that knife in my chest—slides deeper still, straight through my ribs and into my heart. "*None* of you understand. Célie is—she's—"

"Delicate," Frederic finishes, dripping condescension. "Rumor has it she's been through a lot."

She's been through a lot.

I can hardly discharge her.

"She still screams every night. Did you know that?" Jean Luc asks them, and I don't imagine the defensiveness in his tone. "Nightmares. Horrible, vivid nightmares of being trapped inside that casket with her sister's corpse. What Morgane did to her— she should've died. She keeps candles lit around the clock now because she fears the dark. She flinches when anyone touches her. I can't"—he hesitates, his voice deepening with resolve—"I *won't* allow any more harm to come to her."

A beat of silence descends between them.

"That might be true," Lou says softly, "but if I know Célie, you'll cause more harm by keeping this secret. What if this had been her instead of Babette? What if we were discussing *her* corpse right now?" Then, softer still, "She deserves to know the truth, Jean. I know you want to protect her—we all do—but she needs to know the danger. It's time."

It's time.

The words pound in rhythm with my heart as my blood continues to pour, spilling freely, from that wound in my chest. *It never healed*, I realize. It never healed after Pippa, after Morgane, and now my friends—these people I love most in the world, these people I *trusted*—have torn it wide open again. But anger is good. Anger is solvable.

Without hesitation, I shove the door open and storm inside.

CHAPTER EIGHT

A Magical Number

Every eye turns toward me, but I don't hesitate, marching straight to where Jean Luc sits in the center of the room. He nearly falls out of his chair in his haste to rise. "Célie!" Around us, the others draw back, averting their gazes to stare at their boots, the candles, the sheafs of loose paper that litter the council table. A charcoal sketch of Babette's corpse lies on top. "What—what are you doing here? I told you—"

"To wait in my room. Yes, I'm aware."

Part of me relishes the panic in his expression. The rest immediately regrets charging in here to—what, exactly? Witness their betrayal up close and personal? Because they're all here. Every single one of them. Even Beau stands frozen in the corner, looking distinctly undignified with his mouth agape. Though he didn't discuss my position, my past, my *hurt* with the rest of them, his presence still makes him complicit. His silence certainly does. At my accusatory stare, he pushes away from the wall. "Célie, we—"

"Yes?" I snap.

"We—" Steps faltering, he glances helplessly at Lou and Coco, who both watch me with wary eyes. I refuse to look at either of them. "How are you?" he finishes lamely, lifting a hand to rub his neck. Coco elbows his ribs.

I glare at him.

The most powerful players in the kingdom, all gathered together in one room.

All discussing my fate.

"I don't suppose you, er"—he drops his hand in resignation—"did you—did you happen to hear all that?"

Stiff-necked, I stalk to the circular table to examine the other sketches. No one dares stop me. "Yes."

"Right. Well, then, you should know that I didn't want to come, and I wholeheartedly agreed with Lou when she said you should be here—"

"With all due respect, Your Majesty"—I spread the sketches with a hand, staring at the charcoal faces without seeing a single one—"if anyone in this room had wanted me here, I would have been here." If Lou hears the bitterness in my tone—the heartbreak—she doesn't show it. And why would she? She has always been a master of secrets. Just like my sister. "Are these the victims?" I ask Jean Luc. I do not look at him either.

He touches my shoulder tentatively. "Célie—"

I jerk away, fighting tears once more. "*Are* they?"

He hesitates. "Yes."

"Thank you. Was that so very difficult?" Now I do look at him, and the indecision in his gaze nearly breaks me. There is guilt there, yes—perhaps even remorse—but there is also reluctance. He *still* does not want to include me. To confide in me. Unable to bear it another second, I sweep the whole of the sketches into my arms, refusing to acknowledge the ones that I drop. They flutter slowly to the floor as I turn on my heel and march to the door. To Beau, I sniff, "I would say it was lovely to see you again, Your Majesty, but not all of us can lie as adeptly as you."

I ignore the others completely, slamming the door behind me and dropping another few sketches in the process.

This time, I do bend to reclaim them—my entire body shaking—and startle at the moisture flecking each drawing. Tears. I wipe a furious hand across my cheeks and straighten. When hasty footsteps sound from behind the door, I dart up the corridor and into the library room, unwilling to confront any of them again. Not directly, anyway. Some might call it *fleeing*, some might call it *hiding*, but some might be wrong. Some might *say* they want to protect me, but what they *mean* is they want to coddle me. To *manage* me.

I will not be managed.

I will show all of them.

Retreating to the corner of the library—out of sight of the door—I press between two corner bookshelves and flip through the sketches once more. This time, I force myself to study each face as the council room door bursts open, as Jean Luc's boots pound up the corridor. Though he calls for me, I ignore him, shrinking farther into the shelves, staring furiously at the sketch of the loup garou. He lies in the same peaceful supine position as Babette, his hands half-transformed and clasped against his chest. The same puncture wounds at his throat.

"Célie, *wait*." When Jean's resigned voice passes by the library door, I breathe a sigh of relief. "Come back. We need to talk about this—"

I don't want to talk, however. Not anymore. Now I study the trees surrounding the loup garou's corpse instead; I lift the sketch to peer closer at his clawed hands, searching for any sign of a cross. There isn't one, of course. Jean Luc would've asked about Babette's cross if each victim had been found with one. But *why* was the loup garou caught between forms? Was the killer interested in the wolf or the man? Perhaps the man shifted to defend himself?

"Célie!" Jean Luc's voice trails up the staircase, and I relax slightly as it goes, letting my head thud against the bookshelves. I take a deep breath. Perhaps I can creep out before the others conclude their meeting. I flick through the sketches one last time, recognizing none of the crime scenes save one: Brindelle Park, a sacred grove of the witches.

As a child, I stared at the spindly trees outside my nursery window more times than I could count. My mother loathed the faint scent of magic that wafted from their leaves, permeating our yard, but it secretly brought me comfort. It secretly still does. To me, magic smells lovely—like herbs and incense and wild summer honey.

I have not been home in months.

Shaking my head, I study the sketch as Jean Luc's voice fades overhead. Curiously enough, it was not the Dame Blanche found in Brindelle Park, but the melusine. Though I cannot place her silver face, her gills and fins remain intact, which means the killer did not dispatch her here. Melusines' two fins transform into legs when they leave water. He must've killed her underwater and dragged her body ashore, but again . . . *why?*

"Célie?" Jean Luc's voice grows louder once more, sterner, and his feet fall upon the stairs like anvils. "The guards didn't see you come upstairs, so I know you're down here. Don't ignore me."

I tense, eyes darting around the room. I do not want to have this conversation. Not now. Not ever.

He bursts into the library before I can flee *or* hide, and his gaze finds mine immediately. I have no choice but to square my shoulders and step out to greet him, to pretend I've been waiting for him all along. "It took you long enough."

His own eyes narrow. "What are you doing in here?"

I wave the sketches in unapologetic agitation. "Studying." Though he opens his mouth to respond, I plunge ahead, speaking over him loudly. The door remains open but I cannot bring myself to care. "The killer moved the melusine's body. They might've moved Babette's as well, which means we should try to find a connection between each location—"

Crossing the room in three strides, he pries the sketches from my hands and places them carefully upon the nearest shelf. "We need to talk, Célie."

I glare between him and the sketches. "You're right. We do."

"I never meant to involve you in all this."

"That much is *very* clear."

"It's nothing personal." He scrubs a weary hand down his face. Dark stubble shadows his once clean-shaven jaw, and his bronze skin looks ashen, as if he hasn't slept in days. Part of me aches for him, aches at the burden he has carried alone, but a larger part of me aches for myself. Because he didn't *need* to carry it alone. I would have carried it with him. I would have carried it *for* him, if necessary. "This investigation is classified. Father Achille and I haven't released information of these deaths to anyone outside that council room."

"Why is *Frederic* inside that council room?"

He shrugs, and the gesture feels so apathetic, so *detached*, that my spine snaps straighter in response. My chin jerks higher.

"Don't be like this," he mutters. "Frederic found the first body. We couldn't keep him out of the loop."

"*I* found Babette's body!"

He looks away swiftly, unable to meet my gaze. "Two different situations."

"They are *not*, and you know it." I seize the sketches, lifting them to his face and shaking them. "What of the other victims? Who found them? Do they know about the killer, or is that information also *classified*?"

"You wanted me to treat you like a Chasseur." He grinds his teeth, fighting to keep his voice even. Though his temper clearly balances on a knifepoint, my own hands tighten into fists around the sketches. Jean Luc isn't the only one allowed to be angry about this. "This is me *treating* you like a Chasseur—you aren't privy to everything that happens inside this Tower, and to even *expect*—"

"I should be privy to everything that happens to *you*, Jean Luc." Flinging the sketches aside, I lift my ring finger instead, loathing the way it glitters in the torchlight like a thousand tiny suns. That should be the way Jean and I reflect each other—brightly, beautifully, like the diamond in its centerpiece. My stomach sinks horribly at the realization. "Isn't that what you promised me when you gave me this ring? Isn't that what I promised *you* when I accepted it? Regardless of what *either* of us wants, we are more than just our positions, and we have to find a path forward together—"

Scowling fiercely, he drops to his knees to collect the sketches. "I'm not more than my position, Célie. I'm equal parts your captain *and* your fiancé, and you"—his glare turns accusatory, fanning the flames of my own anger and hurt—"*you* of all people should know how hard I've worked to get here. You know everything I've sacrificed. How could you even *ask* me to choose?"

"I am *not* asking you to choose—"

"No?" He clenches the sketches in a neat stack and returns to his full height, stalking to the oblong table and hardback chairs across the room. Though I requested more comfortable seating last month—perhaps a chaise to encourage huntsmen to linger, to *read*—Jean Luc rejected the idea. It did inspire him to have me alphabetize the library, however. He places the sketches beside my current pile of books. "What *are* you asking, then? What do you want from me, Célie? Do you even know?"

"What I *want*"—I snarl the words, no longer in control of my tongue, my vision tunneling on his rigid back, on his stiff fingers as they stack and straighten my pile of books—"is to be treated like a *person*, not a doll. I want you to confide in me. I want you to *trust* me—both that I can take care of myself and that I can take care of *you*. We're supposed to be partners—"

His head jerks. "We *are* partners—"

"But we *aren't*." My voice rises almost deliriously as I wring my hands. The others can certainly hear me—the entire *Tower* can probably hear me—but I can't stop now. I won't. "We aren't partners, Jean. We've *never* been partners. Every step of the way, you've tried to put me in a glass box and keep me on your shelf, untouched and untested and untrue. But I'm already broken. Don't you understand? Morgane shattered me, and I used those shards to strike back. I *killed* her, Jean. I did that. *Me*." Tears stream, unchecked, down my face, but I refuse to wipe them away, instead striding forward to grip his hand. Let him see. Let them *all* see. Because it doesn't matter what they say—I *am* worthy, and I am capable. I succeeded where all others failed.

Jean Luc looks down at me sadly, his eyes pained as he lifts my hand to his lips. He shakes his head, grimacing, with the air of someone reluctant to deliver a fatal blow.

Deliver it he does, however.

"You didn't kill Morgane, Célie. Lou did."

I blink up at him, the righteous anger in my chest withering to something small and shameful. Something hopeless. Out of all the things he could've said in this moment, I never expected that. Not from him. Not from Jean Luc. And perhaps it's the unexpected that knocks the wind from my chest. Until now, the thought has never crossed my mind, but clearly it has crossed his.

"What?" I breathe.

"You didn't kill her. You might've helped—you might've been in the right place at the right time—but we both know she would've slit your throat if Lou hadn't been there. You caught her by surprise with that injection, and that—that sort of luck doesn't last, Célie. You can't depend on it."

We both hear his true meaning: *I can't depend on you.*

I stare at him, crestfallen, as he sighs heavily and continues. "Please understand. Everything I've done is to protect you. You're to be my wife, and I can't"—though his voice breaks slightly on the word, he clears his throat, blinking rapidly—"I can't lose you. I also swore an oath to the people of Belterra, however. I can't protect *them* if I'm worried about your safety, chasing you through cemeteries and rescuing you from a murderer."

When I slip my hand from his, he hangs his head.

"I'm sorry, Célie. Just please . . . go upstairs. We can finish this after the council meeting. I'll bring you dinner, whatever you want.

I'll even—I'll dismiss the chaperone tonight, so we can really talk. How does that sound?"

I stare at him, unable to fathom what more he could possibly say. At least the tears have gone. My eyes have never been clearer.

With another sigh, he strides toward the door, stepping aside to gesture me through it. "Célie?" My feet follow instinctively until I stand before him, the silence between us growing, clanging through my chest like a warning bell. Like a harbinger. He touches a hand to my cheek. "Please say something."

My nursemaid always said seven is a magical number—for dwarves, for sins, for days of the week, and for tides in the sea. Perhaps it is lucky for words too. Though gooseflesh sweeps my entire body, I rise to my toes and press one last kiss to my fiancé's cheek, whispering, "I am going to prove you wrong."

He pulls back. "Célie—"

I have already swept past him, however, into the corridor beyond, where I tug his ring from my finger and slip it inside my pocket. I cannot stand to look at it any longer. Perhaps I'll never look at it again. Either way, I do not turn back as I set out for Brindelle Park.

CHAPTER NINE

Brindelle Park

My childhood home soon towers above me in West End—the wealthiest district of Cesarine—with Brindelle Park inhabiting the flat expanse of land directly behind it. Its trees rustle slightly in the evening breeze, concealing most of the Doleur beyond. Before Pippa and I grew old enough to realize the danger, we would slip through the ethereal, glowing trees to that riverbank, dipping our toes in its gray water. I study the familiar scene now, my hand tightening on the wrought iron fence around my parents' property.

Because the trees are no longer glowing.

Frowning, I creep closer, careful to keep one eye on my former front door.

Though it might be spiteful, I do not wish to see my parents. They . . . *disapprove* of my involvement with the Chasseurs, yet their disapproval feels like more than a difference of opinion; it feels desperate, like manacles clasped on my wrists, bricks tied to my feet, as I plunge headlong into the sea. Whenever I think of them—the last living members of my family—I'm suddenly unable to breathe, and these days, I already struggle to keep my head above water. No. I can't afford to drown in my shame or hurt or anger tonight. I must focus on the task at hand.

If Jean Luc and the others suspect correctly, a killer stalks the streets of Cesarine.

Inhaling slowly, I allow the chill night air to wash over me, *through* me, and freeze the tide of emotions in my chest. Then I place my palm flat against the trunk of the nearest Brindelle tree.

Though I expected cold, the bark nearly freezes my skin, and the color—once luminescent silver—has darkened to stark black. No. It's *withered.* I crane my neck to peer into the bows of the tree. As if sensing my gaze, the wind picks up helpfully, and one of the branches cracks at its touch, dissipating into fine powder. On another gust of wind, the powder swirls toward my outstretched hand and coats my fingers. Its particles sparkle slightly in the dying sunlight.

My frown deepens. My mother petitioned the royal family *many* times to destroy Brindelle Park throughout my childhood. Once, King Auguste even complied. The trees grew back overnight, however, taller and stronger than before—brighter—forcing the aristocrats of West End to accept their spindly neighbors. The Brindelle trees became a stubborn presence in West End. In the very *kingdom.*

What could have possibly caused them to . . . to *die?*

Another branch breaks, and my mind drifts back to the roses in the cemetery, to the way they shriveled upon the earth. Could the killer be responsible for them too? And for the trees? Though I didn't smell witchcraft earlier, the rain might've washed away its scent. Jean Luc thought blood magic could be at play, and all the victims *did* belong to magical species. . . .

When a third branch snaps behind me, I whirl with a squeak.

"Easy." Lou holds up her hands with an uncommonly serious expression. "It's just me."

"Louise." Quickly, I wipe the black powder on my bodice, pretending I didn't just clutch my heart. Pretending I didn't just impersonate a *mouse*. "Did you follow me here?"

Clad in a brilliant white cloak, she treads closer, extending a swath of crimson wool in my direction. Another cloak, I realize, at precisely the same second gooseflesh sweeps my limbs. I left my own cloak in the cemetery with Babette. "Coco sent this," Lou says instead of answering my question. "She would've come with me, but she . . . she stopped by the morgue instead. She needed to say goodbye." Pain flares brilliant and sharp in her eyes as she struggles to collect herself. "To Babette," she clarifies after a moment. "They loved each other once, a long time ago. Before Coco met Beau." She pauses again, waiting for me to speak, and this silence stretches longer and tauter than before. I make no move to accept the cloak. At last, she lowers it to her side with a sigh. "We thought you might be cold."

Sniffing, I resist the urge to shiver. "You thought wrong."

"Your lips are turning blue, Célie."

"Do not claim to care, Louise."

"Do you really want to do this?" Her turquoise eyes narrow as she stalks to my Brindelle tree, leaning against its trunk to peer up at me. A fourth branch crumbles. "You look like you're about to collapse, and a sadistic killer could be marking us at this very second. If you want to have this discussion here and now, though—while we both freeze our delectable asses off—by all means, let's discuss."

Scoffing, I turn to glare at the river. "You're La Dame des Sorcières. I very much doubt anyone who attacks *you* would survive to tell the tale, sadistic killer or not."

"You're angry with me."

I wrap my arms around my torso in response. When the wind strokes my hair as if to comfort me, I repress another shiver. "Not just you," I mutter, sticking my hand out for the cloak. The crimson wool hits my open palm immediately. Bundling it around my shoulders, I inhale the earthy sweetness of Coco's scent. "I'm angry at everyone."

"But you're angrier at me," Lou says shrewdly.

"No," I lie.

She crosses her arms. "You've always been a shit liar, Célie."

"How did you find me?"

"Are you trying to deflect the master of deflection?" When I say nothing, her lips twitch, and I probably imagine the subtle glint of approval in her eyes. "Well . . . *fine*. I will allow this *temporary* distraction from the issue at hand." From the pocket of her leather trousers, she withdraws the sketches—now wadded into a pitiful lump—and gestures to the town house behind us. "I didn't follow you here. I figured you might . . . want to start your investigation with the melusine. Perhaps interview your parents? Jean asked them a few questions after we found her body, but they weren't exactly forthcoming."

"Of course he did." Still shivering violently, I wrap the cloak tighter against the wind, but it does little to comfort me. The cold in my chest creeps through my limbs now, settling into my bones, and I feel impossibly heavy, almost numb. Jean Luc involved my *parents* before he involved me. I close my eyes and breathe deeply, but even the scent of my childhood has gone wrong—the magic has fled, leaving only the faint stench of fish and brine behind. Another branch crumbles to dust. I try not to crumble with it. "I shouldn't have come here."

"This was your home," Lou says quietly. "It's natural that you'd seek solid ground when everything else is, well—" Though she shrugs, the gesture doesn't irk me like it did with Jean Luc. Perhaps because no pity clouds her gaze, only a strange sort of wistfulness. Of *sorrow*.

"Falling to pieces?"

She nods. "Falling to pieces." Pushing from the tree, she comes to stand beside me, and her arm is warm where it brushes mine. Her eyes distant as she too stares out at the Doleur. "The Brindelle trees died with the melusine. I haven't been able to revive them."

The revelation brings me little satisfaction. "Just like the roses."

"Something is wrong, Célie." Her voice grows quieter still. "It isn't just the trees and roses. The land itself . . . it feels *sick* somehow. My magic feels sick." When I look at her sharply, she just shakes her head, still gazing at the water without seeing it. "Did you find anything else in the cemetery? Something we might've missed?"

Instinctively, I slide the necklace from my pocket, dangling the silver cross between us. "Just this."

Her brow furrows as she reaches out to examine it. "Where?"

"Babette had it. She held it in her hands." When she drops her own hand, mystified, I extend the chain more insistently. It isn't right for me to keep it any longer. Despite the overwhelming, inexplicable urge to keep the necklace close, it doesn't belong to me, and it'll do no good hidden in my pocket. "Take it. Perhaps it'll help you locate the killer."

She stares at it. "You kept it from Jean Luc?"

"Yes."

"Why?"

I lift a helpless shoulder, unable to give a true answer. "It just . . . didn't feel right, giving it to him. He didn't know Babette. If you don't need it for the investigation, perhaps you could take it to Coco. She might . . . appreciate such a token."

For another long moment, Lou considers the cross, considers *me*, before carefully pooling the heavy piece in her hand and slipping it back into my pocket. Relief surges through me. It cracks the ice in my chest. "You should trust your instincts, Célie," she says gravely. "Babette didn't worship the Christian god. I don't know why she carried this cross with her when she died, but she must've had a reason. Keep it close."

My instincts.

The words fragment between us, as black and bitter as the Brindelle trees.

"Thank you, Lou." I swallow hard in the silence. Then— "You were supposed to understand."

Though she stiffens slightly at my words, the rest spill from my lips in a sickening torrent that I cannot stop. That I cannot slow. They burst through the crack in my chest, shattering the ice, leaving only sharp, jagged peaks in their wake. "You were there through all of it. You pulled me from my sister's casket. You— you wiped her *remains* from my skin. You followed me into those tunnels toward Morgane, and you watched me walk back out of them unscathed."

"*No one* left those tunnels unscathed—"

"*Alive*, then," I say fiercely, turning to face her now. "After everything, you watched me leave those tunnels *alive*. You watched me claw and bite and scratch my way to the surface, and you watched me plunge that injection into Morgane's thigh. *You*. Not Jean Luc, not Coco, not Reid or Beau or Frederic." My voice grows thicker beneath the flood of grief, of *rage* and regret and resentment and . . . and defeat. "The others, they—they see me as someone who needs protection, who needs a—a glass box and a polished pedestal on the highest shelf, but *you* were supposed to see me differently." Voice breaking, I push up Coco's sleeve to show her the emerald ribbon still tied around my wrist. "You were s-supposed to be my *friend*, Lou. I *needed* you to be my friend."

As soon as the words fall, I regret them. Because Lou *is* my friend—and Jean Luc is my fiancé—and everyone in that council room knows better than me, wants to *help* me. Perhaps I deserve to be treated like a child. I've certainly stamped my feet and screamed like one.

Lou stares down at the ribbon for a long moment.

To my distress, she doesn't speak. She doesn't argue or patronize or reprimand; she doesn't tell me not to worry or not to cry, nor does she sigh and escort me back to the safety of my room. No. Instead, she takes my hand and squeezes firmly, looking me directly in the eye as the sun slips beneath the river. Glittering powder swirls around us as another branch breaks. "You're right, Célie," she says. "I am so sorry."

Seven magic words.

Seven perfect blows.

"Wh-What?" I say, breathless with them.

"I said I'm sorry. I wish I could explain myself somehow, but I have no excuse. I should've told you everything from the start—how you proceeded with it should've been *your* decision, not mine. And certainly not Jean Luc's." Her lips twist as if in memory of something, and my heart sinks in realization. She would've heard our argument in the library. *Everyone* would have heard it. Heat blooms in my cheeks as she adds, "He's an *ass*, by the way, and has no idea what he's talking about. If you hadn't been here"—she gestures around us to the Brindelle trees, and her cloak pulls with the movement, revealing the scar along her collar—"Morgane would've slit *my* throat. Again. I would've died that day, and even Reid wouldn't have been able to bring me back a third time." A wicked gleam enters her eyes as an idea sparks, followed by a wickeder grin. "Do you want me to curse him for you? Jean Luc?"

I chuckle tremulously and pull her toward the wide, cobbled street in front of the town house. An enormous bridge intersects it, spanning the great fissure that split the kingdom in two during the Battle of Cesarine. The Chasseurs—along with hundreds of volunteers—laid the final stone last month. Beau and the royal family held a festival in honor of the occasion, unveiling a plaque at the bridge's entrance that reads: *Mieux vaut prévenir que guérir.*

Father Achille chose the words, a cautionary tale to all who cross.

It is better to prevent than to heal.

I reach out to trace the letters as we pass. There is nothing more to see here, and furthermore, Lou spoke truth—we're freezing off our delectable assets, and our hair now smells of fish. "As much as I'd like to see him squirm, Jean Luc is under a lot of pressure right now. A curse might rather compound things. I *do*, however, give you full permission to curse him *after* we find this murderer."

Lou groans theatrically. "Are you sure? Not even a small one? I came *this* close to dyeing his hair blue last year. Or perhaps we could shave off an eyebrow. Jean Luc would look *ridiculous* without an eyebrow—"

"In fairness, anyone would look ridiculous without an eyebrow."

Chuckling again, I lift Coco's hood to cover my still-damp head. When Lou slips her arm through my elbow in response, forcing me to *sashay* rather than walk across the bridge, that torrent in my chest slows to a trickle—until the cross clinks against the ring in my pocket. A reminder.

My heart sinks once more.

In the distance, Saint-Cécile's bell clangs slow and deep, and Chasseur Tower looms like a shadow behind the cathedral, baleful and imposing in the darkness. There's nothing for it. At the bridge's end, I gently disentangle my arm from Lou's. "I should go. Jean Luc and I need to . . . finish our discussion."

She glances pointedly at my bare finger, arching a brow. "Really? It looks finished to me."

"I—" Cheeks burning once more, I hide the incriminating hand within my cloak. "I haven't decided anything yet." When she says nothing, merely purses her lips, I continue hastily, "Really, I haven't, and—and even if I have—not every choice is a forever one."

Unfortunately, the words fail to evoke Father Achille's steady assurance, and my shoulders slump in resignation. In *exhaustion.*

What a mess.

"Hmm." Taking pity on me, Lou bumps my hip and drags me in the opposite direction. "You aren't wrong, but you also don't need to make that choice tonight. Indeed, I must *insist* you let our dear captain stew in his stupidity for at least a few hours. Coco and Beau are coming over for a nightcap after a *very* long day, and Reid will be thrilled to see you—Melisandre, too, if you apologize for canceling last month. She even caught you a lovely birthday present for the festivities tomorrow. I'm sure she'll drag it out just as we're cutting the cake." Hesitating, she glances back at the town house with its pretty pale stone and ivy vines. "Unless you'd rather stay here?"

"No," I say too quickly.

"Excellent." Beaming, she stuffs a lock of my windswept hair back beneath my hood. "Then I suggest cheese under the table as an olive branch, but slip it when Reid isn't looking. He doesn't like Melisandre eating table scraps—"

My feet slow of their own accord, and reluctantly, I draw to a halt. I don't know why. I miss Lou's cat too—I miss *all* of them—yet I cannot bring myself to take another step. "You go ahead," I tell her, forcing a smile. "I'll catch up." When she frowns, I nod in reassurance and motion for her to continue. "Don't worry. I owe Melisandre an apology, so trust me—I'll meet you there. I can't have her put out with me."

The sun has fully set now, and her eyes flick around the dark street before returning to my person. "You do know it's dangerous to wander alone at night with a killer on the loose?"

"*You* did," I point out.

She hesitates again, clearly deliberating.

"Lou." I squeeze her wrist imploringly. "Whoever killed Babette has little interest in me. They could've snatched me in the cemetery after I found her, but they didn't. I promise I'll be right behind you. I just need a few moments to . . . collect myself. Please."

Lou bobs her head with a quick exhale. "Right. Of course you do. And you *also* have your Balisarda, correct?" When I shake my head, she lifts my left arm with a beleaguered sigh, pinching the hard embroidery on the cloak's hem. "How fortunate that Coco keeps a thin blade in each sleeve. You probably won't need them, but if you *do*, the clasp on the right sleeve sticks. Go for the left."

I try not to look startled. Of *course* Coco keeps knives in her clothing. "I will."

Lou nods again. "I'll see you in an hour?"

"I'll see you in an hour."

"Remember, Célie"—she presses her thumb on the clasp of my left sleeve, and a razor-sharp blade slides into my palm— "everyone has a groin."

After slipping the knife back into position, she hugs me briefly before disappearing up the street. I watch her figure retreat with a wistfulness that only she seems to understand—except, of course, that she doesn't understand at all. Not really. I close my eyes, trying to ignore my leaden feet. Lou has found her place in life—she's found her family, her *home*—and I just . . .

Haven't.

It's a sobering realization.

As if sensing my morbid thoughts, the front door of the town house opens, and my mother steps out, hastily dressed in a glittering black robe. "Célie?" she calls softly, peering out into the shadows of the Brindelle trees. Her bedroom window also overlooks the park; she must've seen me creeping below, perhaps heard me bickering with Lou, and come to investigate. "Darling? Are you still here?"

I stand perfectly still across the bridge, willing her to return to bed.

Indeed, I watch her so fixedly I don't realize that the hair on my neck has lifted, that the wind has fled with Lou. I don't notice the shadow detaching itself from the street, moving swiftly—*too* swiftly—in my periphery. No. As the seventh branch crumbles in Brindelle Park, I see only my mother's forlorn figure, and I wish— I wish, I wish, I *wish*—that I could've found my place with her, my family, my home. I wish I could find it with *anyone.*

I should've known better.

My nursemaid always said seven is a magical number, and these trees—perhaps they aren't quite as dead as I imagine. Perhaps they remember me too. Their glittering powder hangs suspended in the still night air—watching, waiting, *knowing*—as that shadow descends.

As sharp pain explodes across my temple, and the entire world goes black.

CHAPTER TEN

A Bird in Her Cage

Wake up.

The words reverberate through my mind in a voice that's not my own—in a voice familiar, in a voice deep and rich—and my eyes respond immediately, snapping open at the imperious command. Except . . . I blink, recoiling slightly, when the darkness remains absolute. It feels as if I haven't opened my eyes at all. Not even a sliver of light pierces the black around me.

My heart begins to pound.

Thump-thump, are-you

Thump-thump, fright-ened

Thump-thump, sweet-ing?

I slam my eyes shut once more. Because the dark of my eyelids is far better than the dark of the unknown, the dark of my *nightmares*, and—and where *am* I? Confusion scatters my thoughts, heightening my senses until I reel with them, until they converge in a sickening rush. This place smells not of fish but of something sweet and sharp, something oddly metallic, which means I've left the Doleur behind. Perhaps—perhaps I'm safe in Lou's apartment? *Yes.* Perhaps I no longer feel the cold air of Brindelle Park because I fell asleep on her chaise. Perhaps they doused every light because they didn't want to wake me. *Yes, of course—*

Dull pain stirs in my head as I nod deliriously.

Wincing, I touch the knot at my temple, and the entire delusion spins out of control, crashing to the ground at my feet. Because Lou did not give me this lump. She did not creep up behind me, unseen, and knock me unconscious with a single crushing blow.

You do know it's dangerous to wander alone at night with a killer on the loose?

Oh God.

The entire world sways as I lurch from my seat, but small, cold hands descend on my shoulders with startling speed. With startling *strength*. They push me back down, accompanied by a dulcet feminine voice.

"Ah, ah, ah. You mustn't flee."

My heart sinks horribly.

At the woman's words, a single candle ignites across the room—*far* across the room, which spans nearly thrice the distance I expected. Vague shapes emerge in its wake: thick, ornate carpets, heavy drapes, and—and carved ebony boxes. At least two of them, perhaps more. The candle illuminates very little. With that flicker of light, however, the endless dark finally breaks, and my thoughts are able to focus with my vision. My breath steadies. My heartbeat slows.

This darkness—it isn't real. Wherever I am, it is not a coffin with my sister, and Morgane le Blanc is dead.

She is *dead*, and she is never coming back.

"Are you frightened?" the voice asks, genuinely curious.

"Should I be?"

Humorless laughter thrums in response.

How much time has passed? When we parted ways, Lou expected me at her apartment in one hour. If I don't arrive, she'll come looking for me; they'll *all* come looking for me—Jean Luc and Father Achille and the Chasseurs included. I need to stall until then. I need to—to engage the killer somehow. If she isn't interested in conversation, Coco's knives remain tucked in the sleeves of this cloak, and my hands remain free. I can kill if I must.

I have killed before.

"Who are you?" Despite the cold touch on my shoulders, my voice rings hard and clear as the crystal chandelier overhead. I am so *tired* of being afraid. "Where am I?"

The woman leans around me, and her long sable hair falls over my shoulder, a touch lighter and warmer than my own. It smells of marigolds. Of sandalwood. "Why, we're on a ship, darling. Where else?" With a featherlight touch, she plucks the crimson hood from my head, tilting to examine me closer. "I am Odessa, and *you* are every bit as lovely as rumor claims." In my periphery, she rubs a lock of my hair between her thumb and forefinger, and I hear rather than see the frown on her face. "A good deal less scarred, however. The other one had whole constellations of them—she carved all twelve stars of the Woodwose onto her left foot."

Scarred? Constellations? I blink at the words. They seem . . . strangely irrelevant given our situation, in which this woman has assaulted me, abducted me, and stowed me in the belly of a ship like a piece of—

Wait.

A ship?

Oh no. Oh no no no—

When the floor undulates in confirmation, I tamp down on my hysteria swiftly, viciously. I cannot afford to lose my head. Not again. Not like I did with Babette. My eyes flick to the candle across the room, to the wide windows behind it, but the curtains conceal whatever lies outside. I can only pray that we still float in the harbor, that we haven't yet departed for the open sea. If the former, Lou practically lives next door; only a handful of streets separate her apartment and the water. If the latter, well . . .

I force a smile, unsure what else to do.

"It is . . . enthralling to make your acquaintance, Odessa," I say at last.

"*Enthralling.*" The woman seems to taste the word, intrigued, before she drifts away to perch on one of the ebony boxes. "Not quite a lie, but far superior to the truth. Well done."

My breath catches at my first true sight of her face, and I stare at her, rendered momentarily mute. "Er—"

She arches a supercilious brow. "Yes?"

Thick waves frame her large, deep brown eyes—wide-set and upturned, almost feline—and high cheekbones, bow lips. She has painted them plum. They match the satin of her low-cut gown, the jewels of her lavish necklace. Against the pallor of her amber skin, the entire ensemble is . . . well, *enthralling.* I shake myself mentally. "May I ask *why* we are on a ship?"

"Of course you may." Odessa tilts her head, frown deepening, and suddenly, she is the cat and I am the bird in a cage. Despite her words, fresh wariness prickles my skin. Why hasn't she restrained me? Why are there no ropes? No chains? As if sensing my thoughts, she leans forward, dousing half of her beautiful face in shadow. "Such a clever turn of phrase, that—though undoubtedly polite, you simultaneously request my permission to ask and proceed to ask without my permission."

"I—" I blink again, struggling to keep pace with the uncanny woman. "My apologies, mademoiselle." When she continues to simply stare, however—those protuberant eyes *entirely* too intent upon my face—I cast about for something else to say. *Anything* else to say. I need just a few more moments before Lou and the others arrive. "Er, please forgive my ignorance, but you aren't anything like I expected."

"Really? And what did you expect?"

My brows furrow. "To be completely honest, I don't know. Cruelty? A general air of malevolence? You *have* killed five people."

"Oh, she's killed many more than that," another voice—*that* voice—interjects, and I nearly leap from my skin, squeaking and whirling to face the figure directly behind me.

Him.

The cold man.

He stands entirely too close—too *silent*—watching me with a derisive smirk. Cheeks flushing, I clutch my chest and try to speak without gasping, without betraying the sudden spike of my pulse. "H-How long have you been standing there?"

When he laughs, it is low and dangerous. "Long enough."

"Yes, well, it's quite rude to—to—" The words quickly wither on my tongue, however. Though it *is* rude to conceal one's presence among company, it is altogether ruder to knock a defenseless woman unconscious and drag her into one's foul den of iniquity. This man has done both. For all his refinery, he seems to have missed a few crucial lessons in etiquette. "Why am I here?" I ask instead. "Are you planning to exsanguinate me like Babette and the others?"

"Perhaps." Clasping his hands behind his back, he circles me with predatory grace. The candlelight paints his stark colors—the white of his skin, the silver of his hair, the black of his coat—almost golden. It does nothing to soften him, however. His eyes could draw blood as they lock with mine. "Did you tell your little friend about the roses?"

"Why do you want to know?"

"You should answer him," Odessa says from her perch on the ebony box. "My cousin grows quite tedious if he doesn't get his way."

The man's black eyes cut to hers. "A family trait, I'm sure."

"No need to be prickly, darling."

When at last he halts in front of me, I lift my face, pretending to be obstinate when in reality, I cannot look away. I have never met a person with features so fine, so *feral*. Still, unease skitters down my spine as he tucks a single finger beneath my chin. "Who—who are you?" I ask.

"I am much more interested in who *you* are, pet."

With a dramatic sigh, Odessa slides from the lid of her box. "Really, cousin, you should be more specific in the future. I followed your instruction to the letter." She lifts three fingers, revealing black nails, long and wickedly sharp. An onyx gem glitters on her knuckle, connected by a fine silver chain to the bracelet on her wrist. "Black hair, crimson cloak, companion of La Dame des Sorcières. She meets all three criteria—and she certainly *smells* like a Dame Rouge—but . . ." Her plum lips purse as together, the two regard me with what looks absurdly like suspicion. "She bears no scars."

There is that word again—*scars*. And did Odessa say I *smell* like a Dame Rouge? How could I possibly—

Realization swoops low and swift in my stomach—sickening—

as the pieces click into place, but I fight to keep my expression impassive, keenly aware of their scrutiny. Keenly aware that I'm still wearing Coco's cloak.

I am not the only companion of La Dame des Sorcières with black hair.

On the wings of that realization comes another, equally chilling: *The other one had whole constellations of them—she carved all twelve stars of the Woodwose onto her left foot.* These people knew Babette. They knew her intimately enough to see her bare feet, to remember the configuration of her scars. They killed her. Certainty swells in my chest. They killed her, and now—now they're after Coco. Curiously, the knowledge doesn't make my heart pound or my hands tremble like it should. No. It straightens my spine, and I jerk away from the man's touch.

They will not have Coco.

Not if I can help it.

"Is that so?" Despite my best efforts, his grip tightens on my chin, and he tilts my face back and forth in search of scars, his gaze touching my eyes, my cheekbones, my lips, my throat. His jaw hardens at the last. "What is your name?" he finally asks, and his voice is softer now. Sinister. I know better than to ignore him. My instincts tingle all over again, warning me to remain still, warning me that this man is more than he seems.

When I swallow hard, stalling, considering my response, his eyes track the movement. "Why do you want to know?" I finally ask.

"That isn't an answer, pet."

"That isn't either."

Lip curling in displeasure, he releases my chin, but all relief shrivels when instead he crouches before me, his eyes directly in line with my own. I do my best to ignore the way his forearms rest against his knees, the way his fingers lace together as he considers me. Deceptively casual. His hands are large, and I know firsthand how strong they are. He could crush my throat in a second. As if reading my thoughts, he murmurs, "This will be much more pleasant if you play nicely."

I repeat his own words. "And if I refuse?"

"Unlike you, I *do* possess the means to force your acquiescence." He chuckles darkly. "Again, however—they won't be pleasant, and they won't be polite." When still I say nothing—locking my jaw—his eyes narrow. His knee brushes my shin, and even that slight touch bolts up my spine, lifting the hair on my neck. In this position, almost kneeling at my feet, he should look submissive, perhaps reverent, yet he couldn't be more in control. He leans closer. "Shall I tell you *exactly* what I intend to do to you?"

"I told you he could be tedious." Strolling to the candle, Odessa plucks a scroll from the table beneath it. She unfurls it without interest before tossing it aside and selecting another. To her cousin, she says, "*Do* hurry up, Michal. I long to be rid of this foul place."

"You said you longed for fresh air, cousin."

"The air in Cesarine is far from fresh—and don't think I failed to hear the judgment in your voice just now. Air baths have enormous health benefits." She waves an errant hand and sifts through the other scrolls, her attention already drifting. "Really, must you always be so closed-minded? A bit of naked window time might do you good—"

"*Enough*, Odessa."

To my surprise, she complies without protest—without rolling her eyes or muttering an insult under her breath—and that immediate obedience is somehow more ominous than any threat the man could've given. Lou would have laughed in his face. Jean Luc would have attacked in a second.

I suspect both of them would already be dead.

The man—*Michal*—takes a measured, controlled breath before returning his attention to me, but even I can see his patience unraveling. He arches a brow, his eyes darker than before. Flat, frightening black. "Well? How shall you have me, pet? Pleasant or unpleasant?" I stare at him, resolute, until he nods with bleak satisfaction. "Very well—"

"C-Cosette." I force the name through gritted teeth, refusing to break eye contact. A good liar never looks away, never hesitates or falters, but I have never been a good liar. I pray to God now to help me become one. "My name is Cosette Monvoisin."

His expression darkens further at the obvious lie. "*You* are Cosette Monvoisin?"

"Of course I am."

"Take off your cloak."

"I— What?"

Perhaps he sees the panic in my eyes, senses the sudden tension in my body, because he leans closer still. His legs press into mine now. His lips curl in a hard grin. "Take off your cloak, Mademoiselle Cosette, and show us your scars. As a Dame Rouge, you must have them somewhere."

I lurch to my feet—partly to feign outrage, partly to escape his touch—and the chair crashes to the ground behind me. Odessa glances up from her scrolls, curiosity piqued, as my cheeks flame and my hands clench. *Please, please, please*, I pray, but I cannot turn back now. I must lie as I've never lied before.

"How *dare* you, monsieur? I am the Princesse Rouge, and I will not be spoken to in such a lewd and familiar manner. You said yourself that you can—that you can *smell* the magic flowing in my veins. Clearly, I am outnumbered and outmatched, so please, heed your cousin and enact whatever plans you have for this evening. Let us not draw out the unpleasantness. Tell me what you want, and I shall endeavor to oblige—or kill me here and now. I do not fear death," I add, fixing him with my fiercest stare, "so do not presume to—to frighten me with idle threats."

Still crouching, thoroughly unfazed, he watches my tirade with scathing apathy. "Liar."

"I beg your pardon?"

"You're a liar, pet. Every word you've spoken since we've met has been false."

"That isn't—"

He clicks his tongue in gentle reprimand, shaking his head, and rises slowly to his feet like a shadow unfurling. I cannot help but yield a step. "What is your name?" he asks, and something in his voice—perhaps the sudden stillness of his frame—warns this will be the last time.

"I *told* you. I am Cosette Monvoisin."

"Are you eager for death, Cosette Monvoisin?"

I retreat another step subconsciously. "I— Of course I'm not *eager* for death, but death—it's inevitable, monsieur. It f-finds us all eventually."

"Does it?" He closes the distance between us without seeming to move. One second, he stands with hands clasped behind him over *there*, and the next, he stands with hands clasped behind him right *here.* "You speak as if you know him."

I exhale sharply. "How did you—"

"Could it be that he has already found you?" He lifts a pale hand to my collar. Though I stiffen, he merely tugs the strings of Coco's cloak, and it tumbles to our feet in a ripple of crimson fabric. He brushes the hair from my shoulder. My knees begin to quake.

"Wh-Who?"

"Death," he breathes, bending low to—to *scent* the curve of my neck. Though he doesn't quite touch me, I *feel* his nearness like the lightest of fingers trailing down my throat. When I gasp and pull away, he straightens with a frown—unaffected, perhaps oblivious—and glances back at Odessa. "Blood magic doesn't flow through her veins."

"No," she says blithely, still reading her scrolls. Ignoring us completely. "Something else does."

"Do you recognize the scent?"

She lifts an elegant shoulder. "Not at all. It isn't quite human, though, is it?"

I stare from one to the other as silence falls between them, convinced I misheard over the riotous beat of my heart. When neither speaks—when they don't snort in disbelief, or perhaps laugh at their own clever joke—I shake my head and snatch Coco's cloak from the floor. "You're both quite mistaken." Throwing it over my shoulders, I draw my hand into the left sleeve. Cheeks still hot, I press the latch, and her knife slides into my palm.

Lou and the others should've arrived by now. Either they cannot find my trail, or I am already lost at sea. The cause, however, no longer matters. The effect remains the same. I am running out of time, and these—these *creatures* cannot be allowed to roam free. If they leave the ship, they'll undoubtedly resume their hunt for Coco, and here—now—I still maintain the element of surprise. My gaze drifts from Michal's eyes to his ears to his nose to his— lower parts.

He arches a wry brow.

It doesn't matter who you're up against, Célie—everyone has a groin somewhere. Find it, kick as hard as you can, and get the hell out of there.

With a deep breath, I throw caution to the winds and lunge—

Between one blink and the next, Michal moves again, and suddenly, he isn't in front of me at all, but directly behind, seizing my wrist and twisting, lifting the knife in my hand to my own throat. "I wouldn't do that if I were you," he breathes.

CHAPTER ELEVEN

Hell Is Empty

In moments of extreme duress, the human body often triggers the psychological response of fight or flight. I remember Filippa describing it to me as a child—the dry mouth, the tunnel vision, the shallow breaths. Even then, I knew Pip would never flee.

I knew I would never fight.

I react now without thinking—*eyes, ears, nose, groin*—thrusting my head backward, smashing Michal's nose, whirling to knee him in the nether region. He sidesteps before I can connect, however—his arms snaking around my waist, pulling me with him—and I strike hard thigh instead. I nearly *shatter my kneecap* instead. Sharp pain spikes through the bone, but I tear free of his macabre embrace and race past him, stumbling in the darkness, searching blindly for a door, *any* door—

There.

I throw my weight against the heavy wood—once, twice, three times—and when at last it crashes open, I go with it, landing hard on my hands and knees. They shriek with agony as I claw my way forward, upright, as I bolt up the corridor and around the bend. No cold hands seize my shoulders this time; no silvery voice titters a warning.

They've let me go.

No. I push the intrusive thought aside, pushing myself faster, up the stairs, each step between us a breath of relief. *No, I escaped. I escaped the room, and now I must escape the ship*—

Thrusting open another set of doors, I skid to a halt on the quarterdeck, and my stomach plummets with the temperature.

Moonlight glints upon open water.

It yawns before me in every direction, unbroken and unending—except to the west, where a cluster of lights still sparkle on the horizon. *Cesarine.* Never before have I thought the word with such longing. With such *fear.* We've already departed for *God* knows where, which means . . . a hard knot forms in my throat at the realization, making it difficult to breathe.

My friends will never find me.

No.

I dart across the deck to where dozens of sailors work in unison, their movements strangely rhythmic as they handle the sails and steer the helm, as they haul rope and tie knots and scrub floorboards. Unlike Michal and Odessa, their skin flushes with physical exertion, warm and familiar, despite the hollow gleam in their eyes. "Please, monsieur"—I seize the sleeve of the man nearest me—"I—I've b-been abducted, and I desperately need your help." Though my voice climbs steadily higher, shrill now, he doesn't seem to hear it, brushing past as if I haven't spoken at all. Glancing back at the double doors, I cling to his arm helplessly. "*Please.* Is there some sort of lifeboat on board? I must return to Cesarine—"

He shakes free of my grip easily, trudging onward without seeing me. I stare after him with mounting panic before whirling to another. "Monsieur?" This man sits atop a three-legged stool, whittling a piece of wood into a swan—or at least, it *started* as a swan. Where the bird's body should be, the man flicks his wrist mechanically in the same stroke, over and over and over again. Perhaps recklessly, I pluck the knife away, determined to gain his attention. He does nothing to stop me. His gnarled hand, however—it keeps moving as if he still holds the blade, honing the wood into a wickedly sharp point. "Monsieur, can—can you hear me?"

I wave the knife in front of his nose, but he doesn't so much as blink.

Something is very wrong here.

When I slip a hand beneath his scarf to check his pulse, it beats weakly against my fingertips. Alive, then. Relief crashes through me in a violent wave, except—

I recoil, dropping the knife, before wrenching the scarf from his throat.

Before revealing two pinprick punctures.

They still weep gently, trickling blood down his collar. "Oh God. You—you are injured, monsieur. Here, let me—" When I press against the wounds to stem the bleeding, he opens his mouth and mutters something unintelligible. With another hasty glance at the doors, I lean closer despite myself.

"Always sleep at nightfall, darlings, always say your prayers." He slurs the words as his eyes flutter closed, as his head begins to sway to the slow, haunting rhythm. "Always wear a silver cross, and always walk in pairs."

From somewhere in my subconscious, horror dawns.

I know these words. I recognize them as surely as I remember my sister's stubborn face, my nursemaid's lilting voice. *Oh God.*

Oh God oh God oh God

I drop my fingers from his throat, and his hollow eyes snap open. Except they aren't hollow anymore. Absolute terror streaks through them—bright enough to blind, to *burn*—and he seizes my wrist in a punishing grip. A great spasm wracks his frame. "R-Run," he chokes out, his throat working furiously on the word. "*Run.*"

Twisting away from him, I gasp and stumble backward, and he collapses like a marionette. In the next second, however, he straightens. His hands resume their mindless carving, and when he blinks, his eyes empty of all emotion once more. Through it all, his throat continues to drip.

Drip.

Drip.

Spinning wildly, I search for the lifeboat, but now that I've seen those marks, I cannot escape them. Everywhere I turn, they leer back at me, adorning the neck of each sailor—some fresh and still bleeding, others crusted, bruised, and inflamed. It cannot be coincidence. These vacant-eyed men have been attacked and subdued—just like Babette and the others, just like *me*—and these wounds prove it. I clasp a hand to my own throat, shuddering and dashing to the carved handrail. We've been sentenced to death, all of us.

I would rather drown than die as these men will die.

With shallow breaths, I lean over the side of the quarterdeck, staring into the black waters below. The waves are fitful tonight. They crash against the ship's hull in warning, promising retribution for any foolish enough to enter. And perhaps I am a fool. A headstrong, hopeful *fool* for fleeing Chasseur Tower, for believing *I* could succeed where Jean Luc and Lou failed. I glance once more at the double doors, but it seems my captors are in no rush to pursue me. Why should they be? They know I cannot escape.

My resolve hardens at the small insult.

I've never been a strong swimmer, but if I jump, there is a chance—though infinitesimal—that I might survive the water's wrath, that I might follow the current back to Cesarine. I have met the Goddess of the Sea, and I call many melusines my friend. Perhaps they will help me.

Before I can change my mind, I clamber onto the handrail and send a silent, desperate prayer up to Heaven.

Cold fingers wrap around my wrist. They drag me back to Hell.

"Going somewhere?" Michal murmurs.

I choke on a sob.

"L-Leave me alone." Though I try to twist away from him, my efforts prove futile; his hand remains a manacle around my wrist, and I slip on the narrow railing, my stomach plunging as I lose my footing completely and pitch over the side of the ship. Shrieking, I claw at his hand—the only thing keeping me aloft—and dangle midair over the icy waves. He holds my weight easily, tilting his head as he watches me flail.

"I'll admit that I'm curious." He arches a brow. "What now, pet? Do you plan to *swim* to Cesarine?"

"Pull me up!" The plea tears from my throat of its own volition, and my feet search blindly, frantically, for purchase against the side of the ship. "Please, *please*—"

His grip loosens in response, and I slip an inch, screaming anew. The wind thrashes around us. It tears at my hair, my gown, slicing through the thin fabric and piercing my skin like a thousand needles. And suddenly, my resolve doesn't feel like resolve at all. It feels like the violent and visceral urge to *live*. I maul his arm in an attempt to climb up his body, to climb *away* from certain death below.

It seems I wouldn't rather drown, after all.

"By all means"—he drops me another inch—"don't let me stop you. You should know, however, that you'll freeze to death in seven minutes. *Seven*," he repeats coldly, his face a granite mask of calm. "Are you a strong swimmer, Cosette Monvoisin?"

My nails dig into his sleeve, scoring the leather fabric, as a wave rises high enough to kiss my feet. "N-No—"

"No? Such a pity."

Another scream ravages my throat—another swell snatches my hem—before at last I find purchase against the ship and vault upward. He doesn't release my wrist, instead catching my waist with his free hand and guiding me over the handrail in a single fluid motion. Though he deposits me gently on my feet, the ice in his gaze belies the movement. His mouth twists in distaste as he steps away.

When my knees give out a second later, he does nothing to catch me, and I crumple at his feet, wrapping my arms around my torso and shivering uncontrollably. My hem has already frozen in the bitter wind. It sticks to my ankles, my calves, and creeping numbness follows.

I hate him. As fiercely and unequivocally as I have ever hated anyone, I *loathe* this man.

"Just do it." Refusing to bare my throat—refusing to search for those needle-thin knives on his person—I glare up at him. He might take my life, but he will not take my dignity. "Pierce my skin. Drain my blood. Use it for whatever foul purpose you used the others'."

With that same distasteful expression, he crouches, and his sheer size conceals me from the rest of the crew. *Not that it matters*, I think bitterly. The men still move strangely, like puppets on a string. Not a single eye has flicked in our direction since Michal arrived.

He studies me intently now. His expression reveals nothing. "I have never met one so eager for death as you." When I do not speak, he shakes his head. "Never fear, however—I am nothing if not a gentleman. Who am I to deny a lady such as yourself?"

A lady.

The word sparks like kindling under my skin, and I sit up with a snarl, nearly striking his nose again. I have never been a violent person. Indeed, I usually abhor the sight of blood, but when a porcelain doll breaks, she is nothing but sharp edges. A strange, secret part of me wants to hurt this man. It wants to draw blood. Stifling the vicious reaction, I speak between clenched teeth. "Do it, then. Why wait?"

His lips curl in a smile. It doesn't reach his eyes. "Patience is a virtue, pet."

This close, his distinct lack of scent is unnerving—like snow or marble, or perhaps poison slipped in wine. I cannot stand another second in his presence. "I am not your *pet*"—I spit the words in a voice I hardly recognize—"and do not pretend to understand virtue, monsieur. You are no gentleman."

A low noise of agreement rumbles through his chest, or is it— my eyes narrow incredulously—is it laughter? Is he *laughing* at me?

"Enlighten me, mademoiselle. What does make a gentleman?"

"You patronize me."

"It's a simple question."

When I lurch to my feet in response, cold amusement glints in his black eyes, sparking brighter as I stumble and catch his broad shoulder for balance. My hand recoils instantly. I feel sick at that touch—at the rage in my stomach, the *humiliation*. I am not who he wants. Not truly. I am not even important enough to kill.

Taking advantage of his vulnerable position, I try to dart past him, but again—between one blink and the next—he moves in front of me, blocking my path. My gaze darts to the double doors.

I try again.

He reappears.

Clasping his hands behind his back, he speaks with cruel levity. "I can only assume your next step is to seek my cousin, appeal to her compassionate—perhaps maternal—nature. Let me spare you the disappointment: Odessa is the least maternal creature alive. Even if she *did* sympathize with your plight, she would not help you. She answers to me." He pauses with that dark half smile, inclining his head toward the men around us. "They *all* answer to me."

My heart thrashes in my ears as I stare at him.

One second.

Two.

When I pivot and lunge for the railing, he appears before me once more, and I skid to a halt to avoid colliding with his chest. The humor in his eyes gradually fades at whatever he sees in mine. "As you care so little for your own life, allow me to expedite this foolishness."

With the wave of his hand, every sailor on the ship ceases his duties, lurching upright and marching toward the handrail on the starboard side. They don't stop there, however. Without hesitation, without a *word*, they proceed to climb until they stand in a neat row along the handrail, balancing in the gale and awaiting further instruction. The wind heightens to a crescendo as I watch them in horror. Because they look like—like tin soldiers standing there, and suddenly, I don't see their empty faces at all.

I see mine.

Morgane once rendered my body equally powerless. With her magic, she forced Beau and me to duel each other, forced us to *hurt* each other in order to send a message to her daughter. Even as my sword plunged into his chest, I could do nothing to stop it, and I knew in that instant—I *knew*—I would never see such evil again. I knew I would never meet her equal.

When one of the soldiers sways precariously, feet slipping on the handrail, I whirl to Michal with a renewed sense of purpose. "Stop this. Stop this *now*."

"You aren't in any position to make demands, pet. Should you attempt to swim to Cesarine, my men will follow, and they will also—tragically—freeze to death." His eyes harden into something foreign and frightening then, something feral, as he seizes a lock of my hair, testing it between thumb and forefinger. "Of course, anemia will shorten their life span to less than seven minutes. Perhaps four if they're lucky. You'll be forced to watch them all drown." A pause. "Do you understand?"

Anemia? I retreat from the railing like it's grown horns, trying to place the word. When I cannot, the rage in my chest flares irrationally. "Let them down," I snap instead. "I won't answer anything until they're safe on deck."

"There is nowhere safe on deck." Though he speaks the words with quiet menace, the sailors somehow understand his intent; as swiftly and silently as they climbed atop the handrail, they alight from it to resume their eerie dance. No longer tin soldiers, but marionettes. Michal inclines his head. "Have we reached an accord?"

"How do you control them?" I ask. "The men?"

"How do you bear no scars?"

"La Dame des Sorcières cast a spell to disguise me." The lie spills from my lips with unexpected relish. I edge to the left as surreptitiously as possible, eyes lighting on the man with his swan-shaped stake. "We knew you planned to abduct me—"

"Petite menteuse." Michal's eyes darken further at the falsehood. *Little liar.*

Despite alarming evidence to the contrary, I cannot help the way my fists curl. "I am *not* a liar."

"No?" He shadows my steps as a predator stalking his prey. Patient. Lethal. He thinks I am trapped, and perhaps I am. "When were you born, Cosette Monvoisin?"

"October thirty-first."

"*Where* were you born?"

"L'Eau Melancolique. Specifically, Le Palais de Cristal in Le Présage." Obstinance—no, *pride*—drips from each word, from each little detail. *Eternal stars in your eyes,* Pippa always told me, and thank God for that. Thank God I collect stories like melusines collect treasure; thank God I listen when people speak.

Michal's jaw clenches. "Your parents' names?"

"My mother was the fabled witch Angelica. She died in the Battle of Cesarine along with my aunt, La Voisin, who raised me. I do not know my father. My mother never spoke his name."

"Such a pity," he repeats softly, but he doesn't sound apologetic at all. "How did you meet Louise le Blanc?"

I lift my chin. "She threw a mud pie in my face."

"And Babette Trousset?"

"We grew up together in La Fôret des Yeux."

"Did you love her?"

"Yes."

"Who do you love now?"

"His Majesty and king of Belterra, Beauregard Lyon."

"And how did he propose?"

"He surprised me after my initiation into Chasseur Tower—" Triumph flares within Michal's black eyes, and his cold smile returns. Too late, I realize my mistake, missing a step and nearly landing in the enthralled sailor's lap. His wooden stake brushes my hip. Still he moves as if to carve it. Gritting my teeth, I seize the smooth wood and hide it within a fold of Coco's cloak. If Michal notices, he does not say.

Instead, he lifts a familiar golden ring between us. The diamond glitters in the moonlight.

"I did not realize Cosette Monvoisin *had* a betrothed," he says in a voice as frigid as the water below. "How intriguing."

My free hand shoots to my pocket, and bile burns up my throat when I find it empty. My engagement ring and Babette's cross— they're both gone, *stolen* by this man who is not a man at all but a monster. His black eyes aren't quite human as they watch me, and his body has grown too still. My own body responds in kind. I hardly dare breathe. "I did not realize she was a Chasseur either," he says softly. "To my knowledge, only *one* woman occupies that position, and she is not the Princesse Rouge."

In the silence that follows, he inhales my scent again. He tilts his head.

And I throw caution to the wind.

Swinging the wooden stake between us, I brandish it like a child with a toy sword. Between my fingers, the swan's eyes mock me. *You cannot hope to overpower this man*, they seem to say—or perhaps it is not their voice at all. Perhaps it is mine. *You cannot hope to outrun him.*

"Stay away from me." Breathless, I lift my stake higher, furious pressure building behind my eyes. *I can do this. I incapacitated Morgane le Blanc.* "I—I mean *nothing* to you. If you won't kill me, just—let me go. I mean nothing, so let me *go*."

Disgusted now, Michal no longer bothers to move with preternatural speed. No. He closes the distance between us slowly, his cold fist wrapping around mine and capturing the stake with laughable ease. He tosses it into the sea without a word. My heart sinks with it.

I sink with it.

"Do not run again," he warns, his voice softer and deadlier still, "or I will chase you." He leans closer. "You do not want me to chase you, pet."

To my credit, my voice doesn't tremble. "You won't hurt me."

"Such *conviction*."

The words ring in my ears like a promise.

When he straightens and snaps his fingers, the sailor behind me stands abruptly. Without his stake, his hands have stopped twitching, and whatever magic Michal has cast takes full control of him once more. He stares straight ahead without seeing. "Return her to the ballroom," Michal tells him. "If she attempts to escape again, I want you to retrieve your precious stake from the seafloor. Do you understand?"

The sailor nods and starts forward. When I don't immediately follow, he halts, pivoting, and his arm shoots out to snatch my elbow. He wrenches me forward with brute strength. Though I dig in my heels—though I claw at his wrist, hissing and spitting, twisting and kicking and even *biting*—he continues to march me toward the double doors, undeterred. His blood tastes acrid in my mouth.

"My friends will come for me," I snarl over my shoulder, grimacing when Michal appears there without warning. "They've done it once. They'll do it again."

He catches Coco's cloak between pale fingers. It slips from my shoulders easily, draping down his arms, and the way he studies it—

An icy fist grips my heart as at last he smiles—a true smile, a devastating one—and reveals two long, wickedly sharp canines. The world seems to slow in response. The men, the ship, the ocean—it all fades into gray as I stare at him, as I stare at *them*, equal parts horrified and transfixed.

Fangs.

The man has fangs.

"Oh, I'm counting on it," he says, his black eyes glittering.

And in that moment—as I descend into the bowels of his ship—I realize Hell is empty, and the Devil is here.

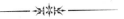

PART II

L'habit ne fait pas le moine.

The clothing does not make the monk.

CHAPTER TWELVE

The Isle of Requiem

I never learned what happened to my sister on the night of her death.

The night of her disappearance, however—*that* night I remember with excruciating clarity. I remember we argued. She'd snuck through our nursery window every night that week, all without a word to me. I still didn't even know the man's *name*. In my kinder moments, I tried to see the situation through her eyes: twenty-four years old and still sharing a nursery with her little sister. Twenty-four years old without a husband, without children, without a home and situation of her own. Perhaps she felt embarrassed. Perhaps the man lacked the title or wealth to procure her hand, so she kept their romance a secret. Perhaps a dozen other things that wouldn't have mattered to me—her *sister*—because I loved her. I would've shared a nursery until the end of time; I would've eagerly championed her mysterious man, regardless of his title or wealth. I would've giggled with her under the blankets, would've oiled the window hinges for their secret rendezvous myself.

She never told me about him, however.

She never told me anything.

In my less kind moments, I wondered if she even loved me at all.

"This has to stop," I hissed that night after the clock struck midnight, after the telltale creak of floorboard. Flinging my coverlet aside, I swung my feet from the bed and glared at her. She froze with one hand on the window latch. "Enough is enough, Filippa. *Whoever* they are shouldn't ask you to creep around in the dead of night to meet them. It's too dangerous."

Relaxing slightly, she edged the window open. Her cheeks glowed with excitement, or perhaps something else. "Go back to sleep, ma belle."

"I will *not*." My fists curled at the term of endearment because lately, it didn't feel endearing at all. It felt diminutive, derisive, as if she mocked me for something I didn't understand. And it *infuriated* me. "How long before Maman and Pére catch you? You know they'll take it out on both of us. I won't be able to see Reid for a *month.*"

She rolled her eyes and hitched a foot over the sill, trying and failing to hide the knapsack under her cloak. "Quelle tragédie."

"What is your *problem*—?"

With an impatient sigh, she said, "Reid isn't for you, Célie. How many times must I tell you? He's for the *Church*, and the sooner you realize that, the sooner you can do us all a favor and move on." She scoffed, shaking her head, as if I was the stupidest girl in the world. "He's going to break your heart."

But it was more than that. For all her sisterly bluster, she used to *like* Reid; she used to take no greater pleasure than forcing the two of us to play with her, to catch snowflakes and pick oranges and call her Votre Majesté, le magnifique Frostine, after her favorite fairy tale. Something had changed between them in the past year. Something had changed between *us.* "Says the woman currently dangling from the drainpipe," I snapped, inexplicably stung. "Why hasn't he introduced himself, Pip? Could it be he isn't interested in a real relationship? At least Reid still wants me when the sun comes up."

Her emerald eyes flashed. "And you'll never know a world without sunlight, will you? Not our darling Célie. You'll live forever safe in the light, and you'll never wonder, never question, never glance behind to see the shadows you cast. That's the problem with those who live in the sun." She stepped from the sill onto the branch outside our window, turning back to add with brutal efficiency, "I feel sorry for you, little sister."

They were the last words she ever spoke to me.

As I watch the candlelight flicker on Odessa's face now— trapped in the dark hull of a ship—I cannot help but wonder if my sister regretted opening that window. If she regretted stepping into the shadows. Though I'll never know, not truly, I can't imagine that she would've accepted her fate. She would've kicked and scratched and clawed against Morgane until her body gave out—because Pippa was strong. Even at her most secretive and infuriating, she was skillful, and she was sure. She was confident. *Convicted.*

As if I'd ever let anything happen to you, Célie.

She'd roll over in her grave if she knew I'd given up.

Straightening in my seat, I say to Odessa, "I don't suppose you'll tell me where we're going."

She doesn't look up at me, still wholly engrossed in her scrolls across the room. "You suppose correctly."

"Or how much longer it'll take to get there?"

"I fail to see how it matters." My gaze narrows at her clipped tone. She's right, of course. Whether we sail for another five minutes or another five hours, I cannot hope to escape until we reach land. As if sensing my thoughts, Odessa arches a sardonic brow. "You've developed the dangerous air of desperation and stupidity that always precedes an escape attempt. It reeks of failure."

I lift my chin. "You don't know that it'll fail."

"I do."

"What are you reading?"

With a barely discernible roll of her eyes, she returns her attention to the scrolls, effectively ending the conversation. I resist the urge to ask again, if only because I have little—no, *zero*—idea how to escape this ship after we dock. I know nothing of these creatures except for a vague, nagging sensation in the back of my mind. *Have I told you the story of Les Éternels?* When I tug on the memory, it unravels slowly into silver brushes and golden freckles and snow-white scarves. Into Evangeline's voice on a crisp October night. *They're born in the ground—cold as bone, and just as strong—without heart or soul or mind. Only impulse. Only* lust.

I twist the fraying ribbon around my wrist, thinking of Michal's black eyes, his adamantine skin, and resist the urge to scowl.

When the ship at last slows, dropping anchor, Odessa takes my elbow in her cold hand. "Where are we?" I ask again, but she merely sighs and leads me above deck once more.

Gray touches the horizon as we step from the gangway, and a truly sordid portrait stretches before us: an isle made of rock, wholly isolated from the rest of the world. On either side of us, dark water churns against sea stacks and a rugged beach. I focus on the waves, on the foam of each crest, to remain calm. To *think*. Because Evangeline had more to say that night in our nursery. The notes of her lullaby still linger in my ears, but I cannot quite hear them.

Not in this onslaught of noise.

My eyes widen at the absolute pandemonium around us.

Just ahead, the sailors dart throughout the harbor, their eyes mysteriously clear, shouting orders and calling to loved ones. Even the man with the stake envelops a small boy in a bone-crushing hug. Relief trickles through me at the sight—that this man has lived to see another day, that he hasn't met a watery grave—but then Odessa pushes me forward, her presence too cold. Too inhuman. Evangeline continues to whisper in my memory.

The first one came to our kingdom from a faraway land, living in the shadows, spreading her sickness to the people here. Infecting them with her magic.

At least Michal has vanished.

Swallowing hard, I track another child as she slips through the adults, nicking the watch from a sailor's wrist. Her skin and hair gleam silver in the pale light, and she—

My mouth falls open.

She has gills.

"Get back here!" Though the sailor lunges for her, she giggles and ducks beneath his outstretched arms, diving into the sea. Beneath her skirt, her legs ripple and shimmer, transforming into two fins, and she flicks them playfully before diving deeper. With a scowl, the man tries to pursue but instead plows into an enormous white wolf, who snaps at his heels in displeasure. "Fucking werewolves," he curses under his breath, lifting his hands and backing away slowly. "Fucking melusines."

I stare after him in disbelief before whirling to face Odessa. "What *is* this place?"

"Rather persistent, aren't you?" Agitated, she prods me past the man as he disappears into a seedy pub. "Fine. Welcome to L'île de Requiem, aptly christened by Michal, who thinks he's enormously clever. Try not to draw attention to yourself. The locals enjoy fresh blood."

The Isle of Requiem.

Though part of me shudders at the macabre name, the larger part cannot help but turn and wonder at the werewolf, at the woman behind who heals a sailor's throat with the flick of her wrist. *A witch.* My mouth parts incredulously. Witches and werewolves and mermaids, all inhabiting the same isle. I've never heard of such a thing.

My father often visited faraway lands as vicomte, of course, but he never allowed Pippa or me to join him. I pored over each map in his study instead—of Cesarine, of Belterra, of the entire continent—and memorized each landmark, each body of water.

There should be nothing but ocean off the eastern coast of Belterra.

"This is impossible." I crane my neck in each direction, determined to see everything, momentarily distracted by this isle that shouldn't exist. "I—I've studied geography. My father practically papered our walls with maps, and I've never—"

"Of course you haven't. This place does not exist *on maps* and *in studies.*" Though Odessa strives to sound indifferent, an edge sharpens her voice as we enter the crush. A bite of tension. Her hand is steel on my elbow. "Honestly, darling, be difficult if you'd like, but never be dense. And for the love of all things holy, stop *staring.*"

She glances swiftly over her shoulder, nodding as two men step into place behind us. No, not men at all. *Les Éternels.* Judging from their hard physiques and the black insignias on their cloaks, they must be some sort of . . . guard. But that can't be right. I can personally attest to Odessa's strength and speed, so why would she need additional protection?

I cut her a sideways glance. "Who are they?"

"No one of import."

"You relaxed when you saw them."

"I never relax."

Unbidden, I sneak another look at the two, frowning as they move even closer—because witches, werewolves, and mermaids aren't the only ones who gather to watch us now. No. A dozen or more Éternels have crept from the shadows to join them. Their cold eyes gleam eerie and strange in the lamplight as Odessa strides past, her chin high and indifferent to their stares. One of the guards' chests actually brushes my back, however, when the nearest Éternel bares his teeth at me. "Am I . . . safe here?" I ask him uncertainly. A ridiculous question.

When Odessa drags me forward, he and his companion follow without answering.

"Dawn approaches, so I fear we have little time for sightseeing." Though she strides purposefully, confidently, Odessa still tracks the Éternels in her periphery. "Tragic, I know. Requiem is a beautiful city—one of the oldest in the entire world and filled with residents of every size, shape, and— Oh, *do* hurry up, won't you?"

She pulls me away from the establishment to our left, where whorls of velvet fabric adorn each balustrade and haunting music spills from doors painted black and gold. From deep within, an audience laughs. The sound is so chilling—so *captivating*—that I cannot help but pause to listen.

My body goes cold, however, as a woman's scream entwines with the music.

A piercing, *bloodcurdling* scream.

Odessa tightens her arm around mine when I move to rush toward the doors. "Ah, ah, ah," she titters again, just as the woman's scream ends in time with the music. The silence lifts the hair on my neck. "Curiosity will kill the cat in Requiem, and no amount of satisfaction will bring you back."

"But she—"

"—is beyond your help," Odessa finishes, tugging me onward. "*Come.* You may walk of your own volition, or one of my guards will carry you. Ivan in particular would take no greater pleasure." She motions to the lean, dark-skinned male behind us. His gaze threatens violence. "The choice is yours, of course."

What kind of magic?

Evangeline's voice drifts back to me as Ivan and I stare at each other. *The worst kind of magic, darlings. The absolute* worst *kind. The kind that requires blood. Requires* death.

His lip curls slowly, revealing fangs.

Right.

I swallow hard and force myself to move, ignoring the odd swooping sensation in my stomach. Because I need to focus. Because I am not *fascinated* by this grim and ghastly place, and this breathlessness in my chest—it means I'm probably about to faint. Yes. I am about to faint, and if Evangeline really *were* here, she'd tell me to twist my head on straight before I lose it.

When I take my next step, however, I fear it might be too late.

Dark liquid oozes around my boot from the moss between cobblestones—dark liquid that looks disturbingly like blood.

With a small shriek, I leap away from it, colliding with Ivan's chest and nearly dislocating my elbow in the process. He shunts me forward none too gently, and when I look down again, blood seeps around his boots too. A trail of our scarlet footsteps follows us along the street. "Is that—is the ground *bleeding*?" I ask in alarm. "How is that possible?"

"It isn't," he says brusquely. "Look again."

Sure enough, the moss no longer bleeds, and the trail of footsteps has disappeared.

Like it never existed at all.

When I gasp, incredulous, he pushes me forward once more, and I have no choice but to stumble after Odessa, shaking my head and spluttering. Because I saw them—they were *there*—yet I must've imagined the whole thing. It's the only explanation. This isle might be different, but even here, the ground cannot have veins or vessels. It cannot be alive, and I—

I swallow hard.

I cannot allow it to unsettle me. The screams, the blood, the cold stares of Les Éternels—they cannot distract me from my purpose, and that purpose is to protect Coco from Michal by any means necessary.

Odessa leads us up a street paved with cobblestone next, where odd little shops line each side. Enormous toads croak from gilded birdcages, live beetles glitter within silver sugar bowls, and incense stands in cut-glass vases, each bundle tied with black ribbon. Another shop sells vials of thick, dark liquid. *Loup garou*, one label reads in spiked handwriting. It joins others marked *human*, *melusine*, and *Dame Blanche*.

My fingers linger on a bottle marked *dragon*, and that tingle of anticipation returns. Or is it dread?

These *are* bottles of blood, after all, and in all my life, only Evangeline has ever spoken of the Eternal Ones. I've since read every book in Chasseur Tower—every book in the entire cathedral—and not a single one mentions them either. Dames Blanches and loup garou, yes, as well as melusines and the occasional lutin, but never Les Éternels.

No, these monsters seem to be . . . new.

I release the bottle and force myself to keep walking.

Or perhaps very, very old.

Always sleep at nightfall, darlings . . . always say your prayers . . .

The familiar verse floats around us in the October market, tangling with the stray cats in the street. One crouches behind the toads, while another meows churlishly at a shopkeeper. Two more watch a three-eyed crow on its perch, completely still except for the twitch of their tails. I hurry to catch up with Odessa. "Do you have a rat problem on Requiem?"

She glances at a nearby tabby in distaste. "Rats are not the problem."

"These cats aren't pets, then?"

"An infestation, more like." When I continue to stare at her, perplexed, she sighs and snaps, "They appeared on the isle several months ago. No one knows how or why—they simply sprang into existence overnight, and no one dares to remove them."

I crouch to pat the head of a long-haired kitten. "Why not?"

"Cats are guardians of the dead, Célie. I thought everyone knew that."

I freeze mid-scratch. I *didn't* know that, but somehow, admitting such a thing to Odessa feels like admitting a grievous character flaw. Withdrawing my hand hastily, I change the subject instead. "I don't understand. How could no one know about this island?"

"Michal," Odessa says simply, nudging the kitten away. "He loves his secrets, my cousin, and this one he guards jealously. No one knows about Requiem unless he wishes it, and even then— they rarely know for long."

"What does *that* mean?"

Before she can answer, however, a handful of Éternels spill from the alley ahead, blocking our path, and the merchants on either side of us scatter. Some crouch by their carts as means of protection, while others flee into their shops; fear shines through their eyes as clear and bright as the crystals in their windows. My stomach clenches as Ivan looms at my back.

"Stay still," he murmurs.

Not a problem.

Odessa, however, lifts her chin once more—supremely unperturbed—and waves a curt hand at the Éternels. "Bonsoir, mes amis. You appear to have lost your way."

A tall, terrifying Éternel with fiery red hair and green eyes tilts his head as he considers us. His gaze feels cold and ancient upon my face, and behind him, his companions stand still and silent. "Who is she?" he asks quietly.

"That," says Odessa, "is none of your concern, Christo."

"I think it is." He points a long, accusatory finger behind us, his lip curling slightly. "The cats follow her."

As one, Odessa, Ivan, and I turn to follow his gaze, and whatever unease I felt at the blood-soaked moss multiplies tenfold—because the Éternel spoke truth. A half-dozen cats trail me like a shadow. No. I shake my head vehemently at the ridiculous thought. They trail *us* like shadows. *Us.* Beyond Lou's pet, Melisandre, cats have never paid me any particular attention, and I have little reason to believe they'd start now. A far likelier explanation would be Ivan hiding anchovies in his pocket.

Odessa casts me a swift, appraising look—there and gone too quickly to decipher—before returning her attention to Christo. "Your imagination runs wild as ever, darling. The cats arrived long before she did."

"Did he bring her to heal the isle?"

"All you need to know," Odessa says, "is that she belongs to Michal, and any creature who touches her will be subject to his wrath—and the wrath of the entire royal family." She punctuates the statement with a chilling smile, her fangs flashing sharp and white in the lamplight. Instinctively, I hold my breath at the sight of them, trying to draw as little attention to myself as possible.

Christo, however, takes a pointed step forward. "And yet, ma duchesse, Michal is still not here. How can the shepherd protect his flock if he refuses to walk among them?" A pause. "Perhaps he cannot protect them at all."

Before I can blink, the other guard lunges, pinning the Éternel against the alley wall with a hand at his throat. Though his companions hiss softly from the street, no one moves to help him—not even when the guard pries the Éternel's mouth open by force. Turning ice-blue eyes to Odessa, the guard awaits her command as the Éternel thrashes and chokes against him.

"Ah, Christo." As if disappointed, Odessa saunters toward them, but her casualness belies the hard glint in her eyes. "Always *such* a cliché, and worse—now *I* must be one too. Shall Pasha and

I deliver your message to Michal personally?"

Christo snarls, trying and failing to bite off Pasha's fingers.

Odessa's eyes spark with delight. "A most definitive yes." Then, in a deft movement, she reaches between Christo's snapping teeth and—and—

My eyes bulge in disbelief.

And rips out his tongue.

The movement is so efficient, so cursory, that the blood spilling from Christo's mouth seems too bright somehow—too shocking, too *red*—to be real. Shaking my head in wild disbelief, I stumble into Ivan again. Only moments ago, Odessa and I were discussing *cats*, and now—now she holds the limp, gruesome organ of a living creature in her hand.

"Next time"—she hands the tongue to Pasha, who releases Christo in disgust—"I shall make you eat it, darling. Consider the delivery a kindness, and never threaten my family again." To me, she says pleasantly, "Come along, Célie."

This time, she doesn't feign her indifference as she glides up the street without a backward glance.

And I—I stand rooted to the spot.

Suddenly, a silly nursery rhyme doesn't seem an adequate weapon against these creatures. What could Evangeline have possibly known about such *violence*? With the Eternal Ones' speed, strength, and—frankly—beauty, how could any one person hope to triumph against them? How could I? Unbidden, my gaze darts over my shoulder, where Christo's companions abandon him to rot in the street.

Next time I shall make you eat it.

"She . . . she tore out his t-tongue," I whisper, stricken.

Pasha slips the tongue into his pocket. "He'll lose more than that. Now *move*."

With little other choice, I follow Odessa toward the center of the isle, where a castle towers above the rest. Thick storm clouds obscure its spires. When lightning flashes, however, the bolt illuminates two wickedly sharp towers through the gloom, and I inhale sharply. Thunder rumbles overhead.

"Welcome to my home." Odessa gazes up at the black fortress with more affection than I've yet seen on her face. "It could be yours too if you're clever. Guests tend to enjoy their stay more than prisoners."

My chest tightens further at the implication. From Odessa's own lips, she admitted few outside the isle's populace know its location. She admitted Michal chooses who lives with that knowledge . . . and who dies with it. "And how long do your guests stay?"

"As long as we wish it."

And there it is—her true meaning, reverberating unspoken between us. As ominous as the thunder overhead. *The longer we need you, the longer you live.* I nearly wring my hands in frustration. Because they don't need *me* at all; they need Coco, and the sooner she arrives, the sooner she dies. The sooner *we* die. I am only the bait, the minnow, the *worm*, meant for bigger and better fish. As we ascend the castle steps—as Odessa finally relaxes, as she floats through the entrance hall and up the grand staircase, as Pasha and Ivan leave us without a word—one thought resolves as slick and sharp as the hook in my back.

Coco must never arrive.

CHAPTER THIRTEEN

Promenade

My room resides in the east wing of the castle.

Though someone has lit a candelabra in the deserted corridor, shadows gather as thick as the cobwebs on the tapestries. A single door looms ahead. Statues of angels carved from black marble adorn either side of it, except—

I draw to a halt behind Odessa.

With broad, membranous wings like a bat, the angels aren't angels at all.

I lift a hand to one of their faces, tracing the harsh contour of his cheek, the palpable anguish in his eyes. The sculptor has captured him mid-transformation, torn between man and demon, and the golden veins and white inlay of the marble do little to soften him. His tortured expression seems to personify the castle itself.

Whereas Requiem is beautiful and strange and *alive*, its castle is stark, dark, with none of the city's whimsical touches. Here, there are no horned toads or three-eyed crows, no stolen kisses between witch and sailor or heartfelt reunions between father and son. There are no strange cats or haunted music or even terrified screams.

Here, there are only shadows and silence. A bitter draft through empty corridors.

The castle reflects the hollow shell of its master.

Any creature who touches her will be subject to his wrath—and the wrath of the entire royal family.

I repress a shudder, dropping my hand from the statue's face. The castle reflects the hollow shell of its *king.*

"Here we are." Odessa opens the door with a screech of hinges. When I make no move to enter, however—peering tentatively into the dark room, lit only by a single wall sconce—she sighs and speaks to the ceiling. "If I'm not sequestered in my room, blissfully alone, within the next three minutes, I will cheerily kill someone. With any luck, it won't be you."

She steps back farther.

I still don't move.

"Someone will return at dusk," she says impatiently, pressing a cold hand against my back and pushing me inside.

"But—"

"Oh, *relax*, darling. As our esteemed guest, you have nothing to fear from anyone inside our home." She hesitates at the threshold before reluctantly adding, "That said, this castle is very old, and it has many bad memories. It would be best not to wander."

I whirl to face her, dismayed. Before I can argue, however, she closes the door, and the small *click* of the lock echoes in the bone-deep quiet of the room. I seize the sconce from the wall, lifting the brass to better see my new cell. As with the ship, the room sprawls before me without end. Entirely too large. Too empty. Too *dark.* The door itself sits at the highest point of the room; wide stairs crafted of the same black marble sweep immediately downward, disappearing into the gloom.

I take a deep breath.

If I'm to remain here indefinitely, I cannot fear my own room.

Right.

When I step forward, however, the air seems to shift—seems to sharpen, seems to *wake*—and suddenly, the room doesn't feel empty at all. The hair on my neck lifts with awareness. I thrust my candle outward, searching for this new presence, but the shadows swallow the golden light whole. My free hand tightens on the banister, leaving a palm print in the dust there.

"Hello?" I ask softly. "Is anyone there?"

The silence deepens in response.

I glance at the marble beneath my feet. Like the banister, thick dust coats its surface, undisturbed except for my own footprints. Clearly, no one has entered this place in many, *many* years, and I have indeed lost my mind. *Breathe*, I tell myself sternly. *You are not in a casket. You are not in the tunnels.*

Still, as I force one foot in front of the other—down, down, down into the shadows—I cannot help but shudder. Never before have I felt such an ambience in a room, like the walls themselves are watching me. Like the floor itself *breathes*. My fingers tingle around the sconce, and I exhale a shaky laugh.

It sounds only semi-hysterical.

I refuse to succumb now, however—not after surviving an abduction and nearly drowning, not after discovering a clandestine isle ruled by creatures who want to kill me. Unfortunately, my chest seems to disagree. It tightens painfully until I can scarcely breathe, but I close my eyes and breathe anyway.

A little dust hurts no one, and this room—it will not hurt me either. I simply need to introduce myself, perhaps coax it to like me, to divulge its secrets. "My name is Célie Tremblay," I whisper, too fraught—too *exhausted*—to feel ridiculous for speaking to an empty room. My eyes sting. My head aches. I cannot remember the last time I slept or ate, and my knee still throbs from striking Michal. "I don't normally like the dark, but I'm willing to make an exception for you." My eyes flutter open, and I take a deep breath, studying the shapes around me. "That said, if I could find a candle or two, it would make this friendship much easier."

Matching screens rise on either side of the staircase, concealing a small dressing area to my left and a wash area to my right. I trail my hand across the paper-thin silk of one screen. It stretches across wooden panes, black as the rest of the room, with a pattern of deep blue violets and golden geese. *Pretty.*

"Our gracious hosts tell me I'll be staying here indefinitely." With a trembling finger, I trace a goose who flies with its mate, or perhaps with its mother or sister. Pippa and I used to stand at our window and watch flocks of them fly south every winter. The memory sends an unexpected pang of longing through me. "I stood at the bottom of the sea last year, yet I've never felt so far from home before," I whisper to the room. Then, softer still— "Do you think birds ever feel lonely?"

The room doesn't answer, of course.

Giving myself a mental shake, I continue my search for candles.

A fresh cloud of dust engulfs me as I pluck the sheets of a lavish bed, coughing and nearly extinguishing my candle. I lift it higher, illuminating a full wall of bookshelves cloaked in cobwebs, two squashy armchairs near the fireplace, and a spiral staircase in the corner. The floor of a mezzanine hangs overhead.

My eyes widen.

Windows.

Three of them, enormous and shuttered tight. If I can open

them, I won't need candles; outside, dawn has surely broken. Thunder continues to rumble around me, yes, but the sun is still *light*, even shrouded by storm clouds. Moving quickly, I cross the room and test the spiral staircase once, twice, before giving it my full weight. Though the metal groans, it doesn't give, and I race up the tight steps until I pitch forward onto the mezzanine, slightly dizzy. "Thank you," I tell the room.

Then I run my hand down the shutters in search of a latch.

Only worn wood meets my touch. With a frown, I try again— feeling inside the seam, along the bottom edge, lifting my candle to search above my head—but no telltale gleam of metal flashes. No hooks. No locks. No battens. I check the window to the right next, then the left, but the shutters on all three remain resolute. Impenetrable.

My frown deepens as I lean the sconce against the wall at my feet.

Using both hands this time, I pry at the seam of the middle window. It refuses to budge. Behind me, the air seems to stir in anticipation. It presses closer, near palpable, until I can *feel* it on my neck, until a lock of my hair actually *moves*. The ache in my head continues to build. I throw myself at the shutters now, claw-ing at them until a sliver of wood slides under my nail and draws blood.

"Ow!" Jerking my hand away, I stumble sideways, and my foot sends the sconce toppling. My eyes widen in panic. "*No—*" Though I lunge for the candle, it skitters from its holder, roll-ing across the mezzanine and pitching over the edge to the floor below. The flame winks out abruptly.

The room plunges into total darkness.

"Oh God." I freeze, still half crouched, as familiar panic claws up my throat. *This can't be happening. Oh God oh God oh God—*

I wrench myself upright before my entire body locks down, darting for the rail and following it to the spiral stairs. *You are not in a casket. You are not in the tunnels.* I repeat the words like a lifeline, but the *smell*—it envelops me with a vengeance, as if the room itself remembers the fetid stench of her corpse. The fetid stench of *death.* I knock into the chair, the bed, nearly break my toe on the first step of the grand staircase. Crawling up it on my knees, I tear the last pin from my hair and lunge for the door. I forget about sharp teeth and black eyes and cold hands. I forget about Odessa's warning, about anything and everything except *escape.*

I am not in a casket.

I have to leave this place.

I am not in the tunnels.

I cannot stay here.

"Please, please—" My fingers shake violently as I shove the pin into the keyhole. *Too* violently. I cannot feel the tumblers of the lock, cannot think beyond the faint glow emanating from the keyhole. "Just let me go," I beg the room, still stab, stab, *stabbing* until my hairpin bends. Until it *breaks.* A sob tears from my throat, and the glow of light flares brighter in response. The softest strain of a violin follows.

It takes several seconds for my mind to catch up with my senses.

Light.

Confusion flares at the sight of it, at the *sound* of it, but relief quickly follows, crashing through me in a hideous wave.

Sinking to my knees, I press my face against the keyhole. This light isn't candlelight; it isn't warm and golden but cold and silvery, like the glow of the stars, or—or the glint of a knife. I don't care. I drink it in greedily, forcing myself to breathe as the strange music builds.

I am not in a casket. I am not in the tunnels.

One breath.

Two.

The tension in my shoulders releases slightly. The pressure in my chest eases. I must be dreaming. It's the only explanation. My subconscious—recognizing the familiar nightmare—has turned lucid at last, creating this strange music and stranger light to comfort me. Both seem to originate from the end of the empty corridor, just around the corner. Unlike my room, however, no windows interrupt these long, gilded walls. The candles in the candelabra have blown out. I settle against the door regardless, resting my cheek against the wood.

I will remain here—kneeling on this hard floor—until Odessa returns for me. I will live here indefinitely if I must.

The silver light pulses brighter as the music grows louder, wilder, and deep voices join in. Feminine laughter. I try to ignore it. I try to count each breath of my lungs and beat of my heart, willing myself to wake. *This isn't real.*

And then—as the music peaks in a bizarre crescendo—*figures* appear.

My mouth falls open.

Human in shape, they waltz around the corner in pairs, their bodies translucent and glowing. Dozens of them. Silver light spills from their skin, from the lavish lace of one's gown, the thick manacles on another's wrists. The chains drag behind him as he lifts a woman in rags overhead. Two men dressed in tunics play violins upon their shoulders, while behind them, a maiden with perfect curls spins a perfect pirouette.

None notice me as they promenade through the empty corridor, laughing, *celebrating*, before the first in their caravan whirls through the wall and vanishes. I watch the rest glide past in horror, no longer convinced my subconscious has turned lucid. No longer convinced I'm sleeping at all. Never before have I conjured spirits—actual *spirits*—in my dreams.

The music fades with the violinists, but the last of the ghosts—a truly lovely woman with clouds of translucent hair—continues to twirl, laughing delightedly as the train of her gown sweeps the floor. It leaves soft circles in the dust there. Just as her hand slips through the opposite wall, however, her gaze catches upon my door. Upon its keyhole.

Upon *me*.

Her smile vanishes as I scramble backward, *away*, but it's too late—swooping low, she fills the keyhole with a single upturned eye. Black spots my vision as it meets mine. "Te voilà," she whispers curiously, tilting her head.

Her words are the last I hear before passing out.

There you are.

Still curled in the fetal position, I wake to a strange man crouching above me. Startled, I jerk away, but something in his grin—in the *tilt* of his dark eyes, the cast of his amber skin—feels familiar. "Good evening, starshine," he croons. "I trust you slept well?"

When he extends a large hand to help me rise, I stare at it in confusion. "Who—who are you?"

"A better question"—he slants his head, those feline eyes still learning my face—"is who are *you*?"

Sighing, I roll over and stare at the ceiling in resignation. Or at least, I *think* I stare at the ceiling. It remains too dark to discern much of anything except the man's silhouette. In the corridor behind him, someone has reignited the candelabra, and golden light diffuses his dark hair and wide shoulders. It casts his face in shadow.

Wretched thunder still rumbles outside.

I'll never see the sun again.

Frustration wells sharp and sudden at the realization, at the injustice of this entire situation. The hopelessness. The lie comes to my lips easier this time, at least.

"My name is Cosette Monvoisin, but I assume you already know that."

He scoffs. "Come now, mademoiselle. We are to be great friends, the two of us. Surely you can divulge your true name?"

"Cosette Monvoisin *is* my true name." When he says nothing, only raises his brows in a vaguely amused expression, I snap, "Well? I told you my name. Etiquette now dictates you tell me yours."

In response, he laughs and wraps cold fingers around my wrist, lifting me into the air like I weigh nothing, like I *am* nothing—not flesh and bone, but ether. *Te voilà.* I stiffen at the intrusive thought, at the ominous words of the ethereal woman, and the events of this morning return in a sickening rush. *Ghosts.*

They weren't real, I tell myself quickly.

A perfect cleft marks the man's chin as he drops me to my feet. "My, my—and Odessa said you were *sweet.*"

"You know Odessa?"

"Of course I know Odessa. Everyone knows Odessa, but alas, I know her more than most." At my blank look, he gestures down his svelte frame, inclining his head in a regal bow. From beneath thick hair and thicker lashes, he winks at me. "She is my twin, Mademoiselle Monvoisin. I am Dimitri Petrov. *You*, however, must call me Dima. May I call you Cosette?"

Twins.

"You may not."

"Ah." He clutches his chest in mock affront. "You wound me, mademoiselle." When he straightens with a dramatic sigh, I hear Odessa in the inflection; I see her in his bearing. Though he wears garnet velvet instead of plum satin—though his eyes glint with sharp interest while hers drift elsewhere—their regal manner remains the same. They *are* cousins to the king, after all, which makes them . . . a duke and duchess? Do Les Éternels prescribe to the same social hierarchy as humans?

I bite my tongue to halt the questions.

"If you insist on falsehood and formality," he continues, snaking his elbow through mine, "I will of course oblige. However, I must warn you—I do enjoy a challenge. From this moment onward, I intend to bother you until we're on a first-name basis. *Coco* shall be the only name on my mind."

I cast him another reluctant glance. Like his sister—like Ivan and Pasha and even Michal—he is almost *too* beautiful, which makes everything so much worse. "I've known you for only ten seconds, monsieur, yet I already suspect *yours* is the only name on your mind."

"Oh, I like you. I like you very much."

"Where is Odessa? She said she would return for me at dusk."

"Ah. I'm afraid there has been a slight change of plan in that regard." His grin fades as he leads me into the corridor, where the soft circles in the dust have disappeared. *Odd.* "Michal has, er . . . *requested* your presence in his study, and Odessa—the wastrel— has not yet woken from her beauty sleep. I volunteered to fetch you in her stead."

"Why?" I ask suspiciously.

"Because I wanted to meet you, of course. The entire castle is humming at your arrival. I heard the name *Cosette* no less than twelve times on my way to your chamber." He peers down his shoulder at me with a sly gleam in his eyes. "It seems the servants have been given the coveted privilege to use it."

As if to punctuate his words, a plainly dressed woman steps from what appears to be a sitting room, a bundle of cloth in her arms. Her eyes narrow when she sees me, and one of the rags slips to the floor. Immediately, I bend to retrieve it, but she moves faster—preternaturally fast—and snatches the cloth from my outstretched hand. "Excusez-moi," she mutters, revealing the tips of her fangs as she speaks. To Dimitri, she bows her head and says, her voice strangely meaningful, "I will return, mon seigneur." Then she darts down the corridor and out of sight.

Unnerved, I stare after her. Fresh blood soaked that rag; scarlet still smears the floor where it fell. When I lean to peer into the sitting room, however—anxious to find the source—Dimitri is there, blocking the doorway with a too-quick smile. "Nothing to see in here, darling."

My eyes fall to the stain on the floor. "But someone is bleed-ing."

"Are they?"

"Is that not blood?"

"Someone else will clean it." He waves a hasty hand, refusing to meet my eyes. "Shall we? I fear Michal has beastly manners, and he doesn't like to be kept waiting." He doesn't wait for me to respond, however, instead tucking my arm firmly into the crook of his elbow and dragging me away.

"But"—I tug fruitlessly against his ironclad grip—"why did she look at me like that? And the blood—where did it come from?" I shake my head, feeling sick, digging in my heels as he tows me down a staircase and across the castle. "There was too much of it. Someone must be hurt—"

"And there is that elusive sweetness. Odessa didn't lie about you, after all." Though he clearly aims to defuse the lingering tension, his arm remains taut beneath my hand. His eyes tight. A curious flush has spread up his throat, and he still won't look at me. I don't know him at all, but if I did, I might say he looked *ashamed.* "Another personal challenge," he says ruefully when I don't respond. "Coax Mademoiselle Monvoisin into being sweet to *me.* Would you do me a favor, darling?"

I stare at him in bewilderment. "That depends."

"Would you mind not mentioning this to anyone? I don't want my sister to worry—nothing is wrong, of course—and Michal and I, well . . ." He shrugs a little helplessly. "We just don't need any more misunderstandings, what with his beastly manners and all. You won't tell him, will you?"

"Tell him *what?*"

He studies me fervently for several seconds, indecision clear in his gaze. "Nothing," he says at last, and that strange color in his cheeks flushes deeper. "Please, forgive me. I should've never—no matter." His jaw flexes as silence descends between us, and we draw to a halt outside a pair of enormous ebony doors. "This is it," he says quietly.

At last, I succeed in wrenching my arm away from him. He doesn't fight me this time. No. Instead he ducks his head in apology, stepping back as if equally keen on putting distance between us. And I feel vaguely nauseous. I don't understand this, *any* of it, and I'm not certain I ever will. This place, these people—they're all sick.

Something is wrong, Célie.

It isn't just the trees and roses. The land itself . . . it feels sick *somehow. My magic feels sick.*

Dimitri winces at my expression and bows low. "I've made you uncomfortable. I am sorry. This—well, I envisioned this all going much differently in my head, and I'm sorry."

My head begins to ache, yet still I must ask, "Why is the castle humming at my arrival? Why are the servants talking about me?"

He does not answer, walking backward in earnest now. At the last second, however, he hesitates, and something akin to regret shadows his features. "I am sorry," he repeats. "Sweet creatures never last long in Requiem."

Then he turns on his heel and leaves.

I have little time to contemplate his warning, however—no matter how ominous—because in the next second, the ebony doors swing inward, and Michal appears between them. For several seconds, he says nothing. Then he arches a brow. "Is it not rude to linger in doorways? By all means . . ." He extends a pale hand, those black eyes never leaving mine. "Join me."

CHAPTER FOURTEEN

A Game of Questions

To my surprise, Michal's study is small. Intimate. Emerald-green panels of silk line the walls, while a dark, lacquered desk dominates the center of the room. On it, all manner of curious objects tick and whirl—a golden pendulum clock in the shape of a beautiful woman, a floating silver-and-pearl egg, an ivy plant with deep green leaves. Beneath the last sits a stack of leather-bound books. They look ancient.

Expensive.

Indeed, everything in this room looks expensive, and I—

I glance down at my snowy white gown, but the delicate lace has been stained irrevocably—soaked, *ruined*—and now resembles the inside of a threadbare shoe. Not quite brown and not quite gray. Not quite comfortable either. It chafes my skin as I shift beneath Michal's cold stare.

"Please." He sits behind the desk with his elbows propped atop it, his fingers steepled as he considers me. When I drag my gaze to his, he inclines his head toward the plush seat across from him. Flames roar in the hearth beside it, flooding the room with light and delicious warmth. As in my chamber, however, shutters barricade the arched windows behind him. They seal us in like relics in a crypt. "Sit."

From my place by the door, I do not budge an inch. "No, thank you, monsieur."

"It wasn't a request, mademoiselle. You will sit."

I still refuse to move.

Because in the middle of his desk, among the books and the ivy and the clock, stands a jewel-encrusted goblet filled with more blood. I try not to look at it—because if I consider *why* there is blood in that goblet, I might scream. I might scream and scream until I cannot scream any longer, or perhaps until Michal tears out my vocal cords and hangs me with them.

With a cold smile, he tilts his head as if sharing the same black fantasy. "Are you always this tiresome?"

"Not at all." Lifting my chin, I clasp my hands behind my back to hide their tremble. "I simply prefer to stand. Is that so difficult to believe?"

"Unfortunately, Célie Tremblay, I don't believe a word that comes out of your mouth."

Célie Tremblay.

Though I blanch at the sound of my real name, he doesn't seem to notice. With one hand, he slowly drags a stack of parchment to the center of his desk. "Such a beautiful name, that—*Célie Tremblay.*" Still smiling, he repeats my name as if relishing the taste of it on his tongue. "Born October twelfth in the kingdom of Belterra, the city of Cesarine. Specifically, born in the home of 13 Brindelle Boulevard, West End. Daughter of Pierre and Satine Tremblay and sister of the late Filippa Tremblay, who perished at the hand of Morgane le Blanc."

I exhale a harsh breath at the mention of my sister. "How do you—?"

"Your parents didn't raise you, though, did they?" He doesn't bother glancing down at his stack of parchment; apparently, he memorized the information there. He memorized *me*. "No, that responsibility fell to your nursemaid, Evangeline Martin, who perished in the Battle of Cesarine earlier this year."

My stomach pitches like I've missed a step.

Evangeline Martin. Perished.

The words sound strange and foreign, as if spoken in a different language.

"What do you—" *Oh God.* I stare at him, horrified, before pressing a hand to my forehead. *No.* I shake my head. "No, there—there must be some mistake. Evangeline didn't . . ." But my voice shrivels to something small and unsure. I never read the final death registry after the Battle of Cesarine. True, Jean Luc *hid* it from me, but I still should've tried harder to find it, to pay homage to the fallen. Evangeline could've been one of them.

Michal arches a wry brow. "My condolences," he offers, but there is nothing sympathetic in his tone. There is only ice. Can this man, this—this *monster*—even *feel* sympathy? Exhaling a deep breath, I somehow doubt it.

I just—need to collect myself. I need to gather my wits. This entire display—my personal history, that startling revelation, his goblet of *blood*—is meant to unsettle me, to intimidate. Dropping my hand, I level him with a dark look of my own before marching forward to settle in his proffered chair. I will not be intimidated. He might hold all the cards, but in demanding I return for a second interrogation, he has revealed his hand: he needs something from me. Something important.

I fold my own hands in my lap. I can be patient.

"Shall we continue?" He doesn't wait for an answer, however; his eyes remain fixed on mine as he lists the pinnacles of my life with scathing indifference—how I fell in love with Reid, how he left me for Lou, how we joined forces to defeat the indomitable Morgane le Blanc. "That must have been very complicated," he says, picking up his goblet, "to work with the man who broke your heart."

When I still say nothing—nearly biting through my tongue—he chuckles low. "Still, I suppose you found vengeance on all parties when you killed his mother-in-law." He swirls the liquid idly before taking a sip. "And when you accepted his best friend's suit."

My mouth parts in outrage. "It wasn't like that—"

"Your captain surprised you with a proposal after your initiation into Chasseur Tower, didn't he?" With a cruel gleam in his eyes, he inclines his goblet in a toast. "The first woman to ever grace its doorstep *and* a future bride. You must be very proud."

Again, he pauses as if expecting me to interject, but I bare my teeth in a furious smile, holding on to civility by a thread. *He wants to unsettle you. He wants to intimidate.* "Are you quite finished?" I ask him tightly.

"That depends. Did I miss anything?"

"Nothing relevant."

"And yet"—he leans forward on his elbows, his voice darkening—"somewhere, it seems that I have."

We stare at each other for a long, taut moment as his pendulum swings between us.

I like silence even less than I like the dark. As if to prolong it, he stands and rolls his shirtsleeves with casual ease, eyes flicking to where my gown ripples against the floor. I cease tapping my foot immediately. With a ghost of a smile, he strolls around his desk to lean against it, crosses his arms, and looms over me. The new position immediately puts me at a disadvantage, and he knows it. His polished shoes—black, like his *soul*—cross scant inches from mine. "What are you?" he asks simply.

My mouth parts in disbelief.

"I am human, monsieur, as you already know by your *deeply* inappropriate invasion of my personal space." Resisting every instinct to flee across the room, I shift closer to spite him, and I lift my nose in my primmest imitation of Filippa. "What are *you*, Your Majesty? Apart from unforgivably rude?"

Uncrossing his arms, he leans forward to mirror my movement, and at his sleek smile, I immediately regret my bluster. We're practically *touching.* Worse still—he no longer feigns apathy, instead studying me in open fascination. As before, his interest feels somehow deadlier, like I balance on the tip of a knife. Voice soft, he asks, "Do you have a temper, Célie Tremblay?"

"I'm not answering any more of your questions. Not until you answer some of mine."

"You're in no position to negotiate, pet."

"Of course I am," I say stubbornly, "or you would've already killed me."

When he pushes away from his desk, I stiffen in apprehension, but he doesn't touch me. Instead, he crosses to the door, opens it, and murmurs something I cannot hear. I refuse to give him the satisfaction of turning, however. I forbid my eyes from following him through the room. "This plan of yours is ridiculous," I prattle into the silence, unable to stand it for another second. "Might I suggest—instead of fixating on me—you turn your attention to poor Christo instead? He is currently without a tongue."

"Without more than that, I think." Michal runs a finger down my neck, and I startle violently, unaware that he crossed the room once more. I still don't turn. I do, however, jerk away from him; my skin tingles where he touched me, and my legs clench along with my fists. "I can hear your heartbeat," he murmurs. "Did you know that? It accelerates when you're frightened."

Standing hastily, I dart around the desk—cheeks hot—and claim his chair instead. "I *want* to know why you've targeted Coco." His black eyes spark with cruel amusement. "I want to know why you didn't kill her—er, *me* in Cesarine with your other victims, and I won't tell you a *thing* until I do. Consider this my leverage."

His grin widens.

"Your . . . leverage," he murmurs.

The word sounds darker from his tongue, insidious.

"Yes." I shift back in his seat, grateful for the lacquered desk between us. My reflection gleams small and unsure upon its surface. Thoroughly out of its depth. "I assume you understand the concept."

"Oh, I understand the concept. Do *you?*"

"Do we have a deal or not?"

With a chilling grin, he sinks into the plush chair I just vacated. It forces him several inches below me. Still, he sprawls wide—entirely too big for the small frame, entirely too at *ease*—and cocks his head, considering. "Fine. Let us play this silly game of yours. I will ask a question—which you will answer *truthfully*—and I will answer yours in turn." He lifts a hand to tap his chest in warning, and his voice lowers. His smile fades. "But never lie to me again, pet. I will know if you do."

I feel myself nod. His eyes track the movement, and—not for

the first time—I remember his ominous words from the ship: *Shall I tell you* exactly *what I intend to do to you?* That question, however, pales in comparison to his next one: "How did you summon the ghosts?"

"I— What?" I blink at the unexpected question, my palms growing damp when his eyes narrow. "What ghosts?"

"Wrong answer."

"Don't be ridiculous. I don't even *believe* in ghosts. Scripture makes it clear that the soul passes directly to the afterlife when the body dies—"

"I am not interested in the Church's relationship with eternal life. I am interested in *yours.*" He leans forward, bracing his elbows on his knees. His fingers lace together. "I felt a shift in the castle earlier this morning, a peculiar charge of energy in the corridors. When I rose to investigate, I found an empty bottle of absinthe"—he points to his sideboard, where a decanter still stands empty—"and my personal belongings strung across the room. Someone drew a rather unfortunate mustache on my favorite uncle." His eyes flick to my left, where an enormous portrait of a severe-looking gentleman glares down at us from the mantel. Someone has indeed painted a thin, curling mustache over his lip.

In any other situation, I might've laughed. "*If* ghosts existed, they certainly couldn't drink absinthe or hold a paintbrush. I am truly sorry for your uncle, monsieur, but as I am not the one who broke into your study—"

"No one enters my study without my knowledge, Célie Tremblay. Are you sure that you felt nothing . . . unusual?"

Though I try to slow my heartbeat, it's no good. I'm still a terrible liar. I lift my chin instead. "Even if I *did* see these ghosts of yours, I certainly didn't *summon* them here."

His body grows still. "You saw them?"

"I—I don't know what I saw." I wipe my hands on my skirt, abandoning all pretense now. "They—*something* paraded past my room this morning in a macabre sort of dance—a waltz, I think." Though his black eyes burn into mine—strangely intent, almost angry—he still doesn't move. Doesn't speak. I wipe my hands again, and the lace of my dress chafes my palms. "Are you saying no one saw them?"

Even I can hear my heartbeat now. It *thump, thump, thump*s through my chest, my throat, my fingers, as he slowly shakes his head.

"Oh." My stomach sinks horribly with the word. "Then how did you— Wait, that isn't another question," I add quickly. He tilts his head, and the quiet of the room deepens, his previous words echoing between us with each tick of the clock.

Tick—

What

Tick—

are

Tick—

you?

Adjusting the collar on my gown, abruptly warm, I grasp for something else to break the silence. "R-Right. Of course no one did. I probably imagined them, anyway. This isle—it does strange things to my head." When his eyes narrow further, I immediately take the defensive. "It's *true*. In the market, the ground seemed to *weep* blood, and the cats—" I stop abruptly, unwilling to share the rest. Because Michal doesn't need to know the details. Despite what Christo said, the cats didn't *follow* me anywhere, and I certainly didn't summon a *ghost* to destroy this study.

"I heard the isle is sick," I say instead, looking down my nose at him. "Perhaps whatever ails Requiem is also responsible for defacing your uncle's portrait. My friend"—I dare not mention Lou's name—"spoke of a mysterious sickness spreading through Belterra. Why shouldn't it be spreading here too? It really *is* the most likely explanation, and—because everything seems to have started with you murdering those poor creatures—I suggest finding a mirror if you want to cast blame. It certainly has nothing to do with me."

Michal steeples his fingers, waiting patiently for me to finish. Which I have. I think. "*Well?*"

"Somehow," he croons, "I doubt this great evil you've concocted would draw a mustache on Uncle Vladimir."

"And a *ghost* would?"

His mouth twists as if in unpleasant memory. "I can think of one. Now—"

"Wait." My hand darts up to silence him before I can stop it. "I have one more question."

"I don't think so," he says silkily.

"But there are *rules* to this game." I square my shoulders in defiance, forcing the ghosts to a small room in the back of my mind. I will revisit them later. Or perhaps never. "You set them yourself, monsieur. You have asked three questions, and I have asked two, which means—"

His teeth click together with an audible *snap.* "You test my patience, pet."

"A cheat is the same as a liar." A sharp knock sounds on the door, however, interrupting us, and a truly evil smile lifts Michal's lips at the sound. I recoil instinctively. Anything that elicits such a mercurial shift in his mood cannot be good. "Who is it?" I ask him, my voice wary.

He inclines his head. "Breakfast."

The door opens, and a pretty young woman slips inside.

Small and round, she flicks auburn hair over her shoulder when she sees me, sauntering to where Michal sits in my chair. Startled, I study her lithe movements, the claw marks down one side of her face. *Loup garou.* When she drapes herself across Michal's lap, her eyes gleam yellow, confirming my suspicion.

I avert my gaze swiftly.

"Good evening, Arielle," he purrs, and at the low timbre of his voice, I can't help it—I glance up to find him looking directly at me. He brushes thick hair away from her throat. Two more scars fleck the ivory skin there. "Thank you for coming on such short notice."

She slants her head eagerly, wrapping an arm around his neck and clinging to him. "It's always an honor, Michal."

Mortified by their intimacy, I try to look away. When he hooks a hand behind her knee, however—when she twists in his lap to *straddle* him—heat washes through me until my cheeks blaze and my skin burns. Because I shouldn't be here. I shouldn't be—*watching* whatever this is, but my eyes refuse to blink. With another cold smile, he skims his nose along the curve of her shoulder, kissing it softly. "Go on," he tells me. "As you said, you have one question left."

"I'll just—I'll come back later—"

"Ask your question." His eyes darken over Arielle's neck. "You will not get another chance."

"But this is *indecent*—"

"You will ask your question"—he jerks his head toward the door—"or you will leave. The choice is yours."

His tone is emphatic. Final. If I flee his presence now, he will not stop me, and I will rot in the darkness until Coco arrives in Requiem and he kills us both. Though he offers a choice, it isn't a choice at all.

I force myself to nod.

Appeased, Michal continues his appraisal of Arielle's neck, and she shivers in his arms. "What—" I clear my throat and try again, attempting to collect my scrambled thoughts, to remember my *imperative* questions, as he cradles her head with one hand. "What do you—"

In the next second, however, he sinks his teeth into her jugular.

All thought vanishes as her back arches into his chest, and she clenches her eyes shut with a sharp moan of pleasure. I lurch to my feet at the sound—knocking over the chair in my haste—and gape at her, at *him*, at the way her hips writhe against him with each pull of his mouth. A drop of blood trickles down her collarbone, and realization punches through my chest like the thrust of a knife. My worst fear has been confirmed.

Michal is drinking her blood.

He's—he's *drinking* it.

I stumble away from the desk, falling over the chair, and rise on shaky feet as Michal releases her throat, tipping his head back and reveling in the taste of her, in the *decadence*. He wipes her blood from his lips. I press into the shutters. Though the wood abrades my back, I do not feel it—do not feel *anything* but the intensity of Michal's stare as he finds me again. As he stands and lifts Arielle in his arms.

"Wh-What—?" But my breath is ragged, sharp, too painful to speak around.

"The word for which you're searching"—he returns her loose-limbed body to the chair, where she sighs dreamily and closes her eyes—"is vampire, though we answer to many names. Éternel. Nosferatu. Strigoi and moroi. The undead."

The undead.

Éternel.

Vampire.

I flinch at each name like it's a physical blow. No books in Chasseur Tower ever alluded to *this*. The puncture marks in the soldiers, in Babette and the other victims . . . their bodies drained of blood . . . I close my eyes, blocking out the sight of Michal's scarlet lips. Of the blood still streaming down Arielle's chest, staining her shirt, the chair.

Loup garou.

Human.

Melusine.

Dame Blanche.

He didn't just kill his victims. He *consumed* them, and those bottles of blood in the market—he consumes them too. I shake my head, unable to catch my breath. My lungs threaten to collapse. Evangeline couldn't have understood the depravity of her story, or she never would've invited such creatures into our nursery, into our very childhood. I've heard of Dames Rouges imbibing blood on occasion, of course—for certain potions or spells—but never like this. Never as *sustenance.*

With an air of black satisfaction, Michal returns to his desk, rights his chair, and sits down. Arielle's breathing deepens in sleep. "I believe it is my turn," he says over his shoulder. "Are you able to summon the ghosts again?"

"I—I—I didn't summon—"

Faster than I can follow, he rises again, flowing to a liquid halt just in front of me. Though he doesn't touch me, the effect remains the same: I'm trapped here, cornered, like a lutin in a cage. "You're lying again," he says.

"I am n-not *lying.*" With the last of my bravado, I move to push through him, but it would be easier to move a mountain, the *ocean,* than the vampire in front of me. He no longer possesses his strange lack of scent. No—he now smells coppery and metallic, like salt, like Arielle's blood. Bile rises in my throat, and I push him harder. "I didn't summon *anything,* but if I did, I w-wouldn't do it again. Not for *you.*"

And it's true.

Through the ringing in my ears, awareness begins to flicker. Resolve.

At last, I understand *why* I'm still alive: as bait for Coco, yes, but also for the ghosts. After this morning, he thinks I somehow raised them, and he desperately wants a repeat performance for some nefarious purpose.

Everyone has a groin somewhere, Célie.

Squeezing past him, I dive behind his desk with breathless triumph. "Why are you after Coco? What do you *want* with her?"

He turns to face me slowly, and despite his impassive facade, something cruel and vicious lingers in the hard planes of his face. It promises retribution as calmly as one discusses the weather. "The blood witches have taken something from me, Célie Tremblay— something precious—and I plan to return the favor in kind." A pause. "Their princesse will do nicely."

I stare at him in growing disbelief. He would kill an innocent woman because a blood witch stole one of his *trinkets*? On the wings of that thought, however, comes another, equally chilling. *He would kill many more than one.* Shaking my head in disgust, I say quietly, "You're a thief *and* a filthy hypocrite. Where is my cross?"

"How interesting. One would think you'd ask for your engagement ring." I inhale sharply, but he merely flicks a hand toward the door. "Get out of my sight. Our game is finished." Then— "Remain in your room until I summon you. Do not attempt to leave this castle."

Torn between a sob and a snarl, I clench my hands into fists. "Why keep me here at all? Why not finish this business in Cesarine? Unless—"

Christo's bloody tongue flares in my mind's eye.

How can the shepherd protect his flock if he refuses to walk among them? Perhaps he cannot protect them at all.

"Unless you can't leave," I finish shrewdly, "because you fear the consequences if you do."

"I do not need to leave. Cosette Monvoisin will come to me." He lifts a piece of parchment from his desk, revealing a letter written in emerald ink. *Masquerade* sprawls across the top in ornate calligraphy. "Indeed, I've sent an invitation to *all* your little friends, welcoming them to Requiem for a ball on All Hallows' Eve. By that time, I will have unearthed all of your secrets, Célie

Tremblay, and will have no further use of you."

All Hallows' Eve.

I quickly tally the days, my heart dropping in realization. *Just over a fortnight.* I have a mere *nineteen days* to undo all of this, to save my friends and myself from a brutal and bloody death. He says nothing as I struggle to compose myself, those black eyes cold and indifferent once more. And for the first time since setting foot in Requiem, I begin to understand the sickness here.

Hatred tastes like poison, like the charred wick of a candle the second before it ignites—and it always ignites. "I will find a way to stop you," I promise him, my mind already whirling forward. In nineteen days, I must learn how to kill the undead—to *truly* kill them, this time. "You will not have my friends."

CHAPTER FIFTEEN

The Twins Petrov

The shelves in my room span to the ceiling, crammed with ancient books and broken trinkets. And dust. Layers and *layers* of dust. I lift the candelabra from the hall as I examine each tome and try not to sneeze. Though hunger wracks my stomach, I ignore it as best I can. Clearly, sustenance is an indulgence on Requiem—unless one happens to drink *blood*—and I would rather starve than ask Michal for anything. Brushing the grime from the spines on a lower shelf, I crouch to read the titles there: *The Resurrectionist*, *Practical Necromancy: A Guide to the Dark Art*, and *How to Commune with the Dead*.

I withdraw my hand abruptly.

Necromancy.

Shuddering, I wipe my palm on my bodice and hurry down the shelf, plucking out another book at random—*Le Voile Écarlate*. With an impatient sigh, I jam it back beneath the bust of an angry, long-forgotten god. This room houses *thousands* of books, yet I only need one—*one* book with detailed instructions on how to kill a vampire. It shouldn't be too terribly much to ask.

Like finding a needle in a haystack.

My stomach gurgles again, but another boom of thunder swallows the sound, rattling a chipped tea set overhead. I yank another book from the shelf. Perhaps this is Michal's true plan—to kill me slowly, painfully, over the next two weeks. At the thought of Arielle and her ravaged throat, her breathless *moans*, I don't necessarily object to the idea. Starvation is infinitely preferable to *that*.

Two hours later, however, I am ready to tear out Michal's throat myself.

I shove *An Illustrated Dictionary of Mushrooms and Other Fungi* back onto the shelf, near delirious with hunger now. My eyes sting and weep, and the candles have melted to stubs. They cast faint, flickering light over the minuscule text of the next book, which depicts the four-step life cycle of . . . mold.

I let out a strangled curse.

"Mademoiselle?" Dimitri's voice drifts down from the stairs, and I startle, lifting the candelabra. He holds a gilt breakfast tray in his hands, laden with what looks to be *food*. I scramble to my feet. Cocking his head with a roguish smile, he asks, "Are you . . . talking to someone?"

"Herself, I think." Odessa steps around him and drags a finger through the thick dust on the banister. Her nose wrinkles. "This is disgusting."

"Yes, it is." I meet her brother halfway up the stairs. "It looked like this yesterday when you tossed me in here to *rot*."

Even to my ears, I sound petulant, but my stomach also threatens to eat itself. When I seize the tray from Dimitri—thrusting the candelabra at him—he runs a hand over his mouth to hide his smirk, glancing sidelong at his sister. "Odessa, that was terribly wicked."

Clearly, he's trying to tidy up any *misunderstandings* from earlier, but after watching his cousin feast on Arielle's throat, I've little doubt who produced those blood-soaked rags in the corridor.

As if reading my mind, he inclines his head with a too-bright smile. "Please believe, mademoiselle, that *I* would have never done such a thing. Look—I have prepared you a delicious, human breakfast."

As one, we all look down at the breakfast in question: honey and cabbage, five hard-boiled eggs, and a vat of butter. "So delicious," Odessa repeats, deadpan, before rolling her eyes and wiping her dusty finger on his coat. Though Dimitri scowls, I leave them bickering on the stairs, stuffing an egg into my mouth and settling into a squashy armchair.

After inhaling the first whole, I force myself to chew the second, to swallow, before skewering Odessa with a glare of my own. "You were supposed to return at dusk."

"I said *someone* would return at dusk, darling, not that it would be me." The train of her gown sweeps over Dimitri's shoes as she descends into the room. She wears crimson silk tonight. The fitted bodice and full skirt gleam slightly in the light of the candle, as does the black paint on her lips, the onyx jewels on her throat. This is the first time I've seen her with her brother, and together— side by side—the two quite literally make the breath catch in my throat.

Tearing my gaze away, I make a mental note that *Vampires are beautiful* right next to *Vampires eat people* and *You are a person, Célie.*

"Dusk was *four* hours ago," I say instead.

"Yes, well, my dear brother insists we all spend the night together, so—lest we ruin a perfectly pleasant trip to Monsieur Marc—shall we let bygones be bygones?"

I frown between them, slowing on the third egg. "Monsieur Marc?"

Trailing after his sister, Dimitri says, "Yes, he—" But Odessa speaks over him.

"—is a dressmaker, of course. *The* dressmaker." She bends to examine the stack of books beside me, tilting her head in idle curiosity before flicking her gaze to my nail beds. "Do you possess a secret passion for horticulture? I myself dabbled with flora for—what was it?" She turns to her brother without waiting for my answer. "Twenty-seven years?"

"Yes," he says tersely. "You abandoned the pursuit after I commissioned a hothouse for you."

She lifts an elegant shoulder, already rising on tiptoe to inspect the tea set. "Why should I visit a dressmaker?" I ask them, suspicious.

Dimitri flashes another devilish grin. "We wanted to—"

Again, however, Odessa interrupts, waving a hand down my body in distaste. "Surely we need not answer such a ludicrous question. Look at the state of your *gown*. It positively reeks, which reminds me"—she flicks her wrist at Dimitri, whose eyes narrow—"you should fetch a servant to run a bath. We cannot introduce her to Monsieur Marc while she smells like a grubby mop."

I try and fail not to huff.

He steps around her hand with thinly veiled patience. "Alas, that stench is your perfume, dear sister. May I speak?" When she casts him a withering look, he grins and continues. "Rumor has it that tonight is your nineteenth birthday, mademoiselle, and my sister and I would like to treat you to a new wardrobe—with Michal's gold, of course." He plucks a piece of cabbage from the tray, lifting it to the candlelight to examine its veins. "He certainly owes you *something* for the state of this room. What does cabbage taste like?" he asks abruptly.

Cabbage. Such a mundane thing to contemplate—and not at all what I thought I'd be eating on my birthday. If not for my abduction, my friends might've prepared a chocolate cake to celebrate the occasion. They might've decorated Pan's Patisserie with pink garlands and everlasting bubbles, and my candles might've sparkled and popped with real fairy dust—they did the same for Beau's birthday in August, except with rum cake and fireworks.

Of course, if not for my abduction, my friends would also still be keeping secrets.

"It tastes a bit peppery." Grudgingly, Odessa flips through *A Book of Old World Gardens.* "Surely you remember cabbage, Dima. We *were* once human, after all."

The admission pulls me from my reverie, and I stare at her incredulously. "You were ... human?"

"A thousand years ago, give or take." Dimitri flicks the cabbage back to the tray as my eyes bulge. A *thousand* years old? Surely I misheard him. He winks at my reaction, adding, "Quite spectacular for our age, aren't we?"

"For *any* age," Odessa sniffs.

Dimitri ignores her. "Though I'm flattered by your attention, mademoiselle—truly—I cannot in good conscience accept it when you still refuse to tell me your name."

Odessa's own eyes roll to the ceiling. "That, and your infatuation with the local fleuriste."

"Ah, Margot," he says dreamily, draping himself in the chair next to me. He drops his head over one arm and swings his legs over the other. With him grinning at me upside down—his black curls tickling my arm, his velvet suit a bit rumpled—he radiates boyish charm.

Except for those rags in the corridor.

I drop my egg in distaste, pushing my tray away at the sight of his sharp incisors. Still, it seems foolish to continue the lie when Michal already knows the truth. "If you must know, my name is Célie Tremblay. And I thank you for breakfast, but I really must ask you to—"

"Célie Tremblay." Like his cousin before him, he seems to taste the words, his mouth pursing in contemplation. "A fitting epithet if I've ever heard one. In your language, I believe it means *heaven*."

And that is when Odessa loses interest in the conversation entirely. "In older, more definitive languages, it means *blind*. Now, shall we go, or did I rise at this unholy hour for nothing?"

Dimitri chuckles. "Loath as I am to admit it, Des, you no longer need beauty sleep." To me, he says, "What do you think, Mademoiselle Tremblay? Would you care to join us for a bit of birthday shopping? It could be fun."

Fun. My gaze flicks to the shadows of my room, the wall of bookshelves, and I almost weep. I have no time for *fun*—if such a thing even exists here. No. I must continue my search and learn how to kill vampires like Odessa and Dimitri; I must somehow warn my friends to stay away from Requiem. Christo didn't seem terribly pleased with the royal family during our trek through the market. Perhaps somewhere on this isle, a witch is equally displeased—perhaps so displeased that she'll magic a note to Cesarine or help me kill her overlords.

Unbidden, my eyes return to Dimitri's upside-down face, to the anticipation there. He looks almost *wholesome*, and a tendril of curiosity unfurls despite myself. *Vampires eat people*, yes, but Odessa studies horticulture. Dimitri has *dimples*.

I give myself a vicious mental shake.

These creatures are monsters, and I hate them. I *do*. They hold an entire *island* hostage, feasting on the blood of its inhabitants, and they plan to lure my friend to her death. They kidnapped me. They assaulted me. They serve a man who undoubtedly murdered Babette, and—and how many more reasons do I need to shoo them from my room?

"Why are you being so kind?" My brow furrows as I straighten the corner of the breakfast tray. "I am still a prisoner here. You shouldn't care about my birthday. You shouldn't care about my wardrobe either."

Odessa speaks to the spines of my books, trailing a sharp nail across them. "Vampires live forever, darling, and you are bright and shiny and new. My dear brother cannot help himself."

"Says the vampire conducting an in-depth investigation of her bookshelves." Sitting up, Dimitri laces his fingers together between his knees and returns his attention to me. "You will remain a prisoner whether you sulk alone in this room or join us in the village. I know which cell I would prefer."

He smiles again to soften the rebuke, and I stare at him, torn with indecision.

A small part of me knows I should send them away. Jean Luc would have done it without hesitation.

Still . . . the thought of remaining here for a fortnight—with only candle stubs, shadows, and rows upon rows of dusty books for company—isn't exactly appealing, and my mother always told Pippa that she'd catch more flies with honey than vinegar. Though

Pip resented the expression, it made perfect sense to me. I needn't be alone on this isle. I needn't rot in the darkness or waste precious time with mushrooms and mold. As vampires, Odessa and Dimitri know more about their species than any book in this castle.

There is only one problem.

Sweet creatures never last long in Requiem.

Perhaps, however—just like my mother said—sweetness needn't be a curse at all. Clearing my throat, I feign a tentative smile and bat my lashes at Dimitri, determined to catch at least *this* fly with honey. "You're right. Of course you're right, and I *would* love to go with you . . ."

"But . . . ?" he prompts.

"Michal told me to stay here," I say reluctantly. "He forbade me from leaving my room."

Dimitri scoffs. "Our cousin is an old bat."

"And *you*, brother, are a rotten liar." Shooting an exasperated look at her brother, Odessa closes her book with a sharp *crack*, and the sound echoes through the room with finality. "*Michal agreed*, did he? I don't know why I still listen to you." She shakes her head and stalks for the staircase. "This has been an enormous waste of time."

"*Des.*" Dimitri leaps to his feet, his voice equal parts outraged and imploring. "You would leave Mademoiselle Tremblay here in this dust and darkness? On her birthday?"

"So bake her a *cake*—"

A sharp pang of regret.

"You cannot be serious—"

"I know it's hard for you, Dima, but do *try* for intelligence. If

Michal said she cannot leave, she cannot leave." She waves a curt hand, her humor growing fouler and fouler with each step. "I shall still ring a bath for her, of course. And perhaps we can arrange for Monsieur Marc to visit tomorrow—"

Dimitri chases after her without decorum, but before he can speak, I rise to my feet, adopting an earnest, pleading sort of voice. "But I am *human*, Odessa. Michal cannot expect me to live in these conditions until All Hallows' Eve. I could catch sickness in this dark and damp—perhaps even my *death*. Is that really what he would want? For me to die before I serve his purpose?"

"And technically"—Dimitri catches her at the bottom of the stairs, looping his arm around her waist and twirling her around— "we *will* remain within the castle grounds. She'll be perfectly safe as long as we do not stray beyond the inner walls. Everyone wins. Isn't that right, Mademoiselle Tremblay?"

I nod fervently. "You *did* say I smell like a grubby mop."

Odessa narrows her eyes at me. "I mistook you for clever, but it seems Michal is right—you have a death wish, and I will not assist you with it."

"Oh, don't be so dramatic." Dimitri cups her cheeks in his hands, flashing her a charming smile. His teeth are very white. Very sharp. "Michal is never right, and furthermore, he'll never know we've gone. He has better things to do tonight than patrol the east wing."

At *that*, a hundred questions rush to the tip of my tongue, but I bite down on them all, unwilling to push my luck so quickly. Odessa already looks prepared to skewer someone. She scowls between Dimitri and me, her cheeks still squashed between his broad palms. "This is a *terrible* idea."

Dimitri releases her instantly, his grin triumphant now. "All the best ones are."

"I want it noted that I objected."

"Duly, of course."

"When Michal finds out, he will skin you, and I will not intervene."

"You may wear my hide as a hat."

"You are a cretin." She pushes him away and stalks toward one of the silk curtains. Behind it, an enormous tub awaits. She pulls on a fringed tassel, and a deep *gong* answers from somewhere overhead. Looking over her shoulder, she snaps, "Well? Are you coming, Célie, or shall Michal follow the trail of your stench to Monsieur Marc?"

I jolt forward just as Dimitri makes a noise of outrage. "Why does *she* get to call you Célie?"

Three-quarters of an hour later—clothed in a gown and cloak from Odessa's garderobe—I stride through the castle arm in arm with Odessa and Dimitri. They sweep me into a vast courtyard, where we have a bird's-eye view of the hillside below—and what appears to be a hidden village.

My mouth parts in genuine awe.

Intricately carved stone ramparts rise to the north, east, and south—shielding the small homes and shops—while the castle itself forms the fourth and final wall of the village. Gargoyles crouch atop each pillar. They leer down at us, flames crackling in their open mouths and ivy climbing up their stone bodies. Though the vines and flowers soften their harsh features, they cannot disguise the gargoyles' scales and teeth and horns. My eyes flit to the three-eyed crow from the market as it pecks at one of their ears, loses patience, and hops instead to the thatched roof of l'apothicaire. When thunder rumbles overhead, it ruffles its wings with an indignant caw.

Below it, two cats detach from the shadows to watch me.

No. I shake myself internally, vehemently. To watch *us*.

Odessa adjusts her parasol just as it begins to rain.

"Wonderful," she says coolly, ushering me down the cobbled street without sharing her umbrella. Dimitri extends his with a long-suffering look at his sister. "Do not start with me, Dimitri. We're already late, and Monsieur Marc detests tardiness. 'Tis a mark of poor character"—her eyes narrow pointedly between the two of us—"and he is an *excellent* judge of character."

Dimitri rolls his own eyes. "You will not melt, Odessa."

"And how do you know?" She glares at the storm clouds overhead, and lightning flashes in response. A great *boom* of thunder shakes the earth. "Hygral fatigue is very real. I may not melt, but my hair follicles will indeed expand from excessive moisture, causing dullness, brittleness, breakage, and—"

"—much-needed humility," he finishes. To me, he adds with a grin, "This is the Old City. Only vampires are allowed to live within these hallowed walls—and only the most revered and respected lineages at that. These roads are nearly as ancient as Michal himself."

Even here, it seems I cannot escape him—or the cats. Despite the rain, they follow us on silent feet, their eyes lamp-like and unblinking.

Still, as I take in the narrow, twisting streets—the moss

between cobblestones, the iron spires, a cracked birdbath—I cannot help but bounce on my toes. Just a little. Odessa's marigold soap washed *years* of grime from my skin, and breakfast dulled the sharp edge of my hunger. I can ignore the cats. After all, I thought I wouldn't live to see sunset just hours ago, yet here I am, strolling through an ancient supernatural hamlet with two creatures who know it best. What better way to uncover their weaknesses than to walk among them?

Does it not feel like you're playing dress-up?

Frederic thought my doe eyes meant ineptitude. He thought I could never assist our brotherhood, could never *belong,* yet the Chasseurs don't even know vampires *exist.* Perhaps doe eyes and dresses are exactly what they've needed all these years.

I reach carefully toward a monarch butterfly flitting through the drizzle. I do not want to frighten it—or Dimitri—away with the wrong question. Never mind that the white specks on the tips of its wing seem to blink at me like . . . like *eyes.* I look away quickly. "And the other inhabitants . . . they came here willingly?"

Dimitri catches the butterfly easily and places it in my palm. It no longer blinks—*thank God*—but its orange color still seems too bright against the dark lace of my glove, the muted grays of the sky and street. "All who inhabit Requiem chose to make their home here, Mademoiselle Tremblay."

"But did they have all the information? Did they know their neighbors would be vampires? Did they know you would *feed* on them?"

"You ask an awful lot of questions." Odessa flicks an arch glance toward Dimitri. "And you shouldn't indulge her. Michal will already be furious—"

"No one forced you to come, darling sister."

She scoffs. "*Someone* must protect your neck, as you're quite insistent on sticking it out as far and as often as possible."

Dimitri chuckles, inclining his head to a pair of Éternels, who bow stiffly to both him and his sister. "And why shouldn't we answer her questions? Aren't *you* the one who always says *curiosity killed the cat, but—*"

"—*satisfaction brought it back*," she finishes irritably. "This is different, and you know it."

"Come on, Des. Who is she going to tell?" To me, he adds, lowering his voice, "You can only leave this isle by ship, and vampire sentries overrun the docks—they'll kill you before you touch the gangplank."

My stomach twists, and I release the butterfly to the wind. It spirals upward toward the crow, who promptly eats it. "I assumed as much."

He turns to Odessa with a self-satisfied smile. "See? She knows better than to flee. And to answer your question"—he squeezes my arm companionably—"their ancestors immigrated centuries ago, but Michal gave each family a choice before bringing them here."

"What sort of *choice* could he have possibly given them? And how could they have refused? According to Odessa, Michal jealously guards the secret of this place. He would have killed everyone who knew of its existence."

Though Odessa tenses slightly at my tone, she pretends to examine her reflection in the window of le chapellerie as we pass. "Have you never heard of compulsion, darling?"

"Odessa," Dimitri warns, his dimples fading. He slides behind me to walk between us. "Don't even think about it."

She shrugs absently, but the set of her jaw, her shoulders, says she isn't absent at all. Her reflection meets mine in the window, and the tiny hairs on my arms rise. *Compulsion.* Even in my thoughts, the word feels strangely forbidden, strangely . . . sensual. But it's only a *word.* Shaking my head, feeling ridiculous, I say, "Of course I've never heard of compulsion. I'd never even heard of *vampires* before this evening."

Those feline eyes flick to mine. "Would you like to know what it is?"

"Odessa, stop—"

"I told you, Dima, I will protect your neck—*and* mine—even if you refuse to do the same. Célie needs to understand the true danger of Requiem. If she plans to continue provoking Michal, she should understand exactly what she risks." She steps closer, offering me her hand. Offering me a *choice.* "Shall I compel you, Célie?"

I glance at Dimitri, whose handsome face has hardened to stone as he glares at his sister. He says nothing, however. He won't stop Odessa from compelling me—whatever *that* is—and he won't stop me from asking her to either. Perhaps I should forgo the whole thing. Clearly, Odessa is still irritated, and even in my limited experience, an irritated vampire doesn't bode well. I already know the danger of their speed, their strength. I know the danger of their *teeth.* What more could there possibly be?

What more could there be?

The question might kill me. Hopefully satisfaction will indeed bring me back, because Odessa is right. I *do* want to know. I take her hand. "Show me."

Squaring her shoulders, she tilts her head with a hard smile. "Excellent."

We lock eyes.

At first, nothing happens. Unsure, I glance at Dimitri, but Odessa catches my chin in her hand, holding my gaze. "At me, darling. Look only at me."

The strangest sensation creeps over my mind in response— like a spectral hand has reached out to touch it, to caress it, to seduce it into tranquility. No. Into *submission*. Part of me wants to lean into that touch, while another wants to recoil, wants to flee as far and as fast as I can. Before I can act on either, she purrs, "Tell me how you plan to strike at us before All Hallows' Eve."

"*Des*," Dimitri says sharply.

She doesn't break our eye contact.

"I plan to warn Coco of Michal's trap." The answer spills from my lips of its own volition, soft and sure and serene. With each word, the tranquility deepens, enveloping me in lovely warmth until I cannot help but smile with it. *This* is the danger? I have never felt more content in my entire life. "I plan to manipulate Dimitri into revealing your weaknesses, and I plan to avenge Babette and the others' deaths by killing you if possible. I plan to kill every Éternel on this island."

"Damn it, Odessa." Dimitri runs a hand down his face, breaking his stone facade. "Why did you ask her that?"

"Isn't it obvious? I wanted to hear her answer."

"But *why*? You know she cannot actually harm us—"

"Of course I do, but now she knows it too." To me, she says, "And there you have it. *Compulsion*. I cannot say I expected a different answer. However, if I were you"—she turns to resume her stroll down the street, twirling her parasol on her shoulder—"I would keep word of my plans away from Michal, and I would leave my brother alone."

The second her eyes leave mine, her thrall over me lifts, the delicious warmth vanishes, and my thoughts crash and spiral in confusion. In horror. *Because she didn't—I couldn't have just told her—No.*

Though I clap a hand to my mouth, it does little good; I cannot take the words back. They live between us now, as slick and dark as the rain upon the cobblestones. My teeth chatter as a wave of cold washes over me, as my heart plummets to somewhere between my feet. I just told them everything. Odessa already knew I wished them harm, of course—and I already knew vampires possessed some form of hypnosis—but the *ease* with which she extracted my innermost thoughts is . . . alarming.

Worse still—she wanted me to know. She wanted me to realize how weak I am in comparison.

I think I'm going to be sick.

"I—" Though I search for the right words to fill the silence, I find none, and treacherous heat creeps through my cheeks at Dimitri's careful expression. "I apologize," I say at last. Even to my own ears, the words sound petulant. "I should never have tried to—well—"

His dark eyes sparkle with good humor. "Seduce me?"

"I wouldn't call it *that.*"

"Your lashes threatened to take flight."

"Like I said," I repeat through gritted teeth, "I am very sorry—"

"Don't be. I quite enjoyed it." His roguish grin soon fades at whatever he sees in my expression. "My sister and I won't harm you, Mademoiselle Tremblay," he says with a sigh, "but you should forget your plans of vengeance. You cannot kill us, and you'll only succeed in angering Michal if you try. Shall we?"

When he extends his arm as an olive branch, I stare at it in cold disbelief. I just admitted to plotting his and his entire family's demise, yet still he wishes to be friends.

I cannot decide whether the gesture is comforting or insulting.

CHAPTER SIXTEEN

Boutique de vêtements de M. Marc

Though golden letters in the window declare it to be *Boutique de vêtements de M. Marc*—and a breathtaking peacock gown rotates slowly on display—the dress shop appears to be falling apart at the seams. Ivy covers nearly every inch of the dark storefront, which has been patched with mismatched stones, and the roof has fallen in on one side. A crooked silver birch curves over the hole, blocking the rain, yet bronze leaves flutter into the shop instead.

I reach out to touch the garland of lovely blue flowers brightening the door. "Careful." With lightning-quick reflexes, Dimitri swats my fingers away as the petals begin to quiver. "The Bluebeard blossoms have started to bite."

I clutch my hand incredulously. "Why on *earth* would they bite?"

"Because the isle has turned naughty." The door opens, and a slight, scowling vampire with wispy white hair and paper-thin skin steps out, crossing his arms at the sight of us. Two dots of pink rouge color his cheeks, and kohl lines his ancient eyes. "You're late," he snaps. "I expected you *sixteen* minutes ago."

Over his shoulder, Odessa arches a smug brow at her brother.

Dimitri sweeps into an impeccable bow. "My apologies, Monsieur Marc. We did not expect the rain."

"Bah! One should always expect rain in Requiem." He lifts his nose in my direction, sniffing disdainfully. "And just who are you? Must I beg for an introduction?"

Dimitri nudges me forward. "Allow me to present Mademoiselle Célie Tremblay, who requires an entirely new wardrobe befitting the castle, as well as a special gown for All Hallows' Eve. She is a guest of Michal," he explains with a devilish smile, "so expense is no object, of course."

With a newfound sense of purpose, I follow Dimitri's lead, dipping into a curtsy. *This* is familiar territory. After all, I've attended a hundred dress fittings in my life, been poked with every needle and cloaked in every fabric imaginable at my mother's behest.

Monsieur Marc considers me through narrowed eyes. "Alas, I do not suffer tardiness from my clients. Not even from guests of Michal." He pulls a large, cumbersome pocket watch from his vest—black silk with ivory stars—and huffs, "Seventeen minutes."

"Did I mention it's her birthday?" Dimitri asks. "She turns nineteen in only a handful of hours, and we thought it right she spend the momentous occasion with *you*." He clears his throat with a covert glance at me, and I straighten, unsure exactly what he expects me to do. I start with a beatific smile. It's only slightly strained.

"They say you're a genius with fabric, monsieur," I offer the dressmaker kindly. "The best on the entire isle."

Monsieur Marc waves an impatient hand. "It's true."

"I would consider it a great honor to wear your work."

"Because it would be."

"Right. Of course." Painfully aware of his silence, I search for something else to say—*anything* else to say—before catching sight of the garland overhead and blurting, "Do you feed them? The

Bluebeard blossoms?" When the silence only deepens in response, I hasten to fill it, cringing internally. "It's just that I—I've never heard of carnivorous flowers before. We obviously don't have them in Cesarine, or—well, perhaps we do, and I've just never seen one. My parents never approved of magical flora. They did plant an orange tree in our front yard, though," I add miserably, my cheeks flushing pink. I force a brighter smile to combat the awkwardness. It doesn't work.

Dimitri closes his eyes with a slow exhale, while Odessa watches with rapt fascination. Her anger seems to have evaporated—a small mercy, as I will need to wear her gowns for the rest of my wretched life.

The dressmaker, at least, takes pity on me. "Oh, very *well*. Come in, come in, and make certain you wipe your feet on the mat. I am an *artist*. I cannot be expected to sully my hands with mud and mops and orange trees. What are you waiting for, papillon?" He seizes my wrist and yanks me inside when I hesitate on the threshold. "Time stops for no butterfly!"

Ducking my head, I hurry after him.

The shop boasts only a single room and two apprentices—a female and male vampire who appear no older than me. But looks can be deceiving in Requiem. These two are probably hundreds of years old. I tear my gaze away from them as a leaf flutters on top of my head.

"Onto the platform, if you please. Hurry up!" Monsieur Marc pushes aside carts of fabric in our path: sparkling muslin, indigo wool, velvet and silk and linen and even pelts of soft white fur. The tips of the fibers glitter peculiarly in the candlelight. "Take off the cloak."

Squeezed between a cluttered table and a shelf full of feathers, buttons, and bones, Dimitri and Odessa sit to watch the proceedings. The former gives me a reassuring nod and mouths, *Well done.* Though I try to return his smile, it feels more like a grimace—a suspicion I cannot confirm, however, as there are no mirrors in this dress shop.

Strange.

Flicking his wrist, unfurling a tattered measuring tape, Monsieur Marc trills, "We are waaaaiting."

I hasten to shrug out of Odessa's cloak, but when Monsieur Marc glimpses the gown beneath, he nearly swoons, pressing a hand to his chest. "Oh, no no no no no. *Non.* Mademoiselle Célie, surely you must *know* that such a warm hue does nothing for your complexion. Tons froids, papillon. You are a *winter*, not a summer. This—this"—he gestures indignantly to my gown of amber lace—"monstrosity must be burned. It is *disgraceful.* How dare you step into my shop with it?"

"I—" I shoot a wide-eyed look at Odessa over my shoulder. "My apologies, monsieur, but—"

"You created this monstrosity for me not six months ago, Monsieur Marc," Odessa says, sounding enormously entertained. "You called it your pièce de résistance."

"And it *was.*" Monsieur Marc stabs the air with his pointer finger, triumphant. And perhaps a little unhinged. "It was my pièce de résistance for *you*, the sun cursed to live in eternal night, not for *her*—the waxing moon, the lustrous crescent, the starlight on butterfly wings!"

I stare at him for a beat, strangely flattered, as new warmth suffuses my cheeks. I've never been called *starlight on butterfly wings* before. It makes me think of the lutins. It makes me think of Tears Like Stars. It makes me think of—

"Your hair is lovely," I say abruptly, and this time, my smile is tentative but true. He blinks in surprise. "It . . . reminds me of snow."

"Snow?" he repeats softly.

My face flushes deeper at the avid curiosity in his gaze.

I don't know why I told him that. It's too personal, too intimate, and I only just met him. He's also a vampire . . . so why did I? Perhaps it's because his fangs are short, and I cannot see them. Perhaps it's because his shop is cozy and warm. Perhaps it's because he calls me butterfly.

Or perhaps it's because I miss my sister.

I shrug casually, trying and failing to explain the situation away. "My sister adored the snow. She would wear white any chance she could—on gowns, ribbons, scarves, mittens—and every winter, she would bundle into her white cloak and insist on building an ice palace."

I hesitate then, feeling more ludicrous with each word. I need to stop talking. I need to at least *pretend* I can adhere to social graces. In the dark whimsy of this shop, however—surrounded by the strange and beautiful—I can almost feel Filippa's presence. She would have loved it here. She would have hated it here. "She once imagined her life a fairy tale," I finish quietly.

Tilting his head, Monsieur Marc considers me with unsettling intensity. No longer curiosity but something else. Indeed, for such a distracted sort of man, his expression grows almost . . . calculating. Though I twist Odessa's cloak with clammy fingers, I keep my gaze fixed on his. Odessa said Monsieur Marc is an excellent judge of character, and this moment—it feels like a test. Another leaf drifts to the floor as the silence in the shop stretches.

And stretches.

At last, a peculiar smile splits his powdery face, and he steps away from the platform. "My apologies, papillon, but I seem to have forgotten my measuring tape in the workroom. S'il vous plaît"—he gestures to the shop at large, his hand mysteriously empty now—"feel free to select your fabrics in my brief absence. Cool tones, mind you," he adds sharply. Then—with the same uncanny smile—he drifts through a door previously hidden behind a rack of costumes.

Uncertain, I stare at the door for several seconds before descending tentatively from the platform.

We have officially left familiar territory.

Not because I stand in a shop full of vampires, of course, but because my mother never allowed me to choose my own fabrics, and this shop bursts at the seams with them.

Cool tones only.

No one speaks as I approach the nearest shelf, trailing my fingers along a bolt of raw vicuña wool. My mother would've absolutely salivated over the mulberry silk beside it. Even as children, she insisted we wear only the most lavish of fabrics—and in silver and gold, mostly. Like pretty coins in her pocket.

Instinctively, I cast around the shop in search of either.

A rack of liquid metallics hangs directly behind Odessa and Dimitri. Their eyes track me across the room, and heat prickles up my throat when I realize they've been watching me this entire time. No—*studying* me. I clear my throat in the awkward silence, sifting through the metallics without truly seeing them. *Copper and bronze. Rose gold. Lavender.* "Do you think I . . . passed his test?" I ask at last.

"No one is testing you," Dimitri says at once.

"That remains to be seen," Odessa says at the same time.

Dimitri casts his sister an accusing look. "*Odessa.*"

"What?" Shrugging, she examines her nails with cool indifference. "Would you prefer I lie? She hasn't yet met D'Artagnan, and everyone knows he's the *real* test."

"Who is—?"

At that moment, however, a truly enormous cat pokes its head up from the basket of fabric between them. With thick charcoal fur, protuberant amber eyes, and a squashed face, it might just be the ugliest creature I've ever seen—and if its low growl is any indication, it feels rather the same way about me.

"*Shoo.*" Hissing the word, I nudge the basket away with the tip of my boot. Because this is getting absurd. The cats on this isle have created a completely unnecessary situation for me, and now one of them has managed to follow me into a *dress* shop. "Go on." I reach down, upending the basket to force the creature out of it, resisting the urge to open my jaw and pop the sudden pressure in my ears. "Get out of here. Leave me alone."

If a cat could scowl, this one would. "Rather cocksure, aren't you?"

The words fall like bricks over my head.

Because this cat—he seems to have *spoken* them, and I must really, truly have succumbed to hallucination now. Surely I must've imagined it. Surely its mouth did not just move like a—like a *human's.* Hearing disembodied voices is one thing, but cats—they cannot speak. They cannot *scowl* either, and—I glance in disbelief to Odessa and Dimitri. "Did either of you hear—?"

"Célie," says Odessa with wry amusement, "please allow me to introduce the magnificent D'Artagnan Yvoire, original proprietor of this lovely little boutique and Monsieur Marc's elder brother."

I stare between them for a beat, convinced I misheard. Surely she didn't just imply that this distinctly four-legged creature once owned a dress shop, and *surely* she didn't imply that said creature is also Monsieur Marc's *kin*. "But"—I feel compelled to state the obvious—"he's a *cat*."

Stretching atop the spilled fabric, D'Artagnan surveys me with scathing apathy. "An astute observation."

I exhale a harsh breath before turning to Dimitri. "And—and you *can* hear him, right? The cat is—er, he's actually talking? This isn't happening inside my head? Or—or perhaps not some strange new sickness of the isle?"

"These voices," D'Artagnan says dryly, "just how long have you been hearing them, precisely?"

Dimitri shakes his head in exasperation. "Just ignore D'Artagnan. Everyone else does."

At the sound of his voice, however, D'Artagnan's ears flatten, and the tip of his tail begins to flick. My frown deepens. I should feel relief, of course—and thank God others can hear this wretched cat too—but gooseflesh erupts down my neck instead. Probably from the chill in the shop. There *is* an enormous hole in the ceiling, after all, and I have too little experience with talking cats to assume anything about their behavior—except that this one boasts *very* poor manners.

"As you can see, he doesn't particularly like me either." Rising from his seat, Dimitri casts a disapproving look in D'Artagnan's direction before patting my shoulder in a sympathetic gesture.

And at that precise second, a gust of cold wind bursts through the branches overhead.

"*Mariéeee...*"

The pressure in my ears spikes to actual pain through my temples, but I bolt upright anyway, glancing around the shop in alarm for any sign of flickering ethereal light. *Not again.* I nearly weep at the pressure, at the looming sense that someone or something lingers just out of sight. *Please not again.*

"Mademoiselle Tremblay?" Dimitri's face twists in concern, and he removes his hand at once, stooping slightly to peer into my eyes. "What is it?"

"Nothing." My eyes continue to dart, however, searching for that damning silver light. "It's nothing."

"Your face has gone white as a sheet."

D'Artagnan's eyes glitter in unapologetic amusement. "Or perhaps as white as a ... ghost?"

I stiffen at the implication, turning slowly to stare at him. "Why would you say that?"

Though he merely licks his paw in response, his silence—it speaks volumes, and it grows loud enough to muffle even the debilitating pain in my head. Because he *knows.* He *has* to know. His use of the word cannot be simple coincidence, which invites the question—can D'Artagnan see them too?

The ... ghosts?

Cats are guardians of the dead, Célie. I thought everyone knew that.

I swallow hard, forcing myself to take deep, steadying breaths through the dread. Whatever D'Artagnan might be, it isn't a simple cat—of *that* much I am now sure. "How—" A trickle of sweat trails between my shoulder blades as I kneel beside him, as my teeth threaten to chatter in the cold. "How exactly did you come to . . . to look like this, monsieur?"

"Oh, it's monsieur now, is it?"

The door to the workroom bursts open in response, and Monsieur Marc strides through with his assistants in tow. Though a measuring tape remains nowhere to be seen, both balance several bolts of fabric in their arms: emerald silk, black wool, and deep lapis-blue satin. "I poisoned him, of course," he says, voice genial. "For seducing my consort."

"After which, of course," D'Artagnan says scathingly, "*your* mistress trapped my soul in the body of a wretched animal for all eternity."

"Ah, Agatha." Monsieur Marc chuckles, and a dreamy look passes over his powdered face. "I've never met a witch with such proclivity to eternal torment. You should never have killed her. Death by cat is a *terrible* way to go—quite slow, you know, and rife with pain." Turning to me, he snaps his fingers and says, "Well? Have you chosen your fabrics, papillon?"

"I—" My eyes fall to the rack of metallics, where my hands clutch both a glittering magenta and a deep emerald green. Swiftly, I forage for any hint of gold, finding a brilliant satin swathe of it at the very end of the rack. I seize it without thinking. "This one, of course—for an evening gown. Don't you agree?"

His misty eyes narrow at the fabric as if it has personally offended him. "Do you suffer from color blindness?"

"Pardon?"

"Color blindness," he repeats emphatically. "Do you suffer from it? Or—perhaps—you come from a realm where *gold* is considered a cool tone?" Wincing, I return the satin to the rack as quickly as possible, searching for a swathe of silver instead. Before I can find it, however, Monsieur Marc shakes his head with impatience and snaps his fingers once more, signaling for his assistants to present the green, black, and blue fabrics. "Soft pink, too, I think," he tells them, "or perhaps a nice teal—"

"Teal?" D'Artagnan makes a derisive sound from his basket. "Tell me, brother, did your good sense die with me?"

"And *what*, precisely, is wrong with the color teal? It symbolizes clarity, originality—"

"There could be nothing less original about this young woman."

"Is that your official verdict?"

"Will it change your mind either way?"

"No, of course. An enemy of my enemy is a friend, which makes you, papillon"—he turns to me, clapping his hands together in delight—"my new favorite customer."

I gape between them, incredulous. And perhaps a touch indignant. "You think I'm *unoriginal*?"

"Oh, come now," says Monsieur Marc kindly. "If everyone were original, no one would be. Which is quite the point."

"Forgive me, monsieur, but it didn't sound like a compliment."

D'Artagnan licks his paw once more, thoroughly unbothered, in the feline equivalent of a shrug. "Life is long, and opinions change. If it bothers you, prove me wrong." When I open my mouth to tell him, well—I don't *know*, exactly—he turns away from me altogether, sniffing Odessa's cloak. "For now, I am afraid you've lost my interest. What *does* continue to interest me, however, are the anchovies in your pocket, Mademoiselle Petrov."

With a supercilious smile, Odessa withdraws a small tin, opening it to reveal a row of small, slimy-looking fish. She offers them to D'Artagnan, who tucks in with the complacent air of having done this a hundred times before. I stop searching the rack abruptly. Again, I *should* feel immense relief at this revelation, yet the indignation in my chest only flares higher. Of course D'Artagnan dislikes Dimitri and me in comparison—we don't carry *fish* around in our pockets. "You're the reason the cats have been following us," I say accusingly.

Odessa's smile fades. "The cats haven't been following *us*, Célie."

"But—"

"Papillon!" Monsieur Marc huffs and plants his hands on his hips. "Focus, s'il vous plaît! My next appointment arrives in *eleven* minutes, which leaves us approximately two minutes and thirty-six seconds to choose the rest of your fabric. Boris, Romi—"

He motions to his assistants, who pull measuring tapes from their aprons and thrust me toward the dais. Their hands are cold as they take my size.

"Silver." I speak the word through gritted teeth, keeping hold of my patience by a very short leash. "I'd like to request a silver gown, please, instead of the teal or pink." I expect him to huff again, perhaps roll his pale eyes and point to an entire cupboard filled with silver fabric, yet he does neither of those things.

Indeed, no one reacts at all how I expect.

The assistants both halt their ministrations, going completely still, while Monsieur Marc plasters a too-wide, too-bright smile upon his face. Odessa and Dimitri exchange a wary glance, and

D'Artagnan—he looks up from his anchovies, whiskers twitching slightly as he considers me. "Yes, brother," he says sleekly. "Where *is* the silver fabric?"

Monsieur Marc clears his throat. "Completely sold out, I'm afraid."

"Is that so?"

"You know it is."

Despite his smile, his voice sounds strained, and though there is nothing inherently *wrong* with his explanation, it doesn't feel right either. Not in a shop like this. Not when he offers at least four different shades of gold in a variety of fabrics. "When will the next shipment arrive?" I ask. "I assume you've placed an order to replenish your stock."

"I fear the borders do not open until All Hallows' Eve."

I blink at him. "Why?"

"So many questions," Odessa mutters.

"And quite the wrong ones," D'Artagnan adds.

After frowning at both of them, I return my attention to Monsieur Marc, whose smile has become rather fixed. "Perhaps a merchant in the village will have—"

"No, no." Clearing his throat again, he waves his hand wildly before plunging it into his waistcoat to retrieve his pocket watch. "I think not, papillon. Silver is a rather—ah, *finite* resource on Requiem, and indeed, we have little need of it. You shall look dashing in *emerald* on All Hallows' Eve. Indeed, I insist on transforming you into a true and proper butterfly—"

"Finite?" A strange sensation settles in my stomach with the word. An inkling. A suspicion. In Cesarine, every dress shop bursts at the seams with ornament—if the fabric itself doesn't sparkle, metallic beads and thread adorn every hem, every waist, every sleeve, and Requiem seems to favor the same lavish taste. It makes little sense that vampires would exclude silver from their repertoire without good reason. "My apologies," I say at last. "Emerald wings will look lovely, of course. I understand completely."

"*Do* you?" D'Artagnan asks.

"I think so."

A beat passes as we stare at each other. His gaze assessing. Mine challenging.

Then, with an abrupt snort, he crouches low over his anchovies once more. "Somehow, I doubt that very much—and I'd go with the pink if I were you. It suits."

Monsieur Marc shuts his pocket watch with the definitive air of someone ending a conversation. "Eight minutes."

I lift my chin in defiance, smiling down at D'Artagnan and ignoring the sharp stab of pressure through my ears. The fresh gooseflesh down my arms. Though a flicker of unnatural light surfaces in my periphery, I ignore it too. Because now—for the first time since arriving in Requiem—I *do* understand.

Vampires have secrets too.

"Teal it is," I say pleasantly.

CHAPTER SEVENTEEN

L'ange de la Mort

Eight minutes later, Monsieur Marc shoos us from his shop, his chest puffing with unmistakable pride. "Excellent choices, papillon, excellent choices—and I shall summon you posthaste for your All Hallows' Eve costume, oui? I am thinking the emerald swallowtail." He splays his fingers wide, wriggling them in emphasis. "The most beautiful butterfly of them all. You shall sparkle like la lune à vos soleils."

The pressure in my head subsides slightly as we step outside. "That would be lovel—"

"Of course it would," he says. "Now get out. Can you not see I must work?"

He slams the door behind us without ceremony, and relief, hesitant at first but growing stronger with each second, loosens the knot in my chest. I tip my face toward the storm clouds—toward the thunder, toward the lightning, toward the three-eyed crow—and close my eyes, inhaling deep. Because Monsieur Marc, at least, seems to like me, and he is an excellent judge of character. Because ghosts are not real, and I smell of marigolds. Because the wretched D'Artagnan will remain a cat forever, and . . . there is no silver on Requiem.

"You were right." I exhale as another bout of thunder rumbles overhead. "Spending my birthday alone would've been horrid, and I quite like Monsieur Marc."

When no one answers, I open my eyes, turning to face Odessa and Dimitri with another smile—

And freeze.

Michal leans against the dark stone of the shop.

Arms crossed, deceptively casual, he studies the three of us with an inscrutable expression. On either side of me, Odessa and Dimitri have gone preternaturally still. They don't even breathe. "As do I, Célie," Michal murmurs. "As do I."

Oh God.

"Michal." Shoulders rigid, Dimitri steps in front of his sister and me. "You shouldn't have—"

Michal lifts a pale hand. "Do not speak."

At that, a flicker of—of *something* stirs deep within Dimitri's eyes. Though I can't quite place the emotion, it looks foreign, unsettling, on his charming face. It lifts the hair on my neck. "Should we have left her to starve?"

With lethal speed, Michal pushes himself from the wall to stand directly in front of him. He does not lift a hand, however. He simply stares down at his cousin, cold and impassive, and waits.

And waits.

I glance to Odessa, who looks straight ahead in a refusal to acknowledge either of them. Her pupils have dilated, and she no longer breathes. Inexplicable flutters erupt in my stomach at the sight, and I move without thinking, placing a hand on Dimitri's chest to—to calm him, somehow. To defuse this strange tension. "I didn't starve," I tell him quietly, "thanks to you."

His jaw clenches in response. After another second, he swallows hard and removes my hand, but his touch remains gentle. His fingers linger upon my wrist. "Remember what I said about sweet things in Requiem."

He steps away before I can answer, bowing stiffly to his cousin in the process. Only then does Michal slide his black eyes to me. "You should indeed take care, Mademoiselle Tremblay, if Dimitri thinks you're sweet." Then— "Did you really think you could creep away unnoticed?"

The relief I felt only seconds before hardens into that familiar tightness as I glare at him. "I was not creeping, monsieur. I walked out the back door."

His eyes flash with anger, or perhaps amusement. They're disturbingly similar with Michal. "No. A lady never creeps, does she?" Arching a brow, lifting an arm to his chest in exaggerated civility, he inclines his head to Odessa and Dimitri. His gaze, however, doesn't stray from my face. "Leave us now, cousins."

Though Odessa casts me an apologetic glance, she doesn't hesitate; looping her elbow around her brother's arm, she attempts to steer him back up the street, but he digs in his heels. "I'm the one who persuaded her to leave her room, Michal," he says, his voice bitter. "Odessa had no part in it."

Michal's answering smile is chilling. "I know."

"It was not the fault of Mademoiselle Tremblay either."

"No." At last, those black eyes break from mine, and he surveys Dimitri with apathy bordering on disgust. "The fault—as always—rests entirely with you, and we shall discuss it at length before sunrise. My study. Five o'clock."

"Dima," Odessa hisses, pulling him harder now. "*Move.*"

"But—"

"Please go," I say. "He won't hurt me. Not yet, anyway." Though Michal's attention sharpens at the last, I ignore him, meeting Dimitri's gaze and adding, "Thank you for the birthday gifts, Dima, and please—call me Célie."

His lips quirk for just a second. Then he sighs, his entire body slumping, and allows Odessa to lead him away with one last inscrutable look over his shoulder. The two quickly pick up speed, blurring around the bend and out of sight. Leaving me alone with Michal.

He extends his arm in a mockery of a perfect gentleman. "Shall we?"

"If you plan to escort me back to my room"—I move away from him, crossing my own arms firmly against my chest—"I will require candles. Lots and *lots* of candles. I am not a vampire, and I cannot see in the dark."

"Who says vampires can see in the dark?"

"No one," I say quickly, realizing I've further implicated Dimitri. Then, unable to resist— "You simply remind me of an old bat. They have night vision, do they not?"

There's no mistaking it now. Humor glints dark in his eyes as he reaches above my head to pluck a sprig of the Bluebeard blossoms. I scowl at the blue flowers, refusing to accept them, until he leans close and tucks the sprig into my hair. "Like bats, these blooms also once ate spiders."

"What do they eat now?"

His fingers brush the shell of my ear. "Butterflies."

I feel that touch all the way to my toes.

Two seconds too late, I jerk away from him, appalled by my

own reaction, and swat the flowers to the ground. "Fortunately for me, I am not a butterfly, and I have no interest in being eaten by *anything* on this island."

"You needn't worry about that. Not *yet*, anyway." At my scowl, he laughs derisively. "Come. We have unfinished business, the two of us, and I am eager to see it concluded." Turning on his heel, he stalks after Odessa and Dimitri without checking to see if I follow. Which I don't.

Unfinished business.

The words have never sounded more ominous.

"I will carry you, Célie," he calls pleasantly, and—at the thought of him *touching* me again—my feet lurch into motion.

"You are grossly informal, monsieur." Hurrying to catch up, I slide a little on the wet cobblestones. I left Dimitri's parasol in Monsieur Marc's shop, and the sky has started to mist once more. "Only my friends call me Célie, and you are most *certainly* not my friend."

"How quaint. You think Dimitri is your friend."

"Dimitri is a gentleman—"

"Dimitri is an addict. He has thought of nothing but your blood since he made your acquaintance yesterday. That lovely throat has become his obsession."

I nearly stumble again, my mouth falling open in outrage. "I— That is *not* true—"

"You should be flattered." Michal ascends the castle steps and passes a quartet of guards, who bow to him in unison. I swiftly avert my gaze. After Michal's vulgar declaration, surely I just *imagine* the hunger in their eyes. "We don't typically crave the blood of humans," he continues, and perhaps I also imagine the way he shifts closer, the cool glance he gives the other vampires. I do *not*, however, imagine the proprietary hand he places on my lower back. "Dimitri is the exception, of course. He craves the blood of everyone."

My cheeks flush inexplicably warm at his touch, and I quicken my step, darting ahead through the entrance hall. "You're lying." I have no idea if he's lying, but I cannot abide Michal speaking ill of Dimitri. Not when Michal is so thoroughly and terribly *Michal*.

His lips twitch as he shadows my steps. "Believe whatever you like."

"Oh, I will." His words have hit their mark, however, and my first memory of Dimitri rears its ugly head once more. The blood-soaked rags. The furtive behavior. I push it all aside with irritation, bursting through the double doors into the night. Dimitri has been nothing but kind to me. Suspiciously, I ask, "Why don't vampires crave human blood?"

"It tastes thinner, weaker, than the blood of magical creatures." Michal extends his arm toward the city below, ushering me forward. "But we've already established you aren't human. Not entirely."

"You sound ridiculous."

"You sound frightened."

My gaze narrows. "If you're *so* sure that I'm not human, please, enlighten me—what am I?"

His own gaze drops languorously to the pulse in my throat. "Only one way to find out."

"You will *never* bite me."

"No?"

"*No.*"

His slow smile doesn't falter as he brushes past without another word.

Four of the five victims have been of magical origin, and all have been found with puncture wounds on their throats and no blood in their bodies.

Vampires don't typically crave the blood of humans. It tastes thinner, weaker, than the blood of magical creatures.

There can be no doubt of his guilt now. That was practically a confession.

And I have no choice but to follow a murderer into the city.

Passersby part for us without hesitation, either bowing in reverence or drawing back in fear. All stare at Michal beneath their parasols, however, as if a god walks among us. He doesn't seem to notice their infatuation. Perhaps he just doesn't care. Hands clasped behind his back, he stalks through the streets with an air of indifference, nodding to some and ignoring others completely. Imperious and insufferable.

Michal has now sought me out *twice* in as many days, however, which means this *unfinished business* of ours remains excellent leverage. Whether he likes it or not, the time has come to receive answers, and if he refuses to give them, I will make him *rue* his immortality. Hurrying to keep up, I say, "Monsieur Marc said silver is a finite resource in Requiem." When Michal says nothing, I nearly clip his heel in my haste to catch him. "Indeed, he doesn't keep it in his shop at all. He doesn't keep any mirrors either."

Michal still refuses to acknowledge me.

"Isn't that odd? No mirrors in a dress shop? Though, now that I think about it"—I step on his heel intentionally this time, remembering when Pippa and I once shattered our mother's hand mirror, coating her armoire in silver dust—"I don't recall seeing any mirrors in my room either. Or in the castle. Or on the entire isle."

"Hence the word *finite*."

"Where is my cross?" I ask abruptly. "You never answered me before."

When I clip his heel a third time, he casts a menacing look over his shoulder. "And I have no intention of answering you now. Tell me, are you always this . . ." His voice trails as he struggles to find the right word.

"Vexing?" I supply it with my sweetest smile, and I relish the way his eyes narrow in response. "*Always*. Now—where are we going?" As if waiting for my signal, the sky opens up in earnest, pelting fat drops of rain on our heads. "To a candlemaker? A parasol shop?"

He chuckles darkly. "No, pet."

We draw to a halt outside the theater.

The velvet swags hang limp from the balustrades—soaked from the rain—and no music pours from the black-and-gold doors. No screams either. Clearly, there is no show scheduled for tonight.

Michal pushes through the entrance anyway, thoroughly unconcerned, just as lightning streaks overhead. It illuminates shadowy shapes in the otherwise empty foyer, and suddenly, I have even *less* interest in this unfinished business of ours. Hesitating on the steps, I ask, "Why are we here? What do you want with me?"

"You know the answer to at least one of those questions." Standing in the threshold, he peels off his jacket and tosses it aside. His shirt beneath is white and—and *soaked*. Mouth abruptly dry, I tear my eyes from the sculpted shape of his chest to find him smirking at me. My cheeks flame. "Feel free to come inside," he says wryly, his eyes a shade darker than before. I glare at him through the downpour, water streaming down my nose. The portrait of aristocratic grace.

"Not until you tell me why we're here."

He chuckles again, rolling each sleeve with slow, deft fingers. "But you're getting all wet."

"Yes, *thank* you for that clever observation. I *never* would've realized if you hadn't—"

"Come inside," he says again.

I push the sopping hair out of my face, resisting the urge to stamp my foot like a child. "Tell me why we're here."

"You're rather obstinate, aren't you?"

"Pot, meet kettle."

Crossing his arms, he leans a shoulder against the open door to consider me. "Shall we have another game, then? If I explain why we're at L'ange de la Mort, will you promise to come inside?"

L'ange de la Mort.

The Angel of Death.

I cross my own arms, slowly drowning in my boots, and try not to shiver in the cold. He thinks himself perfectly reasonable—I can see it in the condescending curve of his lips, the self-satisfied gleam in his eyes. To him, I *am* just a child in need of managing. Under different circumstances, I might've sought to change his opinion, to prove myself capable and competent and strong, but now . . .

I shrug, adopting his devil-may-care attitude, and peer around him into the theater. "I make no promises. A little rain never killed anyone, and I have no interest in helping you do . . . whatever it is you've brought me here to do."

"You shouldn't tempt Death in this place, Célie. He just might answer."

"By all means, do tell me more. You have no idea how willing I am to *not* come inside."

He stares at me for a long moment—his expression inscrutable, calculating—before his lips curve in another cruel smile. For just an instant, I worry I've overplayed my hand—he could *compel* me to come inside, after all, could compel me to do anything he wants—but then he inclines his head.

"Very well," he says. "I am undead, and as such, I exist with one foot in both the realm of the living and the dead. Each calls to me. Each serves the other. When I revel in the warmth of the living—when I feast on its blood—I hold cold death in my hands. Do you understand?"

Any answer I might've given sticks in my throat. This is—not what I expected, certainly, and far beyond anything I'm equipped to handle. *Each calls to me. Each serves the other.* "No, I don't," I say warily, staring up at him. "I don't understand at all."

"I think you do." He pushes from the door, approaching me with his hands in his pockets. "There are always places, however—rips in the fabric between realms—where Death has slipped through and lingered, and L'ange de la Mort is one of them. Many have died here. It should make this process . . . easier."

"What process?"

"The process of summoning a ghost."

CHAPTER EIGHTEEN

The Knife in the Veil

I retreat a step, my eyes wide and my hands cold. "I *told* you that I can't—"

"I have spent the last twenty-four hours scouring this island for any other explanation, and everything—*everything*, down to the last slime-covered toadstool—remains the same as it did two days ago." He shadows my steps with a hard, determined gleam in his eyes. "Everything except for *you*. The veil thinned when you arrived. I felt it then, and I felt it again this evening. Care to explain?"

The veil thinned when you arrived.

I don't like how that sounds. I don't like it at all.

Demanding answers is one thing, but this—this sort of *practical application* is quite another.

A finger of unease trails down my spine, and I glance left and right through the rain, prepared to flee if it means escaping this rather abrupt turn in our conversation. He'll chase me, of course, but my flight might distract him. It'll most definitely lead me away from this—this *rip in the fabric between realms.* Michal already walks with one foot in the land of the dead—as far as I'm concerned, he can follow it straight to Hell. I will not have any part in this. I will not *summon a ghost.*

As if reading my mind, he shakes his head slowly, his voice low. "Never run from a vampire."

Too late.

Lifting my hem, I dart behind a passing couple and sprint for the nearest shop—a quaint fleuriste of painted brick with bouquets of goldenrods on display. Surely Michal cannot exist in such a cheerful place. Surely we cannot summon ghosts in front of the pretty florist, who already rises on tiptoe to watch us—

Cold hands seize me from behind, and before I can scream, Michal wraps impossibly hard arms around my waist, lifting me from my feet and hauling me over his shoulder. Knocking the breath from my lungs. "Let me g—" Gasping, I kick at his hips, pound my fists on his back, but it feels like grappling with a mountain. His body is harder than stone. "Let me *go*! How *dare* you—? Unhand me, you—you appalling *leech*!"

"We seem to have gotten off on the wrong foot, darling." His elbow locks behind my knees—adamantine, unbreakable—as he carries me back to the theater. When I twist upright, aiming a blow at his ear, he catches my fist easily, engulfing it in his hand. "Allow us to start over. I will ask you a question, and you will answer. No more games and no more lies." He tugs on my captured hand, and I tumble into his arms. His face, his *teeth*, loom entirely too close. Though I thrash away from him, he leans closer still, so close I can see the rain in his eyelashes, the shadows beneath his eyes. "Never run from me again," he breathes, no longer smiling but deadly serious.

Kicking open the theater doors, he deposits me on my feet.

I immediately flee behind one of the pedestals in the foyer.

The marble bust of a beautiful woman peers back at me before Michal closes the doors with an ominous *boom* and complete darkness descends. There are no candles here. There is no *light*.

Panic claws up my throat.

Not again.

"M-Michal." My fingers search blindly for the bust, for something to ground myself in the room. "Can we—can we p-please light a—"

Light flares instantly to my left, illuminating Michal beside a life-sized statue; this one lifts a candelabra over her voluptuous form, half-clothed in flowing robes of obsidian. Tilting his head curiously, Michal blows out the match in his hand. "Are you afraid of the dark, Célie Tremblay?"

"No." I exhale heavily, taking in the high ceilings, the gilt edges of the room. A dozen other busts line the walls in an imposing semicircle. *The royal family.* Two at the end with large, feline eyes look acutely familiar, as does the one directly beside me. The sculptor must've been part witch; no ordinary artist could capture the menace in Michal's eyes so perfectly. I turn back to its likeness. "I told you—I am not a vampire, therefore I cannot *see* in the dark."

"Is that all?"

My fingers slip from the bust, leaving tracks down her dusty face. "Yes."

"Then why is your heart racing?"

"It isn't—"

He appears before me instantly and snatches my wrist, his fingers curling around it. They press against the wild beat of my pulse. "I can hear it across the room, pet. The sound is deafening."

When I stiffen at his touch, he tilts his head, and genuine interest sparks in his eyes. *Dangerous* interest. "I can scent your adrenaline too, can see your pupils have dilated. If it isn't the dark that scares you—"

"It isn't," I interject.

"—it must be something else," he finishes, arching a suggestive brow. His thumb strokes the translucent skin of my inner wrist, and a bolt of—*something* streaks through my core. "Unless it isn't fear at all?" he asks silkily.

Mortified, I tug my wrist away, and it slides through his fingers without resistance. "Don't be silly. I simply—I do not want to meddle with ghosts. I don't even know *how*. Regardless of what you felt when I arrived here, I was not the one who *thinned the veil* between realms. I am *human*—a God-fearing Christian woman who believes in Heaven and Hell and hasn't the slightest knowledge of life after death. There's been a"—I skitter around him, unable to stand the fascination in his gaze—"a horrible misunderstanding."

"Is it your emotions that attract them, I wonder? Could it be *any* emotion strongly felt?"

I stand on my tiptoes and wrench the golden candelabra from the statue's hand. "It has nothing to do with my emotions."

"Perhaps you need to hold a personal item of the deceased to make contact."

Pushing into the auditorium, I light every candle within reach. There must be another exit *somewhere*. Perhaps backstage. "I couldn't possibly have held a personal item of every gho—*thing* in that promenade. There were dozens of them."

"Did they speak to you?"

"No."

"Liar." He blocks my path once more, and I cannot help but to stop short and stare at him. Here—gilded in the golden candlelight of the theater, framed by the carved demons around the stage—he looks truly otherworldly, like an avenging spirit or fallen angel. Like the Angel of Death. Exhaling slowly, he stares right back, his black eyes narrowing as if I'm a puzzle he cannot quite solve. "You're doing it again," he says at last.

I look away quickly. "Doing what?"

"Romanticizing nightmares."

Scoffing, I shake my head at my boots. "I have no idea what you mean."

"No? That little sparkle in your eye isn't wonder?" A cold finger lifts my chin, so I'm forced to look up at him once more. His lips purse in consideration. "You wore the same expression when you entered my study yesterday, and again as you left Monsieur Marc's shop—like you'd never seen anything more beautiful than a pendulum clock or bolt of teal silk."

"How do *you* know it was teal silk?"

"I know everything that happens on this isle."

"Can you even hear how conceited you sound?" I jerk my chin away from him. "And you keep that clock on your desk *because* it is beautiful, so I won't apologize for admiring it or—or *romanticizing* it."

He arches a brow. "And the horned toads at market? The carrion beetles? Are they all beautiful too?"

I gape at him, half torn between disgust and outrage. "*Carrion* beetles?" Then, remembering myself— "Have you been *following* me?"

"I told you"—he lifts an unapologetic shoulder—"I know everything that happens here." When I open my mouth to tell him *exactly* what he can do with his great omniscient knowledge, he clicks his tongue softly and speaks over me. "I do not want to force you, Célie, but if you refuse to help me, I will have little choice. One way or another, I will learn how you summoned those ghosts."

One way or another.

I swallow hard, taking a step backward.

He doesn't need to elucidate. Odessa held my mind in her hands only an hour ago, and compulsion isn't an experience I'll ever forget. I shudder to think what might've happened if those hands had belonged to *Michal*—

An unnatural draft sweeps through the auditorium at the thought, leaving tiny icicles upon my wet skin. My stomach plunges at that familiar touch—at the renewed pressure in my head—and I hold my breath, praying I imagined it. "Your eyes," Michal says softly.

"What about them?" Hastily, I look around for some sort of—of reflective surface, but as with everywhere else on this wretched isle, there are none. My hands flutter uselessly near my face instead. "What is it? Is something wrong with them?"

"They're . . . glowing."

"*What?*"

Then someone else entirely starts to speak.

"When shall we three meet again? In thunder, lightning, or in rain?"

Behind Michal, a spectral woman strides onto the stage in dark, opaque robes with chains around her ankles. In her hand, she holds her own severed head. Another woman flickers into existence beside her, this one cloaked in an opulent ruff and pearl jewelry. "When the hurly-burly's done," she recites, seizing the other ghost's head and presenting it to the audience. "When the battle's lost and won."

A dozen more figures soon materialize in the velvet seats, their whispers producing a gentle din.

I close my eyes briefly.

Please, no.

"Absolutely *not*." A portly man with a spectacular mustache storms onto stage next, wielding a skull in his hand like a sword. Except it's a *real* skull—a skull of solid ivory bone—not a spectral one. My eyes dart back to Michal, who still watches me closely. In his black eyes, I see the reflection of my own—two points of eerie, glowing silver. They match the light of the figures onstage. "Elaine, you ridiculous woman, we are in Act Four, Scene One—"

"Yes, all *right*." The bodiless head scowls, rolling her eyes, before snapping, "By the pricking of my thumbs, something wicked this way comes."

"I wanted the Lady of Shalott," the figure nearest me—a man with a monocle on his eye and an axe in his neck—grumbles to his companion. He seems to sense my gaze in the next second, turning in his seat to frown at me. "May I help you, mariée? It's quite rude to stare, you know."

I try to breathe, try to keep the gorge from rising in my throat. Because that axe in his neck, the woman's severed head—how can there be any other explanation for their presence? If not ghosts, what else could they possibly be? Demons? Figments of my imagination? Unless Michal shares the same delusion—unless the silver in my eyes is a mere trick of the light—this is very real. *They* are very real.

At last, understanding dawns, and with it, shards of glass seem to fill my chest.

He called me *mariée*.

"Has anyone seen the cauldron?" With a scowl, the portly man onstage peers into the audience. "Where is Pierre? I *never* should've made him props master—"

My gaze snaps back to Michal, who is suddenly and unequivocally the lesser of two evils. "We need to leave. Please. We shouldn't be—"

At the sound of my voice, however, every ghost in the auditorium turns to face me.

They all fall silent as another draft sweeps the theater, stronger and colder this time. The crystals of the chandelier tinkle overhead in response, and a strand of my hair lifts, blowing gently across my face in the unnatural breeze. Michal stares at it. His entire body stills, tightens. "Are they here now?" he asks quietly.

The pressure in my head builds until it might burst, until my eyes water and burn with it. Unable to pretend any longer, I clutch my ears and whisper, "They call me *bride*."

His brow furrows. "Why?"

"I—I don't know—"

"Isn't it obvious?" Onstage, the portly man plants his hands on his hips and surveys us with stern disapproval. "You're the knife in the veil, silly child—and you probably shouldn't tarry. He *is* searching for you, after all."

"Wh-*Who* is searching?"

"The man in the shadows, of course," says the woman with the ruff.

"We cannot see his face," says the portly man, "but we can certainly feel his wrath."

A whimper escapes my throat, and I clench my eyes shut, struggling to master myself. I will not fear them. As Michal said, this place is a rip in the fabric between realms. Death lingers here. Many have died, and that—that has nothing to do with me. Despite their warning, none of this has *anything* to do with me. This is all just one big coincidence, except—

"You really shouldn't be here at all, mariée," the man with the axe in his neck says irritably. "You need to leave this place, and you need to do it now. Do you want him to find you? Do you know what will happen if he does?"

My heart sinks miserably.

Except they seem to recognize me—*me*, not Michal—and as they drift closer, their voices grow more insistent, echoing all around me, *inside* of me, and impossible to ignore. Just like in Filippa's casket. Indeed, the decapitated woman soon streaks up the aisle, holding her head in one hand, and her eyes burn with silver fire. "You must *look* like the innocent flower, Célie Tremblay, but be the serpent under it."

"*Be the serpent,*" another ghost echoes.

"Leave now," another snarls.

"I"—forcing deep breaths, I choke down my panic—"Michal, p-please, we really need to—"

"How many came through?" Though his voice rises in urgency, I stumble backward, away from him, away from *them*, unable to answer and unable to help. Because the ghosts don't *want* me here. The longer I stay, the colder their touch grows—colder than vampires, colder than *ice*. Too cold to exist in this world. My teeth chatter helplessly. "Where are they?" he asks, louder now. "What are they saying?" Then, abruptly vicious— "Why can't I *see* them?"

He can't see them. The realization crushes the last of my hope, and my breathing hitches, spikes, painful and shallow and— *Oh God.* Vaguely, I can hear him speaking, but his words don't penetrate. Not anymore. A horrible rushing sound drowns out his voice, growing louder with each passing second.

If Michal cannot see the ghosts, cannot *hear* them, it means— he must be right. Somehow, someway, I caused this. I *summoned* them, and now I cannot send them back. They came here for me. *I am the bride,* and—and—

"Leave this place, mariée," the man with the axe hisses.

"You must hide," says the decapitated woman.

The stage manager's voice rises to a shout. "You must HIDE—"

A sob tears from my throat as I wrap my arms around my head, as pain cleaves my skull in two. I am going to die in this theater, where they'll force me to recite dead poets until the end of time. At the thought, hysterical laughter rises until I shake with it, until I cannot tell if I'm crying or screaming or making any sound at all.

Low and strained, Michal's voice reaches me as if through a tunnel.

"Célie. Open your eyes."

I obey the command instinctively to find him standing much closer than before—and motionless. Completely and utterly still. The black of his eyes seems to expand as he stares at my throat, and his jaw locks into place, as if—as if he's trying not to breathe. He doesn't speak again for another moment. Then, through clenched teeth— "You're hyperventilating. You need to calm down."

"I—I—I can't—"

"If you don't lower your heart rate," he says evenly, "every vampire within a three-mile radius is going to descend on this theater. *No*"—the word is sharp, lethal, as his hand seizes my sleeve—"do not run. *Never* run. They will chase you, they will catch you, and they will kill you. Now. Focus on your breathing."

Focus on my breathing. I nod, gulping air until my head swims with it, until the black in my vision begins to fade. At Michal's proximity, the ghosts recoil, muttering bitterly. I choke on an explanation. "Th-They want us to *leave*—"

"In through your nose and out through your mouth, Célie."

I do as he says, concentrating on his face, the hard line of his jaw. He still doesn't breathe. Doesn't move. When I nod again—calmer now—he drops my sleeve and steps backward. I take another deep breath as the ghosts gradually settle into their seats once more. With a grudging look in my direction, the stage manager calls for order. "Please leave," he tells me, and I nearly weep with relief when Michal stalks toward the doors.

Before I can follow, however, another voice emerges from the darkness beyond the brocade curtain. Fainter than the others. So faint I might imagine it. *Come here, sweeting. Such a lovely little doll.*

Like a band snapping, the darkness returns, and I collapse face-first into Michal's chest.

CHAPTER NINETEEN

Rough Day

My dream is cold.

Ice seems to cling to my lashes, my lips, as I rise from my bed and peer around the strange room. It looks familiar—like a place I should recognize—yet it isn't the nursery. It isn't Requiem either. A neat coat and skirt—both brilliant blue—hang within the armoire, and a fireplace crackles merrily from across the room, wafting chill instead of heat and casting strange fey light upon the walls. I lift my hand to watch it dance between my fingers. As with the air, this light feels sharp to the touch, like plunging your hand into snow.

Chasseur Tower.

The thought comes instantly, effortlessly, and on the wings of one realization comes another: I am not alone in this room.

My head turns as though suspended in a substance lighter and thinner than air, yet I have no difficulty breathing. Beside me on the bed, two young women sit with their faces drawn and anxious. They stare at a third woman—this one older, her long black hair beginning to gray at the temples—who rifles through a small desk near the door. "There must be *something*," the woman mutters bitterly, more to herself than the others. "You cannot have looked properly."

The young women exchange a forlorn glance.

"Perhaps you're right, Madame Tremblay," the first says, twisting the moonstone ring around her finger.

The second clasps scarred hands in her lap. "We probably did miss something."

Lou and Coco.

Again, the knowledge simply crystallizes, as does the fact that I know these women. I call them friends. Anticipation gusts to life inside me at the realization, and I shoot to my feet, darting around the bed to face them. As if she can sense my presence, Lou stiffens with a slight frown, but she doesn't look at me. None of them do. I'm not certain if this should upset me. Indeed, I'm not certain if I should feel anything at all, so I sit meekly instead.

At the foot of the bed, a wrinkled green quilt spills over the edge. No one folds it. No one even touches it.

I must have left it like that, I realize suddenly. But why wouldn't they fix it?

Madame Tremblay—no, *Maman*—straightens with familiar pursed lips. They promise a slew of criticisms if Lou or Coco dares put a single toe out of line. Fortunately, the girls remain quiet, watching as Maman piles books and jewelry and two golden lockpicks atop the desk. "The Chasseurs should expect *zero* donations from us this coming year. The entire lot of them are useless." Maman yanks out the drawer too fast and hisses when blood wells on her index finger, a splinter of wood sticking out of her skin like a white flag of surrender.

"Madame Tremblay," Lou murmurs quietly, "please allow one of us to heal you—"

"Absolutely not." Maman straightens, brushing her hair aside, and blood paints the gray ones scarlet. "Pardon my honesty, but magic is . . . well, it is *vile*. Indeed, it is why we're in this mess in the first place. A *week*," she seethes. "My daughter has been missing for a *week*, and what progress have you made in returning her?"

"I promise we have more eyes searching Belterra than you could fit in that magnificent handbag." Lou offers a weak smile—a strained one—and squeezes her moonstone ring so tightly that it begins to melt her flesh. Coco reaches out and snatches her hand. Lou's skin soothes instantly, and the ring returns to its previous impeccable shape.

They don't release each other's hands, however.

The sight of their clasped fingers fills me with a sense of both comfort and longing.

Maman shoves the drawer back in place, and the desk rattles as books—*my* books—wobble dangerously on the shelf above it. Almost magically, however, they shift an inch backward, away from the ledge.

Maman still notices, straightening her shoulders and lifting her chin indignantly. "I do not approve. Whatever you and your . . . your *Dames Blanches* are doing, I *do not approve.*"

"You don't need to approve," Coco says. Anyone else would've delivered the retort under their breath—probably served with an eye roll—but she meets Maman's gaze directly. "We want to find Célie just as much as you, Madame Tremblay, and we're going to do *whatever* is necessary until we do. Including use magic. There is no other option."

Find Célie.

Find Célie?

Confusion dances around my head like a flurry of fresh snow-flakes. I can't imagine why they would need to find me when I'm right here. I drift closer to my friends, resting my hand on theirs. Lou straightens, glancing at Coco with narrowed eyes.

Perhaps I'm not the only one confused. "I'm right here," I whisper to her.

My words ricochet off the walls, met with an echo of deafening silence. I sit in it, certain I'm meant to be doing something too. Searching for something? No, perhaps that isn't right. Perhaps I'm meant to be *sad*. But why? Why can't I remember?

"On *that*, we can agree." Maman nods once, terse but apparently satisfied. "I want my daughter back. No matter the cost."

Coco releases Lou, rising to her feet. She stands taller than Maman, and the latter must look up to meet Coco's gaze. "We *will* find her, madame."

Maman blinks, and I wait for her lips to loosen, to fling sharp words like knives. Instead—to my utter shock—her eyes shine overbright, and a tear slips down her cheek. She wipes it away quickly, but my friends still notice. A sapphire handkerchief drifts across the room on a phantom breeze and lands like a butterfly on Maman's shoulder. She plucks it up and drops it atop the desk.

Though Lou shrugs at the silent rebuke, nonchalant, I know her well enough to spot the concern darkening her blue-green eyes. "There isn't anything I've lost that I haven't soon found, Madame Tremblay. Your daughter won't be any different. One way or another, we *will* find her."

"Thank you." Maman glances away from the desk and moves toward the door as a knock sounds upon it. Once, twice. Then three, four, five times.

I smile in spite of myself.

I've heard this knock a dozen times before. Possibly a hundred.

Jean Luc said we needed it, a way of knowing who was at my door, of knowing whether or not they were safe. Of course, he was the only one who ever used it. And he was only ever safe.

Wasn't he?

Emotion burns like acid up my throat, but I can't discern what, exactly, I am feeling. It hurts too much to contemplate, like an infected wound left to fester. I cannot touch it. That would only make it worse.

The door opens with a flick of Lou's wrist, and—

There he is.

Jean Luc.

Cloaked in blue and silver—a sparkling Balisarda at his side—his eyes widen when he takes in my mother. "M-Madame Tremblay!" He bows instantly. "I had no idea you were visiting the Tower today. You . . . you should have an escort. Let me find Frederic. He can assist you—"

"No need." Maman lifts her chin, and though she stands *much* shorter than Jean Luc, she manages to glare down at him all the same. "And this was *not* a social call. Your investigations are failing, Captain. The time has come for me to conduct one of my own."

His expression falls. "Please, Madame Tremblay, we're doing what we can."

"Oh, I believe *they* are." Maman points grudgingly to Lou and Coco. "But last I saw, your huntsmen were pecking through farm-land and bushes like a flock of useless chickens."

He flinches and looks away swiftly. "They've been ordered to search every inch of Belterra. That includes farmland."

"My daughter has not been *stashed* inside a bushel of *blueberries.*" Her voice cracks, and three more tears leak over her cheeks. Still standing in the threshold, Jean Luc risks a quick glance up at her. His mouth parts when he sees her tears.

Lou attempts to fill the silence with a quiet, "It's true." Then—"Célie would never have risked staining her clothes—uniform, gown, or otherwise."

"Nothing would have made her more violent," Coco agrees.

Jean Luc rolls his eyes at them, ceasing only when Maman jabs a finger in his direction. "I do not care what title you call yourself. I do not *care* if it is captain or fiancé. If you don't find my daughter, I won't rest until this tower has been dismantled and used as kindling."

She pushes past him with an elegance I could never emulate, her anger honed to a knifepoint. Lifting her skirts as she moves into the hallway, she straightens again, her posture impeccable and her spine ramrod stiff. A portrait-perfect stance. She arches her brow at him. "Well?"

"Yes, Madame Tremblay." Jean Luc bows again, lifting his right hand over his heart in a silent promise. "Would you care for an escort back to your carriage?"

"No, I would not."

With that, Maman leaves without another word, and—when she disappears around the bend—Jean Luc slumps against the doorjamb. His forehead, slick with sweat, rests against his arm.

"Rough day?" Coco asks sweetly.

Too sweetly. The words dissolve like candy floss on my tongue. Jean Luc doesn't bother to look up. "Don't start."

"Ah, what a shame." She clicks her tongue gently before she smiles, baring all of her pearly white teeth in a row. "You see, *we've* devoted the day to convincing birds to search the borders for suspicious vessels, enchanting pigs to recognize Célie's scent like she's a damned truffle, and—oh, what else?" She taps her chin. "*That's* right. We spent the last hour trapped in this room with Célie's grieving mother, who just *showed up* while we looked for a personal item with which to scry!"

"Stop it." Jean Luc moves a hand to his Balisarda, as if clutching it for strength. "Don't act like I've done nothing. I haven't been able to eat, drink, or sleep for the past *week*. My entire existence revolves around finding *my* fiancée."

Coco throws her head back with a dry, humorless laugh. "*You've* been suffering? You do realize she only fled because of you and your secrets?" She moves forward then, lithe as a serpent, while Lou rises from the bed with another frown. It looks strange on her freckled face. "None of this would've happened if you'd just told her the fucking truth. What were you trying to prove?"

Jean Luc's hand clenches upon the Balisarda's hilt. "In case you haven't realized, she didn't flee. She was *kidnapped*, which means I had every right to try to protect—"

"No, you didn't, Jean," Lou says. "None of us did. We were wrong."

And I know I should agree with her. I should open my mouth and defend myself—I should assert my presence somehow—but none of them can hear me. And I don't have the energy to fight, anyway. Perhaps I never have. *That's it*, I realize, momentarily triumphant at the realization. *That's the one.*

The singular emotion washing through me as I sit upon this bed. Upon *my* bed.

Exhaustion.

I feel exhausted.

Now that I've acknowledged it, other emotions roll forth like a storm breaking at sea, but for once, I have the ability to stifle them. And it feels like Heaven. I am able to simply watch, entranced, as the three people I care about most in this world argue over me—about where I should or shouldn't have been that night, what I should or shouldn't have been doing. Their voices grow angrier with each word, louder, until they resemble not my friends at all but complete and total strangers. I don't recognize them.

I don't recognize myself.

One thing, however, is for certain: whatever I was doing, I was doing it wrong.

"I didn't come here to fight," Jean Luc says at last, shaking his head and glaring at them. The muscles in his shoulders, his arms, radiate tension as he forces himself to lean against the door. To inhale, to exhale. To disengage from this pointless argument.

"Nor did we." Lou crosses her arms in response, and one of the buttons instantly pops off Jean Luc's coat, landing between their feet. "Just know if we *were* really fighting, Coco and I would win."

"Sure you would." Jean Luc picks up his button, pressing it between his fingers as he glances down either side of the hallway. He won't meet my friends' eyes now. And he won't look past them into the room. "The quilt," he says at last, sighing. "Célie brought it here from her nursery. It should help you scry."

Lou glances back at it. "Of course. It's the only thing not in that hideous shade of blue."

"You should have more respect for the huntsmen. They've all volunteered to help with the search. Even the new recruits have joined."

"Let's make a deal." Lou offers him a mocking hand. "I'll have respect *after* my friend is found. Does that work for you?"

"I'm *trying.*" Jean Luc drags his own hand down his face, and the tension in his body deflates abruptly. "I love her, all right? You know how much I love her."

Retreating to seize the quilt, Coco holds it tightly against her chest. Her eyes still threaten violence. "Well, she isn't in this room, so feel free to look elsewhere."

"Yes, I'm not sure the right tactic for a search and rescue is to linger in doorways." Lou taps her foot against the floor, and it sounds like thunder seconds before another lightning strike. "What do you *want,* Jean?"

Jean Luc clenches his jaw. His gaze lingers on the quilt in Coco's hands. Then— "There's been a new development."

"What?" Coco jolts forward at the words, stumbling slightly— the first time I've ever seen her do so—and knocks into Lou, who steadies her with an anxious hand and wide eyes.

"Where is she?" Lou whispers. "What have you heard?"

Jean Luc peels his own eyes away from my quilt and meets their gazes at last. His brow furrows. "It isn't about Célie. It's—" He swallows. "It's about your family's grimoire, Cosette. It's missing. Someone has—they've stolen it," he finishes quietly.

Coco stares at him for several seconds.

Then she curses—loudly and viciously—as Lou blasts a wave of anger through the room. My books fall off the shelf, one by one by one, and crash into a heap on the floor. My lockpicks roll under the bed and out of sight. I leap to my feet, racing to collect them, but—I swipe at them desperately—my fingers pass straight through the metal. I try again. And again. Each time, my hands refuse to find purchase, and tiny needles of cold spike through my skin.

It seems I can't touch anything here.

Why can't I touch anything here?

And for that matter—why can't they hear me? Why can't they *see* me? Why can't I speak to them at all?

My own frustration breaks free at the last, and I kick at the spine of a leather-bound fairy tale. To my surprise, it moves—just a little, just enough to ruffle the pages. Not enough for anyone to notice, however. And I . . . I feel angry at that. And *sad*. And—and—

A dozen more emotions converge like a wave crashing inside my chest, powerful enough to break my focus. To snap like a band in my belly, pulling me—somewhere else. Somewhere *not here*. It blurs my vision until the scene before me—until Lou, Coco, Jean Luc, my room—bleed into a rainbow of black and gray. I grapple for purchase on anything I can reach, reaching for the desk, the bed, even the floor with a desperate cry. Because I can't leave yet. My friends are looking for me, and *I can't leave.*

"Lou! Coco!" I raise my hands to wave at them, but it's a mistake. The instant I lose purchase with the room, that pulling sensation intensifies, and I can't find it now. I'm not strong enough. "I'm here. Please, *please*, I'm right here!" My voice drifts away, quiet to even my own ears, as though I'm screaming underwater.

The last thing I see are Lou's eyes as they somehow find my face in the dark, and I'm thrust into a deep, dreamless sleep.

CHAPTER TWENTY

A Warning

Golden light dances behind my eyelids when I wake . . . which I do slowly. Gently. Wherever I am, it is lovely and warm and smells of my sister—like beeswax candles and summer honey. Unwilling to open my eyes, I burrow deeper beneath the blanket, rubbing my cheek against what feels like silk. A strand of hair tickles my nose, and I sigh in deep contentment.

Then I remember the theater, the ghosts, *Michal,* and my eyes snap open.

Thousands of candles litter every surface of my room. They trail the grand staircase, line the silk screens, circle the floor around the squashy armchairs. A fire crackles cheerily in the hearth, and branches upon branches of brass candelabras twine together on the mezzanine, their tapers illuminating a gilt-framed gallery. Though the darkness previously hid them, portraits cover every inch of the wall around the windows. Each face regal and exquisite.

I sit up in awe, and black sheets—once coated with dust—slide to my hips. They smell of jasmine now. *I,* however, still smell of rainwater and must. Nose wrinkling, I lift the sheet to examine my damp gown; speckles of mud stain the hem, and the wrinkled lace is probably forever ruined. *Spectacular.* Throwing myself back upon the pillow, I mutter, "Odessa is going to kill me."

I lie there for several more minutes, counting each tick of the clock on the mantel. Dreading the inevitable—that I must rise, that I must continue, that I must eventually face Michal and his isle of vampires again. All Hallows' Eve creeps ever closer, and all I've learned is vampires *might* have an aversion to silver.

Groaning, I roll over to face the insurmountable wall of books.

Without Dimitri and Odessa at my disposal, I have only one option left, and I really shouldn't waste the candlelight. The thought of poring over onionskin pages until my eyes bleed, however, makes me want to scream. I push the blanket away regardless, grimacing, and force myself to slide from the bed. The carpet has been freshly scrubbed too. It feels slightly damp under my bare toes as I trudge to the bookshelves, as I trail my fingers along their infinite books.

And still on *How to Commune with the Dead.*

A chill skitters down my back as I stare at the ancient, peeling letters.

Don't be stupid. The logical part of my mind instantly rejects the idea, and my hand falls from the spine. The ghosts in the theater made their position quite clear—that I need to leave, to flee, or suffer the consequences. Surely they wouldn't help me now, even if I asked. However . . .

I wrench the book from the shelf, throwing myself into one of the squashy armchairs and studying the cover. It would be stupider *not* to ask, right? I need information about vampires, and they could give it to me. Besides, it isn't as if they can scamper off and tell Michal. He can't see them. *No one* can see them except me, which means ghosts would be the perfect allies. True, I passed out the last time I communicated with them, but I hadn't been prepared to meet them in the theater. I hadn't even thought they were *real*.

This time could be different.

With that thought comes another startling revelation—in both of our encounters, the ghosts haven't tried to harm me. Not truly. They've tried to intimidate, to frighten, but they haven't lifted a single finger against me. My hand lingers upon the peeling letters, tracing the *D* in *Dead*.

Can they lift a finger against me? Can they even touch me?

I flick my gaze around the room—hardly daring to hope—but there is no ache in my head, no spectral light or eerie presence or voices of any kind. "Hello?" I call softly. No one answers. Of *course* no one answers—and why would they? I've made my position quite clear too.

Is it your emotions that attract them, I wonder? Could it be any emotion strongly felt?

But how does one *force* strong emotion?

Dismissing the idea, I flip open *How to Commune with the Dead* and skim the pages, landing on one in the middle.

The theory of realms, of course, is one long debated by scholars of the occult. Most agree that realms coexist in tandem, or rather, folded together like the flesh of an onion—layered, identical, impossible to isolate yet separate in identity. As such, the realms of the living and the dead prevail one on top of the other. Rarely do denizens of either realm cross between the two—despite sharing the same physical space—and those who do cross never recover.

I slam the book shut without reading another word. Not that I understood most of them. *Those who do cross never recover,* though—that part seems clear enough. Gingerly, I place the book on the side table, wiping my palms on my skirt for good measure, and comfort myself that it's all conjecture, anyway. Even vampires do not know how this strange new ability of mine works. These *scholars* probably grasp even less.

Perhaps I can simply *ask* the ghosts to appear.

Clearing my throat, feeling ridiculous, I adopt a tone of polite inquiry. "If anyone is there, could you, er—could you please show yourself? I'd like to speak with you."

When still no one speaks, I clasp my hands together and try again. "I understand your . . . reluctance to appear, but I think we all want the same thing. With your help, I'll be able to leave this isle much sooner—tonight, in fact, if we're very clever. We just need to work together."

Silence.

Irritation begins to prick at my patience. "I need to know about silver on Requiem. Everyone here turns rather evasive when I mention it, but I assume ghosts are no friends to the vampires." Repressing a shudder, I add, "Michal himself probably put that axe in your neck, after all, when he tricked you and your family here." More silence. "Perhaps silver could be a weapon against him? Monsieur Marc mentioned poisoning his brother—I assume that means vampires *can* die. Unless the poison just weakened D'Artagnan somehow? How *does* one trap a soul in the body of a cat?"

When *still* no one answers, I straighten my shoulders, lift my chin, and scowl at the empty room. If the ghosts *are* here, listening out of sight, they certainly don't care to participate in their half of the conversation. "There's no reason to be difficult, you know," I tell them irritably. "All you've done since I've arrived is terrorize me—blathering on about how I need to *listen* and how I need to *leave*—yet here I present an actual opportunity to do those things, and you choose to ignore me. It's perfectly asinine behavior."

Only the clock chimes from the mantel in answer. When it finishes, plunging the room into quiet once more, my temperature rises with each steady *tick, tick, tick* of its second hand.

Losing patience completely, I pick up *How to Commune with the Dead* and hurl it across the room.

It doesn't thud against the bedpost as expected. Indeed, it doesn't thud at all, and I watch incredulously as the corner of the cover seems to *pierce* thin air, ripping through the ether of the room and vanishing into an outstretched hand. "Do you kiss your mother with that mouth?" a light, feminine voice asks, and a familiar head stoops to appear in the impromptu gash between my bedroom and—somewhere else.

With a squeak, I scramble backward, but it's too late.

The strange gash near my bed continues to spread, stretching into a gaping maw, and with it, the temperature in the room plummets. The air thins and sharpens until I can scarcely breathe, until my lungs threaten to collapse, until reality blurs into dreamlike delirium with its muted colors and flickering eerie light. Indeed— instead of smoke—ash seems to drift from the candle flame. It lands like snow in my hair.

A ghost perches against the iron whorls of my footboard, her legs crossed as she peers at me intently.

"It's you," I whisper, my eyes widening in recognition before darting around the room once more. *Because it worked.* It *must've* worked, yet I feel no building pressure in my ears, no splitting pain in my head. "You're the one who—who looked through my keyhole on the first night. You spoke to me."

The woman's laughter is bright and infectious, like chimes in the wind, and her dark eyes gleam with mischief. "You make looking through keyholes sound indecent. Have you ever tried it? It's quite my favorite thing to do."

"What? Er—no. No, I haven't." My breath comes easier now, along with the sneaking suspicion that I need not breathe here at all. Wherever *here* is. "Apologies, but . . . where *am* I?"

"You're through the veil, of course."

"Through the what?"

"Do you really not know?" She sets the book aside, tilting her head curiously to consider me. Though youth radiates from her smooth skin and shining hair—long and thick and opaque, probably rich brown in life—there is something distinctly elegant about her too. Something wise. She could be my age, yes, or perhaps a few years older. *No.* A few years younger? I frown at her while trying to decide. "How is that possible after the theater?" she asks. "Did no one explain?"

"Forgive me for asking, but who—er, who *are* you? Were you at the theater too?"

She scoffs. "Absolutely not—and you shouldn't have been either. L'Ange de la Mort is raucous at the best of times, suffused with all manner of rude and unsavory creatures. And my name is Mila." She pauses with an air of great importance, sweeping the hair back from her face. "Mila Vasiliev."

Mila Vasiliev.

The name is clearly supposed to mean something to me, but as

I have *no* idea what, I curtsy to hide my ignorance. "It is a pleasure to meet you, Mila Vasiliev."

"And to meet you, Célie Tremblay."

She flashes a radiant smile before sweeping upward into a flawless curtsy. Though I open my mouth to ask *how*, exactly, she knows me, I change tactics abruptly, plunging straight to the heart of the issue instead. Who knows how long I have before Dimitri or Odessa or even—God forbid—someone *else* returns? "Michal said L'Ange de le Mort is a rip in the fabric between realms. He took me to—to summon the ghosts there, somehow."

Mila's smile vanishes into a scowl, and when she rolls her eyes, I know I've calculated correctly—this ghost, at least, is no friend of Michal. "You cannot *summon* us anywhere," she says in distaste. "We are not dogs. We do not answer to any master, and we do not come when called. That you can see us at all is because *you* have approached *us*, not the other way around."

When she arches a brow at my rigid stance, I force myself to bend at the knee, to sit on the edge of the squashy chair as ash continues to drift around us. "But I *haven't* approached you. As a matter of fact, I've been doing my very best *not* to—"

"Of course you haven't *meant* to tear through the veil." She waves a curt hand before settling back upon the bed. Or rather, hovering several inches above it. "Really, though, what do you expect when you repress your emotions? They have to go somewhere eventually, you know, and this realm *is* rather convenient—"

"Wait, *wait*." I grip my fingers in my lap, knuckles turning white, and lean forward in my seat. Though my head remains miraculously without pain, it does start to spin at the ease with which she discusses the veil and—and—everything else. "Slow down. What do you mean *this* realm? How many realms *are* there? The book just mentioned the realms of the living and the dead—"

"The authors of said book were presumably alive at the time of its writing. How could they possibly claim authority on the complexities of the afterlife?" Another bright, infectious laugh as she weighs the enormous book in her palm. When it falls open to a page at random, an illustration of a skull with a wide, gaping mouth leers back at us. I look away quickly. "Even *I* do not understand the whole of it, and I am quite thoroughly dead. What I do know"—she speaks louder when I open my mouth to interrupt, incredulous—"is this realm, *my* realm, acts as an intermediary of sorts. It exists between the realms of the living and the dead, and as such, we spirits can see glimpses into both your realm and . . . beyond."

"Beyond," I repeat blankly.

She nods and examines the skull as if we aren't discussing the whole of *eternity*, as if she didn't just throw my entire creed and covenant into question with two simple sentences. "Your realm is much clearer, of course, as we've already lived there, and the two are near identical." She snaps the book shut. "But you didn't come here to talk about life, did you? Rather the opposite, I think."

Death.

Of course, death is the reason I sought an audience with ghosts in the first place. *Focus, Célie.* I force myself to unclench my fingers from my skirt, to dust the strange ash from my knees and square my shoulders. Despite all of this—this *distraction*, Coco must remain my first priority, and to protect her, I must first find a way to protect myself.

Before I can find a clever way to begin the interrogation,

however, she tosses *How to Commune with the Dead* aside and says, "I don't blame you for seeking violence, but you must first allow me to apologize for my coven's wretched behavior. Vampires always have been beastly creatures."

My brow furrows at the word. *Coven.* "But does that mean— Are you a witch?"

"A witch?" She flashes another smile, this one with teeth, revealing two sharp points. I recoil slightly. "Of course not. I'm a vampire—or at least, I *was.* Do try to keep up, won't you, darling? As previously discussed, I am now dead."

I am now dead.

Despite her rebuke, the words are everything I wanted to hear.

I force my features to remain carefully blank, nonchalant, as I settle back into the squashy armchair. On the shelf across from me, the teapot begins to hiss and steam of its own accord, but I hardly hear it. Hardly see it.

If Mila was once a vampire, that means . . . *Les Éternels can die.*

Despite the claims of Michal, Odessa, and even Dimitri, it seems they aren't *quite* as eternal as they want me to believe. The proof of their deception sits only three feet away, fluffing her hair and awaiting my response. I study her innocently as the teapot starts to rattle. No blood or gore marks her skin, and—unlike the ghosts at the theater—no axe protrudes from her head, which remains firmly in place on her neck. Indeed, nothing whatsoever hints at the manner of her death. If not for her silvery, incorporeal form, she would look perfectly healthy. Perfectly *alive.*

I clear my throat, adopting—*I hope*—just the right amount of sincerity. "I am very sorry to hear that, Mademoiselle Vasiliev. If you don't mind me asking . . . how did it happen?"

Her grin stretches wider, like the cat that got the cream. "You *are* clever. I'll give you that."

My heart sinks. "I don't know what you're—"

"A horrid liar, though. You should stop immediately." She points a finger toward my eyes. "One needn't hear your heartbeat or scent your emotions to know exactly what you're thinking. They are the *loveliest* shade of green, though." With a sly glance at the candles around us, she adds, "His Majesty must agree."

I smooth my skirt as the teapot pours pitch-black tea into a chipped cup. "What does *that* mean?"

"It means you mentioned silver earlier," she says, her voice a bit too innocent, "which seems an unusual request. Tell me, is that truly what you wish to discuss? If so, I could summon the others. They're all quite anxious to speak with you, and they'll just *love* to describe how foolish you've been in painstaking detail."

"The others?" Unbidden, my gaze flicks to the shelves, where iridescent faces have started to flicker, hiding among the books and bric-a-brac. The chipped cup no longer sits between them, however. No—it now stands on the table beside my chair, glittering innocently. "I—I don't understand. I was under the distinct impression they wanted me to leave. Why does it now seem like *you* want to help me?"

"Do you consider pride a fault or a virtue, Célie Tremblay?"

Startling at the question, I tear my gaze from the cup, which almost touches my hand now. I snatch my fingers away from the armrest, and the soft scent of orange blossoms wafts from the tea in its wake. "Neither, I suppose."

"And what of yourself? Do you consider yourself prideful?"

"What? N-*No*. Not at all."

Though I'd never admit it, I actually consider myself quite the opposite. How could I otherwise? Only three-year-olds fear the dark, and even then, they don't descend into fits of hysteria when the candles go out. They don't speak to *ghosts*.

"Well, then," Mila says, "it should take little imagination to realize even the departed have loved ones to protect."

"Of *course* you do, but what does that"—I resist the urge to gesture wildly toward the floating ash, the icicles along the mantel, the muted gray light—"what does *any* of this have to do with me?"

"Come now, Célie. Every tongue in our realm has been wagging about a bride for weeks—and I wouldn't drink that tea if I were you," she adds sharply.

I blink, startled, and realize my hand has reached instinctively for the strange little cup. "Why?"

"Because it's poison." She shrugs delicately as I push the cup away with a strangled sound, spilling its black liquid across the tabletop. Upon contact, it quite literally *eats* through the wood with tiny, razor-sharp teeth. "Did you think yours was the only realm affected by this blight?" Mila asks.

"But I thought—apologies, of course, but as everyone here is already *dead*—"

Mila flings *How to Commune with the Dead* across the room, where it lands with a painful blow upon my legs. Heavy and real and alarming. "While you are in this realm," she says seriously, "you are *of* this realm, which means you need to be very careful. The ash, the teapot, the poison—none of this is as it should be, which means our realm is no longer safe. Not even for a Bride."

The teapot still whistles from the shelf, punctuating her words and growing louder—screaming now—with each turn of its porcelain feet. I stare at her incredulously, trying and failing to keep my voice even. "What are you *talking* about? And why do you all keep calling me bride? I am still very much unmarried—"

"Not that kind of bride." Mila shakes her head, and ash settles around her in a macabre sort of bridal veil. "You're a bride, as in a Bride of *Death*." When I blink at her, nonplussed, she heaves a long-suffering sigh. "Death and the Maiden? Filles à la cassette? Oh, come now, Célie, did you merely skim that wretched book?"

My mouth parts indignantly. "You said I couldn't learn about the afterlife from a book! You said the authors—"

"—can of course postulate correctly on occasion!" She flips the book open to a section near the end, turning it around to reveal another ghastly illustration of a woman with a serpent in her mouth. "Look, they penned a whole section on Brides at the end. I won't pretend to know what happened to you, but clearly, you've been touched by Death. He does that sometimes," she explains, "on very rare occasions with beautiful young women. Instead of snuffing out her life, he lets her go—he lets her *live*—except she's never quite the same after Death visits her. She becomes his Bride."

His Bride.

Touched by Death.

Do you have a death wish, mademoiselle? Or is it the dead themselves who call to you?

I rise hastily to my feet.

This is not the direction I wanted this conversation to take.

"Do you not wonder why you can cross between realms and no one else can?" Mila throws her hands in the air before I can answer. "Never mind. It doesn't matter. Well, it *does*—you should really read more—but the details aren't relevant to this particular conversation. What *is* relevant is that you find a way off this island before he comes for you."

"Before *who* comes for me?" Losing my temper completely, I throw up my own hands because I am tired and damp and hungry again. Because every time I turn a corner in this god-awful place, I find more questions than answers. Because I wanted to learn about silver, and now I shall dream about *snakes* for the rest of my fleeting life. "And I want a real explanation this time," I add angrily, "or you and the rest of these filthy eavesdroppers"—I raise my voice, addressing the bookshelves—"can float right back through those walls and out of my life. I'm serious. I don't yet know how to purify a space, but I'll find sage if I must. I'll—I'll sew up these *rips*, so none of you can ever bother me again!"

Mila regards me shrewdly for several seconds. "The rips generally heal on their own."

"I'm warning you, Mila—"

"Yes, all right, *fine*," she says at last. "If I *must* say it . . . we don't truly know what approaches. Spirits aren't omniscient, but we—we *do* often see things, sense them, in ways you cannot." She floats from the bed, drawing closer, and her next words lift the hair at my neck. "Darkness is coming for us, Célie. It is coming for us all, and at its heart is a figure—a man," she clarifies.

"Who is he?" I ask a bit breathlessly. "Death?"

"Of course not. I told you—Death rarely interferes." She sighs again, frustration filling her voice, as she brushes the ash from her shoulders. "The man of whom I speak . . . we cannot see him clearly through the veil. Grief seems to shroud his face."

I exhale a shaky laugh, a relieved one. "Then how do you know he's looking for me? This is probably a complete misundersta—"

"He needs your blood, Célie."

The words fall brutally simple between us, like the blade of a guillotine. They sever every thought in my head, every question, leaving me to stare at her in stunned silence. Perhaps I misheard her. Because this man, this—this *dark figure* who even ghosts fear—cannot possibly want my blood. Perhaps she'd meant to say Lou's blood, or Reid's blood, or even the all-powerful Michal's blood. Perhaps then I'd believe her. But *mine?* A snort of laughter escapes me in the silence. "There has been a terrible mistake."

Mila's eyebrows pull together.

Before she can argue, however, a knock sounds at the door, and Michal's dry voice echoes through the quiet room. "Are you alive?"

All desire to laugh shrivels into an angry knot in my chest.

As always, Michal has impeccable timing.

Instantly, the ghosts in the shelves scatter out of sight, but Mila remains, her eyes darting toward the door. Something akin to fear flashes through them, there and gone too quickly to identify. She swallows hard as if deliberating. After several more seconds, her shoulders slump, and—decision made—she bolts toward the ceiling.

It isn't fair, however—*none* of this is fair—and why should she get to flee when I cannot? Gesturing furiously toward the door, I mouth, *He wants to speak with a ghost.*

A small, mournful smile touches her lips. "I know."

And I can do nothing but watch as she rises higher and higher, beyond my reach in more ways than one. Once again, I am left with more questions than answers, and the gore of that guillotine has left a mess behind. *He needs your blood, Célie.*

Ridiculous.

"Célie?" Michal asks again.

"I promise to return. To explain." Mila hesitates beneath the gilded ceiling, right next to the chandelier, just as my doorknob begins to turn. Her last words reach me in a forlorn whisper before she slips out of sight. "But I cannot give him what he wants."

CHAPTER TWENTY-ONE

A Gift

She vanishes just as Michal appears behind me, and I cannot keep the sharp bitterness from my voice as I whirl to confront him, crashing back into the realm of the living. Heat washes through me in a violent wave, and my eyes burn at the sudden burst of bright and saturated color. "I didn't give you permission to enter."

He arches an imperious brow. "I didn't ask for it."

"That is *entirely* the problem—" I startle as he moves in front of me with inhuman speed, his black eyes tracking upward to the chandelier. The movement bares the broad, pale expanse of his throat above his cravat. Black, as usual, though he has changed into clean, dry clothes since I last saw him. I glance down at my sullied gown in resentment.

"Did I interrupt something?" he asks casually.

I cannot give him what he wants.

And now I know—Michal doesn't want to speak with just any old ghost. No. He wants to speak with only one, and he wants to speak with her very badly. Though I don't know why, I also don't care.

"You interrupted nothing," I lie.

"I could've sworn I heard you speaking."

"I talk in my sleep."

"Is that so?" Clasping his hands behind his back, he strolls around me with a quiet sort of self-possession. His eyes still study the ceiling. "Interesting. You didn't utter a word when I tucked you in this morning." My cheeks burn almost painfully at the revelation—at the thought of Michal anywhere near my sleeping form, my blankets and *bed*. "What?" he asks, a mocking curl to his lips. "No expression of gratitude?"

In my periphery, the rip between realms flutters slightly in a nonexistent breeze, its edges knitting together slowly. *Healing*, I realize in disbelief. As if I really *am* a knife in the veil, as if my crossing created an actual wound between realms. I force myself to turn away. "For leaving me in a damp gown? Yes, Your Majesty, I am *eternally* grateful for a chest cold and cough."

He halts mid-step, casting me a curious, sidelong look. "Would you have preferred I undress you?"

"*Excuse* me—?" If possible, my cheeks flame hotter, but he only tilts his head, and that curl of his lips transforms into a fully-fledged smirk. "I— You are despicable, *monsieur*, to talk of such things. Of course I wouldn't have *preferred* that you—you—"

"Undress you?" he finishes salaciously. "You need only ask, you know. It would be no hardship."

"Stop looking at me like that," I snap.

He feigns innocence, beginning to circle once more. "Like what?"

"Like I'm a piece of *meat*."

"More like a fine wine."

"I thought vampires didn't crave human blood."

He leans closer, cruelly amused, and his gaze dips to my throat once more. He is trying to unsettle me. I *know* he is trying to unsettle me, yet instinct still roots me in place. Instinct and—something else, something liquid and warm and not entirely unpleasant. Michal's smile widens as if he knows. "There are exceptions to every rule, Célie."

I can scent your adrenaline too, can see your pupils have dilated.

I curl my fists tighter, startled by the inexplicable and unwelcome urge to reach out and touch him. I blame it on his mystery. Michal is truly and thoroughly horrid, but . . . do the shadows beneath his eyes feel as cold as the rest of him? And what causes them? Exhaustion? Hunger? My eyes flick to his teeth, to the pointed tip of each fang. They look sharp enough to pierce skin with the slightest stroke of my thumb. Would it hurt?

As if reading my thoughts, he murmurs, "You're too curious for your own good, pet."

"I don't know what you mean."

"Are you not wondering how it feels? The kiss of a vampire?"

Arielle's moans rise, equally sharp, in the forefront of my mind, and my skin flushes hotter.

No. It didn't seem to hurt.

"Don't flatter yourself." Storming away from him, I realize too late that I've veered toward the bed instead of the fireplace. *Mother of God.* I grit my teeth, smoothing the sheets and straightening the blanket to make the error seem intentional. "As I said before, I am not interested in being bitten by anything on this island—especially you."

Michal's laughter is dark, rife with promise I don't understand. "Of course."

"Why are you *here*? Do you have no other prisoners to provoke this evening?" I glare at him over my shoulder, adding, "It *is* evening, correct? It's impossible to tell, as apparently those shutters are integral to the structure of this godforsaken room."

"It is seven o'clock in the evening." He returns his attention to the ceiling. "And I came to ensure you survived," he says wryly. "After your collapse at L'Ange de la Mort, I feared your heart might give out, and I cannot allow that. Though we made progress, our work remains unfinished."

"Progress," I repeat flatly.

"When did you develop nyctophobia?"

"How is *that* relevant?"

His black eyes fall back to mine. "It is relevant because nyctophobia seems to be your impetus. I realized as soon as I entered your room. Both shifts I felt occurred immediately after you'd been left here in the dark, and the third occurred in the theater—again, in the dark."

I fluff my pillow with a vicious *thwack*. "Many people fear the dark."

"Not like you do. Never before have I witnessed such an intense psychological reaction." His eyes grow brighter, hungrier, as they search my face, and—seemingly unbidden—he drifts closer to the bed. To me. "I believe your fear allowed you to slip through the veil. It allowed you to see the ghosts. To speak to them."

A beat of silence.

What do you expect when you repress your emotions? They have to go somewhere eventually, you know.

Though I open my mouth to refute his claim, it isn't . . . *entirely* ridiculous, and it seems to fit with Mila's explanation too. Each time the ghosts have appeared, with the most recent exception,

I've been in the throes of a panic attack. Indeed—safe in the golden light of the candles—I might even admit that I never feel closer to death than I do in darkness.

"Is that your plan?" Lifting my chin and straightening my spine, I feign bravado. "Will you plunge me in darkness until you get what you want? Or is that what you *really* want—to watch me cower and hear me scream?" His expression cools instantly in response, but I press forward anyway, determined to—to *rile* him somehow. To *shake* him the way he has shaken me. "Does our fear make you feel powerful? Is that what you did to Babette before you killed her?"

All interest in his eyes flickers out. "You ask a lot of questions."

"Why light these candles at all?" I fling my arms outward, reckless, perhaps foolish, and gesture to the candlelight all around us. "Aren't you just prolonging the inevitable?"

"Perhaps," he says coldly, inclining his head. "Nevertheless, I appreciated your efforts at the theater, and as such, I've decided to open my home to you. From this night onward, you may move through the castle freely. Consider it a token of my good faith. Do not, however"—he steps closer, his voice softening in that horrid and lethal way—"trespass on my hospitality, pet. Do not attempt to flee. You will regret it if you do."

"Stop *threatening* me—"

"It isn't a threat. The isle is dangerous, and I have business elsewhere tonight. I will not be able to intervene should you wander too far."

It takes several seconds for the words to penetrate the thick haze of my anger.

"What sort of business?" I ask suspiciously, envisioning Babette's bloodless body, the charcoal sketches of his other victims: human, Dame Blanche, loup garou, and melusine. Five species in total. No vampires.

All of their bodies drained of blood.

A hard edge of urgency hones my anger. If Michal plans to leave this isle, there can be no doubt that a sixth body will soon turn up in Belterra. I need to—stop him somehow, to incapacitate him, but short of finding a deadly and magical weapon—

I tense in realization. If Michal really *does* plan to leave, I can take this opportunity to search for my cross. He has hidden it somewhere, and though Mila didn't confirm my suspicion about silver, I have little else to go on. I cannot save this victim—my stomach twists with regret—but perhaps I can save the next. Perhaps I can *kill* Michal the moment he returns to Requiem. Fierce purpose resolves at the thought. If silver is the key, I will find it, and I will stop him. "What sort of business?" I ask again, my voice harder this time.

"None of yours."

With another imperious look, he stalks past me to the armoire behind the second silk screen. I hesitate only a second before charging after him. "What are you doing back there?"

"For you." He flings a bundle of emerald lace and silk at me before I've taken two steps, and the fabric spills from my hands, revealing the most beautiful gown I've ever seen. Delicate black diamonds sparkle along the sweetheart neckline, down the fitted bodice, so small they look like flecks of stardust. "Monsieur Marc sends his regards and bids you return tonight with Odessa to collect the rest of your trousseau—for which you are also welcome."

His voice drips with disdain. I clench the exquisite train in my fists. Despite his *galling* arrogance, I shouldn't continue to goad him. He is a vampire, a *murderer*, who relishes control above everything else. He won't leave until he reestablishes dominance over this situation, and I need him to leave in order to search for my cross. If I must express my gratitude to quicken his departure, I should do it—I should smile, I should apologize, and I should submit. I should lose this battle to win the war.

It would be the sensible thing to do. The logical thing.

Scoffing, I spin on my heel. "No gift can absolve the things you've done, monsieur. Your heart is as black as these diamonds."

He snakes a hand through the silk, catching it—catching *me*—with fingers like ice. "Forgive me. I thought we had started over. Shall I return the gown for you?"

"No." I tug on the dress, mindful of the delicate fabric, but he doesn't release it. Instead, he draws it toward him slowly, forcing me to face him once more. I scowl and dig in my heels. He continues to pull, reeling me closer, closer, until I must crane my neck to see his beautiful face. "You most certainly will *not* return the gown," I hurl at him. "It belongs to me now, and I hope you spent a *fortune* on it."

With his free hand, he slides long, luxurious evening gloves from his pocket, dangling them in front of my nose. I cannot decide if the glint in his eyes is amused or angry. Perhaps both. "I did," he says softly.

Just angry, then.

"*Good,*" I snarl because I am angry too—I am *furious*—and he—he—

He slides the gown from my hands with laughable ease. Before I can stop him—before I can so much as utter a startled curse—he tears it neatly in two, dropping the beautiful lace and silk and *dia-mond* to the floor at my feet. His eyes never leave mine. "My heart is blacker. Enjoy your freedom, Célie Tremblay."

He leaves without another word.

CHAPTER TWENTY-TWO

The Curio Cabinet

I wait half an hour before peeking my head outside the room, searching for any sign of Michal. Dozens more candles illuminate the deserted corridor beyond, which has been cleaned to perfection since yesterday—the cobwebs swept, the tapestries scrubbed, the statues polished—without me hearing so much as a peep. It seems the servants move just as soundlessly as their master. Taking a tentative step from my room, I close the door behind me with a soft *click*.

True to Michal's word, no guards loom outside to hear the sound.

In the folds of Odessa's skirt, my new pins jingle eagerly as I hasten down the corridor.

Quieting them with a hand, I follow the candlelight and attempt to trace Dimitri's steps on that first evening. He led me directly to Michal's study, which seems the best place to start my search for hidden things. The *only* place to start my search, really, as I've visited nowhere else in the castle except the entrance hall. If Michal's confidence in my ability to escape is any indication, however, he probably hasn't hidden the cross at all—or he's already cast it into the fire.

At that, I almost laugh.

Michal is too arrogant to destroy such a trophy, but as they say, pride always goeth before the fall. If the cross still exists, if Michal has hidden it somewhere, I *will* find it, even if I must tear apart this castle brick by brick. I will find it, and I will use it to my advantage somehow.

I *will*.

My confidence quickly fades, however, when I turn a corner unexpectedly, skidding to a stop in a corridor lined with suits of armor. Their shields gleam dark and strange in the candlelight, where my own pale face reflects back at me from each one, both familiar and—different, somehow. My features wild and fey. When I look for too long, my reflections' eyes seem to bleed, and—*no*.

With a gasp, I shake my head to clear it before turning to retrace my steps around the corner. Because this is just another perversion. Of course it is. Mila, Lou, and even *Christo* spoke of a darkness—a sickness—spreading through the realms, and the castle wouldn't remain unaffected. I just—I need to pay attention. I need to take better care, and I need to—

I lurch to a halt, and my eyes grow wide at the blank stretch of wall before me.

I need to stay calm.

Because the corner around which I just came—it has somehow vanished, *moved*, like the corridor itself grew legs as a spider and fled. Leaving me here with only suits of armor and shadows for guidance. *Right.* I swallow hard and turn slowly to face them. My reflections, at least, have returned to normal, and I choose to interpret that as a fortunate sign. Perhaps the castle isn't trying to terrorize me, after all; perhaps it's trying to *help* me, and this corridor will take me where I need to go.

When the nearest helmet turns to watch as I pass, however, I abandon *that* foolish thought and bolt down the corridor out of sight, not stopping until I reach a staircase that looks vaguely familiar. Except it isn't familiar at all. And neither is the next one, or the next. Blowing a damp strand of hair from my eyes, I plant my hands on my hips and glare at the portrait of the woman in red before me. It *definitely* wasn't there a second ago, and sure enough—between blinks—it disappears again, leaving only empty wall behind.

This is getting ridiculous.

If I haven't already passed a vampire without realizing—and if said vampire hasn't already contacted Michal or Odessa or Dimitri through some sort of macabre mind control—I'll eat my left shoe. Any one of them could appear at any moment, which means this little excursion has an expiration date. With a reluctant sigh, I whirl to face the corridor at large, loathing myself for what I'm about to do. "Mila? Are you here?"

She doesn't answer, but after her rather dramatic exit, I expected no less. Indeed, when a bud of irritation blooms in response, I focus on it with every fiber of my being. It really shouldn't be this difficult. *Nothing* should be this difficult, yet here I am, attempting to coax forth enough emotion to pierce through a metaphysical veil and ask a ghost for directions. I scoff. My friends would never believe me if I told them. A week ago, I never would've believed *myself.* And perhaps I should be ashamed by such an admission— that no one, including me, would've ever thought I'd be tangled up in such a mess.

As swiftly as the realization comes, the temperature plummets, and all color seeps from the corridor as familiar ash begins to drift from the candelabra on either side of me. I brush it away with a weakened sort of triumph. Because I did it—*I crossed*—and I should be enormously pleased with myself. And I *am* pleased, but I am also . . . not.

Which leaves me feeling quite lost.

But I haven't time to focus on that now. Shaking the thoughts aside, I hiss Mila's name again, and—in true Célie fashion—a gangly, speckled-face ghost answers instead, floating up through the stairs with his hands in his pockets. "How do you know silver will kill them?" he asks.

"I don't." Hurrying past him in search of Mila, I make it only two steps before hesitating. Because like it or not, I cannot afford to waste this opportunity. I cannot afford to feel sorry for myself. Not yet. "Do *you* know how to kill them?"

He gestures to the twin gashes at his throat with a sheepish grin. "A friend once told me garlic."

"Right." I look away quickly, grimacing as I tuck that bit of information away. "No garlic. Perhaps you could direct me to Michal's study instead?"

Grin widening, he jerks his narrow shoulder to the right. "Perhaps I could."

Drifting into the wall, he vanishes just as quickly as he appeared, and I pause at a fork in the next corridor. Repressing a shiver, I forget about garlic and glance down each passage.

To the left, candles continue to burn, casting warm light on a passage that *might* lead to the entrance hall. The tapestry there looks vaguely familiar. I don't remember Dimitri and me crossing the entrance hall to reach Michal's study, however.

Biting my lip, I glance to the right, where shadows cloak the unlit sconces.

The ghostly boy didn't *seem* to have malevolent intentions. With a deep, steadying breath, I snatch up a candelabra and veer to the right, picturing Jean Luc in my mind—and Lou and Reid, Coco and Beau. They crept through the dark of those tunnels for me, and I can do the same for them. I can find my silver cross, and I can save my friends from Michal's wrath. I can save the lives of his future victims. He knows I fear the dark.

He left this passage in shadow for a reason.

I lift the candelabra higher, casting light farther up the passage. This place—it looks familiar too. I recognize that turbulent tapestry, this sprawling family tree. I move past them quickly, darting down another flight of stairs. Still no vampires spring out to stop me. The ash continues to settle, however, and the temperature continues to drop. Gooseflesh rises on my arms at each creak in the walls. "You're being ridiculous," I mutter to myself, gripping the candelabra with two hands now. A groan echoes overhead in response, and I tense, remembering Odessa's warning: *This castle is very old, and it has many bad memories.*

"Ridiculous," I repeat.

When peculiar laughter erupts behind me, I let out a strangled squeak, swinging my candelabra around like some sort of cudgel. It sails through empty air, however, nearly slipping from my hands and colliding with familiar ebony doors. I skid to a halt and stare up at them in awe. They tower to the ceiling—spanning just as wide—ominous and impenetrable and black as night. Just like their owner. "Found you," I breathe.

As if the castle itself is listening, a gust of cold air sweeps down the corridor in response.

It extinguishes each and every one of my candles.

"*No—*"

Before I can panic, before I can demand that it somehow— I don't know—*reignite* the flames, another head pops straight through the ebony doors, sending me sprawling backward. I wield the candelabra at it like a sword and huff, "Can you *please* give some sort of forewarning before you leap out at me like that?"

"I do not leap." The ghostly woman sniffs and lifts her haughty chin, pearl earrings bobbing within the perfect ringlets of her hair. Except for the odd cant of her neck, she is the portrait of civility. "You warmbloods are always so presumptuous, disparaging death in front of the dead. It isn't the worst thing to be, you know." She begins to withdraw.

"Wait!" I scramble to my feet, hastily smoothing my skirt and hair beneath her critical gaze. To be frank, she reminds me of my mother, albeit several years younger. Or perhaps several years older? It's impossible to tell. "Er, please, mademoiselle, I—I apologize for the offense. You are entirely right, but if you could remain for just a moment, I would be forever in your debt."

She wrinkles her pert nose in distaste. "Why?"

I gesture to the doorknob. Her silvery form provides *just* enough light to see the keyhole there, and she must have a good reason to linger in Michal's study—presumably a vengeful one. He doesn't strike me as the type to treat his lovers with affection. "The master of this castle has stolen something from me, and I should like to retrieve it. I need light, however, in order to pick the lock."

A vicious sort of glee sparks in the woman's eyes. "You want to steal from Michal?"

I nod warily.

"Ooh, excellent. Where shall I stand?"

I exhale in relief as she glides through the door, casting proper light over its handle. Peculiar ridges line its perimeter. I examine each carefully before turning to the keyhole, feeling unexpected camaraderie with this dead woman. Those of us who loathe Michal must stick together. "Pardon my candidness, but"—I fish the lockpicks from my skirt—"did he kill you too?"

"Who? Michal?" The woman laughs as I work the picks into the lock. "Of course not. He broke my heart, not my neck, though I would've gladly wrung his." She lifts a hand to her hair, twining a ringlet around her finger almost dreamily. "Such a shame. The *wicked* things he could do with his tongue."

Choking, I nearly drop the picks.

"Oh yes," she says impishly, "and his teeth—"

The lock opens with a click, and I straighten hastily, my cheeks hot. On second thought, she most certainly *doesn't* remind me of my mother. "Yes, well—thank you very much for your help. After I find my necklace, I promise to give Michal your love."

She swells up like a toad. "You most certainly will not *give him love*—"

Twisting the handle, I leap across the threshold into his study, tearing back through the veil and landing firmly in the realm of the living. To my relief, the ghost merely pokes her head through the rip before sticking out her tongue and vanishing back the way she came. And as this rip is smaller—almost neater—it heals too quickly for her to change her mind.

Leaving me alone.

True darkness doesn't descend, however, as a low fire still smolders in the hearth and a taper flickers weakly on his desk. It drips black wax upon the lacquered surface.

Right.

Summoning the last of my courage, I steal around his chair and wrench open each of his desk drawers.

Unlike the room itself, they remain unlocked, filled with neat and conventional supplies: an eagle-feather quill, pot of emerald ink, and needle-thin dagger in one; a velvet pouch of coins in another. I pour a handful into my palm. They bear not the crown on Belterra's couronnes but the crude silhouette of a wolf in gold and bronze. No silver. I replace the pouch carefully and move on to the next items.

A box of matches and bundle of incense.

A skull-shaped seal and black wax.

An iron ring fashioned into a claw—I slip it over the tip of my thumb, examining its lethal tip in morbid fascination—and last, a charcoal sketch of Odessa and Dimitri. I recognize the thick waves of their hair, the feline shape of their eyes, though they look younger here than the vampires I've met. Perhaps my age. Even in pencil, their smiles transcend the page—their *human* smiles. No fangs interrupt the straight white lines of their teeth. They look . . . happy.

I tuck the sketch back beneath a jade paperweight, gritting my own teeth.

The cross isn't here.

Though a fresh decanter of absinthe sits atop the sideboard, the cross isn't there either. It isn't among the cut glassware beside it, the dense books on the shelf above. It isn't tucked beneath the carpet or tacked behind the portraits, isn't hidden within the enormous curio cabinet.

It isn't here.

Swallowing a scream of frustration, I nearly hurl my candelabra into the fireplace. It isn't *here*, and I am running out of time. Already, Michal could be returning to the castle. Thanks to his carnivorous *doorknob*, he'll know of my trespass the instant he steps foot in this room. He gave permission to explore the castle, yes, not break into his private study and rummage through his personal belongings. It has to be here.

It has to be.

I fling open his curio cabinet once more.

Even if I flee, he will find me, and without silver in my hand, he will be able to punish me, to lock me in darkness and throw away the key. I have to keep searching. I have to—

My candelabra knocks into the floor of the curio cabinet with a hollow *thunk*.

Hardly daring to breathe, I drop to my knees and search the shadowed recesses of the cabinet with clumsy fingers. The wood sits flush against the floor, and—*there*. A small button hides at the very back. When I press it—my eyes wide—gears crank from deep within the wall, and the floor of the cabinet pops open.

"A trapdoor," I breathe.

And it is.

Below, an impossibly narrow stairwell plunges straight into darkness, the air thick and earthen, laced with the sweet, metallic scent of blood. My stomach flutters at that scent. My mouth dries at the absolute absence of light. Whatever lies at the bottom of this tunnel, it cannot be good. Still . . . I should investigate. This is surely where Michal has stowed my silver cross—in this damp and dark *lair* beneath the castle. Before I can change my mind, I race back to his desk, fumbling with the box of matches and relighting the tapers of my candelabra.

I'm halfway down the stairs before I realize what I've done.

Panic creeps up my throat.

No. Taking a deep breath, I focus on counting each tread. Reid always counts to ten when his temper flares. Unfortunately, my own anger has fled, leaving me as cold and hollow as the cavernous room into which I step. My hand clenches around the candelabra. The last time I journeyed underground, Morgane had knocked me unconscious, and I woke in the catacombs. I woke in a casket.

I shake my head against the memory. *This isn't like that.* Though Michal has carved his lair into the very rock beneath the castle, these walls aren't those of a crypt or casket. These walls sparkle with veins of mineral and specs of mica, and across the room, dark water extends smooth as glass beyond the glow of my candles. Whether it's a pool or secret inlet of the ocean, I cannot tell, but a simple boat has been tethered at the shore. My heart leaps into my throat at the sight of it.

Dimitri said I could only leave Requiem by ship. He said vampire sentries would kill me before I reached the gangplank.

He conveniently forgot to mention this little rowboat hidden beneath the castle.

Forcing my feet into motion, I descend a second, wider set of stairs that feeds into the main level before picking up a pebble at the water's edge. With a quick glance over my shoulder, I throw it as far as I can, holding my candelabra aloft to watch its trajectory. It does little good, however; even with the distant splash, I have no way to gauge whether this inlet connects to the sea. Except—

I crouch abruptly, dipping my fingers into the water before bringing it to my lips.

It tastes of salt.

Tears of overwhelming relief prick my eyes as my entire body slumps forward. Because this grotto *must* lead to the sea, which means—*this is it.* I hardly allow myself to think the words, to *hope,* but there it is, materializing just as clear and bright as my candlelight on the water. Michal is gone, and I can escape.

I can *leave.*

My foot is halfway in the boat before the reality of the situation swiftly follows, crashing down on my head and stunning me. I can flee Requiem tonight, yes—every instinct in my body screams for me to go, go, *go*—but my flight won't stop Michal. He will not give up. He will still hunt for me, and worse—he will still hunt for *Coco.* Eventually, he will find us, and I will not be able to stop him from hurting her.

Not like I can now.

My fingers clench white upon the boat's lip, and I stare determinedly at the dark water, deliberating. Michal needn't know I uncovered his trapdoor, his secret chamber and private grotto. For all intents and purposes, he believes I am trapped, helpless, or he never would've allowed me to roam the castle unattended. And now—if I *do* find a weapon against him—I have means to escape. *True* means. If I killed him, no one would think to look for me here. They'd flock to the docks, and by the time they realized I vanished, I could be halfway back to Cesarine. Would they even *try* to avenge his death?

This could work.

Gingerly, I step back to shore, turning to examine the grotto with newfound urgency. I'll need to be very careful, of course. Michal cannot know I've been here, or my entire plan will be ruined. Creeping forward, I approach the vast bed in the center of the cavern—ebony wood and lustrous emerald silk—before hesitating, loath to touch it. I cannot envision Michal *sleeping* either.

Focus, Célie.

Swiftly, lightly, I run my hands over the coverlet and pillows in search of my silver cross. *Nothing.* I turn away again. Though a thick carpet softens my footsteps, Michal has included little other decor: no statues, no pillows or settees, no candlesticks. A haphazard row of paintings leans against the far wall, but he's hidden them with black cloth. Unable to resist, I uncover one of them, staring into two faces I recognize in pieces: his nose and her eyes, his jaw and her mouth. Michal's parents.

His *human* parents.

A sense of wrongness pricks my scalp as I stare at them. I cannot picture Michal as human. The image simply doesn't make sense—like an ugly Coco or a bashful Beauregard. Without his preternatural strength, his stillness, his intensity, the Michal I know doesn't exist, yet here is proof that he did. Michal was born human. My fingers trace his mother's eyes as I envision his compelled soldiers on the ship, his teeth in Arielle's neck. The shadows in his gaze and the blood on his lips. Was he always this twisted up inside? This sadistic? How does one *become* a vampire?

How does a man become a monster?

Shaking the strangely mournful thoughts away, I note the names written in the lower right-hand corner of the portrait: *Tomik Vasiliev and Adelina Volkov.*

My gaze narrows.

Vasiliev.

My stomach pitches like I've missed a step. It cannot be coincidence.

With trembling hands, I flip to the next portrait, exhaling slowly at the familiar faces gazing back at me, at the matching names scrawled in the corner. *Michal and Mila Vasiliev.* He stands behind her, his pale hand resting upon her shoulder, while she sits regally in a velvet chair. Rendered in full, vibrant color, her eyes are no longer translucent, but instead gleam the most perfect shade of brown. Her hair—dark brown, just as I imagined—flows long and thick down her seafoam gown, and her cheeks flush dusky rose. She is breathtakingly beautiful.

My chest contracts painfully.

She is Michal's sister.

Her eyes are larger, softer, than his—her skin darker—but there is no mistaking the bold angle of her brows, the straight line of her nose, the strong shape of her jaw. They belong to Michal too. They belong to their father. And suddenly, Michal's obsessive quest to speak to her makes sense. His sister died. He is . . . grieving.

I replace the cloth hastily, feeling sick. Unless he hid my silver cross beneath his mattress, it isn't in this room, which means I shouldn't stay here any longer. Rifling through his desk is one thing; creeping into his bedroom, learning his family's faces, is quite another. Instinctively, I know that if Michal finds me in this place, he won't simply lock me away until All Hallows' Eve. He will kill me, and I cannot say that I'd blame him.

With one last perfunctory sweep of my candelabra, I leave his secrets in darkness.

CHAPTER TWENTY-THREE

The Celestials

My parents hired a specialist when I returned from the catacombs. My mother quickly realized she wasn't equipped to help me, and my father tired of waking each night from my screams. *My little fits,* he called them, and the specialist—a healer of the mind called Father Algernon—dutifully confirmed my condition, diagnosing me with hysteria. "A uniquely female complaint," he told my parents, who in turn dutifully paid him for prescribing a tonic instead of an asylum—or worse, an exorcism.

I still heard them whispering in my father's study, however, about demonic possession.

"It is not uncommon," Father Algernon said gravely, "among those touched by witchcraft. We see it often in their victims—a corruption of the soul. A black seed planted in the weak and immoral. You must know it is not your fault, my lord, as rotten fruit grows in even the halest and heartiest of families."

My mother shooed Father Algernon from our house after that, but nearly a year later, I still haven't forgotten his words. *Weak. Immoral.*

They seem to swirl with the leaves as Odessa and I approach Boutique de vêtements de M. Marc later that night.

Overhead, paper bats hang from the silver birch tree in honor of All Hallows' Eve, their tiny wings fluttering in the crisp wind.

Below, pumpkins and gourds litter the doorstep. Someone has carved wide, leering mouths into the fruit, along with eyes that flicker from the tea lights within. Live spiders skitter across the window—which now displays a breathtaking gown of aubergine crepe—and garlands of black roses wind around the lamppost across the street. Above the door, a human skull dangles from rosary beads.

Odessa, who notices me staring up at it, offers, "The skull is an All Hallows' Eve tradition in Requiem—and the rosary."

"Why?"

Why doesn't Mila want to see Michal? Why will she not speak to him? And—more important—why won't she speak with me now?

I tried reaching back through the veil. After returning from Michal's study empty-handed, I focused on every single emotion welling inside me: confusion and anger, even hope and expectation.

Fear.

No matter how I entreated her to appear—or the dozens of ghosts who peeked through my shelves to watch the spectacle— she refused to answer, leaving me to stew and pore through *How to Commune with the Dead* until Odessa arrived. *Leaving me,* I think bitterly, *one step closer to my demise.*

My plan doesn't work without a weapon.

"I suppose you could say vampires have a dark sense of humor." Odessa's eyes linger too long on my face. If I didn't know better, I might think she seems concerned. Perhaps I look too pale, too drawn, since discovering Michal's secret. Perhaps I'm not asking enough questions. When I still cannot bring myself to answer, however, she plunges onward with an air of determination. "The early Church attempted to absorb the ancient pagan rite of Samhain by choosing October thirty-first and November first for All Hallows' Eve and All Saints' Day—for ease of conversion, they explained. Quite a nasty little habit they developed. Of course, they never expected the undead to participate as well." She smirks and raises her brows at that, but when I merely nod, she heaves a sigh. Then, like she'd rather pluck out her own eyes and nail them to the door— "Do you want to talk about it? Whatever is bothering you?"

Whatever is bothering me. I almost laugh, instead forcing myself to ask, "The early Church knew of vampires?"

"Briefly." Lips pursed, she studies me for another second before caressing the skull's cheek fondly and passing into the shop. "Hello again, Father Roland. You're looking well."

And there it is—*exactly* why Mila wouldn't want to speak to her family. My stomach churns as I watch the skull swing gruesomely back and forth, and I resist the urge to remove it, to lay poor Father Roland's head to rest. Michal may grieve his sister, but how many others grieve because of him?

"Oho!" Monsieur Marc's exclamation rings through the shop when I follow Odessa, and it takes several seconds to find his wispy white hair among the bodies packed inside. He kneels at the hem of a beautiful vampire on the middle platform, while Boris and Romi flit to and fro between his worktable and two other vampire patrons, measuring, pinning, nipping, and tucking with supernatural speed.

"Bonjour, monsieur—" I begin, but he blurs past Odessa and me, seizing a length of golden chain from the wall behind.

"You are *early*, ladies!" He darts to a bin of beads next. "How terribly rude of you. Do you not realize All Hallows' Eve approaches? Do you not realize the entirety of the Old City clamors for my attention? Do you not understand the concept of punctuality? Your appointments do not start for another *ten* minutes—"

"And we are happy to wait, monsieur. Aren't we, Célie?" Odessa glides a hand down the garnet damask bodice near the door. A lavish sapphire cloak—sewn of velvet so dark it appears nearly black—hangs beside it, complete with a diadem of gold and pearl. The entire ensemble feels oddly familiar, though I cannot place where I've seen it before. "We understand true genius takes time. This is stunning," she adds, lifting the cloak for me to see. "He never fails to exceed all expectations."

"You flatter me." Though Monsieur Marc pretends to grumble, impish glee sparks in his eyes at the compliment, and he puffs out his chest in unmistakable pride. "And flattery will get you everywhere. Boris"—he snaps his fingers at his assistant—"finish fitting Monsieur Dupont for me, would you? I must prepare our Madonna for her final fitting before entrusting Mademoiselle Célie with her trousseau."

"Madonna?" I blink between Odessa and the blue-black cloak, the garnet bodice. *Blue of the divine. Red of Christ's blood.* I snort in the most unladylike way possible. My mother would be ashamed. "You're dressing as the *Madonna* for All Hallows' Eve? As in the Madonna and child? The Mother of God and Jesus Christ?"

"Would you believe that Dimitri refuses to participate?" Costume in tow, Odessa tosses her hair as Monsieur Marc leads her into the back room. She winks at me conspiratorially. "You must convince him that he'll make a darling newborn babe when he arrives with the carriage. With his keen intellect, he's already halfway there. Just imagine him in swaddling clothes."

Chuckling, Monsieur Marc closes the door, ending our conversation.

Leaving me alone in a shop full of silent vampires.

Moving in a blur, Boris extends the train of Monsieur Dupont's gown—molten gold, the fabric so sleek it looks liquid—all the way to the door of the shop. I step around it carefully, all too aware of Monsieur Dupont's dark eyes on me. Atop his smooth head sits a coronet shaped like rays of light.

I could never tolerate silence for long.

"Your costume is beautiful," I tell him with a tentative smile. "You look like the sun." When he says nothing in return, only stares at me, I clear my throat and start again. "Of course, you have no idea who I am, which makes this rather inappropriate, doesn't it? My apologies. Please, allow me to introduce myself. My name is Célie Tremblay, and—"

In a voice as dark and smooth as his skin, he says, "I know who you are."

Boris and Romi exchange a wary glance.

"Ah." I look between him and his companions, my smile fading. "I see—"

"He allows you into the Old City?" The second vampire—pale, tall, and svelte, with ice-blond hair and bloodred lips—tilts her head curiously. Romi rearranges a fold in her soft white gown. The fabric seems to glow slightly, and a delicate black headpiece glitters across her head. It falls into a crescent moon pendant above her brow. "His human pet?"

I stiffen slightly. "His *pet?*"

I dislike the nickname from Michal's lips. I absolutely loathe it from hers.

"A Chasseur," Monsieur Dupont says, his expression unreadable. "A huntress."

"Why has he brought a *huntress* to Requiem?" the third vampire hisses. Raven curls fall in wild disarray down her round and voluptuous form, and the bodice of her gown is fitted and sheer— dove gray but iridescent, with flecks of diamonds sewn into the gossamer. They look like stars.

Because they are *stars*, I realize with irritating and irrational interest.

Together, these vampires will form the three celestial bodies on All Hallows' Eve. They also look like they want to kill me. And suddenly, I refuse to admit that I'm a prisoner, a *pet*, while they lord over me with their lovely gowns and lovelier faces. I force another smile at each in turn. "Michal invited me here as a guest in his household. I shall return home after the masquerade ball on All Hallows' Eve."

It is the wrong thing to say.

Instantly, the raven-haired vampire hisses, and her ice-blond companion's lip curls. I force myself to remain exactly where I am. *Never run from a vampire.* "He invited you to the All Hallows' Eve celebrations?" the former asks in outrage.

"Should he not have done so? I've seen humans in the market."

"As chattel," she snarls. "Never guests."

"Priscille." Monsieur Dupont lays a broad hand on her shoulder before turning those fathomless eyes to me. Though they aren't openly hostile like Priscille's, they aren't exactly kind either. "Take care, humaine, for we are not the Vasiliev king or his family.

We have not the blessing of celebrating with our kin this All Hallows' Eve."

Swallowing hard, I glance to the back room. "Oh?"

"*Oh.*" Priscille bristles beneath Monsieur Dupont's hand. "Vampires from all over the world should already be arriving in Requiem, yet this year, Michal has closed our borders. Without his blessing, no one comes in, and no one goes out."

"Except you, of course," the blonde says coldly. "Will your brethren try to follow you here?"

"I—I am hardly a Chasseur, mademoiselle."

"Would you still taste like one, I wonder?"

"Juliet," Monsieur Dupont warns. "Not here."

Not here. My mouth dries. He didn't say *not ever.*

But surely Odessa and Monsieur Marc can still hear us; surely they'll intervene if I'm in true danger. My gaze darts again to their door. Though a shop full of angry vampires isn't ideal, perhaps their hatred of Michal can work in my favor. An enemy of my enemy is a friend, after all. "Why has he closed the borders?"

Monsieur Dupont shakes his head slowly. "We do not discuss such things with humans."

"Why shouldn't we?" Priscille pushes his hand from her shoulder. "Michal flouts his own rule despite the danger to his people, yet he expects us to follow blindly? I think not." She lifts her nose, nostrils flaring. "If you ask me, he is not himself. His servants have started to whisper, Pierre. They speak of strange happenings in the castle, of his reclusiveness and restlessness. They speak of *ghosts.*"

"*You* should not speak of them, Priscille."

"My cousin even overheard that he invited La Dame des Sorcières and La Princesse Rouge to the masquerade on All Hallows'

Eve. Can you imagine? Witches walking the streets of Requiem, thinking themselves our equals? Whatever happened to our sanctuary, our *secret*?" She glares at me with withering disdain. "I did not want to believe it, yet now I fear it must be true—Michal is truly unhinged, and I no longer feel safe here."

Juliet shakes her head in disgust. "The Chasseurs will follow their huntress. Mark my words. When the enchantment lifts on All Hallows' Eve, they will come with their swords of—"

Monsieur Dupont speaks sharper now. "*Juliet*—"

"And how can Michal protect us?" Priscille's beautiful face twists in scorn. "He couldn't even protect his own sister—"

The door to the back bursts open with a mighty *bang*, and Odessa stands in the threshold, still and slight and utterly terrifying. She no longer smiles. Monsieur Marc appears grave and silent behind her. "Oh, darlings, don't mind me," she says, her voice light and deceptively pleasant. It lifts the hair on my neck. "Please continue. I am ever so interested to hear more of this *fascinating* conversation."

Monsieur Dupont bows his head, baring his teeth at Priscille and Juliet when they don't immediately follow. Juliet grimaces as if pained before dropping into a curtsy. Odessa's attention flicks to Priscille, who still stands on the platform with her back ramrod straight, her shoulders proud. Boris and Romi retreat from her slowly, their gazes fixed upon the floor.

"Do you challenge him, Priscille?" Odessa asks. "Shall I summon our king?"

Wide-eyed, I watch as Priscille's jaw clenches, as she refuses to break eye contact with Odessa. It all feels terribly important—terribly *foolish*—like I am watching the last moments of this immortal creature's life. If Michal were here instead of Odessa, Priscille would already be dead. Echoing my thoughts, still bowing, Monsieur Dupont murmurs, "Do not be rash, mon amie. Yield now."

Priscille's throat works furiously. "Michal is not fit to lead us."

"And you are?" he asks.

"Perhaps."

Odessa's smile hardens. "Take care how you speak, celestials. Hundreds have challenged Michal in his thousand-year reign, yet Michal alone remains—for the sun, moon, and stars do not exist in Requiem. Here there is only darkness, and darkness is eternal."

An inexplicably eager chill sweeps my body at that. Perhaps I *am* immoral. Because I cannot tear my gaze away from Priscille, from Odessa, from the palpable threat of violence between them. If the situation escalates much further, Odessa might not wait for Michal. She might dispose of Priscille with her bare hands, and I—well, I simply cannot muster proper horror at the prospect.

Leaning forward, I wait with bated breath for Priscille to respond.

When a small hand clasps my elbow instead, I tense, my heart leaping to my throat. Monsieur Marc coughs pointedly. "Go, papillon," he says, his voice uncharacteristically quiet. "Some conversations are better left unheard, and I have assembled your trousseau in the back. Please wait for me to join you there."

He doesn't allow any argument, pushing me forward with strength that belies his white hair. Not a single vampire in the room acknowledges me as we pass. Odessa and Priscille remain locked in silent challenge, even as Monsieur Marc closes the door behind me.

⇥╫⇤

Resisting the urge to press my ear to the door, I glance around the tiny room. *His office*, I realize. Dozens of garment boxes spill over his desk, beneath his chair, across his rug in organized chaos, and emerald ribbon adorns each one with a pretty bow. An unexpected surge of affection fills me as I blink at them. They match the ribbon on my wrist exactly.

"My brother suffers from that one malediction which cannot be cured," D'Artagnan muses from a basket half-hidden behind the door. Startling, I whirl just as he yawns wide, stretches in a leisurely fashion—thoroughly unconcerned—and sits up to lick his paw. The tip of his tail flicks. "Sentiment."

Though my eyes narrow, I resist the urge to tug my sleeve down over my own ribbon. Because I have nothing of which to be ashamed, and besides—I don't much like this disdainful little creature and his opinions. I've always known cats to be rather standoffish, of course—with the exception of those on this isle— but this one wins the crown. "It isn't the worst of sins, you know. To care for someone."

He pauses in licking his back leg to blink up at me. "Is that what you think is happening? Vampires caring for you?"

"Don't be absurd—"

"Oh, good. Then we're in agreement." He resumes licking himself in a rather offensive manner, taking care to gift me his back end. "I worried for a moment, but it *would* be rather absurd—even delusional—for either of us to pretend a vampire has your best interests at heart. Even your beloved Monsieur Marc poisoned me in a fit of malicious temper, and we shared the same womb."

Unbidden, my eyes flick to the shop door, but no sound comes from beyond it. No footsteps. No voices. No screams of anguish, no cries of rebellion. Perhaps the celestial vampires have left the shop in peace, or perhaps—more likely—I simply cannot hear them; Monsieur Marc *did* admit to dallying with a witch, after all. Perhaps an enchantment lies upon this door, and they cannot hear me either, which means . . .

Edging toward the tattered desk, I nudge aside the boxes there as covertly as possible.

It couldn't hurt to have a poke around. Though my search of Michal's study didn't yield my silver cross, it still proved useful, and Monsieur Marc doesn't seem quite as scrupulous with his belongings as Requiem's benevolent ruler. He *did* poison his vampire brother, after all. Could he still possess whatever he used? Powdered arsenic? Nightshade berries?

Rat droppings?

Please let it be rat droppings.

"You seduced your brother's wife." Determined to maintain a casual air, I trail my hand along the crystal bottle of ink, the peacock-feather quill, in search of anything immediately out of the ordinary. A crude portrait of two teenage girls—presumably Monsieur Marc's daughters—sits framed with pride behind a leather-bound portfolio filled to the brim with sketches. "He had every reason to be angry with you."

"Yes, well, he stole my favorite pocket square."

My hand stills on the handle of the desk drawer, and I crane my neck to stare at him incredulously. "You cannot be serious."

"As opposed to what?"

"You ruined your brother's marriage because he stole your favorite *pocket square*?" I shake my head and resume my search, dipping into Monsieur Marc's drawer now. "That's despicable,

D'Artagnan. You should be ashamed of yourself as both a vampire and a cat."

"Tit for tat—though if you *must* know, it wasn't his marriage I ruined. His human wife died long before either of us transitioned to vampire, and she never allowed such antics."

He blinks his great amber eyes at me in distaste, and though he has no way of knowing—he cannot read *minds*—a shadow of doubt still spreads through my chest in response. No. Of *shame*. Only moments ago, I relished the thought of Odessa hurting that celestial vampire, so who am I to shame D'Artagnan for his behavior?

My throat tightens at the realization.

I need to escape this island as soon as possible.

As if indeed sensing my bleak thoughts, D'Artagnan says, "More to the point of despicable behavior, however, has my brother stowed your trousseau in his desk? Is there perhaps an evening gown folded among the envelopes?"

I nearly slam my fingers in the desk drawer as I hasten to shut it. "Of course not," I say quickly—*too* quickly—and I loathe myself as I adopt a wide smile, as I pat the nearest garment box with one hand and slip the blank sheet of parchment into my pocket with the other. It rustles against the inkpot and peacock quill already there. "I simply hoped to catch a glimpse of my costume before All Hallows' Eve. Is it here in the shop? Has he finished it?"

If a cat could roll his eyes, this one would. "At least have the sense to steal more than a quill."

"I beg your pardon?"

"Stupidity does not become you." At last, he finishes his bath, bestowing me with his undivided—and, frankly, inconvenient—attention. "Go on, then. I will not stop you. I assume you intend to procure a weapon for some madcap escape attempt—all the while failing to realize, of course, that no weapon in this shop can help you."

Now it's *my* turn to give him undivided attention. Because he didn't say *no weapon in general*; he said *no weapon in this shop*, and D'Artagnan doesn't strike me as one to speak without thinking. "For your information, I *do* have a plan," I tell him. "Or at least"— abandoning all attempts at subtlety, I fling open the cabinet beside the desk to widen my search—"I'm in the process of forming one, and it isn't madcap at all. It's rather simple, actually."

"Does it involve the quill and ink in your pocket?"

"It might."

"Then I regret to inform you, foolish girl, that there is nothing simple about sending a letter on Requiem."

I move swiftly to the bookcase, pulling out each tome in hopes of loosening something. A packet of powder, perhaps, or a secret lever. "Nonsense. Do you not have an aviary?"

"Of course we have an aviary, but it resides on the northern shore of the isle, which—in case such trivial matters as revolt and rebellion have escaped your notice—is no longer safe. The streets are restless, and the citizens are eager for a martyr. Without Michal as protection, you will be ... marked."

Marked.

The word should lift the hair at my neck, but I return the last book to its shelf before whirling to face the rest of the room, scouring the cramped space anxiously. Despite D'Artagnan's rather unexpected warning, there are no true safeguards here. Michal marked me the instant he saw Coco's scarlet cloak. I am no more *safe* with him than I am in the streets.

Dropping to my knees, I begin to feel along the floorboards with increasing desperation.

Monsieur Marc and Odessa could break up this little chat at any second, and even if they don't—my eyes dart to the back door, where the former arranges deliveries—Dimitri will be here soon. My fingers scrabble at the wood as disappointment rears its ugly head. Perhaps D'Artagnan didn't mean to hint at a secret weapon at all—or perhaps he *did*, and he now delights in watching me crawl about on my hands and knees.

"You're ruining your gown," he says disdainfully, "and you look like the little match girl as well. Are you familiar with the tale? I used to read it to my nieces every night. It's about the hopes and dreams of a dying child—"

"Though I appreciate the concern, D'Artagnan," I say through gritted teeth, "I don't care about my gown, and I don't need your encouragement. I *will* warn my friends of what awaits them here. I don't expect you to understand, of course, but—" Something bright glints in my periphery, and I stop short, turning sharply toward the underside of Monsieur Marc's desk. Eyes narrowing for one second—two—I lean closer to investigate. *Odd.* Long and sharp and narrow, it appears to be some sort of . . . of *pin*, except—

No.

My eyes widen as I scramble to my feet, as I crack my skull on the desk and nearly crash to my knees once more, clutching my crown through tears. Because it isn't a pin at all.

It's a *stake.*

And it isn't just any stake. It's a *silver* stake, and I don't know whether I weep with pain or giddiness, concern or jubilation. It hardly matters either way; seizing the weapon from its perch, I resist the urge to kiss D'Artagnan all over his cantankerous face. Because there can be no doubt now—if Monsieur Marc has taken such care to hide it, this stake must be dangerous. *Silver* must be dangerous.

"I knew it." Still slightly dizzy, still clutching my head, I twirl among the boxes before remembering the ink, quill, and parchment in my pocket, upending them all on the desk. "I *knew* it."

"Oh dear." To my surprise, however, D'Artagnan makes no move to swat the stake from my hand or otherwise alert the vampires next door of my newfound weapon. Instead, he kneads the edge of his basket dispassionately. "It seems you've found my stake."

"*Your* stake?"

"You insult me, mademoiselle. If my brother hadn't poisoned me that morning, I would've staked him that very night. Indeed, the plans were already in motion."

"Despicable," I repeat, shaking my head, but my heart is no longer in it. No—my heart now flies across the parchment with my hand as I finally, *finally*, set my plan into motion.

Coco,

You must not come to Requiem. The killer is here—a vampire called Michal Vasiliev. He drinks the blood of his victims, and he intends to kill you on All Hallows' Eve. Armed with silver, I myself am in no imminent danger. Please know that I will escape this wretched place, and I will see everyone in Cesarine soon.

All my love,

Célie

At the last stroke of my quill, D'Artagnan steps languorously from his basket—yawning once more—and saunters toward the delivery entrance. "What are you doing?" I ask suspiciously, folding the parchment into quarters before slipping it into my corset with the stake. "You aren't coming with me."

"Of course I am." He stretches upward to catch the door handle, and cool night air spills between us as it opens to the shadows of the alley. "Once a vampire, always a vampire, after all."

Frowning at his back, I quietly follow him from the shop. "What does *that* mean?"

His tail flicks in the darkness like the feu follet of lore. Like an omen. "I quite enjoy the scent of blood."

CHAPTER TWENTY-FOUR

Ma Douce

Anticipation swells in my chest as D'Artagnan leads me toward the seven-tailed gargoyle, parting the ivy beneath it and ducking through the crack in the wall. Perhaps it's foolish to feel so . . . *buoyant* after his warning, but the city feels different now. A harsh, almost painful laugh escapes as we climb through the shrubbery on the other side of the wall, as we dart into the wider street beyond. The colors here—the yellow of the gourds, the amber of D'Artagnan's eyes—appear richer than before, beautifully saturated, while the salt in the air tastes sharper, and a distant rumble of thunder promises another storm.

But not yet.

The streets are perfectly still tonight. Peaceful, even. The moon herself peeks out from behind her clouds, glistening upon the wet cobblestones, and a black cat follows us as we cross to another street. When she purrs, brushing against my skirts, I know in my bones this is it. This is my moment. Reaching a hand into my skirt pocket, I double-check the folded letter there. When D'Artagnan arches his back and hisses, frightening the poor creature away, I triple-check the stake in my corset.

"You didn't need to do that," I whisper to him. "She wasn't harming anyone."

He looks smug. "I know."

Shaking my head, I glance around the landscape to gain my bearings—and thank God that the Old City sits on the highest peak of the isle. From here, just outside the wall, I can see the whole of Requiem sprawled out below us. D'Artagnan said the aviary lies on the northern shore, which means—I turn and squint in the moonlight—*there*. I can just see it rise along the rocky beach. With a slow exhale, I memorize the stars above it: a constellation called Les Amoureux. The same star forms the tip of the serpent's tail and the dove's wing. I allow it to guide me as I plunge into the city and lose direct sight of the aviary.

Beau renamed the constellation as a wedding gift to Lou and Reid last summer.

A pang of longing shoots through me at the memory, but I push it aside. I bury it deep. Nothing can dampen my spirit tonight—not rain, and certainly not regret.

This is my moment.

After sending this letter, I'll slip back to Michal's grotto and wait.

Though candlelight flickers from the shops on either side of us, I duck my head and resist temptation; I hurry past the bookshop and perfumery, glance only twice over my shoulder at the diamond and pearl collars on display in the bijouterie. The celestials might be distracting Odessa for now, but eventually, she *will* notice my absence. Quickening my step, I nod politely to a passing gentleman, who tips his hat to me with a curious expression. His face is pale as bone.

Maintaining my calm, measured pace, I refuse to glance back at him. Refuse to give him a reason to stop, to speak to me. For all he knows, I've done nothing wrong; I'm a simple human pet out for a stroll in the moonlight, perfectly commonplace and dull. What had Priscille said? *Like chattel.* I wait several more seconds. When no cold hand grasps my arm, I turn my chin slightly, exhaling in relief at the empty street behind me. "Second thoughts?" D'Artagnan murmurs. "It isn't too late to turn around."

"You'd like that, wouldn't you?"

"Not at all." He rubs his side along a gargoyle in perfect contentment. "Why deprive myself of the entertainment? There is nothing quite so satisfying as watching a plan go awry—not that yours would qualify as a plan, of course. A letter and a stake seem more a farewell." He pounces on an errant leaf. "I've always envisioned my own swan song with rather more pomp and circumstance— perhaps in haute couture, my brother's tonsils in hand."

"Lovely."

No other creatures cross our path as we continue down the sloping streets.

It seems the crowds of the lower markets avoid wandering too near the Old City—an advantage, I tell myself, nodding and walking faster still. It would be much harder to maintain secrecy while traipsing through the hustle and bustle of witches, werewolves, and mermaids near the docks. Still . . . I glance around us. According to Odessa, vampires rise with the moon. Shouldn't there be more of them outside tonight, perusing these lavish shops near the wall? Surely not *all* vampires reside within the Old City? Dimitri claimed only the most revered and respected lineages lived inside.

Cold awareness pricks my nape.

Then again . . . perhaps vampires *are* here. Perhaps I just can't see them.

As if in response, movement stirs in the shadowed alcove across the street, and I tense, drawing the silver stake from my corset. But . . . no. I relax again, my cheeks growing warm. The couple—a man and a woman—seem to be locked in a passionate embrace, far too occupied with each other to notice us. Their hips move in synchrony. Even to my human ears, the man's breathing sounds labored and uneven, and when the woman pulls away, he moans and topples sideways, blood streaming down his chest. My heart lurches into my throat. They aren't embracing at all. The woman is *feeding* from him, and the man appears to be dying. "Quelle tragédie," D'Artagnan purrs.

Holding my breath, I nudge him forward and tiptoe past as quietly as possible. It takes several moments to slow my heartbeat, to regain my sense of purpose. I cannot save that man—I cannot save Michal's victim tonight—but I can save Coco. I *will* save Coco, and I will save myself too.

The stake is slick in my palm when another gentleman passes halfway across the city. He wipes blood from the corner of his mouth with a silk handkerchief and a salacious grin, his teeth gleaming long and white. "Bonsoir, ma douce."

"Good evening, monsieur." I clutch the stake tighter, hiding it in my skirt, as I stride around him. When he continues to stare—the breeze tousling his raven-dark hair—I force a pleasant smile and murmur, "Beautiful night, isn't it?"

"Indeed it is."

He watches as I turn the corner, but thankfully, he doesn't follow. "See?" I ask D'Artagnan with strained optimism. Except gooseflesh rises along my arms, my legs, and pressure starts to build in my ears with each erratic beat of my heart. I struggle to control my fear, to steady my breathing, as color leeches from the street around us. "If any vampire wanted to bite me, it would've been that one, and he was a perfect gentleman—"

"Except for the blood on his collar," Mila says, her voice sharp.

I startle violently as she materializes beside me, her eyes narrowed and—and *angry*. "Mila!" My own eyes dart around us as the spirit realm fully descends, and I slink back a step, slipping a little in ash and trying not to look too disappointed. *Now* she deigns to speak to me. "What are you—?"

"The better question is what are *you*, Célie Tremblay? Do you think you're being *brave*, sneaking away from the others? Do you think you're being clever?" When I move to walk around her, she shoots in front of me, and I cringe at the unpleasant, icy sensation of her skin against mine. "And to think I mistook you for intelligent."

"It's wonderful to see you too." Lifting my chin—ignoring the hot spark of anger at her words—I bare my teeth in a smile before continuing down the street. Ahead, the shadow of the aviary looms closer, larger. I fix my gaze upon it, refusing to look at Mila. She cannot ruin this. Coco, Lou, Jean Luc, Reid—they're almost safe. *I'm almost there.* "Thank you for telling me about your *brother*, by the way. I really appreciated that little lie of omission."

Her brows snap together in surprise. I've shocked her. *Good.* "I didn't lie," she says, recovering quickly and squaring her shoulders. "I told you my name. It isn't my fault you didn't recognize it."

"Such *modesty*. Must be a family trait." I quicken my step, eager to escape her. "I'm rather busy at the moment, though, so if you'll excuse me—"

"I will most certainly *not* excuse you. What are you doing out here all alone?"

D'Artagnan clears his throat, detaching himself from the shadows and startling us both. "Hello again, Mila."

"D'Artagnan." If possible, Mila's expression hardens further—she resembles actual stone now—but their cold greeting only confirms my suspicions: D'Artagnan *can* see ghosts, which means I'm not quite as alone here as I feared. Not quite as *wrong.* The realization fills me with a strange sense of kinship with the beastly little creature. "Of all the meddlesome—I should've known you'd be here." Mila's voice drips with accusation. "I assume *you* put her up to this?"

D'Artagnan rubs languorously against a streetlamp. "Her reasons are her own."

Throwing up her hands, she streaks after me in exasperation. "*Well?* What are they?"

"I'd rather not discuss them with you."

"I'd rather not be dead, yet here we are," she snaps. "Did Michal not impress upon you the danger of this place? When we agreed you'd leave the isle, I assumed you meant *alive.*"

"Listen, Mila," I say tersely, practically sprinting from her now. "Michal might be your brother, but this really doesn't concern you. I can't let him kill my friends, and I thought you of all people would understand that. Clearly, he wants to speak with you—and I could've translated—but you refused to see him earlier. It must've been for a reason."

Angrier now, she streaks in front of me once more. "This isn't about me and Michal. This is about *you.*" *Wrong answer.* I skirt around her, clenching my jaw, but she merely follows like a bat out of Hell. "Vampires *eat* people, Célie. Just because my family has treated you with kindness"—I scoff aloud—"does not mean *vampires* are kind. If you stumble across the wrong sort, even my brother will not be able to save you. Do you understand *that*? Do you understand how unpleasant it is to die?"

"I can do this." I lift my chin stubbornly. "I *have* to do this." Then—unable to keep the frustration from my voice— "Why do you even care? You don't know me, and your brother plans to kill me in less than a fortnight. Clearly, you still feel some loyalty toward him, and—" Realization dawns swift and cruel and—and *oh my God*. "Is that it? Are you worried that my friends won't arrive if I die before All Hallows' Eve? That Michal will never get his vengeance?"

Mila's eyes narrow once more. When she moves to stop me this time, she draws to her full height, looming over me with a look so cold and so familiar that I almost miss a step. "You really are a fool," she says, every inch her brother, "if you think I'm here for vengeance."

I skid to a halt to glare up at her. "Why *are* you here, then? To help your brother choose his next victims? To drag those poor souls to Hell?"

"My brother didn't kill those creatures. You think him beyond absolution, but you're wrong. Michal can still be saved. I *know* he can."

You think him beyond absolution.

No gift can absolve the things you've done.

D'Artagnan clicks his tongue in disapproval.

"Were you *eavesdropping* on us?" I ask indignantly, but when she opens her mouth to answer, I realize I don't want an explanation. Mila was Michal's sister—of course she thinks he deserves absolution; of course she doesn't want to believe him capable of such irrevocable evil. If the roles were reversed, I'd never believe it of Pippa either. But—no. I don't have time for this. Odessa could arrive at any moment.

Lifting the silver stake, I say decisively, "Let me be clear. Even if it *were* possible—which it isn't—I would never help you absolve Michal. If I could, I would drive this silver straight into his chest to rid the world of his black heart."

"My brother's heart is many things," she says vehemently, "but black it is not."

But I refuse to tolerate Mila *or* her brother for another second. With a vicious, instinctive push, I thrust out with my anger, feeling righteous—feeling *vindicated*—for the first time in ages. Feeling like perhaps I *could* drive this silver into Michal's chest if he appeared. Mila's mouth parts in shock as the veil splits in a swift, brutal cut behind me, and I leap through it, away from her, seizing the edges and forcing them back together again.

Eyes widening, she bolts forward two seconds too late. "What are you doing?"

"I'm sorry, Mila. I wish we could be friends."

She shakes her head—tries to force a hand through—but the veil repairs itself at rapid speed now, stoked by the fire in my chest. "Don't do this, Célie, *please*—"

"*Leave.*"

With a final, ruthless swipe, I force the veil to close completely, leaving the path to the aviary clear. I take another deep, steadying breath—tamping down on my guilt—and inhale warmer air before striding toward the aviary. To my inexplicable relief, D'Artagnan follows.

"Loath as I am to admit it," he murmurs, "that went . . . well."

"You didn't tell me you could see ghosts."

"You didn't tell me you could either."

Heavy silence descends as we step through the door together.

Unlike the aviary in Cesarine, this one isn't built like an enormous cage. No. It's built like a rook, tall and narrow and slightly crooked, with a concave ceiling and stone walls. A peculiar smell fills the place—one I can't quite place—but it probably belongs to the birds. And there are *hundreds* of birds: hawks and owls and pigeons and ravens, each face illuminated by the basin of fire in the middle of the room. Some of them blink at us within cages, while others perch along the rickety staircase that circles the walls to the top of the structure. Above us, chains rattle faintly before falling silent.

I peer at the dark ceiling cautiously. Though the firelight doesn't reach the top of the aviary, I assume the keeper tethers his deadliest birds up there, away from the others. Already, my fingers itch to set them all free. The cages, the chains—they've always seemed particularly cruel for creatures with wings.

Unfortunately, I can only release one tonight.

Quietly, I follow D'Artagnan up the stairs, searching for a larger bird to make the voyage across the sea. Even D'Artagnan seems reluctant to speak in this place. Crude windows pock the walls the higher we climb, and a leak trickles from somewhere overhead. Its steady *drip, drip, drip* joins the soft flutter of wings, the gentle crackle of fire.

A sharp, sudden *caw!* from above nearly stops my heart. D'Artagnan hisses, darting up the stairs and out of sight as my face snaps toward the sound. The three-eyed crow from the market peers back at me in a cage near the shadowy ceiling. Tilting its head inquisitively, it ruffles its feathers and hops from foot to foot. *Odd.* I frown and start toward it, whispering, "How did you get up there? I thought you were someone's pet."

Voice low, D'Artagnan says, "Should I be insulted you think the bird will speak?"

"Why shouldn't it? You certainly never stop."

It caws again in response, sounding strangely urgent as I climb higher into the gloom. As the *drip, drip, drip* of water grows louder. "You're making a terrible racket, you know. No wonder that merchant got rid of you." The bird's only answer is to caw and attack the bars of its cage. I hesitate beside the agitated creature.

There are other birds, *better* birds, that could deliver my letter, yet I feel an inexplicable kinship with *this* one.

"Stop that," I tell it firmly, extracting the folded parchment and poking its beak with the tip. "You're going to hurt yourself, and I have a job for you."

Though it pecks my letter in irritation, it also seems to understand my words, growing still and quiet on its perch. Watching me. *Studying* me. "Right." I eye it apprehensively before sticking the silver stake back in my décolletage. "I am going to unlock your cage now, and you are *not* going to attack me. Do we agree?"

"This should be good," D'Artagnan says.

"Ignore him," I tell the bird.

It ruffles its wings with some importance.

Interpreting that as *yes*, I lift the latch and swing the door open. When the bird doesn't move, I loose a breath of relief. "See? It's quite easy to be civil. Now"—I slip the letter into the pouch around its foot—"I need you to deliver this to Cosette Monvoisin." The bird tilts its head. "La Princesse Rouge? You can find her at

7 Yew Lane in Cesarine—or at the castle," I add, feeling stupider by the second. If witches and mermaids and *vampires* can exist, however, surely this bird can deliver a letter. "She often stays with His Majesty there. Or—or she could also be up past Amandine. Have you heard of Chateau le Blanc? I don't *think* she'll be there this time of year, but just in case—"

The bird *caw! caw! caw!*s to put me out of my misery, and before I can duck, it hurtles past my face and out the nearest window. I watch it go with a mingled sense of triumph and unease. Something isn't quite right about that bird—and I don't just mean its extra eye. Indeed, something isn't quite right about this *place*.

I try to shake the feeling, climbing to the window and forcing myself to appreciate the view. Because I did it. *I did it.* With any luck, the bird will find Coco quickly, and my friends will heed my warning. I've procured a silver stake to end Michal's evil reign, and I'll soon be rowing home to Cesarine. Everything will end perfectly. Everyone will live happily ever after, just like in the fairy stories Pip and I read as children. *We'll all be fine.*

As the three-eyed crow disappears, however, my sense of hope refuses to return. A peculiar sense of awareness settles over my skin instead. The longer I stand here, the stronger it grows. My gaze flicks to the owls on either side of the window. Though their wings quiver, they stand wholly and totally still on their perches. Shouldn't animals—even birds—make more noise than this? And where is Odessa? Shouldn't she have found me by now? "Come on," I whisper to D'Artagnan, turning toward the stairs. "We should go back to Monsieur Marc. . . ."

But a gentle lapping sound has joined the steady *drip, drip, drip* of water. Frown deepening, I glance down at my feet, where

D'Artagnan crouches, licking up a pool of . . .

My entire body goes rigid.

A pool of blood.

Unbidden, my head snaps upward to find the source, and— from the darkness of the ceiling—the wide eyes of a corpse stare back at me. For the span of a single heartbeat, my mind refuses to accept the scene overhead: the corpse's limbs tangled in chains, his throat torn open, his mouth twisted in agony and *fear.* Then a drop of his blood hits my cheek. My eyelid, my *lips*—

The reality of the situation crashes over me, and I choke, stumbling away from him, crashing into the cages along the walls. The owls shriek with terror. They catch my cloak in their talons, my hair in their beaks, but I cannot feel the sting, cannot feel *anything,* because the corpse's blood—it's in my mouth. It's on my *tongue,* and I can taste its bitter tang. I can—I—

I crash to my knees, heaving, but there is blood here too. It coats my palms as I push to my feet once more. It seeps across my vision and paints the aviary red as my eyes instinctively return to the man.

No.

Behind him—just visible in the shadows—a vampire clings to the ceiling, his body, his *head,* contorted unnaturally to watch me. *Just because my family has treated you with kindness does not mean* vampires *are kind. If you stumble across the wrong sort . . .*

A jagged grin stretches across the vampire's face. Bits of the man still remain in his teeth, and blood pours down his chin in a dark wash of crimson.

This is the wrong sort.

My knees unlock, and I seize D'Artagnan, turning and sprinting down the staircase. "What are you *doing?*" He twists wildly in my arms, hissing and spitting indignantly. "Unhand me this *instant—*"

"Don't be *stupid—*"

Though I fumble for the stake in my corset, I only manage to cut my chest before the vampire lands in front of me on silent feet. His pale eyes glint with hunger at the line of blood on my décolletage, and he licks his lips greedily, dragging his gaze back to mine in a slow, wicked taunt. That simple movement—the sight of his lust, his *tongue*—sends me reeling backward, near delirious with panic. "I will not be quick," he promises, his voice guttural and deep. And I believe him. Oh *God*, I believe him, and I should've listened to Mila—to D'Artagnan, to Odessa and Dimitri, even to *Michal.*

Do you understand how unpleasant it is to die?

When he lunges, I don't stop to think.

I simply jump.

The floor rises swiftly to meet me, but I bend my knees, pressing my feet together to brace for impact. Jean Luc taught me how to fall during training. He taught me to relax my muscles, to angle toes first, to do a hundred other things that I forget the instant my feet hit the ground. Pain explodes up my legs, and I pitch forward, rolling and landing hard on my elbow. The bone shatters instantly. Yowling, D'Artagnan leaps from my arms and bolts through the open door. Though the vampire's cruel laughter echoes above, I drag myself upright, the ground pitching and swaying beneath my feet.

My elbow is broken. My left ankle too. The force of the collision pushed the stake deeper into my breast, and blood pours freely down my bodice. By some miracle, however, I'm still alive; I *survived.* Leaning against the basin of fire, I wrench the stake from my skin with my good arm. I cannot run, but I will not die here. *Not yet.* "Where would you like it, monsieur?" I ask him through gritted teeth, lifting the stake. Black spots bloom in my vision. I taste blood in my mouth. "Eyes, ears, nose, or groin?"

He drops to the ground by the basin. Though I prepare for his attack, it never comes.

Instead, his eyes dart over my shoulder, and his salacious grin vanishes at something behind me. My fingers tighten around the bloody stake. I hardly dare hope. I hardly dare *breathe.* Turning slowly, I follow his gaze across the aviary, but it is not Odessa who steps through the door. It is not Monsieur Marc or Dimitri or Michal either.

No.

The two gentlemen from the street tip their hats to me, devastatingly handsome, followed by the woman with the lover. All three stare at the blood on my chest with palpable hunger. "Oh dear." Extending his handkerchief with long, graceful fingers, the raven-haired vampire clicks his tongue sympathetically. His smile, however, is pure evil. "You seem to be bleeding."

CHAPTER TWENTY-FIVE

A Natural Aphrodisiac

The vampire beside me snarls, every muscle in his body taut and tense. "I found her first," he tells the others, his guttural voice dropping another octave. Near unintelligible now. Blood still spills down his chin, and I choke back bile at the sight of it. At the *scent*. "She is mine."

The raven-haired vampire's eyes never leave my face. His handkerchief remains extended. "Nonsense. I marked her on the street half an hour ago." To me, he purrs, "Ignore the others. Come to me, ma douce, before you waste another drop of that lovely ichor. I shall take your pain away."

He shall take my pain away.

The words are delicious, lovely and warm and—and *compelling*. When my head starts to empty and my feet begin to move, I wrench my gaze away and seize the rim of the basin. Pain radiates up my leg, down my arm, but I force myself to feel it, to remain in control, and stare determinedly at my scraped knuckles. I cannot run. I cannot even *walk*. The stake still bites into my palm, but the possibility of stabbing even a single vampire with it was slim; the possibility of stabbing four is nonexistent. The reality of the situation washes over me, and with it, my knees threaten to buckle.

I am going to die here, after all.

I can only pray Coco receives my note.

"Odessa will be here any moment." Swaying on my feet, I lie through my teeth. "She just needed to finish up a bit of business with Monsieur Marc, but she said she'd be along soon. You don't want to anger Odessa." The last I deliver with as much bravado as I can muster. It's what Jean Luc would do, what Lou and Reid and Coco would do too. They'd stare Death in the face, perhaps laugh at him, before striding into the afterlife with their chins held high.

I force my own chin up as the woman's brow furrows.

"Fortunately for me, this will only take a moment." The second gentleman removes his hat and gloves, draping them across the nearest cage. "Unfortunately for all other parties, however, etiquette dictates that you belong to the first vampire who marked you, and I've been tracking you since you crawled out of that hole in the Old City. What *were* you thinking?"

The feral vampire sinks into a half crouch before I can answer. "I don't care for etiquette."

The second gentleman glances at the ceiling—at the mutilated corpse still dangling high above us—in distaste. "Clearly."

"Gentlemen," the woman says warily. "She doesn't look willing."

"I don't *care*," the feral vampire repeats with a snarl, sinking lower.

The raven-haired vampire sighs in resignation. "Let us be civil about this. Etiquette is subjective, of course, but I should still hate to destroy other vampires. The girl is no more than a mouthful— hardly enough to satisfy any one of us—so perhaps we can *share* her. I personally favor the femoral artery in the thigh." He licks his lips, staring at my legs, and inches closer. "Which leaves her underarm and throat unattended, as well as that *delectable* wound above her heart."

"I suppose the blood *is* much sweeter under the arm," the second gentleman says grudgingly. He looks to the feral vampire. "What say you, Yannick? We shall even allow you first bite."

The feral vampire hisses in agreement.

All three turn to the woman. "Madeleine?" the raven-haired vampire asks.

But the woman, Madeleine, edges toward the door, shaking her head with thinly veiled fear. "If what she says is true—if Odessa tracks her to us—Michal will not be far behind." She waves a brown hand in my direction, inhaling deep. "Can you not smell the castle on her? She is his guest."

The raven-haired vampire strolls toward me with an elegant shrug. "He has not yet bitten her. She remains unclaimed."

Hesitating, Madeleine swallows hard and glances once more at my bleeding chest. "Michal will not like this."

"Michal is not *here*," the other gentleman says impatiently, "but if you so fear him, by all means . . . leave her to us. I am hungry. Yannick?" Cold hands seize my shoulders from behind, and I cannot help it—I close my eyes, the last of my bluster vanishing. Because I am not Jean Luc or Lou or Reid, and I cannot laugh in Death's face, cannot pretend to be brave as the feral vampire lowers his mouth to my throat. His breath is foul.

I will not be quick, he promised.

I tense, waiting for the first brutal lash of pain—and something streaks past my ear instead.

It imbeds in Yannick's skull.

My eyes snap open as he releases me, as his head quite literally *explodes* in a shower of blood and gore. It douses my face, my throat, my chest in cold viscera. Whirling—clamping my mouth shut, clutching the basin for dear life—I watch a wooden stake clatter from the carnage to the ground, followed by his decapitated body. Before my very eyes, his figure begins to age, to desiccate, until it resembles not a man but a shriveled husk several hundred years old. *His true age.*

I stare at the dead vampire as if from underwater, a terrible ringing in my ears. His innards remain on my skin. I cannot acknowledge them. Cannot acknowledge *him.* The entire scene is so familiar—so *gruesome*—that my mind simply . . . withdraws. Between one blink and the next, the outside world stills, and I fold into that small, quiet place I discovered in my sister's coffin. That place where I cease to exist.

No one is coming to save you.

The other vampires freeze instantly, their eyes darting in unison to the aviary door, where Michal leans casually against it.

"Forgive me." In the dark leather surcoat from earlier—not a single hair out of place, his boots polished and his tie pristine—he pushes from the doorjamb with the grace and repose of an aristocrat. If not for the lethal glint in his eyes, he might pass as one. "Loath as I am to crash the party, I must say, I felt quite distressed at not receiving an invitation." He pauses to pick a nonexistent speck of dirt from his sleeve. "I am the host, after all. And as such, a host *might* take offense to his guest being stalked, cornered, and terrorized in the street like common prey. A host might seek . . . restitution."

Slowly, the vampires begin backing away—from him, from

me, from each other. Madeleine's eyes flit to the nearest window, while the raven-haired vampire lifts placating hands. "We meant no offense, Michal, of course. We would never *dream* of harming your esteemed guest."

"Of course," Michal repeats silkily, shadowing his steps.

The second gentleman bows, careful not to break eye contact. "We meant only to save her from the clutches of *Yannick*, Michal. The poor creature was unhinged." He gestures to the ceiling, shaking his head with regret. "You did us all a service, really, by ridding the isle of such boorishness."

Michal nods almost pleasantly. "No one will miss Yannick."

"*Exactly*—"

"You are, however, wrong about one thing, Laurent."

The second gentleman's eyes widen. "I—I am?"

"The curve between neck and shoulder"—suddenly, Michal stands directly in front of him, lifting a hand to caress the slope of the gentleman's neck—"is where blood tastes the sweetest."

Laurent is going to die.

The realization comes slowly at first, then all at once, as Laurent's pallid face loses the last of its color. He knows it too. The predator has become the prey, and Michal—he relishes this moment, relishes the wild, panicked gleam in this weaker vampire's eyes. Part of me relishes it too. Indeed, something dark stirs in my subconscious as I watch Laurent go completely and utterly still.

Part of me hopes Michal will not be quick.

"Michal." Though Laurent's voice drops to a whisper, the aviary has fallen quiet enough to hear every word. Even the birds sense imminent danger. "Please, mon roi. We just wanted to play with her."

We just wanted to play with her.

To *play* with her.

The words are like needles, pricking my subconscious and jolting me back into my body. Yannick's blood drips from my fingers as I tighten my grip on the stake. "I am not a doll," I say quietly.

Frowning, Michal turns his face toward mine—just the slightest tilt of his chin—and in that split second, Laurent moves. He lifts his arms with lightning speed, breaking Michal's hold on his throat, and lunges with bared teeth. Michal, however, moves faster. He plunges his fist into Laurent's chest like a knife through butter, twisting, and when he pulls it back out again, he holds Laurent's beating heart.

I stare at it in mute horror. In disbelief.

The raven-haired vampire bolts for the door, but Michal is somehow there too, repeating the process with brutal efficiency. Both bodies—shriveling, desiccating—fall to the earth in unison. The birds nearest them shriek and strain against their chains, collide with the bars of their cages, but Michal ignores them all. Tossing the hearts aside, he turns to the last remaining vampire, Madeleine, who still hovers across the aviary. Perhaps she knows better than to flee. Perhaps she knows she is already dead.

With alarming ease, he tears a wooden tread from the staircase, snapping it in half with his bare hands. It forms two crude stakes. "Please," Madeleine begs, backing into the wall. "I'm sorry—"

"As am I, Madeleine." Michal shakes his head in disappointment. "As am I."

Apprehension flutters in my stomach.

Because Madeleine—she isn't Laurent.

"Wait!" Before I realize what I'm doing, I lunge after him,

grimacing at the fresh bolt of pain up my leg. It instantly crumples. The ground rises up with alarming speed, but then Michal is there, catching me. He doesn't glance down—doesn't acknowledge our embrace at all—his eyes instead narrowing on Madeleine, who risks a quick step toward the door.

"Do not move," he warns her. Or perhaps me. Black blooms in my vision as I try and fail to escape his hold. My broken arm dangles uselessly at my side, the other trapped between us. My head throbs in time with my heart. Recognizing the battle lost, I collapse against him and nod weakly toward Madeleine.

"This woman—she told them not to hurt me. She respected your—your *claim* on me. She told the others there would be consequences."

His arms tighten slightly around my waist. "She was correct."

"You would truly kill a loyal subject in cold blood? An innocent?"

A cruel twist of his lips. "You know I would."

Mila could not have been more wrong about him. Even *Morgane* cared about the lives of her people. This man—this *creature*—has completely lost whatever once made him human. "If you really want to send a message," I say through gritted teeth, "you need a messenger."

"A messenger," he repeats coldly. At last, he deigns to look at me, his eyes flicking from my twisted ankle to my shattered elbow, the bloody gash above my breast. His jaw clenches almost imperceptibly, and too late, I realize his chest doesn't move against mine. *He isn't breathing.* "She inflicted none of these injuries?"

I shake my head, and another wave of black crests through my vision.

"You wish her to live?"

"I do."

"Why?"

"Because"—I struggle to keep my eyes open, my head upright—"she doesn't deserve to *die*."

Michal stares down at me in disbelief.

I don't know whether Madeleine killed the man outside; I hope she didn't. I hope he consented to the feeding, just as Arielle did. *I hope.* Though Michal's lip curls at whatever he sees in my expression, he finally jerks his chin to Madeleine. "Fine. Go. Tell the others what you saw here tonight. Tell them their king still protects this isle—from dangers both within and without—and tell them Célie Tremblay spared your pitiful life."

Madeleine's mouth parts in confusion, but she doesn't hesitate. Bowing hastily, she casts me one last grateful look before streaking past without a word. Unlike her peers, she kept her life today. She escaped certain death.

And so did I.

Exhaling in relief, I unclench my limbs, but Michal doesn't release me. Indeed, the tension radiating from his body only seems to build. He struggles to empty his expression, to school his features into that cold mask of calm, but fails miserably. His eyes glint colder than I've ever seen them as he stares at the door. We stand that way—still and silent—for several more seconds before he says, "I told you not to leave the castle."

Frowning, I try again to extricate myself. "I thought you had business elsewhere tonight."

"I returned only moments ago."

"How fortunate for all of us."

"How *fortunate* that Odessa scented Yannick," he says tightly, "and rushed to find me. If she hadn't, this night would've ended very poorly for you. Yannick's tastes ran darker than most."

The information shouldn't surprise me—it *shouldn't*—yet disgust still twists low in my belly. *Birds of a feather.* "You knew Yannick tortured and maimed his prey, yet you did nothing to stop him? You allowed him free rein of the isle?"

Without warning, Michal sweeps me into his arms, crosses the aviary, and deposits me carefully on the stairs before stripping off his coat. Though each of his movements remains carefully controlled, carefully *leashed*, his jaw looks hard enough to shatter glass. "It is not my job to rein in Yannick. Where are you hurt?"

"You are the *king.* It is your *only* job to rein in Yannick. You're supposed to ensure the safety and well-being of your subjects, to maintain law and order—"

"Vampires are not humans." His tone brooks no argument. "We possess none of your tender feelings, and we abide by only one law—a law you have undoubtedly broken tonight. Now, where are you *hurt?*" When I glare at him stubbornly, his eyes flash, and he tears his sleeve up his forearm, sinking into another crouch before me. "Your left ankle and wrist are broken, and you've lacerated your chest, both palms, and eight fingers. Shall I conduct a more thorough examination, mademoiselle, or will you answer my question?"

We scowl at each other for a beat.

"My knees," I say grudgingly. "I scraped my knees as well."

His eyes flick to my torn skirt. "Your knees."

It isn't a question, but I answer it regardless. "Yes."

"How did you scrape your knees, Célie Tremblay?"

"I jumped down the stairs fleeing Yannick."

"I see." His hands—still bloody and cold and *wrong*—lift to my jaw with surprising lightness, probing the bones there, pushing my matted hair away from my face. I wince at the slight indention he finds at my crown, at the pain that explodes behind my eyes. His mouth sets in a grim line. "And your head?"

"I jumped down the stairs," I repeat stupidly, the words slurring a bit as my adrenaline fades. The pain builds in earnest without it. "Do you think I have a concussion?"

"That seems likely."

I'm going to lose consciousness soon. I know it as certainly as I knew Laurent would die. As if sensing the same, Michal slides a knife from his polished boot, dragging the blade along his wrist, and crimson blood wells upon white skin, stark and startling. I recoil instinctively as he lifts it to my mouth. "What are you—?" Though I try to scramble backward—up the stairs, *away*—he moves in a blur to sit on the tread above me, blocking my escape. His uninjured arm snakes around my shoulders, and he traps me in the cradle of his legs. His mouth tickles my hair.

"Drink."

"I will *not*—"

"My blood will heal you."

"I— *What?*" I shake my head, convinced I misheard, only to pitch sideways as delirious pain bolts through my temples. "I can't—I'm not going to—to drink your blood," I finish weakly. Though Lou, Reid, and Beau have occasionally drunk Coco's blood mixed with honey to heal themselves—a magic unique to Dames Rouges—this is not the same. This is not Coco; this is *Michal*, and the thought of consuming such a vital part of him, of taking him into my body, is unthinkable. Perverse. I watch the blood drip slowly down his forearm, repressing a shiver. *Isn't it?*

"We have no healers on Requiem, Célie. If you don't drink my blood, your bones could set incorrectly, and your wounds could become infected, resulting in a slow, tedious death—and that's only if your head injury doesn't kill you first." Though I open my mouth to argue, to refuse, I fall back against his shoulder instead—the entire world tilting—and stare at his blood as the wound begins to close. I do not want to die. I've never wanted to die.

Jean Luc won't like this.

"Going once . . . ," Michal says quietly, holding his wrist within my reach. "Going twice . . ."

At the very last second, I struggle to lean forward, to seize his wrist. I needn't bother. The second he feels my intent, he presses it to my lips, and the strange, metallic taste of his blood explodes on my tongue. My head instantly reels with it. Stars burst in my eyes as the pain in my temples vanishes, along with the pain in my elbow. My ankle. My hands and chest and—and—

A small, shameless noise escapes my throat.

My eyelids clench shut at the sound, and I pull his arm closer, drinking deeper. With each pull of my mouth, delicious heat spikes through my belly until I'm near delirious with it, until I'm on *fire* with it. When I press backward, into his chest, his thighs—desperate for his cool skin—his body shifts subtly in response, tightening like a snake about to strike. "Célie," he warns, but I don't hear him. I feel lighter than I have in weeks—in years—yet heavier too, aching and tingling and *needing* something I cannot name.

Frustrated, I lave his skin with my tongue, and he curses, his voice lower and harsher than before. Though he rises to his feet, I move with him, my mouth feverish upon his skin. Unable to stop. He pulls his arm away, murmuring, "Enough," but I whirl to face him with a gasp, my cheeks flushed and my skin tight. *Too* tight. A pulse throbs deep in my belly as I stare at him. As he stares at me.

He still doesn't breathe.

The sight should've frightened me. Though my injuries have healed, blood still drips down my chest, and Michal is a vampire. He can hear my heartbeat. He can scent my emotions. And when his eyes narrow, flicking almost reluctantly to my neckline, the sight doesn't frighten me at all. No. It fills me with a strange, heady sense of power instead. Like if I don't kiss him this very instant, I might combust.

So I stretch up to my toes and do just that.

CHAPTER TWENTY-SIX

Reunion

His hands descend on my shoulders before I can touch him, and he forces me down a step. Two. Through clenched teeth, he asks, "What did your note contain?"

"What note?" I ask breathlessly, struggling against his ironclad hold. My brow dips in confusion. In *despair.* Though my hands still reach for his rigid chest, he keeps me firmly at arm's length, so I settle for stroking his forearms instead. His elbows. His biceps. "Please touch me, Michal. Please."

Those black eyes grow impossibly darker. "No."

"*Why?*"

"Because you don't actually want me to touch you. The blood of a vampire is a natural aphrodisiac—it makes transition easier. The older the vampire, the stronger its effect." A bitter smile twists his mouth, but it doesn't reach his eyes. "I am . . . very old, making my blood more powerful than most." When he speaks again, his voice is cool, almost dispassionate, and his gaze slides away from me altogether. "Your body's response will soon pass."

The strange words pierce the thick haze of my thoughts. *Aphrodisiac. Transition.* Like a lightning strike, Jean Luc's face follows, searing my mind's eye with his disbelief, his *disgust* that I could ever act so selfishly. I lift a trembling hand to my swollen lips. I can still taste Michal's blood on my tongue.

Your body's response will soon pass.

"No." Exhaling the word on a whisper, I close my eyes in revulsion, unable to look at him for another second. Unable to look at *me*. My hands fall limply to my sides. "This—this didn't happen. This *can't* have happened."

"Say it again," he says shortly. "Perhaps you'll make it true."

Releasing my shoulders, he stalks past me down the stairs, but even the slightest brush of his arm sends a fresh bolt of heat through my core. And shame. Hideous, *horrifying* shame. It curdles in my stomach as I force my eyes open, staring down at the smooth, newly healed skin of my palms. Envisioning Jean Luc and broken Balisardas and Babette. I suck in a sharp breath.

Babette.

The forgotten silver stake glints at my feet.

"In the meantime"—he unrolls his sleeve without glancing back at me, thrusts his arms into his leather surcoat—"you will tell me *exactly* what your note entailed. You chose the aviary for a reason." His careful control never falters as he stoops to retrieve the handkerchief from the vampire's desiccated body, as he calmly wipes the gore from his hands. "What did you tell your friends about us, Célie Tremblay?"

Slowly, I bend to retrieve the stake. My heartbeat pounds a relentless beat in my ears. Michal plans to murder those friends, and I just—I just drank his *blood*. I just tasted his *skin*, and even *worse*—I'd wanted to—to—

Visceral loathing courses through my veins, and I refuse to finish the thought. My hands shake with purpose as I descend the stairs, as my vision narrows on his broad leather-clad back.

On the spot directly behind his heart.

"I told them how to kill you," I snarl, lunging as he turns.

For the span of a single second—perhaps less—I relish the surprise on his beautifully cruel face as the silver strikes his chest. The stake pierces his thin shirt easily, and where it touches his bare skin, smoke curls in a startling plume. Pain flares briefly in his eyes. Then anger.

Bright, biting anger.

He catches my wrist before I can drive the silver into his heart, wrenching the stake from his chest and hurling it across the aviary, where it shatters instantly against the door. The resolve in my chest shatters with it. *Shit.* Stumbling backward, I stare up at him with wide eyes.

He bares his fangs in a feral smile.

Shit, shit, *shit.*

Though I try to flee, he moves too quickly, and the entire aviary blurs until we lurch to a sickening halt just before the door. Spinning me with those impossibly strong hands—one capturing my wrists, the other my nape—he walks me leisurely into the door. Silver powder from the stake still clings to the wood. It abrades my cheek. "Clever girl," he says, his voice tight at my ear, darkly amused, "but you really shouldn't play with sharp objects, especially with vampire blood in your system. You might hurt yourself."

"Let me *go*—" I snarl, but he only presses closer. His body coiling tighter.

"No."

"I swear if you don't unhand me, I'll—I'll—"

"You'll what?" Smoke still undulates between us. It curls

around my hair and shoulders. Much more concerning, however, are his *teeth*. They linger just above my head, taunting me, as his chest rumbles with derisive laughter. I feel every inch of it down my spine. "What, *exactly*, is your plan, mademoiselle? Your stake is gone. You have no other weapons, and even if you did—you are human on an isle full of vampires. The scent of your blood has already attracted unwanted attention. At this very moment, a dozen Éternels wait just beyond this door, each of them eager to learn your fate. Each of them *hungry*." His hand on my wrists falls away, as does the one at my nape. "Shall I leave you to them?"

I press closer to the door, repressing a shiver. Goose bumps erupt down my arms. As gently as his hands touched me, they tore into Laurent's chest cavity only moments ago. *To protect you*, a small voice in my head argues, but it isn't enough. And in the end, it doesn't matter what happens to me. "What did she take from you?" I ask quietly, bracing myself against the wood. My fingers curl. The silver powder clings to the blood still there, coating each tip of my nails. "Coco?"

"Something she can never give back."

"Are you going to kill her?"

"Perhaps."

One breath.

Two.

I whirl, raking my nails across his cheek, but when he rears backward—roaring in pain—the door blows open unexpectedly, toppling me into his open arms. Angry red claw marks burn and smoke across his features as he seizes my arms and snarls.

"Michal Vasiliev." Mila's furious, *unexpected* voice fills the aviary in the next second. "You cannot hear me, but if you don't release her this *instant*, I'll drag your enormous corpse into the afterlife for good."

I gasp, whipping my head around to face her, and she descends on the aviary like a breaking storm—her expression dark, her eyes flashing—as the cages around us rattle. The birds shriek. I can still hear Michal's sharp inhalation of breath, however. I can feel his hands tighten on me. Heedless, Mila swirls around us, gusting my hair in all directions. "Did he hurt you, Célie? I swear on everything holy, if that's *your* blood—"

"It isn't," I say quickly, following her agitated circles, but stop short when Michal's head turns to follow her too. All emotion empties from his face. He blinks once, twice, as she draws to a halt beside him to inspect the blood on my chest. I gape at her. Because this shouldn't be possible. I haven't slipped through the veil—we're most *certainly* still in the realm of the living—and none of this makes any sense. "How are you—?"

"You mended *one* tear in the veil, Célie, not all of them." She speaks over me without drawing breath. "They exist everywhere— all around us—and some heal faster than others. How else could Guinevere destroy Michal's study last week? Don't answer that." She slashes a hand. "It doesn't matter. Do you have *any* idea how lucky you are that Yannick didn't eat you? No? Because I'm going to haunt you until you understand that actions have real consequences—"

"Mila." I say her name louder now, and she hesitates, her eyes snapping to mine. Pointedly, I incline my head toward Michal, who stares at her through the smoke rising between them. The burns on his face leap out in sharp relief, but he stands still enough to have been carved from stone. "I think he can see you," I continue with a tight smile, "and I know he can hear me."

Her brows snap together. "But that's impossible. He isn't— Can he—?" She waves a hand in front of his face, recoiling slightly when his eyes follow the movement. "Michal?" she whispers.

His lips barely move around the words, "Hello, little sister."

Her eyes widen in disbelief, and they stare at each other for several agonizingly long seconds. The rest of the aviary seems to fade beneath the intensity of their stare—the owls no longer shriek, the fire no longer crackles. Even the wind seems to pause, apprehensive, as if dreading what comes next. I try not to breathe. Perhaps they'll forget I'm here altogether.

At last, Mila exhales.

"How is this possible?" she asks, her voice still quiet, as if the moment might break at any second. "You've never been able to see me before."

Michal's hand still clutches the bare skin of my arm. The lace sleeve that should've been there hangs limp around my elbow, shredded from my fall. Slowly, he eases his fingers away—his face still granite—before clenching his jaw and replacing them swiftly. "It would seem," he says, staring hard at his hand on my skin, "we have a common acquaintance to thank for that."

"Oh." Mila follows his gaze to where we touch, alabaster against ivory. "It makes sense, I suppose."

"Nothing about this makes sense," Michal says tersely.

And the moment breaks.

Mila's eyes narrow. "Do try to keep up, won't you, brother?

Surely you've realized by now that Célie is a Bride." Though Michal opens his mouth to respond, she speaks over him quickly, determinedly, with the air of someone trying to steer the conversation away from something. Or perhaps flee the conversation altogether. "She's been touched by Death, which is why she can reach through the veil—and also why she can see me here. If this encounter is any indication, that neat little trick of hers temporarily extends to whoever *she* chooses to touch." She humphs, casting a withering glance at his clenched hand. "Or *doesn't* choose to touch. Please tell me you aren't responsible for the gore all over her person, Michal, because if you are, those marks on your face are the least of your worries."

"Mila." He speaks her name with surprising patience, but again, she ignores him, turning away with a toss of her opaque hair.

"If you are, I'll simply have to tell Guinevere about this little development, and every time you touch Célie—even the slightest brush of her arm—Guin will be there, breathing over you like a rabid dog."

"Mila," he says again, his voice darkening slightly. "You're deflecting."

I watch him in rapt fascination. Though he tries to remain hard, impassive, his eyes have begun to burn with strange emotion as he looks at his sister. Exasperation, yes, but there is also a softness there. Never before have I seen him look so—so *human.* The realization would've knocked me back a step if he hadn't been clutching my arm. I scowl up at him, tugging fruitlessly against his hold. I'm the worst sort of idiot for trying to humanize a monster.

But even monsters care for their sisters.

"She'll draw another mustache on Uncle Vladimir," Mila

continues hotly, pacing by the stairs in agitation. "I swear she will. Maybe she'll draw horns and black out his teeth this time too. Maybe I'll give her the ink." Michal exhales heavily, but he doesn't say her name again, instead waiting with thinly veiled patience for her to pause for breath. Which she doesn't. "Guin is the ghost who helped you break into Michal's study," she says to me, and I tense at the betrayal, shooting a quick glance at Michal. He will not be distracted, however. His gaze remains fixed solely upon Mila. "Michal broke her heart, and she never forgave him, even after death. She still moons around his study, raging and weeping and fawning over him in equal measure, even though he can't hear a word she says. It's *heartbreaking.*"

"Are you finished?" Michal asks.

Mila lifts her chin. "No."

Yet it seems, at last, that she's run out of things to say. Undeterred, she opens her mouth to try again, but Michal shakes his head slowly. "Enough, Mila." The words are less command than plea, but Mila still floats to a halt by the door, her shoulders curling inward. Defeated. "Tell me what happened. Tell me why you went to Cesarine."

She refuses to look at him, instead glaring at the nearest stair tread. "You know why I went to Cesarine."

Cesarine? Brows furrowing, I glance between them as Michal's lip curls. "Dimitri," he says.

"You say his name like a plague."

"Because he *is* a plague. He never should've asked you—"

"Stop it, Michal." Mila whirls, gesturing angrily to the sky beyond the door. Thick storm clouds have rolled in since I left Monsieur Marc's shop, and thunder rumbles in answer. "You act as if we've never sought the help of witches before. Wasn't it *your* brilliant idea to ask them for eternal night?"

"Hundreds of years ago—since which time we've carefully culled our existence from their memories. You threatened to expose our entire race for the sake of *one* vampire."

"For Dimitri. For the sake of *Dimitri*. He is your *cousin*, and he needs your help—"

"What he needs is self-restraint, not a mystical cure from the hand of our enemy." Michal's nostrils flare as his careful self-control begins to slip. "He left you there. Did you know that? Half-hidden in the refuse behind Saint-Cécile, where I assume you thought to find La Dame des Sorcières. He *left* you."

"It wasn't his fault." Mila rises to her full height now, casting the force of her defiance upon Michal. Opaque tears sparkle in her eyes. "He was *frightened*—"

"Who was it, Mila?" Between blinks, Michal seizes my hand, dragging me along behind him as he advances on his sister. His expression grows blacker than the storm clouds outside. "Who did this to you? *Tell me.*"

But I cannot keep quiet any longer. Cesarine, Saint-Cécile, La Dame des Sorcières—the words are familiar to me, *sickeningly* familiar, yet somehow half-formed, like trying to fit together a puzzle without all the pieces. My chest tightens with the confusion of it all, and I dig in my heels, trying and failing to slow his approach. "What does Lou have to do with any of this?" I ask wildly. "Why were you at Saint-Cécile? And who did *what* to you?"

Michal slows to a halt, glowering at his sister, and an unspoken question passes between them. Mila sighs.

Then, reluctantly, she brushes aside her hair and pulls down her collar, revealing perfect twin puncture wounds at her throat.

Just like Babette's.

I stare at the marks as if through a tunnel, unable to understand. They feel *wrong* somehow, aberrant, and even I can sense they shouldn't be there. Vampires can die, yes—I just watched Michal kill three—but to drain one of its blood? How could such a thing happen? They're too strong, too fast, too *lethal* to be hunted as they hunt others. A slick, slimy sensation unfurls in my stomach as I grasp at the only other explanation, the only possibility that still makes sense. Recoiling from Michal, I breathe, "You killed your own sister?" Then, to Mila, louder now— "Is that why you refused to see him? He *killed* you? He drank your blood?"

"Don't be disgusting." Mila releases her collar to hide the offensive marks once more. "Vampires only drink from vampires in *very* nonfamilial situations—"

"You refused to see me?" Michal asks in a quiet voice. He sounds almost *hurt*.

"But he still *killed* you, right?" I ask over him.

She waves a curt, impatient hand at both of us. "I *told* you, Célie—my brother didn't kill those creatures, and he didn't kill me either." Her lips purse, and she glares once more at the stair tread, carefully avoiding Michal's gaze. "But I also can't tell you who did."

Michal instantly closes the distance between them. "*Why?*"

"Because I don't remember. My last memories—they're just . . . gone."

"Witchcraft," Michal snarls.

And there it is. The final piece. His quest for vengeance at last clicks into place. Trying and failing to wrench my arm from his grasp, I settle for glaring up at him instead. "Coco didn't kill those people. She loved Babette, and even if she hadn't, a blood witch would never *drain* a creature of its blood." My eyes flick pointedly to Yannick, to Laurent. "Not like a vampire would."

"A vampire," he says, his voice dripping disdain, "would not have killed a member of the royal family."

"How do you know? I overheard the celestials talking in Monsieur Marc's—"

"Because Mila is not *me*." He says the word through clenched teeth. "Everyone who gazed upon her loved her."

I snort at him in disbelief—and pity. "You're allowing your opinion of your sister to cloud your judgment. Even if the killer had no personal grudge against Mila, they would've known her death would affect you." I turn apologetic eyes to Mila, who watches us with a peculiar expression. "You can't remember your final moments, but perhaps someone else can remember theirs. Is Babette beyond the veil? Can you bring her to us?"

"Not every soul chooses to remain near the realm of the living, Célie." For the first time since I've met her, something akin to regret shadows Mila's beautiful features. "Most choose to go . . . on."

"Oh." For some inexplicable reason, the words feel like a blow to my chest. They shouldn't. Of course they shouldn't. The final resting place of spirits shouldn't *matter* right now—not with a bloodthirsty vampire currently holding my hand—yet I can't help it. *Pippa.* Her name echoes through my mind like a phantom hand, as if she herself has reached through the veil to touch me.

But she didn't.

And she won't.

Because if anyone has ever been brave enough to go on, it would be my sister.

As if sensing my thoughts, Michal tightens his fingers around mine ever so slightly. "I would hazard a guess," he says, voice low, "that Babette isn't available for questioning in this realm or the next." At my frown, he adds, "Two nights ago, her body vanished from the morgue."

"*What?*" Mila and I gasp in unison.

Michal tilts his head, studying me with an unreadable expression. "She was Babette's lover, you say?"

"Coco *didn't do this*," I snap, losing patience entirely, but he doesn't allow me to pull away.

"We'll see." He extends his free hand toward the door and motions for Mila to exit before him. "Come. We must discuss next steps, the three of us, and it should be done away from prying ears."

Mila, however, doesn't move.

"Michal," she says softly.

Unlike his sister, Michal doesn't bother with deflection. "Don't do this, Mila."

"You asked why I didn't want to see you." She draws closer, reaching out to touch her brother's cheek. Whether or not he can feel her, I don't know, but he braces in the doorway just the same, his hand tight and cold around mine. A tether. *Or perhaps*, I realize with an unpleasant start, *I am his.*

"You know better than this, Michal," Mila says, her gaze uncharacteristically solemn. "I am dead. *Truly* dead this time, which means there's nothing left for us to discuss. I'm not Guinevere; I refuse to haunt you, and no amount of vengeance will bring me back. Darkness stirs on the horizon, looming closer each moment, and this realm will need you—*both* of you"—her eyes flick briefly to mine—"in order to survive it. You must let me go, brother. Please."

"I will *not*." Eyes blazing brighter than I've ever seen them, he lifts our linked hands, and her hand passes straight through his face. "Because I *have* brought you back—twice now—and I have no intention of losing you again. I *will not* lose you again."

Mila looks at him sadly.

"Loath as I am to admit it"—I step between them before Michal can do something truly stupid, like try to kidnap his sister—"I agree with him. You and the other ghosts see things from the other side that could help us find the killer." I hesitate then, unsure how to communicate the strange, niggling pressure in my chest. Something still bothers me about Mila's death, about Babette's, about this mysterious killer and looming darkness. About my own strange powers. They can't all be isolated incidents, but I can find no immediate connection. I exhale hard. None of it makes *sense*. Like a sore tooth, I bite down on it all again and again, yet I gain no relief.

Perhaps I'm imagining things. Perhaps there's no connection at all.

Perhaps I just don't want to be alone with Michal.

"What if—what if they're the same person?" I ask Mila tentatively. *Please don't leave.* "The killer and the man who follows me? The dark figure?"

Michal looks at me sharply.

Mila, however, shakes her head in resignation. Whatever fire she had during her confrontation with Michal has vanished, leaving only a small, defeated woman in its wake. "I've told you everything I know, Célie. The rest, I fear, is up to you."

With that, she floats upward—where even Michal cannot follow—drifting farther and farther until she melts into shadow and out of sight.

CHAPTER TWENTY-SEVEN

Michal's Promise

Half an hour later, Michal pours himself a tumbler of absinthe in his study.

He doesn't speak—doesn't look at me—as he unstoppers the crystal decanter, pours the foul liquid, and throws the whole thing back in one swallow. I watch the pale column of his throat work in grudging fascination. I didn't know vampires could drink liquor, yet here he is, unhinging his jaw like a snake.

The burns on his face shine slick and angry in the firelight.

I can't bring myself to feel guilty.

His silence soon stretches too long, however, and I shift in my seat, the soft rustle of my skirt joining the steady *tick tick tick* of the clock on his desk. I cross and uncross my ankles. I knot my fingers in my lap. I feign a cough to clear my throat. Still he ignores me. At last, unable to bear the awkwardness another second, I ask, "Why did you bring me here? And why haven't your wounds healed?"

He pours himself another glass of absinthe in response. "Silver."

I wait patiently for him to explain; when he doesn't, I resist the urge to roll my eyes. "Will they just . . . remain on your face forever, then? You'll look like you've been mauled by a bear for all eternity?" I don't remind him that *I* was the bear, not when his shoulders look so tense and forbidding.

After Mila left us, he led me from the aviary to his study without a word, refusing to touch me again. "She'll be back," he said ominously. "The temptation to meddle is too great."

Despite his certainty, however, she didn't reappear. Not then and not now.

"My wounds will remain until I drink something stronger than absinthe." Michal cuts an arch look over his shoulder. "Are you offering?"

The shadows beneath his eyes seem deeper after his encounter with her, the planes of his face sharper. Harder. He looks . . . tired. "No," I say. Because I don't feel sympathy for him. His sister completely and thoroughly dismissed him—*and me*, I think mutinously—but he still doesn't deserve my sympathy. Even if he isn't *the* killer, he is certainly *a* killer, and—and I don't exactly know where that leaves us.

Or why he's forcing me to sit with him.

"Why did Mila want to heal Dimitri?" I fidget with the ribbon at my wrist, unwilling to look at him any longer. "Why did they need to find Lou?" *And at the Church, of all places?*

At last, Michal turns to lean against the sideboard, considering me. I watch him swirl his absinthe leisurely from my periphery. My mother always called it the Devil's drink. It makes sense that he'd like it. "Dimitri suffers from bloodlust," he says after another long moment.

I don't wait for the awkward silence this time. "And what is *bloodlust?*"

"A uniquely vampiric affliction. When Dimitri feeds, he loses consciousness. Many vampires forget themselves in the hunt, but a vampire affected by bloodlust goes beyond that—he remembers nothing, feels nothing, and inevitably kills his prey in gruesome and horrific ways. Left too long, he becomes an animal like Yannick." I can't help it—now I do glance up at him. Shadows cut sharp beneath his cheekbones as his gaze drops to his glass once more. He stares hard at the emerald liquid. "Usually, we dispatch those infected quickly and quietly. Vampires with bloodlust are a liability to everyone. They cannot keep our secret."

"But Dimitri is your cousin."

A hard, self-deprecating smile twists his features. "Dimitri is my cousin."

"You love him," I say shrewdly. "You blame him for Mila's death, but you still love him, otherwise he'd already be dead."

Michal's lip curls at that, and my hands twist the fabric of my skirt as another thought, altogether unwelcome, intrudes in the space between us. Love blinded Michal to his sister—he still cannot fathom why anyone would want to hurt her—but what if it also blinds him to Dimitri? Michal might not have killed his sister and the others, but *someone* did. Someone drained the blood from their bodies and left those bodies all over Cesarine. How long, exactly, had Dimitri and Mila been in Cesarine before she died? A week? Longer?

Enough time to feed on a human, Dame Blanche, Dame Rouge, melusine, and loup garou?

Beneath Michal's black stare, I don't dare voice my suspicion—not after Mila—but there it is, growing stronger with each tick of his maiden clock.

Dimitri has bloodlust.

Dimitri was the last person with Mila before she died.

Though Mila claims vampires only feed on other vampires

in strictly nonfamilial situations—whatever *that* means—would Dimitri know who he fed upon in the throes of his bloodlust? Michal himself just said vampires with the affliction often lose consciousness, so it stands to reason that he wouldn't.

Dimitri is an addict. Michal's ominous words drift back to me on a chilling whisper. *He has thought of nothing but your blood since he made your acquaintance yesterday. That lovely throat has become his obsession.*

Mila's voice soon joins. *At the heart of it all is a figure. A man.*

Grief shrouds his face.

He needs your blood, Célie.

A shiver skitters down my spine, and I sit rigid in my seat, clenching my hands in my skirt. *Does Dimitri know I'm a Bride?* But—no. Michal didn't know until Mila told him earlier, and he certainly won't be sharing that information with his estranged cousin any time soon. I relax a little, exhaling soft. For now, my secret is safe.

"And what do you know of love, Célie Tremblay?" Michal asks softly. I startle at the question, returning to the room with an unpleasant lurch. Nothing good ever comes when Michal uses that voice. Indeed, a cool, calculating gleam has entered his eyes, and without warning, he crosses to his desk. When he sets his empty tumbler upon it with a decisive *clink*, I recoil slightly in my seat. "Humans always speak as if they're experts on the subject, but in my experience, nothing is so fickle as the human heart." In a blur of movement, he opens the top drawer, clicks something within, and withdraws—

My heart plummets to the floor.

He withdraws my engagement ring.

It sparkles between us in the firelight like a thousand tiny suns, bright and pure and eternal, and my throat grows thick just looking at it. *Jean.* Cheeks flushing, I lurch to my feet to seize it, but of course, Michal moves faster. The ring is there and gone again before I can take a single step. "Prove me wrong, mademoiselle," he says, lifting it into the air between us. "Tell me why you didn't wear it, and I'll gladly return it to you."

Pressure burns behind my eyes, but I refuse to cry in front of this wretched man. He needn't know that I haven't thought about Jean Luc, *really* thought about Jean Luc, since I arrived here. He needn't know about our confrontation in the library, about Jean's failures as a partner, about my own horrible failures as one too. He needn't know that I didn't wear the ring because I—because—

I can't even think the words.

"I don't know," I snap instead, crossing my arms tight against my chest. "Why do *you* care so much either way? That's twice now you've mentioned my engagement. Do you have nothing better to do than pry into the relationship of two people you don't even know? Aren't you the *king* of all vampires?"

The cruel gleam in Michal's eyes fades at whatever he sees in my expression, and after another moment, he shakes his head in disgust. Perhaps at me. Perhaps at himself. And I hate him—I *hate* him—because part of me hates myself too.

When he tosses the ring to me in the next second, I jolt and almost drop it. He pretends not to notice. "Take it. I have no use for such a silly trinket anyway."

My hand trembles slightly as I stare down at it, torn with hideous indecision. If I slip the ring onto my finger, I'm admitting something to Michal. If I don't, I'm admitting something else altogether. He spares me the humiliation of an audience, however, by turning and stalking back to his sideboard, busying himself with something I cannot see.

Self-loathing courses through me as I push the ring down my corset and out of sight. "Where is my silver cross?" I ask him, surprised at how steady my voice sounds.

He doesn't turn. "That depends entirely on you."

"Then give it to me. I want it."

"No," he says calmly, sliding the silver cross from his pocket and dangling it aloft by its chain. His fingers smoke slightly at the contact, and the pendant spins and winks in the firelight like a mirage. "Not until we reach an agreement."

"What kind of *agreement?*"

At last, he turns, clenching the cross in one hand and offering me a tumbler of absinthe in the other. "Quite a simple one. Are you with me, Célie Tremblay, or are you against me?"

My eyes dart incredulously from his face to his clenched fist, where the silver continues to sizzle and smoke against his skin. Part of me wants to draw this moment out. Part of me wants to see how long it'll take before his entire hand bursts into flame. The other fills with inexplicable dread at the prospect. I have never seen someone catch fire before, and I don't necessarily want to change that, even with Michal. "Do you still plan to kill Coco?" I ask breathlessly, ignoring the absinthe altogether.

"If the situation calls for it."

My expression hardens. "It doesn't."

"I remain unconvinced."

"And *I* remain unconvinced that you aren't a blackhearted, sadistic madman intent on destroying all that's good in the world. You might not have killed your sister, but you've certainly killed others. I would no sooner trust you than trust an adder."

"Hmm." He considers me for a moment—his expression cool, calm, despite his smoking hand—before tipping my tumbler of absinthe back and pocketing the silver cross once more. He shakes his head in disappointment. "Such a pity. To think, I was going to take you with me."

I wrench my gaze away from his charred palm. "Where?" I ask suspiciously. "*Why?*"

"It doesn't matter now, does it? I'm a blackhearted, sadistic madman who can't be trusted." He tilts his head. "Though, curiously enough, I haven't tried to destroy *you*. Do you not consider yourself among what's good in the world, Célie Tremblay?"

"Stop twisting my words."

"I would never." Then— "Tell me everything you know about Cosette Monvoisin and Babette Trousset."

My eyes narrow at the unexpected turn. "Excuse me?"

"Cosette Monvoisin," he repeats, his own eyes glittering with sudden malice, "and Babette Trousset. You wanted to know why I brought you here, why I want you to accompany me off the isle. I need information on their relationship. Specifically, I need to know why Cosette would've stolen Babette's body from the morgue."

"You think . . . Coco stole Babette's body—?" But the words die swiftly, and realization bursts to life in their wake. "You really are insane. Coco would *never* impede a murder investigation by—by running off with Babette's corpse—"

"Blood witches have peculiar burial rites, do they not? Called ascension?"

"Well, yes, they burn their dead and hang the ashes in secret groves throughout La Fôret des Yeux, but I *repeat*: Coco would not have taken Babette's body without permission."

"Is it true that they believe a witch's soul remains trapped on earth until they ascend? Would Coco wish to subject Babette's soul to such torment, even temporarily? You said they were lovers."

I scowl and lift my chin. "*Anyone* could have moved Babette's body. Just because you have a personal—and extremely misplaced—vendetta against Coco doesn't mean she is guilty. Perhaps the *real* killer returned for her body. Did you ever consider that? Perhaps the healers missed something in the autopsy, something that would've implicated the killer, so he returned to destroy the evidence."

Michal spreads his hands, leaning forward upon his desk. "Enlighten me, please, mademoiselle. If not Coco, who?"

I glare at him, opening and closing my mouth like a fish. Because obviously I don't know *who*. No one in the kingdom knows *who*—not even him—and that is the *entire* godforsaken problem.

"I have two viable paths before me, Célie Tremblay." Straightening, Michal clasps his hands behind his back and strolls casually around his desk. Except there is nothing casual about Michal. Not ever. Each step falls precise, ominous, as he draws to a halt before me. "I can either investigate Cosette Monvoisin, or I can investigate Babette Trousset." His face remains deceptively calm. "Perhaps your friends are innocent. Perhaps they are not. Either way, I *will* avenge the death of my sister, and I pity all those who stand in the way of that vengeance. Now," he says, softer still, "which path will it be?"

A beat of silence.

Dimitri, I almost say, but I catch his name on the tip of my tongue. I have no real evidence that Dimitri killed Mila or anyone else, and until I do, I cannot betray his friendship. Michal tolerates Dimitri's tangential involvement in Mila's death; if I tell him that Dimitri actually *killed* her, Michal won't hesitate. He'll tear the beating heart from his cousin's chest without waiting for proof.

Neither can I betray Coco.

Michal continues to wait, clearly expecting an answer.

"You don't need *me* to tell you anything about Babette Trousset." Frustration spikes, sharp and sudden, at his complete and utter obstinacy. "You can compel any one of the witches in her coven to tell you everything you need to know about her—not that it matters. We have a greater chance of finding a needle in a haystack than finding her body now."

"Let your idiotic brethren find her body. Her body isn't important. What we need to know is why the killer returned for it and not the others."

"They are *not* idiotic," I say hotly.

He waves a dismissive hand. "They are inept. For months now, they've skirted around the periphery, searching for our mystery killer without unearthing a single suspect. In a week, you've managed to position yourself in the very heart of this investigation—as well as learned how to kill vampires, walk through the veil, and communicate with the dead. You also have a unique knowledge of witches, mermaids, and—unless I'm much mistaken—werewolves, all of whom call you friend."

My cheeks flush at the unexpected words. I stare at him, confused, as his praise washes through me in a hot wave. I'm not quite sure if I'm floating or drowning in it, however. Never before has anyone been so—so *flattering* to me, yet from Michal, it somehow isn't flattery at all. By his curt, matter-of-fact tone, we could be discussing the weather. "I"—I blink stupidly, unsure how to respond—"I don't think—"

"Yes, you do," he interrupts. "You *think*, which is why you're twice as valuable as every huntsman in Chasseur Tower. I will not force your hand, however. If you don't wish to join me, I'll return you to your room, and I'll personally ensure you remain unbothered until All Hallows' Eve." A pause. "Is that what you want?"

The soft *tick, tick, tick*s of his maiden clock are the only sounds that punctuate the silence. And my heartbeat. It beats a treacherous rhythm in my chest, threatening to burst forth and ruin everything. *Is that what you want?* No one has ever asked me *that* question before either, and I—I stare at him helplessly. In a handful of hours, I've gone from plotting to kill Michal to—to *what*? Absolving him of guilt? Seeking his praise? I nearly weep with frustration at the impossible choice before me.

If I agree to join Michal, we might find the killer.

If I agree to join Michal, I'll be helping one too.

"Promise you won't kill anyone," I whisper. "P-Promise you'll let the Chasseurs have the killer if we find them, and promise you won't interfere with their sentence."

His reply is swift, instantaneous. His eyes dark. "I promise I won't kill *you*, Célie Tremblay, and that is the only promise I'll ever make. Do we have a deal?"

I close my eyes briefly.

In the end, however, it isn't a choice at all. I cannot simply return to my room, to my shelf, and collect dust while a killer roams free. I cannot ever go back to that place again. *I won't.* "We have a deal," I say quietly, opening my eyes and lifting my hand toward his. It trembles only a little.

A small, dangerous smile pulls the corner of his mouth, and he shakes my hand with his blackened one, his fingers wrapping firmly around mine. No ghosts rise up to meet us this time. No. This touch, this *binding*, is ours alone.

When he pulls away, the silver cross rests in my palm, as brilliant and familiar as ever, and I frown down at the faint initials etched along one side. I've never noticed them before—indeed, wouldn't have noticed them even now if not for the exact angle of the firelight—yet there they are, winking up at me. *BT.*

If we're going to work together, Michal needs to know everything.

"I don't know why the killer returned for Babette and not the others, but Babette . . . she was the only victim found with one of these." Together, we gaze down at the cross. "She didn't worship the Christian god."

Michal's eyes snap to mine. "You think she knew something."

"I think she feared something." *Like a vampire.* I tuck the cross into my skirt pocket, where it lies heavily against my leg. It tethers me to the floor of Michal's study; it tethers me to *Michal.* But I can't turn back now. "Serial killers typically choose victims that fit a certain profile, but the huntsmen have found no discernible pattern among the dead. Perhaps this killer chooses his victims a different way. Perhaps he has a . . . personal connection to them."

Michal doesn't need further explanation. His mind races ahead, his black eyes glinting with anticipation. "Where did Babette live? In Cesarine?"

"No." *And thank God for that.* I shake my head, tears of relief welling up behind my eyelids. Thank God that Babette moved far,

far away from Coco after the Battle of Cesarine. Thank God that Michal has forgotten my friend for now. I can only pray it remains that way. "She lived in Amandine. I overheard her telling—telling someone," I say quickly, "about a place called Les Abysses, but I don't know the address. My parents sold our summer home in Amandine when I was a child."

"I doubt your parents would've approved." Michal steps away from me with a cold smile. "The Abyss is no place for genteel, politely bred ladies."

"You know it?"

"Oh, I know it." He gestures to the door, which opens of its own accord, spilling deep shadows into the room. I rise quickly. "And soon, you will too. We're going to Amandine, pet. If there is any connection between Babette and our killer, we will find it. You should know, however"—his hand snakes up my arm as I pass through the doorway—"if there is nothing to find, only one path remains. Do you understand?"

Our eyes lock in the semidarkness, her name passing between us unspoken.

Coco.

I resist the urge to burn a cross into his cheek forevermore.

"Yes," I say bitterly.

"Good." He releases me with a dismissive nod. "We sail to Belterra tomorrow evening, then. Seven o'clock. Wear something . . . green."

---— ❈ —---

PART III

---— ❈ —---

L'appétit vient en mangeant.

Appetite comes with eating.

CHAPTER TWENTY-EIGHT

To Go Below

I dress in scarlet as an act of rebellion. It's a small thing, perhaps a trivial one, but just because I'm working *with* Michal doesn't mean I'm working *for* him. It feels important to start on equal footing, to remind him that he cannot simply order me around like I'm his servant, or worse—I tug at the silk bodice irritably—his *pet*.

When I meet him in his study at seven o'clock sharp, he appraises my gown with a wry look, as if trying not to grin. My eyes narrow to slits. "Red is my favorite color," I tell him haughtily.

Silhouetted in the doorway, he fastens his black traveling cloak with deft fingers. "Liar."

"I am *not* lying." A pause. "How do *you* know when I'm lying?"

"You make too much eye contact. It's disconcerting." He plucks another thick black cloak from a hook by the door, holding it aloft and gesturing for me to slip my arms through the sleeves. Startled, I do just that, hesitating when he says, "Is there nothing I can say to change your mind?"

The burns across his face have vanished, as have the ones on his hand, leaving behind only smooth, pale skin. My stomach turns slightly at the sight. *They'll remain until I drink something stronger than absinthe.* Perhaps Arielle visited him again. Perhaps someone else. The thought brings bile to my throat, and I pull away from his touch, chastising myself inwardly. I didn't think to bring my own cloak, a beautiful creation of ivory wool and silver buttons. I'd been too determined for Michal to see the scarlet. "Not a thing."

Unable to conceal his smirk any longer, he brushes past me into the corridor. "As you wish."

"Why did you want me to wear green?" I ask him suspiciously. His only answer is a dark chuckle.

As when we arrived in Requiem, a single ship floats in the harbor. Michal doesn't pause to see if I follow as he strides up the gangplank to the sailors who stack simple wooden boxes along the bow. Clutching a stitch in my side, cursing Michal and his preternatural speed, I hasten to follow. My teeth ache from the bitter wind. "Michal! Could you *please* slow—?"

The question dies on my tongue, however, as the wooden boxes take shape in the lamplight. I skid to a halt atop the main deck, staring at them. "Caskets," I breathe.

They're stacking caskets.

Michal's traveling cloak billows behind him as he turns. "Yes. Requiem, Ltd., is the majority supplier of caskets to Belterra." When he smiles, his fangs glint coldly in the bolt of lightning overhead. Already, freezing mist coats our clothes, our hair. The storm tonight promises to be a nasty one. "We have quite the monopoly on the market. No one can compete with our prices. Come along." His gaze flicks irritably toward the sky. "The storm is almost upon us."

A deafening clap of thunder sounds in response, and I jolt forward, catching his sleeve as he speaks a command to one of the sailors. They work in that same rhythmic fashion as before— clearly under compulsion—stacking and stacking and *stacking* the caskets until I can hardly see beyond the deck. "M-Michal." My teeth chatter now, and my entire body trembles. It isn't from the cold. "Why do you need to export c-caskets?"

"We don't," he says shortly, frowning and leading me belowdecks to the ballroom. Though someone has lit another lantern here, the light does nothing to assuage the knot in my chest. It only illuminates more caskets—these grander than the ones upstairs, carved from ebony and sandalwood with gilt trim, silk and satin linings. "We export them to smuggle vampires into Cesarine. Inspectors rarely look *inside* the caskets." A distant part of my mind registers that he says *rarely* instead of *never*, but I can't worry about those inspectors who do look inside. Not right now. "It's much simpler this way. Cleaner. After the ship passes inspection, we slip into the city without notice. We won't need to climb inside for another couple of hours, however. Not until we near the city." He slips leather gloves from his pocket and hands them to me. "Here. Take these."

But gloves are useless against the cold that grips me.

"Michal, I can't—" The words die as my gaze lands on the coffin nearest him. It looks just like Filippa's: rosewood, with two life-sized swans carved atop the lid, each wearing a laurel crown. *Did Requiem, Ltd., produce her coffin too?* Hot sick rushes up my throat at the thought, and I clamp my mouth shut to stop from vomiting all over Michal's pristine boots. "I—I can't just climb into a casket. I can't."

"I remember." At this, he withdraws something else from his pocket—a strange glowing jewel. Perfectly round, it looks almost opaline, shot through with veins of luminous white and iridescent hues of blue, green, and purple. "Here. The last of the witchlights.

A show of good faith from La Dame des Sorcières of old." He presses the jewel into my hand, and another boom of thunder drowns out the sailors' shouts as the ship lurches out to sea. When I tumble sideways, Michal steadies my arm, casting a dark look at the ceiling. "Along with the weather."

I thrust the jewel back at him with trembling hands. Because light won't help inside a *casket*. Nothing will keep away the scent of death, the feel of Pippa's brittle hair in my mouth. Already, I choke on it, stumbling back a frantic step and knocking into the casket behind me. With a strangled noise, I leap sideways—*away* from it—but I trip on my cloak and nearly crash to my knees instead.

Michal catches my elbows before I can fall.

His brows draw together as I sink to the floor anyway. He descends with me, kneeling now, his eyes tracking the rapid rise and fall of my chest. I know my pupils have dilated. His nostrils flare, and I know he scents my fear. I can do nothing to stop it, however, nothing to battle my body's response when all I can see are *coffins*. When all I can smell is summer honey and *rot*. "What is it?" he asks in confusion. "What's wrong?"

No one is coming to save us.

"I c-can't get into a casket, Michal. Please, there must be another way."

His frown deepens. "Your fiancé has ships all over these waters looking for you. The king has ordered inspections of every vessel. Squadrons of soldiers patrol the kingdom as we speak, and both huntsmen and witches alike scour the streets of Cesarine on orders from the Archbishop and La Dame des Sorcières. You're the most sought-after person in the whole of Belterra—and that doesn't even include the vicomte, who has offered a reward of a hundred thousand couronnes for your safe return. I believe you're familiar with him."

A shuddering laugh wracks my frame.

Yes, I'm familiar with him.

Lord Pierre Tremblay, humble servant of the Church and Crown, devoted husband and father, and a man I haven't spoken to in almost a year. Under different circumstances, his reward of a hundred thousand couronnes for his daughter's return might be touching. As it is, the vicomte doesn't have two couronnes to rub together, and I still remember his last words to me, low and furious: *No daughter of mine will disgrace herself with the Chasseurs. I won't allow it. Do you hear me? You will* not *be joining—*

"I can compel ordinary men to forget your face," Michal says, replacing my father's baleful green eyes with his black ones, "but if a Chasseur or Dame Blanche sees you, I'll have to kill them."

"No." Gasping, I struggle to my feet, and Michal releases me instantly. "No killing."

In any case, the risk is too great; we have no idea who'll inspect this ship, and if anyone recognizes me, they'll drag me back home to West End. I'll never uncover the truth about the killer. I'll never make sense of my strange new ability or the looming darkness, never have another chance to prove myself to my parents and Jean Luc and Frederic. I'll be thrust once more into a glass box—no, *locked*—and this time, my parents will throw away the key.

No. That cannot happen.

My eyes dart wildly for another solution and land upon Odessa's desk in the center of the ballroom. Her mountain of scrolls still lie atop it, but beside them, glinting dully in the lantern's light—

Another bottle of absinthe.

Thank God. My heart leaps, and I lunge for the foul green liquid as if my life depends on it. When my hand closes around the bottle, however, Michal's hand closes around my wrist. He shakes his head with a sardonic twist of his lips. "I don't think so."

"Let me *go.*" Though I jerk and twist to weaken his hold, it remains unbreakable. Surprisingly light, yes, but unbreakable all the same. I lift my chin. "I changed my mind. I *can* do this. I can climb into a casket."

He snorts derisively. "With absinthe?"

"*You* drink it."

"I drink all manner of things that you don't, and let me assure you—absinthe is perhaps the *most* offensive among them. Have you ever tried it?"

"No." I plant my feet determinedly, stubbornly, and at last, he allows me to wrench the bottle away from him. I clutch it to my chest. "I stole a sip of my mother's wine once, though. It can't be much different."

Michal stares as if I've lost my mind, perhaps plucked it from my head and tossed it out the window. And perhaps I have. Perhaps I don't care. I wrestle with the bottle's cork beneath his critical gaze, just managing to unstopper it when a distant crash sounds outside.

Both of our faces snap upward.

"What was—?" I start to ask.

In the blink of an eye, however, Michal disappears up the stairs. I hasten to follow, clumsy and slow in his wake, and some of the absinthe spills onto my hands. Its spicy scent—anise and fennel and something else—wrinkles my nose as I dart up the stairs and skid to a halt on the quarterdeck, sliding a little in the rain. It comes down in great sheets now, as if God himself pours buckets of it upon our heads. In seconds, it soaks me to the skin, but I push sopping hair from my face to follow Michal's line of sight.

To the north, just visible through the gale, another ship struggles to remain aloft in fifty-foot waves. Its foremast has splintered in the winds, and the entire vessel pitches sideways, precariously close to capsizing. My entire body goes cold with realization.

"Michal!" The wind carries away my shout, however, and I duck swiftly as another bolt of lightning flashes. Caskets slide in every direction. The crew—half-drowned—rush to secure them, but even compulsion is no match for the storm. With another ear-splitting crack, one wooden box crashes into another, and both pitch over the railing and into the sea. "Michal!" Wind tearing at my cloak and hair, I fight to reach him, to seize his arm. "That ship—the entire crew is going to drown if we don't—"

"We cannot help them."

At his words, the splintered mast of the other ship separates completely, and a vicious swell drags the bow under, along with half of the ship's crew. The other men shout and charge forward to secure the vessel, but it's too late. Their ship sinks in earnest now. In the next second, lightning strikes another mast, and its sails spark and catch fire. Horror fills my belly at the sight, and my hand tightens on Michal's sleeve. "But we have to help them! Michal!"

But he only gestures dispassionately to the churning water around us. Sharp, broken bits of other ships pierce the waves like tombstones rising up in a cemetery. And that's what it is, I realize—a cemetery. "There is no saving them," Michal says. "No one finds Requiem except those who are born or created there."

"*What?*"

"The isle is secret, Célie." Voice curt, Michal turns his back on the sinking ship, on the dying men, but I can't tear my eyes away. He seizes my elbow and steers me to the sheltered alcove by the stairs. "Your precious Louise's ancestor cast a spell of protection around it many years ago. Most simply drift off course when they near Requiem, but others—like our friends here—are too skilled to be dissuaded. And so the enchantment kills them. They never reach the isle."

"It—it *kills* them?" I repeat in disbelief.

"Except on a witch's holy days." Lightning bleaches Michal's hair bone white, casting shadows beneath his eyes and cheeks, and when his mouth twists viciously, he truly looks like a denizen of Hell. "A clever loophole, that. La Dame des Sorcières claimed it as a protection for her people—a counterbalance to the enchantment. For three weeks of the year, Requiem lies completely exposed and vulnerable to the outside world." He arches a meaningful brow. "Samhain is one of those days."

I clench the bottle of absinthe so hard that my fingers ache. The sea has claimed all but the ship's stern now. My stomach plummets as the men's shouts fade beneath the roaring wind, the deafening thunder. Though I stumble forward, determined to— to *help* them somehow, to lower the lifeboat, I manage only three steps before Michal catches my cloak and drags me back to shelter. A wave surges up and over the handrail a half second later. I cling to him helplessly as our ship pitches in response. "So Lou and the others—they won't be able to pass through the enchantment until All Hallows' Eve?"

"At midnight precisely."

"And if they come early?"

Together, our eyes follow the last man as the sea swallows him whole. "Pray they don't," Michal says simply.

By the time he finishes speaking, the entirety of the ship and its crew have vanished. Just . . . vanished. My heart beats a heavy, painful rhythm in my chest. It's like they never existed at all.

We stay that way for another long moment, staring out at the waves as wind and rain lash around us. I only realize that I still clutch Michal when he firmly disentangles himself and turns to stalk belowdecks. At the last second, however, he hesitates, casting an unreadable look over his shoulder. "The lifeboat wouldn't have saved them," he says.

My chest aches because it's true.

And when he disappears down the stairs, I lift the bottle of absinthe to my lips and drink.

CHAPTER TWENTY-NINE

La Fée Verte

I take a shot for each person I've seen die.

Michal—who has apparently grown a conscience in the five minutes since I've joined him—stops me after three.

"How *dare* you?" Swaying with the turbulent waves, I thrust my wet hair from my cheeks indignantly. They already feel warm, flushed, as if I've been lying in the sun for hours instead of drowning above deck. My throat, too, burns like I've been drinking acid. I peer suspiciously at the bottle now clutched in Michal's hand, squinting at the green fairy on the label. Her smile appears innocuous enough. "I am *trying* to honor the dead, but you"—a particularly violent swell rocks the entire ship, and I stagger into him—"you wouldn't understand that, would you?"

He rolls his eyes and steadies my elbow. "Probably not."

"Typical." I push away from him to seize Odessa's desk instead, stripping off my heavy cloak before it suffocates me. "Death doesn't affect you anymore. You've killed too many people."

"Whatever you say."

"Yes, I *do* say. I really do." A pause. "Out of curiosity . . . how many people *have* you killed?"

The corner of his mouth lifts—more grimace than smile—and he stalks around me, tucking the bottle of absinthe inside Odessa's desk. He shuts the drawer firmly. "That's a very personal question, Célie Tremblay."

"I'd like an answer." I lift my chin. "And my bottle back. I only drank for Ansel, Ismay, and Victoire, but I still need to drink for—"

"And I'd like you not to vomit on my shoes." His eyes narrow when I sway again, blinking as the heat from my cheeks washes through the rest of me. It happens quite suddenly, quite unexpectedly, and—I hesitate, glancing around the semi-lit ballroom in surprise. It seems pleasantly distorted around the edges now, almost like I'm in a dream, or—or perhaps seeing it through lovely, clouded glass. Michal scowls at something in my expression. Snatching my wrist, he drags me around Odessa's desk and forces me into her chair. "It looks like both of us are going to be disappointed."

I lift a hand in front of me, examining it curiously in the flickering lamplight. "I feel . . . strange. I've seen other people intoxicated, you know, but I never expected it to feel so—so *nice*." I leap to my feet and whirl to face him, stumbling slightly. He catches my elbow once more. "Why don't people do this all the time?"

Impatient, he exhales hard and pushes me back down. "A sip of your mother's mulled wine didn't make you feel *nice*?"

I wave an airy hand. "Oh, I lied about that."

"You what?"

"I lied." A muscle in my cheek begins to twitch as his expression darkens. Ignoring him, I open Odessa's desk drawer to steal back the bottle of absinthe. He nearly slams the drawer shut on my fingers. "You said I couldn't lie, but I can and I *did*. And you had no idea." I cannot help it now—a giggle bursts from my lips as I turn in my chair to poke his stomach. He swats my hand away. "I told you I tried my mother's wine, but I never did. She doesn't drink wine. She doesn't drink alcohol at all—she doesn't approve of it— so I've never had a *sip* in all my life before this." I clasp my hands together in delight. "It's *wonderful*, though, isn't it? Why didn't anyone tell me it's so wonderful? Have *you* ever been drunk?"

He glares at the ceiling with a pained expression, as if questioning how, exactly, an ancient and all-powerful vampire could land himself in such a situation. "Yes."

I gaze at him intently. "*And?*"

"And what?"

"Well, and *everything*. How old were you? How did it happen? Was it absinthe too, or—?"

He shakes his head curtly. "We aren't discussing this."

"Oh, come on." Though I turn to prod him again, he sidesteps in a blur, and I'm forced to merely point my finger at him instead. "*That* isn't fair," I tell him. "You may be able to—to dart around with your *super-special speed*, Michal Vasiliev, but *I* can be super and specially *vexing* when dismissed, which is quite unfortunate for you because I'm *always* being dismissed"—I wave my finger emphatically—"which means I'm quite comfortable being vexing, and I'll simply keep asking and asking and *asking* until you tell me what I want to—"

He seizes my finger before I accidentally poke him in the eye with it. "That much is *painfully* clear." Exasperated, he drops my hand back into my lap. "I was fifteen," he says irritably when I try to jab him again. "Dimitri and I stole a keg of mead from my father and stepmother. The entire village came out to celebrate their tenth wedding anniversary, and they never noticed it was gone."

He was fifteen. "You drank all of it?" I whisper in awe.

"No. Mila and Odessa helped."

"Were the four of you the very best of friends?"

He scoffs, though the sound isn't nearly as cold and dispassionate as he wants it to be. No, he almost sounds *fond*, and I bite my cheek to hide my smile. "We almost set the barn on fire, and we spent the rest of the night vomiting in the hayloft. Our parents were furious. They made us muck the stables for hours the next day."

Despite the vomit and horse muck, I cannot help but sigh at the story—inexplicably wistful—and lace my fingers together in my lap. "Did your father love your stepmother very much?"

"Yes." He casts me a long, probing look. "He loved my mother too."

"He sounds lovely."

"Yes," Michal says after another slight pause. Then, more reluctant— "He was . . . much like Dimitri in that way."

Huh.

I purse my lips, considering him with keen interest for several seconds. The absinthe still blurs his features into a dark painting of sorts—all alabaster and obsidian—until he doesn't look entirely real. I shake my head in bemusement. Because he *is* real, of course, even if the thought of him at fifteen with exasperated parents and mischievous cousins and a barrel full of mead fills me with an inexplicable and unexpected sense of loss.

I laugh reflexively.

"And to think—when *I* was fifteen, I still slept in a nursery and played with dolls." I laugh again, unable to stop myself, and tip back abruptly to balance on my chair's hind legs. Though he opens his mouth for a scathing reply, I speak over him, faster now. "Lou and Reid and Beau played a game of truth or dare with whiskey last year, but I was sleeping in the other room. I wish I hadn't been, so I could've played too. I'd like to play a game like that sometime—and you'd think it would've been awkward, all of us traveling together, but it wasn't awkward at all. Do you know why?" I pause dramatically, craning my neck to look at him upside down, waiting for his eyes to widen, riveted, or perhaps for him to lean forward and shake his head in anticipation.

"No," he says, his voice strangely quiet instead. "I don't."

"Do you want me to tell you?"

A wry twist of his lips as he pushes my chair back to all fours. "Do I have a choice?"

"No"—I spring to my feet once more, and he takes a step back to avoid the collision—"and it wasn't awkward because Lou and Reid are *soul mates.* Just like your *parents,* Michal."

"Is that so?"

I nod enthusiastically. "You already know Reid and I dated because you—well, I don't know how you know, exactly—but I bet you don't know how perfect they are for each other. I bet you don't know that Lou plays four instruments. I bet you don't know that Reid dances *splendidly* around the maypole when he thinks no one is watching." I poke him in the chest again, daring him to contradict me. "He dances better than you, I'm sure. *And* he's taller."

His lips twitch. "A god among men."

"Reid would never invite that comparison. He's too humble." Lifting my nose in the air, I turn and snatch the bottle of absinthe from the drawer. This time, Michal doesn't even try to stop me. He leans against the nearest coffin instead, folding his arms across his chest and watching me. "And don't forget about his brother, Beau," I tell him, unstoppering the absinthe for another drink. It doesn't even burn my throat now. Indeed, my tongue has gone completely numb. "Beau just might be the funniest person in the entire world. He's a gentleman *and* a rogue, and when he smiles, he looks exactly how I imagine a dashing pirate to look—all charm and dimples and danger. And Coco—*Coco*"—I shake the bottle for emphasis, unable to stop myself—"Coco is so much *more* than a beautiful face, you know? She has this razor-sharp wit and tough exterior, but it's only because she doesn't like to feel vulnerable." I cradle the bottle against my chest now, leaning against the desk and tracing the green fairy's wings with my thumb. Perhaps I'll dye my hair emerald like hers for the masquerade on All Hallows' Eve. Perhaps Monsieur Marc will sew all of us matching wings. I sigh happily at the thought. "I just love them all so much."

"Really?" He arches a sardonic brow. "I never would've guessed."

Startled, I glance up at Michal and frown. Because I'd quite forgotten he was here. Because judging by his tone, he doesn't love my friends like I do, and because he—he plans to—

The room swirls dangerously as I seize a letter opener from Odessa's desk drawer, brandishing it at him like a knife. It's much lighter than the lances and longswords of Chasseur Tower. Much more agreeable. "I will not let you kill them, monsieur," I say abruptly.

He rolls his eyes, but otherwise, he doesn't move. "Put that away before you hurt yourself."

My own eyes flash at the dismissal. "You can't tell me what to do. Everyone is *always* trying to tell me what to do, but only one of them is my captain—*you* are not my captain—which means I don't have to listen to a word you say."

At mention of Jean Luc, all humor in Michal's expression flickers out.

"Ah, yes." Clasping his hands behind his back, he stares down at the tip of the letter opener against his chest. Regretfully, it's made of steel and not silver. "Célie, the huntswoman. For a moment there, I forgot. How many people would *you* have killed, I wonder, if you'd stayed in Chasseur Tower?" He steps pointedly into the letter opener, and it—my eyes widen in disbelief—it bends against his chest. It *bends*. I drop it hastily, scramble backward, and careen into Odessa's desk. He doesn't stop strolling toward me, however, slowly closing the distance between us. "You certainly never hesitate to attack *me*. Why is that?"

"Because you're a monster." Still backpedaling, I throw the bottle of absinthe at him to stop his approach. I don't even know *why* I want to stop his approach. He promised he wouldn't hurt me, yet something in the determined set of his jaw sends a delicious skitter down my back. He catches the bottle with one hand and throws it into Odessa's desk drawer. "And I'm *not* a Chasseur," I tell him stubbornly, darting behind a coffin. "Not anymore."

"You certainly think like a Chasseur. Does your beloved captain know you've broken your vow?"

"No, he—" My brows furrow in confusion, and I recoil, blinking hard. I forgot to tell him about Jean Luc. I told him all about the others, but somehow, I forgot to mention how driven Jean is, how steadfast and capable and devoted. *Does your beloved captain know you've broken your vow?* A low hum fills my ears at the question, making it impossible to think. "What—what do you mean by that?" I ask him suspiciously.

He plants his hands atop the coffin. "You tell me."

But—no. I don't like his question. I don't like it at all. Indeed, this conversation has grown irrevocably dull.

"I—I'm not telling you anything, and I don't want to talk to you anymore." Resolute, I turn away from him into the aisle. He will not ruin this moment for me, no matter how hard he tries. It doesn't matter that I'm nineteen instead of fifteen, that my only companion here is la fée verte—I too can light a metaphorical barn on fire. I look around desperately for something to do. The ship has stopped pitching, which means we must've outstripped the storm, and beyond the stairs—somewhere on the sodden deck—a sailor plays a lively jig on his harmonica. *That's it.* I bounce a little on my toes at the sound. We *are* in a ballroom, after all, and I haven't danced in ages.

I don't hear Michal move behind.

"Let us hope," he says, his voice unexpectedly strained, "that Monsieur Diggory didn't teach you how to dance."

Leaping from my skin, I whirl again—this time to push him away—but stop short at the last second. He stands very close to me. *Too* close, yet my feet grow roots as I stare up at him. Standing this near, this still, I could count his eyelashes if I wanted. I could sweep my thumb across them, could trace the line of his cheekbone to the corner of his mouth.

I could graze the tips of his teeth.

My breath hitches at the intrusive thought, and unbidden, my gaze falls to his lips. Though his expression remains carefully empty, he doesn't move either. He doesn't breathe.

He didn't breathe in the theater when he scented my fear. Or the aviary when he scented my blood.

Because he's a monster, my mind repeats, thrashing wildly against me. *A monster.*

Stomach fluttering, I lift a tentative hand anyway.

In that instant, however, a knock sounds on the door, and a sailor pokes his head inside the room. "Your Majesty," he says, and the unnerving tension between us shatters. *Your Majesty.* I snort loudly at the designation and step back. Michal turns stiffly to look at the sailor, who cowers beneath his black glare. "Apologies, Your Majesty, but three ships approach with the Belterran flag. They've signaled for a cargo search."

A cargo search.

The words flit in my ears like bees, urgent and unpleasant and unwelcome. They clearly mean something important to Michal and his crew, however, which means they should probably mean something important to me. I can't quite remember *what,* however— not with all this humming—or why they've started to sting. So I swat the words aside, bounding across the room and reaching for the sailor. "What is your name, monsieur?" I ask him eagerly.

Warm and calloused, his hands accept mine after a brief hesitation. When I squeeze them, he returns the pressure with a small smile and a furrow between his brows. "My name is Bellamy, mademoiselle."

"You have an *excellent* name, Bellamy." I lean into him conspiratorially. "And you're very handsome too. Did you know that? Do you have a family at home? Do you dance with them? I *love* to dance, and if you'd like, I can teach you to love it too."

He blinks at me, nonplussed, and glances at Michal. "Er—"

"Just ignore Michal. I always do." When I swing backward, pirouetting under his arm, the vampire in question catches me instead. He yanks me toward him. His lips have pressed together in a hard, flat line, but I don't care; I spin beneath his arm too, still laughing and speaking to the handsome sailor. "If *I* were a vampire, I'd compel everyone on the isle to ignore Michal. It would be marvelous."

"How fortunate that'll never happen." Michal waves a curt hand at the sailor, who backs hastily out of the room. "Now"—he inclines his head toward something behind me—"stop bewitching my crew and get in the coffin."

Instinctively, I cast a glance over my shoulder, and my heart crashes to somewhere around my navel. A familiar rosewood coffin leers back at me. I blink at it rapidly. The bees in my ears buzz in earnest now, and the room grows abruptly, intolerably hot. Scrambling away from Michal, I press my hands to my feverish cheeks. Why *is* it so hot in here? Have we somehow transcended Cesarine and sailed straight into Hell? "Get in the coffin, Célie," Michal says again, softer now. His black eyes glint with impatience. And something else. Something I cannot name.

I snort again.

"Your Majesty, *darling,* has anyone ever told you no?"

He steps toward me with purpose. "Never."

"I'm not getting into that coffin."

"You drank a pint of absinthe for no reason, then?"

"A lady would never drink a *pint* of absinthe. I partook sensibly, and moreover—I said I wouldn't get into *that* coffin. I never said I wouldn't get into a different one." Feigning a serene smile, I pat the lacquered ebony casket beside it. The floor begins to shift beneath my feet as the fourth shot of absinthe hits my stomach. "I'll be getting into *this* one, thank you."

"That's my coffin."

"It *was* your coffin. Now it's mine." Still smiling, still swaying, I fumble with the brass clasps and heave the lid open as shouts sound again from above. The royal fleet must be almost upon us. I lift my skirts and step into the casket before hesitating, turning to extend an expectant hand. "And I'll take that witchlight now."

"Your Ladyship, *darling*, has anyone ever told you no?" To my surprise, to my *horror*, Michal blows out the lamp before I can answer—plunging us in total darkness—and steps into the coffin with me.

"What are you *doing*?" I seize his arm as he moves to sit, pushing him away and clinging to him in equal measure. I can't see a thing beyond the sickening spin of the darkness. "You can't just— *Michal*," I hiss, "this is highly inappropriate, so go somewhere else! And give me the witchlight before you do!"

"I refuse to spend the next hour cramped in another coffin when I built this one specifically to accommodate me. If you prefer not to share, by all means"—he extracts the witchlight from his pocket and shoves it into my hands—"choose another."

I stare at him in the eerie white light, wide-eyed with disbelief, but he doesn't wait for my decision. No. He sinks into the coffin like a person might sink into silk sheets, and *that* is not a comparison I need right now. I give myself a vicious mental shake and nearly stumble to the floor. It isn't a comparison I need *ever.* Of course I can't share such a small, intimate space with a vampire, especially one as domineering as Michal. Besides—I glance into the coffin—there isn't even room to lie beside him. If I do this, I'll have to lie, well—*flush*. My cheeks burn hotter.

If I don't, however, I'll spend the next hour alone in the semidarkness, trying not to remember those things la fée verte has kept away.

Perspective is a wonderful thing.

Before I can change my mind, I drop like a stone onto Michal's chest, shimmying flat against his front—or trying to, at least. I nearly knock him in the forehead with my witchlight, and my knees prod first his stomach, then his hip, in their battle to contain my skirts. The red silk and chemise bunch up in the tight space, baring my calves, and I twist to straighten them in alarm, accidentally jabbing Michal in the throat with my elbow. "Sorry! I'm sorry!" But my knee jerks to the left with the words, grazing the place between his legs, and he inhales sharply. I gasp in horror. "I am *so*—"

"*Stop*"—he seizes my waist and lifts me straight into the air above him—"*moving.*"

Without another word, he shifts my weight, pressing me against the coffin wall, and reaches a hand between us to tug my skirts back into place. His fingertips brush my bare legs. My hair kisses his furious face. Neither of us acknowledge either, however, and when he lowers me back against him, I want to leap from the coffin and flee.

As if reading my thoughts, he pulls the coffin lid shut with a decisive *click*, and thank goodness he does—within seconds, the ballroom door opens, and heavy footsteps land upon the carpets.

CHAPTER THIRTY

Confessional

"See anything?" a hoarse voice asks. I imagine a gnarled old man lifting a torch or lantern, its golden light sweeping over the rows upon rows of caskets.

His companion sounds disgusted. And much younger. "Coffins. This has to be bad luck."

"Don't know what he thinks we'll find with these searches." The first man's footsteps grow closer, and I tense, my eyes clenching shut when he raps his knuckles atop our coffin. The witchlight flickers and spins against the dark of my eyelids, and it's harder to swallow now than it was before. Michal's hand creeps over my back. "Notice *he* isn't out here in the middle of the night, freezing his balls off with the rest of us."

"Better him than the one upstairs," the second says bitterly, "wearing that blue coat and acting like a king on high. If he calls me *boy* one more time, I swear I'll take that silver stick of his and shove it straight up his ass. You just watch. I'll do it." A pause. "Should we search the coffins?"

Another sharp rap on the lid. "No. The only thing we'll find in here is a stiff, and I won't be the one to tell Toussaint his little fiancée has kicked it."

"You think she has?"

He scoffs. "I think he does too, deep down. Women who disappear rarely turn up again, do they? Not alive, anyway. Just look at her sister. I heard the witches got ahold of her, cursed her to age until her heart gave out. It's only a matter of time before we find this one dead too."

Cold, gentle fingers touch my hair now, sliding through the heavy mass to my nape. It takes several seconds for me to realize why—to notice that my entire body has started to tremble, that my hands clamp bone white around the lapels of Michal's coat. I didn't know I held him. I didn't think I could move at all. "I don't know," the younger man mutters. "She already disappeared once. No one knows where she went then either. My dad thinks she ran away. He thinks she left him—Toussaint. She wasn't wearing his ring when she fled the Tower. My mom says Toussaint deserves someone better for a wife." He chuckles grimly. "She volunteered my sister."

The buzzing in my ears pitches higher with each word. Sharp and painful now.

Before they can continue debating the faults of my character, however, the ballroom door opens once more, and a third pair of footsteps joins them. "Gentlemen."

A violent shudder wracks my body at the word, and I abandon all pretense, burying my face in Michal's cloak. Because *this* voice I recognize. It's a voice I would give every couronne of my father's reward to never hear again.

"Frederic," the first man grumbles. It sounds as if he pushes from our coffin, straightening reluctantly. The younger man says nothing. "She isn't down here."

"You've checked every casket."

It isn't a question, and the two men—unsure how to answer—hesitate briefly before the second clears his throat and lies with relish. "Of course."

"Good." The word drips with disdain, and I can picture Frederic strolling down the aisle now, trailing his hand along the ornate boxes. Perhaps inspecting his fingers for dust. "The sooner we find her body, the sooner Toussaint resigns."

"You think he'll resign, monsieur?" the first asks dubiously.

Frederic laughs—a short, humorless sound that makes my stomach twist. "How can he not? A captain who fails to protect not only his subordinate but also his fiancée? It's humiliating."

"It's hardly his fault the girl ran out on him," the second mutters.

"And that, boy," Frederic says, his voice sharpening, "is exactly where you're wrong. It is his fault. This *entire* fucking mess is his fault. He brought a woman into a brotherhood of men. He gave her a Balisarda *and* an engagement ring." He scoffs bitterly. "You aren't a Chasseur, so you wouldn't understand."

The second man, the *boy*, only takes further offense. "Oh yeah? Try me."

Another mirthless chuckle. Another pause. "Fine. I'll try you. Do you remember the bloodshed in December and January? After that redheaded Chasseur allied himself with a *witch?*" He snarls the word like a curse, and to Frederic, it is. "The kingdom lost all faith in our brotherhood when he killed the Archbishop on Christmas Eve, then again when his mother-in-law slaughtered our king in the New Year. Toussaint was his friend. Toussaint sided with Diggory and his witch in the Battle of Cesarine, and the kingdom suffered."

A tendril of anger cracks open in my stomach, churning with the absinthe. It rises up my throat, but I choke it back down, my breathing growing louder. Harsher. How *dare* Frederic criticize Jean Luc and Reid? How dare he hold *any* opinion on the Battle of Cesarine—a battle in which hundreds of innocent people lost their lives, a battle in which he didn't even *participate*? Michal's fingers tighten on my nape in warning. He breathes something in my ear, but I can't hear anything beyond that wretched humming, can't *see* anything beyond Frederic's hateful face in the training yard.

This scrap of wood won't debilitate a witch.

Basile's leering grin.

Only two scraps of wood will do that! A stake and a match!

My brethren's laughter—all of their cruel laughter—as I struggled to lift a longsword.

"You don't have to tell *us* about Reid Diggory," the second man snaps. " My brother lost several fingers in that battle."

"I wasn't a huntsman then," Frederic says. "If I had been, your brother might've kept his fingers. Regardless, I've worked very hard to restore the kingdom's trust, but Toussaint's actions have cast doubt upon our brotherhood all over again." He makes a low, disgusted noise in his throat as his footsteps recede. "Perhaps it's for the best. Even if Toussaint fails to resign, he'll have no choice but to rededicate himself to our cause without Mademoiselle Tremblay as a distraction." He pauses at the foot of the stairs, and for a split second—less, even—I can almost feel his brilliant blue eyes settle on our coffin. Bile rises in my throat, and this time, a violent heave rocks my stomach, my chest. Michal pulls back in alarm. I clamp a hand over my mouth, his face blurring into sickly lines of white and black. My mother was right. Absinthe *is* the Devil's drink.

"It really is a shame," Frederic says with a sigh. "She would've been a lovely wife."

With that, his footsteps retreat above deck, and the ballroom falls into silence.

She would've been a lovely wife.

The words pulse with the stabbing pain in my temple like a sickening poem. No. I swallow the bile, and it burns all the way down. Like a prophecy.

A lovely wife.

She would've been

lovely

if she'd been his wife.

"I thought you were going to shove that silver stick up his ass," the first man grunts after a moment, "*boy.*" The second curses in response, followed by the dull thud of his fist hitting the other. They chuckle companionably for another moment before trudging after Frederic.

Leaving us alone.

"Célie?" Michal murmurs.

But I can't seem to speak. Each time I open my mouth, I see Frederic's face, his blue coat, and my throat constricts. On the third attempt, I manage to whisper, "I hate them." Dragging my hands from my mouth, I scrub my eyes and cheeks viciously until my face burns. Anything to subdue the poison coursing through my veins. Through my *stomach.* "I hate all of them, and I *hate* that I hate them. They just—they're so—"

Michal's fingers resume kneading my neck, distracting me.

They feel like ice against my overheated skin. "Breathe through the nausea, Célie. In through your nose. Out through your mouth." Then— "Who is Frederic?"

"A *Chasseur*." I spit the word with venom, then cringe, remembering the similar way Frederic spat *witch*. I take a deep breath. In through my nose and out through my mouth, just like Michal said. It doesn't help. It doesn't help because I'm *not* like Frederic, and I can't—I *won't*—condemn all the huntsmen with him. Jean Luc is kind and good and brave, as are many of the men who reside in Chasseur Tower. And yet . . .

I force back another surge of bile. Unless we reach land soon, there's a very real possibility that I'm going to vomit all over Michal.

I can only pray it'll be his shoes.

"I gathered as much." His hand moves from my nape to my hair. A small part of my mind wonders at the gesture, wonders why Michal is trying to—to *soothe* me, but the other, larger part refuses to complain. "Who is Frederic to you?"

Though I cannot close my eyes in defeat—not while the world spins—the fight collapses in my chest without warning, and my shoulders slump against him. Who *is* Frederic to me? It's a valid question, one that immediately prompts another: Why should I let him affect me anymore? My voice grows small at the truth. "He's no one. Truly. He liked to provoke me in Chasseur Tower, but that hardly matters now. I'm never going back."

Michal's hand stills in my hair. "You aren't?"

"No." The word falls freely, without hesitation, as if it's always been there waiting for permission. Perhaps it has. And now— hidden in a coffin with a half-sadistic vampire—I finally give it.

"No one ever tells you how hard it'll be to blaze a trail, how lonely it is." I rest my cheek against his leather-clad chest and concentrate on my breathing. And the words keep coming, more destructive than the liquor in my stomach. "I just wanted to do something good after Filippa. It's why I told Reid to focus on the Chasseurs at her funeral; it's why he left me to fall in love with Lou instead. It's why I followed them to that lighthouse in January, and it's why I fought against Morgane in the Battle of Cesarine." Sighing, I trace the collar of his coat for something to do with my hands. Because I can't look at him. Because I shouldn't be admitting any of this, especially not to him, yet I can't seem to stop. "I told myself it's why I joined the Chasseurs afterward—I wanted to help rebuild the kingdom. Really, though, I think I just wanted to rebuild my life."

After a brief hesitation, he resumes stroking my hair. It should feel strange. No one has really touched my hair like this since Filippa—not even Jean Luc—but somehow, it doesn't. "I met Morgane le Blanc once many years ago at a night circus." As before, he seems reluctant to continue, but this is our game. A question for a question. A truth for a truth. "She'd just turned eighteen, and her mother, Camille le Blanc, had passed the title and powers of La Dame des Sorcières to her freely. She loved her daughter. Morgane had no idea what I was, of course, but even then, her blood smelled . . . wrong. I watched as she stole a trinket from an elderly peddler. When the woman confronted her, she lit the woman's cart on fire."

I swallow hard. It takes little imagination to envision the scene in my mind.

She trapped me with fire, too, when she took me—a ring of

it around my bed in the nursery. The smell of that smoke still suffocates me at night. The heat of those flames sears my skin. Clearing my throat, I whisper hoarsely, "She—she crept into my room while I was sleeping, and she took me like she took Filippa, except she didn't really want me. She wanted Lou and Reid." The words grow thicker in my throat, lodging there and refusing to move, but I need to say them. I *want* to say them. Michal doesn't try to fill the silence; he simply waits, the stroke of his hand steady and calm. "She used me as bait, and she locked me in a casket with my dead sister. I stayed there in the dark with her for over t-two weeks before Lou found me."

The words land heavy and brittle between us.

For several seconds, I don't think Michal is going to reply. How *does* one reply to something so horrific, something so wholly and completely evil? Jean Luc, my friends, even my parents—no one ever knows what to say. No one knows how to comfort me. On most days, I don't even know how to comfort myself, so on most days, I say nothing too.

Pressure burns behind my eyes as the silence grows, and I really do think I'm going to be sick now.

Then Michal slips a finger beneath my chin, tilting my face up to look at him. His eyes no longer appear cool and impassive; they burn with black fire, and the sheer violence in his gaze should send me running. And why wouldn't I? Frederic and his search party have probably disembarked by now, which means there's no longer a reason to keep . . . *embracing* like this. I pull away half-heartedly at the realization, but Michal refuses to release my chin. "You said you fought against Morgane in the Battle of Cesarine. How did she die?"

I stare at his shoulder. "You know how she died. Everyone knows how she died. Lou slit her throat."

"Tell me what happened."

"There's nothing to tell," I repeat weakly, glancing at him. I once made the mistake of . . . overstating my involvement to Jean Luc, and it isn't one I intend to repeat with Michal. The thought of *him* sneering, shaking his head—or worse, feeling *pity*—brings fresh pressure to my eyes. "Lou confronted Morgane, and they fought. It was awful," I say, quieter still. "I've never seen a person so intent on killing another, let alone a mother and her daughter. The magic Morgane used was lethal, and Lou—she—she had no choice but to defend herself."

"And?"

"And"—I resist the urge to weep, or perhaps hit him—"and nothing. Lou slit her mother's throat, just like Morgane slit hers on her sixteenth birthday."

Michal's eyes narrow, as if he senses the half-truth. "How?"

"How *what*?"

"How did Lou slit her mother's throat? Morgane le Blanc was one of the most formidable creatures to ever walk the earth. How did Lou do it?"

I exhale a bit helplessly, my eyes darting between his. "She— Michal, she's La Dame des Sorcières. Her magic—it—"

"*How*, Célie?"

"I stabbed her!" The words burst from me loudly and unexpectedly, but I can't take them back. Fresh anger flares in response—because the words are true, because I shouldn't *want* to take them back, because it shouldn't matter what Jean Luc thinks, yet it does. It did. "I stabbed her with an injection of hemlock, and it incapacitated her long enough for Lou to finish the job. I would've done that too," I say bitterly, wiping away furious tears, "if Lou would've faltered. I would've slid that knife across her mother's throat, and I wouldn't have regretted it for a single second."

Though my tears fall thick and fast upon Michal's hand, he doesn't move to wipe them away. Instead, he leans forward until our faces are nearly touching. "Good," he snarls. Then he thrusts the coffin lid open and propels us both into the ballroom, igniting the lamp and seizing my cloak from the floor before I can blink. "Here. Take it. We've docked in Cesarine, and we have approximately seven hours until sunrise. It'll take at least four for us to reach Amandine."

The sudden movement, however, sends my vision spiraling. Saliva coats my mouth, and my stomach lurches violently as I seize Michal's arm to steady myself. Dizzy and disoriented.

Suddenly, it doesn't matter that Amandine lies across the entire kingdom, that we can't possibly reach it before sunrise. It doesn't matter that my cheeks still glisten with tears; indeed, it doesn't even matter that I just shared entirely too much with my mortal enemy—that he *patted* my *hair.*

No. I clap a hand to my mouth. The situation has grown too dire.

If you're listening, God, I pray fervently, screwing my eyes shut in fierce concentration, *please don't let me vomit in front of Michal. I'll never drink another drop of alcohol again, just please, please, don't let me vomit in front of—*

"Célie?" Alarmed, Michal tugs on his arm from my grip. "Are you going to—?"

But God *isn't* listening, and I am an *idiot*, and—and—a moan escapes from between my fingers in answer. I never should've closed my eyes. I force them open now, but it's too late: the room tilts, my throat tightens, and my entire body heaves. Before I can stop myself—before I can turn away, or perhaps throw myself in the sea—I spew acid-green vomit all over Michal's shoes.

Just like he said I would.

CHAPTER THIRTY-ONE

Eden

Michal doesn't lie about reaching Amandine in four hours. It should be impossible, but I'm beginning to understand there is no such thing as *impossible* anymore—not when Les Éternels rule the night. After cleaning the mess from his shoes in long-suffering silence, Michal gestures for me to climb atop his back—which I vehemently refuse—before sighing, sweeping me into his arms, and whisking me into Cesarine.

"*Wait—!*" The wind takes my cry, however, and Michal only pushes faster, the city passing in a blur of browns and blacks and grays. At least it isn't raining here; at the speed with which we now move, the drops would've bruised my face. As it is, Michal lurches to a halt twice, twisting me around just before I empty my stomach onto the street.

"Finished?" he asks dryly.

I've barely wiped my mouth the second time when he sets off again.

I suppress another low, pitiful moan, and Michal's mouth twitches again like he wants to laugh. This entire evening has been humiliating, *debasing*, and I swear on everything holy that I'll never drink another *drop* of alcohol again.

My stomach gradually settles as we cross into La Fôret des Yeux and its whispering pines. I hardly notice the way they've sickened, their bows turning black and curling inward. What possessed me to drink *absinthe* as my first crusade in the land of vice? Why did I ever agree to climb into a coffin with Michal? And why—*why*—did he treat me with such kindness inside it? Why did he *comfort* me? My stomach twists anew at the gentleness with which he touched my hair. At the fierceness in his gaze when he forced me to admit the truth—that Lou couldn't have killed Morgane without me. That we'd needed to do it together, or not at all.

It would've been so much easier if he'd been cruel.

A different kind of sickness spreads through me at the direction of my thoughts, and I shake myself mentally. Because it doesn't matter if he showed me kindness tonight. He still plans to kill Coco, to lure my friends to their deaths—he still *kidnapped* me—and one kind deed doesn't outweigh a lifetime of horrid ones. Michal is still Michal, and to forget that would be the last mistake I ever make. He is not my friend—he will never *be* my friend—and the sooner we find the true killer, the sooner we can part ways forever.

I take a deep breath and nod.

It's for the best.

Michal doesn't take any road through the forest. He doesn't need one. Though my hair grows wilder and wilder in the wind—which wrests tears from my eyes and the breath from my chest—Michal never slows, and he never tires. His footsteps never falter as the trees drift farther apart, and the hills around us rise into mountains.

Somewhere after Saint-Loire, I succumb to exhaustion and fall asleep.

⇥⧈⇤

He wakes me at the edge of the city with a murmured, "We're here."

Blearily, I blink at the streetlamp nearest us. It marks the beginning of Amandine, a glorious, sprawling city in the mountains. Warmth blooms through me at the sight of it, at the familiar smell: lichen and moss and damp earth, the sharp sting of cypress. Cesarine might be the political and industrial capital of Belterra, but I've always preferred Amandine's libraries and museums and theaters. Before my father sold our estate here, my mother would host parties filled to the brim with artists—actual, genuine artists who painted and wrote and acted—and Filippa and I would fall asleep on the staircase, listening to their stories. They always seemed so magical. So *fantastical.*

Michal sets me on my feet now.

Tonight, I suspect he's going to show me an entirely different side of the city. Babette was a courtesan in Cesarine. It makes sense that she would've continued her work in Amandine. My heartbeat accelerates a bit at the possibilities, and by the wry slant of Michal's lips, he hears it. "Three hours until sunrise," he says before striding into the darkened street.

Mouth dry, I smooth my crinkled skirt and hurry after him. I've never stepped foot in a brothel before—my parents wouldn't allow it—let alone a brothel called Les Abysses. It sounds positively, delightfully *thrilling.*

"Try not to skip with glee." Though clearly attempting to sound superior, the amused glint in Michal's eyes quite ruins the effect. "We're here for reconnaissance, nothing more."

"What's it like?" I ask, burning with curiosity. "The brothel? It *is* a brothel, isn't it?"

He casts me a probing glance. "The absinthe wasn't adventure enough for you?"

My face flushes, and I abruptly remember that it smells like something died in my mouth. "You don't have any mint, do you?" When he shakes his head, I snatch his arm and steer him left, toward an apothecary I used to know. Then I stop short. Because it won't be open at three o'clock in the morning. Indeed—I peer around the street in growing hopelessness—the city has turned into a veritable graveyard. Not a single creature meanders past. Not even a cat. A groan of frustration builds in my throat. What am I going to *do*? I can't very well make my debut at Les Abysses reeking of *sick*.

Sighing heavily, Michal drags me toward the shop anyway. I dig in my heels. "What are you—?"

Before I can finish the question, however, he breaks the lock on the door with a quick flick of his wrist. I gape after him as he sweeps inside and reappears seconds later with a toothbrush and mint paste. He thrusts them both at me, closing the door firmly behind him. "Happy?" he asks.

"I—" My hands close around the items. "Well, yes—that was very—very—" He rolls his eyes and paces several feet away. Giving me privacy, I realize with another start. "Thank you," I say awkwardly. "Did you, er—did you happen to pay for these?"

Slowly, he turns to look at me.

"Right." I nod hastily, making a mental note to repay the apothecary on my next trip to Amandine. Preferably without Michal breathing down my neck. *Add thief to the list,* a supercilious little voice in my head says, *along with kidnapper and potential murderer.* My eyes, however, cannot help but drift back to his perfect profile—and that's when I see it. My own face staring at me from the shop across the street. Inked in large, crisp handwriting, the notice below it reads:

MISSING

CÉLIE FLEUR TREMBLAY

NINETEEN YEARS OLD

LAST SEEN ON 10 OCTOBER

I turn away quickly, pretending not to have seen, and scrub my teeth a bit harder. Of course there are notices. My father cannot pretend to distribute his ludicrous reward without notices. The street remains dark and empty, however—no bounty hunters descend—and five minutes later, I follow Michal down a side alley and through a trapdoor in the cobblestones.

I try not to shudder at the thick, suffocating air in the stairwell beneath. It always feels like this belowground, like the walls and ceiling might collapse upon me at any moment, like the earth itself wants to swallow me whole. Thank God torches line the passage. Thank God we slow almost immediately, drawing to a halt at an unmarked crimson door. It boasts no knocker, no keyhole, not even a handle. Just smooth, painted wood.

It matches the precise color of my dress.

"Is this it?" Whispering, I resist the urge to fidget. To straighten my bodice and tame my snarled hair. It's one thing to read about the unknown in books, to dream of exploring it yourself someday. It's quite another to stare it right in the face. "Is this Les Abysses?"

"It is." He arches a brow at me. "Are you ready?"

"I—I think so."

Michal nods once before lifting a hand to the door, which swings open silently. Without another word, he steps inside, leaving me no choice but to follow. My mouth falls open as I cross over the threshold, and my breath leaves in a sudden *whoosh*.

The unknown is a whole new world.

Polished marble floors of swirling white give way to a shining gilt banister, where vines creep along the most magnificent staircase I've ever seen. I resist the urge to gasp, to gape and point and make an utter spectacle of myself. I spent my childhood surrounded by wealth, of course, but this single room—we appear to be on a landing of some sort—puts my father's entire estate to shame. To my left, stairs lead down into shadow. To my right, they curve upward and disappear around a bend, but that hardly matters—not when a fresco of brilliant clouds and blue skies opens up on the ceiling above us. Two enormous trees sprawl outward from the center, and cherubim soar between their limbs. Each carries a great flaming sword.

"Welcome to Eden," a light, feminine voice says.

I startle, clutching Michal's elbow, as a white-skinned woman with peculiar eyes of gray smoke materializes in front of us. In her hands, she holds a beautiful red apple, and the pieces finally click into place. The vines, the trees, the cherubim . . .

Eden.

My breath hitches.

As in the *Garden* of Eden.

Smiling at the woman, I speak in an undertone to Michal. "I thought we were going to Les Abysses?"

He bows his head toward mine and replies in a mocking whisper. "That depends entirely on you. Ladies first."

"What?"

He makes his meaning clear, however, by pushing me forward without ceremony. The woman turns her gaze to me instead, and upon closer inspection, I realize her eyes don't have pupils or sclera. I try and fail not to stare. The gray smoke simply swirls, uninterrupted, throughout the whole of them, each lid fringed with pale lashes. They linger curiously on my crimson dress as I drop into a curtsy. "Bonjour, mademoiselle," I say, studying her through my own lashes in fascination. She looks almost like a melusine with her monochromatic complexion, but I've never seen a melusine with eyes like hers. I *have* heard whispers of melusines who possess the gift of Sight, however. Though rare, they must exist; their queen is an oracle, after all—*the* Oracle—a goddess of the sea who glimpses tides of the future.

Straightening, I smile wider now. "It's a pleasure to meet you."

With a small, enigmatic smile of her own, she says to Michal, "You know the rules, roi sombre. The maiden is not welcome here."

"The maiden is with me. That makes her welcome."

He speaks the words coldly, absolutely, as only a king could, and my chest pinches unexpectedly as his cruel mask slips back into place. As his eyes flatten to terrifying black, as his face hardens into that of the vampire I met aboard the ship and in the aviary. Gone is the spark of interest, the reluctant amusement. This is the Michal I know. No—this is the Michal he *is*.

It takes several seconds for me to realize what the woman said. *The maiden is not welcome here.* An odd sentiment, as I do not know her at all. Could she mean—are *humans* not welcome here either?

Those eerie eyes study Michal for several seconds more—or

at least, I think they do—before flicking once more to me. "Very well." She inclines her head in submission. "Bonjour, Eve." When she presents the apple to me with both hands, her fingers have one too many knuckles. *Definitely a melusine.* In water, webs will grow between those long fingers. Her legs will transform into fins. "Will you partake of the apple and gain the Knowledge of Good and Evil, or will you resist temptation and seek Paradise?"

I tear my gaze away, blinking rapidly. Because something just *moved* in her eyes—something shapeless and shadowed at first, but growing clearer each second. Something familiar. No. *Someone* familiar. But—that can't be. I shake my head to clear it, and when I risk another look, the melusine's eyes are clouded once more. I must've imagined the face I saw there.

"Will you partake of the apple," she repeats, her voice a touch louder now, "and gain the Knowledge of Good and Evil, or will you resist temptation and seek Paradise?"

Clearly, she expects an answer.

Focus, Célie.

I look determinedly at the apple now instead of her eyes. I know this story, of course, and it doesn't end well: *Now the serpent was more subtle than any beast of the field which the Lord God had made.* The melusine even wears swathes of iridescent black fabric to complete the effect; they glisten like scales in the candlelight, stark against her white skin. She is paler than even Michal.

"This is blasphemous," I whisper to him, ignoring the eager flutter in my belly. We stand in a metaphorical Eden, which means the stairs to my left must lead to Les Abysses, while the stairs on my right must lead to Paradise. All I need to do is partake of the apple like Eve, who cursed the whole of humanity in a moment of weakness, and we can be on our merry way.

To the Abyss.

Hesitating, I crane my neck to peer into the shadows below. *It's just a clever metaphor*, I remind myself quickly. *It isn't actually Hell.* And yet... "What does she *mean* by 'gain the Knowledge of Good and Evil'?" I ask Michal.

"Just what she said. If you eat the apple, you gain truth but lose eternity. If you resist temptation, you enter Paradise."

"You couldn't be *more* vague, could you? There are parts of this I still grasp."

He clicks his tongue impatiently. "You're stalling, pet. Make your decision."

"The decision is already made, though, isn't it? We need to go below." I exhale a shaky breath, still hesitating to take the apple. This situation—though different—reminds me of another on the shores of L'Eau Melancolique. If I learned anything from those mysterious waters, it was that the truth isn't always helpful. It isn't always kind. "I just— I want to understand. What will happen after I bite the apple? What does 'gain truth' mean?"

"It means something different to everyone." When I continue to gaze at him, expectant, his tone grows rather scathing, and irritation pricks my chest at the sound of it. "After you bite the apple, our lovely pythoness, Eponine"—he gestures to the melusine, who still watches us—"will tell you a truth about yourself. Is that clear enough?"

Oh, it's perfectly clear now, and I don't like it one bit.

"Have *you* partaken of the apple before?" I ask with a note of accusation.

"Many times." As before, his lips twist into a not-quite smile.

"For example, our pythoness once predicted that I would take a bride—a mortal woman with hair of onyx and eyes of emerald, not unlike yourself." My cheeks blaze instantly at the ridiculous image—at the two of us, *together*, bound forever in holy matrimony—before he reaches out without warning, tucking a strand of hair almost affectionately behind my ear. His black eyes glitter with malice. "She also predicted that I'd kill her."

"*What?*"

When I recoil from him, horrified, he drops his hand and chuckles darkly. "Then again, five hundred years ago, she told Odessa that she'd fall in love with a bat. To my knowledge, that hasn't yet happened. Now, shall we stand here debating Eponine's ploys for the rest of the night, or have you made your decision?"

Eponine's smile does not falter. "They are not ploys, roi sombre, and that is not all I told you about your bride."

The last of Michal's laughter fades at that. "And as I told *you*," he says softly, "it will not happen."

"The future oft reveals itself in strange and unexpected ways."

"Take the apple, Célie," Michal says, abruptly curt, "and let us be done with this."

Eyes narrowing, I glance between them. They obviously don't want to discuss the rest of Eponine's prediction aloud, but as that prediction concerns *me*, their secrecy hardly seems fair. And what could possibly be worse than him *killing* me? No. I repress a shudder. It cannot be true. Odessa hasn't fallen in love with a bat, and what's more—Michal promised he wouldn't hurt me. Indeed, it was his *only* promise, and I have no choice but to believe him at the moment. Besides, his suspiciousness makes sense. I learned melusines can be crafty during my time in Le Présage; they can be sly. Each word from them often holds a double meaning. Michal found a mortal bride, yes, but not in holy matrimony. He found a Bride of Death, which is something altogether different. Perhaps the second part of Eponine's prediction relates to that.

It doesn't mean Michal will *kill* me.

Or perhaps, says the supercilious voice again, *her predication isn't about you at all.*

Strangely agitated, I ignore that voice, and my fingers close instinctively around the apple. "To your health," I tell Michal, and without further ado, I lift the sweet fruit to my lips.

It tastes just like any other apple.

I chew quickly, ignoring the way Eponine's smile widens—like a cat who has cornered a particularly juicy mouse. The impression only intensifies when she begins to circle me, her long and glittering robes trailing behind her. "Take out what is in your pocket."

I hesitate for only a second before extracting the silver cross and dangling it from my fingertips, where it spins and glints in the lamplight. Eponine studies it in silence for a long moment. Beside us, Michal tracks her every step. I cannot decide if he dislikes her or simply distrusts her; either way, I do not envy the pythoness. "Tell me what you see," she says at last.

I frown at her. To be completely frank, I expected much worse. "It's a silver cross."

"And?"

I hand the apple to Michal. "And it's . . . ornate, bright, with filigree around the edges. It belonged to Babette Trousseau." I trap the cross pendant in the palm of my hand, extending it to her. "She etched her initials along the side. See? Just there."

Light, delighted laughter spills from Eponine's mouth. "Are you sure?"

Brow furrowing, I angle the cross toward the nearest lamp, and golden light spills upon the markings. "Quite. Her initials are faint, but they're right there, etched into the silver like I said. BT."

At last, Michal looks away from Eponine, lifting my wrist to examine the cross. Despite his fit of temper with the prophecy, his touch remains carefully light. "This doesn't say BT."

"Of course it—"

"Someone tried to carve over the original letters, but the strokes are different." He regards me almost warily. "I don't think Babette was the original owner of this necklace."

I snatch my wrist away from him, unaccountably offended. "Don't be ridiculous. What are you talking about?"

"Why didn't you give the necklace to your brethren after you discovered Babette's body?"

"I—" My frown deepens as I look between him and Eponine. "It just didn't feel right to turn in something so personal. The necklace plainly meant something to Babette, or she wouldn't have been carrying it with her. I was going to give it to Coco instead," I add defensively. "She would've wanted it."

"But you didn't give it to Coco. You kept it. Why?"

"Because *someone* abducted me before I had the chance." My voice echoes a touch louder than necessary in the still and quiet of the landing. Perhaps because I've developed a strange connection to this cross, and I don't relish the idea of it belonging to someone else. Perhaps because I shouldn't have kept it in the first place.

Or—perhaps the most disturbing—because I cannot unsee my sister's face in Eponine's smoke-filled eyes. "What does it *matter* why I kept it? Shouldn't we be descending into Les Abysses now? I partook of the apple, which means we're free to go below."

"It matters," Michal says firmly, catching my sleeve when I move to shove past him, "because the original initials are FT."

FT.

FT.

Oh. He means—

FT.

The letters wash through me like a flood, but instead of carrying me away, they freeze my insides solid. "Filippa Tremblay," I whisper, turning slowly to face him. "You think the necklace belonged to my sister."

He answers with a small nod.

"No." I shake my own head abruptly, forcefully, the ice in my chest melting to molten-hot conviction. I plunge the cross into my pocket and seize the apple from his hand. As it turns out, there is such a thing as *impossible*, and we've stumbled upon it in this exact moment. Michal isn't going to kill anyone—not if I can help it—and my sister—my dear, *departed* sister—couldn't have owned this cross before Babette. Without a doubt now, Eponine is a charlatan, and Michal needs his vision checked. "It seems you've already forgotten our cozy little confessional. Let me remind you: Filippa has been dead for over a year. The murders started last month. She isn't involved in this."

"Célie," Michal says quietly, but I refuse to hear another word. Not about this. As far as I'm concerned, this conversation never happened, and our pythoness is a mermaid in a gauche costume. Impulsively, I sink my teeth into the apple once more, chewing the sweet fruit without tasting it.

"*There.*" I lift the apple to show the pythoness my second bite. "I partook of your wretched apple again, so I demand another truth—an *actual* truth this time, and not about me. I want to know about Babette Trousset."

Eponine tilts her head, irritatingly calm despite the circumstances. "You may only partake of the apple once per night, Célie Tremblay."

"You recognize me from the notices outside. Excellent." I cross my arms in my best impersonation of my sister, of Lou and Coco and every other stubborn woman I've ever met. "You're about to learn much more than just my name, however. I can be quite stubborn when I want to be."

Though he says nothing, Michal moves to stand behind me. To *loom* behind me.

Eponine pretends not to notice. With another curious smile, she says, "My own sister, Elvire, speaks highly of you, mariée. I believe you met her in January when you visited Le Présage. You showed her kindness."

Perhaps not the notices, then.

"It wasn't difficult. Elvire is lovely."

"There are many humans who disagree." A pause. "However, for the sake of my little sister, I must ask . . . are you certain you wish to enter Les Abysses? I am not the first pythoness to warn the descent to Hell is easy, and I will not be the last. If you continue on this path, you will not be able to turn back."

"Babette has *died*," I say emphatically. *As if any of this has been easy.* "Any one of us could be next if we don't find her killer."

"Hmm." Her smile fades as she considers me, but she no longer seems to see *me* at all; her gaze has turned peculiar, almost *inward*, as if she stares at something we cannot see, and her voice takes on a strange, ethereal cant. "You seek someone, yes, but forget someone seeks you. If you are to succeed, the killer will too."

My heart drops like a stone. "What did you say?"

Behind me, Michal radiates such cold that I can practically *feel* him burn down the length of my back. "Do you know the name of the killer, Eponine?"

She lifts her face toward the ceiling, still lost in the otherworld. Her hands shoot upward as well, and her fingers twitch as if searching for something, plucking at invisible strings. "No . . . his is not the name you need. Not yet."

Michal steps around me now. "And yet it is the name I *want*. You will give it to me."

"I will not."

"Be very careful, pythoness." Though she cannot see him, his eyes flash with the promise of violence. "I cannot compel you, but there are other ways of extracting information."

Slowly, she lowers her hands, and her own eyes seem to clear, returning her to the present. When they finally land upon Michal, they narrow, and she draws herself up to her full and considerable height. "How very foolish you are, *vampire*, to risk the ire of my queen. You live on an isle, do you not?"

Michal suppresses a snarl, but even he seems reluctant to provoke the goddess of the sea. After several seconds, he forces his features into a mask of indifference, but I know—I *know*—that if Eponine invoked any other name, this night would've ended very different for her.

Which leaves it solely to me.

"I'm not leaving this spot until you explain." Widening my stance, I plant my hand on my hip and glare at her. "*Properly* explain. No more riddles." When she arches her pale brows, unimpressed, I resist the urge to shrink beneath her stare. Because I don't care if her patience has grown thin. Mine unraveled hours ago. "I'll stand here all night if I must. I'll frighten away all your customers. For all your pomp and pageantry, you still need customers, don't you? This *is* a place of business. I'll tell everyone both brothels are *full* of humans like me, or I'll"—inspiration strikes like a bolt of lightning—"I'll tell them the Chasseurs are on their way!" I thrust the apple toward her for emphasis. "Is that what you want? Huntsmen running amok?"

She scowls between me and Michal. "You dare invite even their name into this sacred place?"

"Oh, I'd dare a lot more than that. Perhaps I'll invite the real thing." *A lie.* "At this very second, half the kingdom searches for me. I'm quite certain that a huntsman or two will answer my call. Isn't—isn't that right, Michal?"

Though he doesn't look at me—though his gaze remains cold, remote, as he considers Eponine—there is almost . . . satisfaction in the set of his jaw now. Perhaps triumph. "She means every word," he says softly, strolling to the wall beside the stairs to lean against it. He tips his head at me infinitesimally before picking a crimson thread from his sleeve.

"That's right." My stomach swoops low at his assent. "I can be *incredibly* vexing."

Without warning, the apple flies from my hand to Eponine, who clenches it tight in her fist. "I can see that." Her voice has lost its light, ethereal quality, and she sounds very ugly now. Very ugly, indeed. "Though even I cannot see why Elvire dotes on you. I will not give you the name you seek, but—if you leave my presence this instant—I will give you another: Pennelope Trousset. She is Babette's cousin and confidant, and she will lead you where you need to go."

Pennelope Trousset. I commit the name to memory, and—for Elvire's sake—force myself to take a deep, calming breath and curtsy once more. "Thank you, Eponine. It was . . . interesting to meet you. Please tell your sister I'll visit soon."

"I will not lie to my sister, Célie Tremblay. Now go." She waves a skeletal hand, dismissing us, those eerie eyes burning into mine even as the rest of her begins to fade, to dissipate like smoke in the wind. Her voice, however, lingers after her body has disappeared. "And take care of the company you keep. We will not meet again."

As I follow Michal down the stairs, her true meaning rings clear and ominous behind me: *Because you will be dead.*

CHAPTER THIRTY-TWO

Les Abysses

I often understand why my father fell prey to magic.

Though I hate him for it—though I blame him entirely for my sister's death—I understand its lure. It lingers like a toothache when you're surrounded by extraordinary people, when you yourself are thoroughly and irreparably ordinary. When Lou beckons the stars with the crook of her finger, I cannot help but gasp and clutch my jaw. When Reid catches them in a glittering bouquet, I bite down hard, again and again, until that toothache consumes my entire body. Until I cannot think of anything else, cannot *do* anything else but want.

Sometimes, I think the wanting will kill me.

It certainly killed my sister.

"Are you afraid?" Voice low, Michal pulls me toward another crimson door. This one stands at the bottom of a narrow spiral staircase of black stone, and when he pushes it open, I force myself to march past him, to enter the room first with my chin held high.

"No," I lie, breathless.

Michal smirks and follows after me.

We step onto a metal platform that runs the circumference of the room. Enormous fireplaces curve along the walls—built of the same black, rough-hewn stone as the corridor—and inside their hearths, strange black fire crackles, casting stranger light on the center of the room. *The pit,* I realize with a sudden stab of delirium. Several feet below the outer platform, it spans wide and deep; dark velvet pillows scatter across its floor between low chaises and settees, and atop them, creatures I've never seen. Most writhe and twist so closely that I can't tell where one body ends and another begins, but some simply lounge and watch. My cheeks flush hotter with each second. There are witches and werewolves and melusines, yes, but there are also . . . others. Creatures I've never before seen.

You know the rules. The maiden is not welcome here.

Any doubt of Eponine's meaning flees when a pallid woman laps at the bloody palm of a scarred courtesan. When a dragon-esque man flicks a forked tongue in the ear of another. When a horned woman digs sharp nails into the latter's hips. Behind them, a fully transformed werewolf throws their head back, howling as a man with scales strokes his tail. No human—at least, no discernible one—joins the revelry.

Wait.

It takes several seconds for my eyes to see past the—the *relations* occurring below us, but when they do, they dart between the different creatures with rising panic. In a sea of black fabrics, the courtesans burn bright like beacons in the night . . . because each one of them wears brilliant crimson.

My eyes widen at the realization, and I sway on the spot.

Each and every courtesan wears a crimson gown, crimson suit, or crimson cape. Two melusines wear crimson roses in their silvery hair, while crimson jewelry drips from a broad-shouldered loup garou's neck. Indeed, crimson is the only color in the entire room other than black, which is *most* startling for anyone else wearing it.

Namely *me.*

Whirling toward Michal, feeling rather light-headed, I hiss, "Why didn't you *tell* me?" I seize my skirt and quell the urge to wrap it around his marble throat. "Give me your cloak!" I paw at his black traveling cloak instead. Tragically, I left mine aboard the ship. "Give it to me!"

A smirk still plays on his lips, and his black eyes glitter almost impishly as he evades my attack. "I told you to wear green."

"You didn't tell me the courtesans wear *red.*"

"According to you, I couldn't have said a thing to change your mind."

"If anyone here thinks I'm a courtesan, they'll"—I wince and shake my head—"they'll—"

"They'll *what?*"

I stare hard at my shoes, at the scuffed leather along the toes. At anything other than Michal, who sees too much and also nothing at all. "They'll be very disappointed," I whisper, my voice growing smaller with each word. I hate him for making me say them. For making me even *think* them. "Because I'm—I wouldn't know the first thing about helping them, because I'm—because I'm a"—my voice is almost inaudible now—"a virgin."

Michal still hears it. When I dare to glance back up at him, his smirk has faded. To my surprise, however, no pity has crept into his expression. No. That same strange intensity from the casket burns in his gaze, and he lifts a hand as if to touch my cheek before his fingers curl inward and he drops it back to his side. "No one would be disappointed," he says shortly. Then he flags down a nearby courtesan, a lovely man with glowing violet eyes and lustrous dark skin. Bare-chested, he wears ruby studs in the shape of flowers through his nipples. "We need to speak with Pennelope Trousset," Michal tells him.

The man dips his head—his ears are pointed—toward the pit. "Of course, monsieur, but Pennelope appears to be already engaged this morning. I'm late to an appointment myself, but might I suggest Adeline? We've been told her blood tastes sweetest." He pulls a jewel-encrusted pocket watch from his belt, checking the time, before turning those beautiful violet eyes upon me. They flick down my dress curiously. "Is tonight your first shift, chérie?"

I swallow hard. "Er—no, monsieur."

"No?" He blinks in confusion. "But how can that be? I never forget a face." Leaning closer, he sniffs delicately, and his confusion only deepens at whatever he smells. I send up a fervent prayer of thanks that I brushed my teeth. "A *human* face, it would seem. However did you convince Eponine to let you in?"

Helpless, I glance to Michal for an answer, but he only rumbles with laughter and starts toward the pit.

"Do the courtesans know what you are?" Trying not to hyperventilate now, I clamber down the stairs after him. "You said you've been here before, and that woman"—I jerk my head to our left—"is drinking that man's blood."

"They do not have a name for our kind, but they know and respect our tastes." Among the bodies in the pit, a dancing couple threatens to separate us, but Michal's hand snakes back to seize mine. He pulls me to his side, murmuring, "I thought you weren't afraid?"

"I'm *not* afraid. I'm—I—" But the words stick in my throat as I glance right, and the dragon man shifts, affording me an unobstructed view of his—of his—I turn my face away quickly, breath hitching, and lift a trembling hand to my forehead. What I *am* is woefully unprepared for a situation like this. Just like my mother and father wanted me to be, just like Evangeline and my governesses wanted too. In all my years, in all my education, I've never once learned—never once *seen*—

Filippa slipped through our window each night, yes, but she never told me what she *did* with her mysterious paramour. I've heard about sex, of course—read every book I could sneak into the house—but it's much different to imagine it than to *see* it with my own eyes. *Seeing* it makes the room feel much smaller than it should be, much hotter, as if I'm standing in an open flame, burning slowly alive.

It makes me feel faint.

When I stumble, Michal catches me, pulls me across the room toward a courtesan who arches in the lap of a loup garou, his form caught halfway between man and wolf. His eyes gleam yellow. His teeth glint sharp. Though they aren't quite in the *act*—at least, I don't think they are—they still seem to be enjoying themselves. "Do you want to wait outside?" Michal asks, and his *thumb*—he slides it up my wrist to soothe my rapid pulse. "Eponine gave you her blessing. She won't bother you again."

"No." I shake my head fervently and pull away. "No, I have to do this. I *want* to do this." Then, because I cannot help it— "Does Eponine own this place?"

"She is its mistress, yes."

"And Paradise?"

"She presides over it too."

"What's it like up there?"

He gestures around us. "Much like this. The courtesans wear white instead of red, and a choir of melusines puts all who enter into a sort of trance." He pauses. "I confess, I've only visited Paradise once. It . . . felt much like a dream."

It felt much like a dream.

A dream is exactly what this entire night has felt like.

When I fall silent, Michal sinks into a nearby settee, spreading an arm along its camel back while I stand awkwardly beside him. Unbidden, I glance toward the werewolf and courtesan. This must be Pennelope. She shares her cousin's heart-shaped face and golden hair, her scarred and ivory skin. And the way she *moves* . . . a heavy weight settles in my chest as I watch her. I could never hope to move like that.

I force myself to look away, to give them privacy. As the violet-eyed courtesan above pointed out, she seems . . . somewhat preoccupied at the moment, and quite unable to answer our questions. Perhaps we should've made an appointment. Who knows how long they might take to—to finish? Michal seems prepared to wait, but as he said, daybreak rapidly approaches. Could I just . . . tap her on the shoulder? I shift from foot to foot, considering my options. Perhaps I can simply clear my throat, and the two will magically break apart.

Voice casual, Michal says, "It isn't a dirty word, you know."

"What word?" I ask distractedly.

"*Virgin.*" He arches a brow at me. "No one here cares one way or another, so you needn't whisper it like a curse."

My mouth falls open in shock, in mortification, and my hands curl to fists at my sides. Just like that, I quite forget about Pennelope and her companion undulating behind us. "I never should've told you that. I never *would've* told you that if I'd known you'd want to—to *discuss* it."

"Why wouldn't we?" He tilts his head curiously. "Does it make you uncomfortable to talk about sex?"

"And if it does? Will you cease this conversation?"

"It's rude to answer a question with a question, pet."

"I am not your *pet*, and it's ruder to continue addressing me as such."

He studies me with rapt interest. "Do friends not take sobriquets? If I recall correctly, you called my dear cousin *Dima*."

"You cannot be serious." I stare at him in disbelief—both that he remembered the *one* time I shortened Dimitri's name and that he could ever, even in the warped depths of his mind, consider *pet* as a term of endearment. "You are not my friend, Michal Vasiliev."

He arches a brow. "No?"

"*No*," I say emphatically. "That you would even *think* of friendship while you plan to maim and murder my loved ones proves you are quite incapable of it."

He waves a dismissive hand. "Every relationship has problems."

"*Problems?* You kidnapped me. You blackmailed me." Indignant, I lift a finger for each offense. "You locked me in a room, and you goaded me into summoning ghosts. Only a few moments ago, you revealed a *prophecy* in which—"

Before I can finish, however, a square-jawed gentleman approaches us—no, approaches *me*—and extends a broad hand. The sharp bite of incense, of magic, trails in his wake. "Hello," he purrs without preamble, kissing my fingers. "May I have your name, humaine?"

I stiffen at the word, abruptly and painfully aware that I'm not supposed to be here—and that my face and name litter the street outside. Cursing myself for forgetting my cloak, for wearing this silly dress, I duck my head. "Fleur," I say, pulling my hand from his as politely as possible. "My name is Fleur . . . Toussaint."

I cringe internally at the slip.

"Toussaint?" The witch furrows his brow, trying to place the name, before brushing it aside and inhaling deeply. A wide, unctuous smile spreads across his face at my scent. *Humaine.* "Might we spend some time together this morning, Mademoiselle Toussaint? I am . . . eager to know you better."

"Er—no." I shake my head apologetically. "No, I don't think so. I don't actually work here, monsieur."

The witch's smile slips. "I beg your pardon?"

"I don't work here. This dress—it—"

"—is crimson in Les Abysses," he finishes, scowling now. "As you stand alone in the pit, I can only assume you seek companionship." A dark pause. "Unless witches are somehow offensive to you? Is that what this is, Madame Toussaint?"

"No, *no*, not at all! This dress"—I glare at Michal in accusation, and he gazes right back, completely at ease—"was a very poor joke, and I apologize for any misunderstanding it caused."

"Humph." Though the witch's eyes narrow, his face relaxes slightly after hearing the earnestness of my words, and he edges closer to try again. "In that case . . . are you *sure* I might not persuade you to leave your companion for the remainder of the morning? I promise you will not regret it."

Now *I* resist the urge to scowl. Apparently, he didn't hear the part where *I don't work here*, or else he's conveniently forgotten in the last thirty seconds. Grudgingly, I look again to Michal, who has once more, somehow, become the lesser of two evils. Enormously entertained, he suppresses a smirk—still reclining against the settee—and in his black eyes, I see my own reflection snapping, *You are not my friend, Michal Vasiliev.*

Perfect.

Exhaling hard through my nose, I say, "My apologies, monsieur, for not explaining properly"—the witch leans forward eagerly— "but I've already made an appointment with *this* gentleman." I drop stiffly to the settee beside Michal and force a would-be convincing smile. The witch still eyes the space between us in suspicion. Scooting a bit closer, I give Michal's knee an awkward pat. "I shall be spending the rest of the morning with—with him."

"So leave," Michal tells the witch coolly.

For a second, it looks as if the witch might argue, but with one last disgruntled look in our direction, he turns and stalks away. I remove my hand from Michal's knee at once. "I think I'm going to kill you," I say pleasantly.

"I think I might enjoy it," Michal says as another patron— this one a scaled creature with round, glassy eyes—approaches. When she asks for my name, my hand darts back to Michal's knee. When she asks if I'll join her by the fire, it creeps higher, clutching his thigh for dear life. When she brazenly asks for a kiss, I crawl straight into Michal's lap, and he shakes with laughter underneath me.

"You are *insufferable*," I whisper as the woman sighs and slinks away. I brace my shoulder against his chest, unable to look at him, as this is quite possibly the most humiliating moment of my life.

And yet—as absolutely *revolting* as it is to admit—he did tell me to wear green. "Do you mind if I just—er, sit here until Pennelope finishes her appointment?" Then, unable to keep a note of desperation from my voice— "*Has* Pennelope finished her appointment?" Michal's laughter gradually subsides. "No."

Damn it.

I sit there for a moment—trying not to notice the chill of his skin through my gown—before he shifts slightly, his free hand sliding around my back. "We're starting to draw attention."

I cast a panicked glance around, and—sure enough—more than one pair of eyes has settled upon us. Perhaps because I'm human, or perhaps because we're not locked in passionate embrace like all the other couples. Instinctively, I press my cheek into Michal's shoulder, praying my hair hides my face. It'll be a miracle if I leave this place unrecognized. My stomach plunges as my mind plays out the consequences: Chasseurs swarming, Jean Luc shouting, Frederic seizing my arm—

"Would it be horribly rude for you to interrupt Pennelope?" I ask quickly.

Would it really be so terrible to see Jean Luc again?

"No one here will report you to the huntsmen, Célie."

"A hundred thousand couronnes is a lot of money, Michal."

I feel rather than hear his low rumble of agreement, and his arm—it tightens subtly around me, angling my face further into his chest. *Shielding me,* I realize with a start. "Loup garou are territorial by nature, occasionally aggressive, and he could perceive it as an insult if I interrupt. He could attack." Instantly, I envision the enormous loup garou charging Michal, who stands still and silent, waiting, before tearing him in half. "Yes," Michal says, correctly interpreting my shudder. "I doubt anyone here would help us after that."

My throat tightens at our distinct lack of options. "So . . . we wait."

"So we wait."

It is the longest hour of my life.

Never before have I been so aware of a man's proximity—of his hard thighs beneath mine or his cool hand on my spine. I try not to think about either, try not to acknowledge the way my heartbeat slowly descends to my belly. The cries of pleasure all around us do little to help the situation. If this is how they indulge in public, I cannot imagine what happens in the courtesans' private rooms . . . unless the exhibition makes it *better* for some? I squirm a little at the thought, still flushed and restless, until the hand on my back seizes a lock of my hair and tugs. Hard. I gasp and pull away to face him. "What was that for?"

"Stay still."

"Why?" I jerk my head toward Pennelope, who moans in time with the werewolf. "*She* isn't staying still."

His fingers wrap more firmly around my hair, and he pulls harder, tilting my face upward and baring my throat. His eyes glint like shards of glass as he holds my gaze. "Exactly." When I open my mouth to tell him *exactly* where he can put his arrogance, he flexes his hips against me, and I nearly choke on the words. Something—something *hard* presses against my leg. "Shall we do what they're doing? Is that what you want?"

Heat floods my cheeks, but I don't answer. I don't *need* to answer. Of course I don't need to answer, and of course I don't *want* to—

"Interesting." His eyes drop to the pale column of my throat, and that casual arm along the sofa moves to my knees. He drapes it across them, his fingers lightly brushing the back of my thigh; gooseflesh erupts down my legs. I shift in his lap again, unable to help it. Unable to *breathe*. Because this is Michal. I should fear the open hunger in his gaze, should push him away from me—should do it *now*—but the fluttering in my belly doesn't feel like fear. It feels like something else, something tight and urgent and powerful. The realization catches in my throat as I stare at him. I feel *powerful*. "They're almost finished," Michal murmurs.

He dangled you over the sea, I remind myself fervently. *He threatened to drown every sailor.*

My hands still ache to touch him, however, not unlike how it felt when I drank his blood. Except I haven't drunk his blood this time, and that—*that* should send me fleeing into the sunrise.

"How can you tell?" I ask instead.

"Do you really want to know?"

"Yes." Though I hesitate on the word, I realize it's true—I *do* want to know more about this strange, secret world that has been kept from me. I want to understand, I want to *learn*, but most of all, I want—

No.

I dare not admit what I want, even to myself.

Because if I admit that I want Michal to keep looking at me like this, I'll have to admit other things too, like how the name Madame Toussaint chafes against my skin. It shouldn't, of course.

Someday, it'll be mine. Madame Célie Toussaint, devoted wife, mother, and huntswoman. A future as neat as it is pretty. As I told Michal, however, I have no intention of returning to Chasseur Tower, of pining for respect I've already earned. Which means . . .

Guilt spears the flutter in my stomach.

Would it really be so terrible to see Jean Luc again? The answer hides in the darkest part of my mind, waiting for me to look at it. To look at myself. I've been too scared to admit it—to lose the only place I have in this world—but here, straddling the unknown, the truth creeps out from the shadows. Ugly, yes—the ugliest thing I've ever done—but impossible to ignore.

I don't want to marry Jean Luc.

My heart lifts and cracks simultaneously as I finally acknowledge the truth. "Célie?" Michal drags his gaze from my throat as I lift his hand to the feverish skin of my cheek. His fingers are cool. Lovely. The guilt twists deeper.

"This isn't real," I tell him. "We're just pretending."

It felt like a dream.

He tilts his head languorously to consider me. "Of course we are." His thumb, however, brushes my bottom lip in the next second, parting it from the top and lingering there. Daring me, I realize, to make the next move. I should recoil from the challenge—that small, hateful voice in my head urges me to stop, stop, *stop*—but instead, I take his thumb into my mouth. If possible, his eyes darken further, and that same heady sense of power surges through me, washing away everything else. Without knowing why—without understanding the impulse at all—I suck gently, my tongue laving his skin with a confidence I shouldn't feel. He tastes cold and sweet from the juice of the apple. I suck harder. "Easy," he says through clenched teeth.

Reluctantly, I release his thumb. "Why?"

"*Because*"—he presses it hard against my bottom lip—"I've been imagining how you taste since I met you."

I swallow, and he tracks the movement hungrily. "I thought vampires didn't like the taste of human blood."

"I think I'd like the taste of yours."

I certainly liked the taste of *his*. We stare at each other, and from his expression, we're remembering the same thing: how I climbed up his body in the aviary, drunk on his blood and desperate to kiss him. Would he let me kiss him now? Would I let him *bite* me? In a seemingly reflexive reaction, his hips jerk up at the memory, and heat stabs through me like a knife—I catch his thumb between my teeth and bite down violently.

In an instant, I know I've made a mistake.

His entire body clenches, and he wrenches his thumb from my mouth with preternatural speed. Ice creeps back into his voice as he says, "Never do that again."

"Wh-What?" With that single cold command, reality crashes down upon my head, and I blink at him, confused and disoriented. The cries and grunts around us magnify as I return to the room, to *myself*, and realize what I've done. *Oh God*. I glance hastily at his unblemished thumb. "Did I—did I hurt you?"

His expression softens slightly. "No."

Abrupt pressure burns behind my eyes, but I refuse to acknowledge it. Because I don't deserve to cry, because this is my fault—this is *all* my fault—and my shoulders curl inward as the guilt returns tenfold, twisting my insides until I can't look at anyone or anything. We were just pretending, yes, but we still—*I* still—

"I'm sorry," I whisper to him. To Jean Luc.

Jean Luc.

I bury my face in my hands.

"Célie. Look at me." When I don't respond, shaking all over, Michal pries my wrists apart and forces me to meet his eyes. They burn into mine, stark and brutal with unfamiliar emotion, and I don't like it. I don't like the way it makes me *feel*—like my skin has shrunk too small, revealing the exact shape of me, and he can see every imperfection. "You cannot ever bite a vampire. Do you understand? You cannot consume my blood—or *any* vampire blood—ever again. It's too dangerous."

"But in the aviary—"

He shakes his head fiercely. "It was an emergency in the aviary. You might've died without it. But if something happens to you with vampire blood in your system, yours will be a fate worse than death."

"What will happen?"

"You'll become like us. Like me." He clenches his jaw and glares determinedly over my shoulder. "That cannot happen."

"Michal—"

"It *will not* happen, Célie." Without another word, he lifts me from his lap and returns me to the settee. I fall silent, staring at the rigid lines of him, and nod. Because I don't know what else there is to do. Because I couldn't have *actually* pierced his skin—not without wood or silver—yet even the possibility has upset him beyond anything I've seen.

Most of all, however, because he's right—this can never happen again. This *will never* happen again.

Brushing aside a tear, I glance back to check on Pennelope, only to find her standing directly behind the settee. She arches a golden brow, watching us, as a smile plays on her lush, red lips. "It seems I've missed the fun part. What a pity."

CHAPTER THIRTY-THREE

A Brief Interview

"Pennelope!" I leap to my feet and curtsy, praying she hasn't been standing there long. Judging by the amused gleam in her golden eyes, however, she heard every word between Michal and me. I wish the floor would rise up and swallow me whole. "It's lovely to meet you."

"Is it? It sounds as if I'm interrupting something."

Beside me, Michal rises in stony silence.

"Not at all." I smooth my gown in a self-conscious gesture, my limbs still trembling. Her own is much simpler with its crimson gauze, but much lovelier too—it floats down her hourglass figure like a cloud, glittering and sheer. Despite the claws of her paramour, the fabric remains wholly intact, probably spelled; the biting scent of blood magic wafts from it. I wipe away another tear. "We've been waiting for you, actually."

"Oh, I'm aware."

"You—you are?"

She waves a flippant hand. Unlike her cousin, she hasn't attempted to cover her scars with cosmetics, leaving them bare to glow in the firelight. They wind up her fingers, her wrists, her arms with intention—as if she planned the exact location of each mark—before ending in a delicate filigree across her chest. "I might not be a creature of the night like your *friend* here"—she eyes Michal appreciatively—"but I still have ears. The two of you haven't exactly been subtle. Not that it's entirely your fault, of course," she adds. "We always notice when night children come to call. Two more just arrived upstairs."

Her tone holds no reprimand, merely keen interest. Though beautiful, her face is almost fey-like with its sharp eyes and pointed nose, and when she waggles her eyebrows mischievously, the impression only intensifies. "If you'd like to make an appointment, however," she continues, "I'm afraid it'll need to be for tomorrow night. Dear Jermaine is already waiting in my room, and he hates to share."

I glance around us, looking for the staircase that leads to the courtesans' chambers, but there isn't one. No doorways either. Just rough black stone and crackling black fire. And shadows—disembodied shapes that writhe against the walls of the outer rim, unaffected by the firelight. I didn't notice them before. *Can't imagine why*, I think bitterly.

"We aren't here to make an appointment," Michal says, his tone imperious once more. "We're here to ask about your cousin."

"My cousin?" Instantly, the impish smile vanishes from Pennelope's face, and the golden glow that surrounds her hardens to flinty silver. Her eyes narrow between the two of us. "Which cousin?"

"Babette Trousset."

Her lips press flat.

"We want to give our condolences," I start quickly, but Michal interrupts.

"Tell us about the days before her death." Ignoring my scowl, he prowls around the settee to close the distance between them. If he means to intimidate, it doesn't work; Pennelope refuses to cower at his approach. No, her golden eyes spark in silent challenge instead. Michal's reputation as a *creature of the night* apparently means very little to her—which means she must know very little about him. Still, I resist the urge to step between the two. Only once have I seen the true wrath of a blood witch, and it isn't an experience I'd like to repeat.

"Did she share anything that might've caused you unease?" Michal presses. "Perhaps introduced you to a new lover, or an old one?"

My scowl deepens. This sort of conversation requires delicate handling, and Michal is displaying as much finesse as a blunt axe.

"Our apologies, mademoiselle," I say before he can speak again. "We realize speaking about Babette must be difficult—"

Michal, however, interrupts once more, his voice growing colder with each word. "Perhaps she spoke of a business arrangement gone wrong, or a family member who needed help."

At this, Pennelope's expression twists, and I hasten to smooth the tension, skirting around the settee myself. I knit my fingers together to keep from wringing my hands. Or strangling Michal. "We're investigating her death, so any information you can give us about her final days—any unusual behavior, any new faces—would be most helpful."

"Would it?" Pennelope sneers around the question, and even I can tell the expression doesn't belong on her cheerful face. "I'll tell you the same as I told your brethren, Célie Tremblay: I didn't know Babette even *went* to Cesarine, let alone who stole her body."

I sigh in resignation. *Of course* she knows who I am. My chances of discovery climb steadily higher.

"The Chasseurs came to Les Abysses?" Michal asks sharply.

Pennelope scoffs. "They certainly tried—on a tip-off from *your* friends, I might add," she snarls at me, "but you know Eponine. She saw the pricks coming, and everyone vacated the premises before they arrived. Everyone except me." She lifts her chin with pride. With defiance. "I stayed, and I answered their questions because no one—*no one*—wants vengeance on the bastard who hurt Babette more than I do. She and Sylvie are like sisters to me, and I'll gut anyone who ever harmed them."

"Sylvie?"

Pennelope looks away quickly, cursing the slip under her breath. "Babette's little sister."

I frown at the revelation. "I didn't know Babette had a sister."

"Perhaps you don't know Babette as well as you think you do."

"Where can we find her?" A drunken melusine stumbles into Michal, who shunts him away without blinking. "Sylvie?"

A mixture of triumph and heartache creeps into Pennelope's eyes. "You can't. Sylvie died three months ago." Before we can ask, she adds tersely, "Blood sickness."

Oh.

I've heard of blood sickness only once before—it took the life of a little boy named Matthieu, whose death twisted his mother into one of the most evil creatures alive. She died in the Battle of Cesarine with her mistress, La Voisin, otherwise known as Coco's aunt, who once ruled the Dames Rouges with an iron fist. "I'm so sorry, Pennelope," I say quietly. "To have lost both of your cousins in such a short—"

But Pennelope jerks as if I've struck her. "We don't need your *pity*."

"Of course you don't." Frown deepening, I lift my hands in a placating gesture. Though my heart aches for her, we'll need to take a more direct approach if Pennelope refuses to cooperate. I shudder to think of what Michal might do otherwise. "Is there somewhere more private we can talk? Somewhere more comfortable?" Nudging aside the pouf at my feet, I inspect the floor beneath it as surreptitiously as possible. Perhaps their chambers lie below, and pillows cleverly hide any door. Except—I bite back a groan of frustration. There are no doors here either. "Jermaine is in your bedchamber, but perhaps we can retire to Babette's?" A careful pause. "Have you cleaned out her rooms yet?"

"That's none of your business, pig."

My brow furrows at the slur. Given the situation, an emotional outburst is perfectly understandable, but this one also feels . . . exaggerated, somehow. Overwrought. She didn't seem to have a problem with Michal *or* me until we mentioned Babette, and she would've known my connection to the Chasseurs right away. "There's no need for hostility, Pennelope. We're just trying to help. If you could answer our—"

"I already told you everything there is to know." She speaks with a sharp, cutting air of finality, her voice just shy of drawing blood. "Are we finished here? Jermaine likes waiting even less than sharing. Who knows *what* he might do if I leave him alone for much longer?" A forbidding smile. "And we all know how much Eponine abhors violence—blood never really lifts from the furniture, does it?"

"White vinegar does the trick." Far from being deterred, Michal continues to study her, clasping his hands behind his back and refusing to move. Though casual, his body has gone completely still again. "I presume the huntsmen searched the premises during their interrogation?"

Pennelope scoffs as if unimpressed. "Of course they did."

"All of it?"

"Everything." She sweeps her arms to encompass the entire room, glaring directly into Michal's eyes for emphasis. Almost *too* much emphasis. "They found nothing of interest. Now—this conversation is over, and I am leaving." She charges toward the stairs but halts just before ascending. Her lip curls. "And Eponine *will* be hearing about this, nightwalker. I hope you like to swim."

CHAPTER THIRTY-FOUR

And a Long Grudge

We stare after her for a beat of silence. Then—

"What was *that*?" I whirl to face him incredulously. "Are you completely without sense? The entire *point* of this exercise was to seek her help, to commiserate with her and to charm her, to apply *gentle* pressure if all else failed—"

He rolls his eyes and steps around me. "We're investigating a killer, Célie, not asking him over for tea."

"And now?" Storming after him through the pit, I nearly step on his heel—then I *do* step on his heel, and he growls, turning with lethal speed and sweeping me into his arms once more. Perfect. All the better to poke him right in his idiotic chest, which I proceed to do. Most vehemently. "What now, O Ruthless One? Eponine sent us to Pennelope for a reason, and because of *you*, she and Jermaine are probably plotting our painful and untimely ends at this very second." I poke him again. Then again for good measure. "Well?"

He glares down at me as we climb the stairs. "Well *what*?"

"What did you hope to accomplish by bullying her that way? What did we gain?"

"Much more than you think," he says coolly, "O Brilliant One."

"I'm wounded, truly"—I clutch my chest in feigned injury—"but as the courtesans have hidden their rooms, I doubt we'll be able to just stroll into Babette's without permission, let alone conduct a thorough search of it. We needed Pennelope for that too."

"How quickly you forget I've been here before."

"How is that relevant?"

"I know where the courtesans' rooms are."

"Oh." I blink at him, and heat rushes to my face at his meaning. "*Oh.*"

"As delicious as I find that look"—his eyes darken as we draw to a halt beside one of the enormous stone fireplaces—"it's incredibly distracting, and we have only an hour and a half before sunrise." Setting me on my feet, he nods to the black fire before us. "The courtesans' rooms lie beyond the flames—one of Eponine's more ingenious security measures. One cannot enter without the blessing of a courtesan." His subtle emphasis on the word *blessing* makes me frown, but he continues before I can question it. "Those who try burn to death within seconds. This is Hellfire, eternal fire, cast many years ago by La Voisin herself."

"I know what Hellfire is." Earlier this year, the same black flames ravaged the entire city of Cesarine, including my sister's crypt. I stare at the deadly tendrils in trepidation, and at that precise second, the violet-eyed courtesan steps out of the fireplace next to ours—*out* of it, passing straight through the flames, like the back of the chimney is some kind of door. *Which it is*, I realize, returning the courtesan's puzzled wave. A golden doorknob winks at us behind the flames. My gaze darts back to Michal. "What sort of *blessing* could possibly allow us to pass through Hellfire unscathed?"

"It isn't really a blessing. It's a loophole in the magic." He runs his hand along the mantel as if inspecting for dust, but his fingers linger over its elaborate whorls and shapes too long to be casual. His eyes probe them too intently. Some I recognize—like the serpent and the wide, yawning mouth of Abaddon, demon of the abyss—while others I don't. "Like all witches, La Voisin wove a gap into her enchantment: courtesans can pass through the flames without harm, as can anyone they bless with a kiss."

A kiss.

I echo the words faintly. "You— You're saying that in order to enter Babette's rooms, a courtesan will need to . . . kiss us." He nods once, curt, before stalking to the next fireplace. But that isn't answer enough. That isn't *near* answer enough, and this is suddenly the most asinine plan I've ever heard. A hundred more questions spring fully formed to my lips as I hurry after him. "Can only the courtesan to whom the room belongs bestow their blessing, or are all courtesans given access to all rooms? If the former, how on earth are we going to procure the blessing of Babette, who is, in fact, *dead*?" When I step on his heel again, he turns to glare at me. Perhaps that look would've once stopped me cold, but now it only spurs me faster. "Won't asking to enter her rooms raise suspicion? And what are you *looking* for, exactly? Because if it's the latter, we don't need to locate her individual rooms at all. We could simply *ask* someone for their blessing to enter any one of these fireplaces—"

"By all means"—tension radiates from his shoulders, his neck, his jaw—"go ask a courtesan for a kiss. I'm sure they'll give it without question, and no one will run to Pennelope when you ask to enter her dead cousin's rooms."

"Sarcasm is the lowest form of wit, Michal." Lifting my chin, I tilt my head toward the pit, where a handful of courtesans pretend not to watch us, and two more stare outright, their faces taut with suspicion and anger. Either they overheard our conversation with Pennelope earlier, or they don't appreciate a pale, imperious man prowling around outside their bedchambers. "We aren't exactly being inconspicuous as it is, and"—I lower my voice—"and couldn't you just *compel* a courtesan to tell us where to go?"

"Doest my ears deceive me, or did the holier-than-thou Mademoiselle Célie Tremblay just suggest we take away free will?" He casts me a sidelong glance. "I had no idea you were so wicked, pet. How delightful."

Though I flush at his words, chagrined, he continues to feel along each mantelpiece, as thorough and composed as ever. Sweat trickles between my shoulder blades. If the heat from the fire bothers him, however, he doesn't show it. "I don't mean we *should* compel her," I say hastily. "I'm merely asking, *hypothetically*, what would happen if we did."

"Hypothetically," he repeats, his voice dry.

"Of course. I would never *actually* suggest we force someone to do something against their will. I'm not"—I cast about for the right word, failing to find it—"I'm not *evil*."

"No, no. Just hypothetically evil." He rolls his eyes again as I sputter indignantly. "Compulsion requires much greater effort on supernatural creatures than humans. Their own brand of magic protects them. When a vampire slips through their mental shield, he often shatters it, which in turn shatters their mind. It takes supreme self-control to leave a creature intact, and even then, the compulsion might fail."

Helpless to resist, I ask, "Could *you* do it, though? As a last resort?"

"Are you implying I'm beyond hypothetically evil?"

Scowling, I try not to sound as flustered as I feel. "And it would work? You wouldn't shatter anyone's mind, and the compulsion wouldn't fail?"

"Hypothetically."

"If you say the word *hypothetically* again—" I exhale hard through my nose, straightening my shoulders and wresting control of myself once more. Bickering will get us nowhere. "How many hours until sunrise?" I ask again.

"One and a quarter."

Neck still prickling from the courtesans' gazes, I turn to count each fireplace. Over a dozen overall, closer to a score. "And . . . what happens if we stay past daybreak?"

"Guests cannot remain in Les Abysses past daybreak." A low, frustrated noise reverberates from his throat, and his fingers curl upon the mantel like scythes. A piece of stonework crumbles into his palm, littering the hearth in black dust. "Each fireplace is identical," he murmurs. "No distinguishable markers."

"Can you scent blood magic through the smoke?" I repress the urge to fidget, to bounce slightly on the balls of my feet. We'll need at least an hour to search Babette's rooms properly, if we can even find them at all—and that's only if Pennelope doesn't swoop down upon us and ruin everything, which she could do at any moment. Now I do begin to bounce, knitting my fingers together and clutching them tight. "Babette wasn't particularly trusting. She might've placed additional protections on her door, especially after falling in with someone dangerous."

But Michal only shakes his head. "Too many smells."

He stalks to the next fireplace. And the next. With each one, he grows more agitated, but his agitation looks different from mine—instead of growing flustered and animated, he grows cold and quiet. Succinct. No emotion whatsoever flickers across his expression as he studies each curve in the stone, and he refuses to hurry. Every step is deliberate. Calm and controlled. Part of me wants to shake him, just to see if he'd crack, while the rest knows better. This might be our only opportunity to learn about the killer, and we cannot waste it.

I pace behind him, searching for anything he might've missed, but of course there's nothing—the stonework on each mantel *is* identical, as are the shadows dancing on the walls between them. I glare at each one in turn. They seem humanoid in shape, almost like ghosts, except—

I bolt upright at the thought. *Ghosts.*

What was it Michal said about his sister? *She'll be back. The temptation to meddle is too great.* Unexpected hope swells in my chest. Nothing could be more meddlesome than this exact situation, and evidently—if Mila died in Cesarine but chose to haunt Requiem—ghosts aren't confined to the land on which they died. Could she have followed us here? Could *she* tell us which fireplace belonged to Babette?

Shooting a furtive glance at Michal's back, I focus with single-minded intensity on that bubble of hope, which grows larger by the second. In the castle, in the theater—even in the Old City, stalked by vampires—my emotions allowed me to slip through the veil. They allowed me to banish Mila in a moment of pique. Perhaps they'll allow me to call her again.

Only one way to find out.

"Mila?" I whisper eagerly. "Are you here?"

At the sound of her name, Michal's face snaps toward mine, and he appears at my side in the span between heartbeats. I extend my hand without looking at him. He nearly crushes my fingers in his haste. "Mila?" I try again, searching the walls, the ceiling, even the pit, waiting for her to pop into existence with a *tut tut* and supercilious expression. "Please, Mila, we need your help. It's just a simple favor—quick and easy."

Nothing happens.

"*Mila.*" Hissing her name now, I turn in a slow circle. Irritation pricks at my hope like needles. She had no problem following me to the aviary and berating me—*twice*—but the moment I actually need her? Silence. "Oh, come *on*, Mila. Don't be like this. It's terribly rude to ignore a friend, you know—"

Michal squeezes my hand, and my attention sharpens on the wall nearest us. The shadows there continue to writhe and twist, but one of them—it looks different from the others. Silver instead of black, its form more opaque. I smile in triumph as the ghost materializes, twining her arms over her head in a peculiar manner. My smile falters. Eyes closed, face contorted with passion, she sashays her hips rather awkwardly and bobs her head to music I cannot hear. Perfect ringlets bounce to and fro with the movement, and she flips one of them with the practiced air of a stage actor.

She also, tragically, isn't Mila.

"Guinevere." I fix my smile back into place, praying for a miracle. "How lovely to see you."

Her eyes flutter open at my voice, and she pretends to startle. "Célie!" Clutching her chest, she says, "What are the *chances*, darling? Mila mentioned you might be here, of course, but I never expected *Michal* to accompany you." An obvious lie, accompanied by a saccharine smile. "Are the two of you . . . official, then?" Before I can answer, she clicks her tongue sympathetically. "Quite the choice for a first date, isn't it? He took *me* to a candlelit dinner in Le Présage, complete with a choir of melusines—such angelic voices, such rapture that night—but never despair, darling. Never despair." She drifts forward to pat my head in perhaps the most condescending gesture ever made. "Very few will ever experience a love as cosmic as ours. Star-crossed, you know."

"How . . . nice." I risk a glance at Michal, who looks as if someone has clubbed him over the head. Brows furrowed in disbelief, he recoils and tries to twist his fingers from mine, but I clamp on to him like a vise. Though he glares at me—half-furious and half-pleading—I whirl and seize his other hand too, lacing our fingers tight. If I cannot escape, neither will he. "I believe the two of you are already acquainted," I say pleasantly, "but allow me to offer reintroductions—Michal, meet the ghost of Guinevere, and Guinevere, meet Michal Vasiliev, His Royal Majesty and king of Requiem."

Guinevere's eyes dart between us in dawning realization, growing wider and wider until—

Gasping, she swoops level with Michal's face, hovering an inch or two from his nose. "Can you *see* me, cherub?"

He stares determinedly at the fire, at the ceiling, at anything other than the vibrating ghost in front of him—and a good thing too. His eyes would've surely crossed if he tried to meet hers. Heedless of his reaction, she adds gleefully, "After all this time, can you hear me?"

He grimaces when she tickles his ear. "Hello, Guinevere."

"Egad, you *can*!" Breathless with triumph, she quickly twines several ringlets around her finger, pinches dark silver spots upon her cheeks, and smooths her pristine gown. "Oh, happy day! Happy, happy day indeed!" Then—with the efficiency of a gardener in spring—she plants herself directly between Michal and me, which stretches our clasped hands directly through her stomach. Gooseflesh erupts up my arms. "You needn't worry about *her* anymore, Michal darling." She tosses her hair in my face before nuzzling her cheek against his rigid chest, purring in contentment like a cat. "Not now that we're reunited at last. Why bother with cheap pyrite, after all, when you can have real gold? I forgive your boorish behavior, by the way," she says to him, elbowing me aside further. "I know you didn't *mean* to change the locks on every door in the castle, just as you know *I* didn't mean to smash every window on the first floor."

Lip curling, Michal levels her with a black look. "And some on the second."

She bats her lashes sweetly. "Shall we let bygones be bygones?"

"That depends. Did you also destroy the portrait of Uncle Vladimir in my study?"

She swells instantly, as if he insulted her mother or perhaps kicked her dog instead of asking a perfectly reasonable question. "Did I—? How *dare*—?" Clutching her chest once more, she retreats backward into me, and now it's my turn to grimace. She feels like a bucket of ice water dumped overhead. "'Tis a question boldly spoken from the man who destroyed my very *heart*! But oh no, poor Uncle Vladimir has a mustache now! Let us all grieve his countenance, for the paint on his face means more to Michal Vasiliev than the pure and enduring love in his paramour's chest!"

Michal shakes his head in exasperation. "We were never *paramours*, Guinevere—"

"Ah!" Guinevere swoons as if he stabbed her. Unsure what else to do—but quite sure I need to do *something* before she reaches full-blown hysteria—I release one of Michal's hands and wrap my arm around her shoulders; she deflates dramatically at the contact, turning her head to sob loudly into the crook of my neck. "And now for the salt! Inflicting the wound never was enough for him, Célie darling. Always, *always* he must deny our connection, deny the very *heartbeat* of our *souls*. I implore you to run, not walk, away from this wretched beast before he cleaves your heart straight in two, as he has mine!"

When Michal starts to retort, I shoot him a menacing look and mouth, *Stop talking*. He clenches his jaw impatiently instead. "You have nothing to fear of that, Guinevere," I say soothingly, stroking her silver hair. "My heart is quite safe. Michal kidnapped me to use as bait, after all, and as soon as I serve my purpose, he'll probably try to kill me."

Too late, I remember Guinevere's fit of temper outside Michal's study—*You warmbloods are always so presumptuous, disparaging death in front of the dead*—but she no longer seems to care about disparaging anything except Michal. I can empathize.

"You see?" Her sobs grow somehow louder, and for the first time since I learned of my gift, I feel enormously grateful that no one can see or hear ghosts except me. Though one or two courtesans in the pit still watch us—confused, probably, by my oddly suspended arm and our conversation with thin air—the rest have lost interest or retired for the morning. As if she senses my attention drifting, Guinevere pretends to gasp for breath. "He cares not for the feelings of anyone but himself!"

I nod sagely. "I'm not fully convinced he has feelings."

"*Or* friends."

"Or even a basic understanding of what friendship entails."

"Ha!" Guinevere straightens and claps her hands in delight—her eyes mysteriously dry—and we gaze at each other with a strange new sense of kinship. "I knew I liked you, Célie Tremblay," she says, reaching out to smooth a lock of my hair, "and I've henceforth decided—we shall be the very best of friends, you and I. The very best indeed."

I bow my head in a half curtsy. "I would be honored to call you friend, Guinevere."

Michal looks seconds away from hurling himself into the fire. With the air of a man trying and failing to reclaim control of the situation, he asks in a terse voice, "How familiar are you with Les Abysses, Guinevere? Do you visit often?"

She whirls toward him in an instant. "Why? Are you implying I followed you here? Is that what you think? *Poor, pathetic Guinevere, she must've been pining after me for all these centuries—*" She snaps her fingers under his nose, eyes blazing bright and liquid silver. "A woman has *needs*, Michal, and I will not be shamed for seeking companionship in the afterlife. Do you hear me? I will not be shamed!"

I touch her arm lightly before she can gouge his eyes out. Or before Michal can open his mouth again. "No one is trying to shame you, Guinevere." Though how, exactly, a ghost seeks companionship among the living *is* something I plan to ask about later. "We just— We need a favor."

She arches a narrow brow. "Oh?"

"We need to know which of these fireplaces leads to Babette Trousset's rooms."

"*Ooooh*," she repeats with relish, looking infinitely more intrigued. "And whatever do you want *there?* Rumors abound that the girl is dead." At this, she cuts a sly, significant look at Michal, twirling another ringlet around her finger. The gesture reeks of nonchalance, but—much like Michal's performance with the fireplaces earlier—there's nothing nonchalant about it. My eyes narrow slightly.

Guinevere knows something we don't.

Worse still—if I know her at all, she'll try to bait us with her secret for as long as possible, relishing in our struggle. We don't have time to dangle on the end of her hook, and even if we did, Michal would need to crawl on his belly and beg before Guinevere told him anything. She'd want him to squirm. To suffer. Our friendship has lasted all of three seconds; it'll do nothing to heal a centuries-old grudge.

Michal's face darkens with the same realization.

"We want to search her rooms, to see if she left anything behind that might point us to her killer." I watch Guinevere's face carefully, frowning at the way her lips quirk slightly at the corners. Her eyes glitter with malice, or perhaps glee; perhaps the two are one and the same with Guinevere. "Can you tell us which way to go?"

"Of course I can, darling. Anything for a *friend*." She twists the word in her mouth like a barbarous thing, and I tense, waiting for the sting. Instead, she taps the tip of my nose with her finger before pointing it at the fireplace directly beside us. "*That* is your entrance, though I am loath to inform you that no courtesan here will give their blessing to enter. 'Tis bad luck to meddle in affairs of the dead—just a word to the wise, cherub," she adds to me, winking viciously.

"Any courtesan can give their blessing?" I ask.

She shrugs a delicate shoulder. "The enchantment got a little sticky when the evil hag tried to personalize it to each fireplace—plus the turnover of staff, you know. It turned into a logistical nightmare. No, a one-for-all enchantment fit best, and anyone who wears the color red can bestow—" She stops abruptly, clamping her lips together and blinking hastily between us. She needn't finish the thought, however.

Michal does it for her.

His gaze descends to my rumpled crimson gown, and at the sight of it, he smiles. It's a lethal smile—a victorious one—and it trails gooseflesh down my spine like a cold finger. *His* cold finger. Though he raises his brows at me, expectant, he makes no move in my direction. *Waiting*, I realize with a flush of familiar heat. It collides with the chill of his gaze into a tempest.

Anyone who wears the color red can bestow their blessing.

Scoffing in a rather panicked way, Guinevere darts between us. "I don't know *what* possessed you to wear such a garish color, Célie, but it really doesn't suit—"

"Excuse me, Guinevere."

"But Célie, *darling*, you shouldn't—"

I step around her, hardly hearing her, and walk with purpose toward Michal. Though my heart thunders, I cannot hear it either. I cannot hear anything except the deafening roar in my ears. *You're being ridiculous*, I tell myself firmly. *It's just a kiss. It's for the investigation.* He still doesn't move. Still doesn't speak. His smile widens, however, as the tip of our boots touch, as I stretch onto tiptoe, as I lift my face toward his. No one should be this beautiful up close. His lashes fan thick and dark against his eyes as he lowers his gaze to my lips.

"I have to kiss you," I whisper.

Again, he tucks a strand of hair behind my ear with startling affection. "I know."

He isn't going to do it for me, however. He can't. And if I wait much longer, I'll lose my nerve—or worse, Guinevere will drag me away by my hair, and the two of us will never know what lies in Babette's rooms. *It's for the investigation*, I repeat in desperation, and—before I can change my mind—I press my lips to his.

For a second, he doesn't move. I don't move. We simply stand there, his hand still cupping my cheek, until humiliation flares swift and hot in my belly. Though my experience is limited, I *have* kissed one or two men before, and I know it isn't supposed to be so—so stiff and awkward and—and—

I move to pull away, cheeks burning, but his free hand rises swiftly to capture my waist, pulling me flush against him. When I gasp, startled, his hand slides into my hair, and he tips my face back to deepen the kiss. My mouth parts instinctively in response, and the instant our tongues touch, a deep and potent heat unfurls inside me—slower than before, but stronger, suffusive. An ache instead of a throb. I close my eyes against it—*helpless* against it— and wrap my arms around his neck, pressing closer and reveling in the strange feel of him. His breath is colder than mine. His body larger, harder, deadly enough to kill. Though I mold my own against it, desperate to find friction, to welcome his heavy weight, I cannot move close enough to ease the ache, cannot coax him to envelop me completely. No, he holds me like glass until I think I might scream. And perhaps I already *am* screaming. Because this is Michal. *Michal.* I can't— I shouldn't be—

Gasping again, I wrench my lips away and stare at him in shock. He doesn't release me, instead staring right back for one heartbeat. Two. The room falls away even as Guinevere sputters behind us, indignant, until only Michal and I remain. His hands tighten upon my waist infinitesimally. This close, I should be able to feel his heartbeat, should be able to see a flush in his cheeks, but of course, he remains as pale and strange as ever. Not a hair out of place. At last, with a slightly mocking smile, he brushes a thumb across my cheek and says, "No one would be disappointed, Célie."

Without another word or backward glance, he strides into the fireplace without me.

CHAPTER THIRTY-FIVE

A Spell to Resurrekt the Dead

I lift trembling fingers to my lips as he goes. They still feel cold. They ache and they tingle. Exhaling the breath I'd been holding—an odd heaviness settling over me—I open my mouth to say something to Guinevere before closing it again, shaking my head.

"Not quite what you were expecting?" Though Guin sneers, her eyes shine with—not longing, precisely, but perhaps ruefulness as she too watches Michal disappear through the flames. "It never is with him. Others often pity me—I know they do," she adds as if expecting me to contradict her, "but truly, it is not me they should think upon. It is him." She sighs and sets to arranging her curls in a silver cascade down her shoulders. "I have loved often and loved deeply throughout my being, but Michal . . . I've known him for a very long time, cherub, and his heart—if he has one—beats differently than yours and mine. There have been moments when I wondered if it even beats at all."

"He loves his sister." My voice sounds higher than usual. "His cousins."

She waves a hand in distaste. "A distant, eternal sort of love. The love of a guardian. A patriarch." She arches that narrow brow again, fixing me with a scornful look. "Is that the love you desire? A love that turns you to ice instead of setting you to flame?"

Once more, I open my mouth to argue, and once more, I close it again without finding words. Because there was nothing icy about how he kissed me just now. Nothing icy about how he touched me in the pit either, nor my own body's response.

No one would be disappointed, Célie.

Dropping the hand from my lips, I step into the hearth before I can hesitate. Because if I hesitate, I might turn and flee instead— Les Abysses and this horrid situation, yes, but also Michal. This raging guilt in my stomach.

"Of course," Guinevere says slowly, wickedly, as if trying to salt a wound, "Michal never looked at me the way he looks at you."

"Goodbye, Guinevere." The flames tickle my skin, harmless and pleasantly warm, as I turn and curtsy in farewell. I don't yet know if I like Guinevere very much, but she *did* inadvertently assist us; someday, perhaps we'll call each other friend in truth. Part of me hopes so. "Thank you for your help."

She floats forward to kiss my cheek. Tapping my nose again, she says, "Take care of yourself, darling, and remember what I said—crimson really isn't your color. Next time, choose a lovely shade of green."

The familiar words stop me in my tracks. "Why green?"

Her answering grin is sly. "To match your eyes, of course."

Unlike the stark metaphor of the pit, with its black stone and crimson courtesans, Babette's chambers feel straight from a fairy-tale cottage. My eyes widen as I step through the door—is that lavender I smell?—and join Michal in the middle of the first room. Warm and circular, it boasts burnished wooden floors and a charming fireplace with bric-a-brac along the mantel: dried roses and candle stubs, a broken mirror and a glass box full of letters and shells and rocks. A golden staircase to the left spirals upward to a painted door in the ceiling. "Where do you think that leads?" I ask Michal hesitantly. "To Paradise?"

He doesn't answer, and that inexplicable guilt in my chest bites deeper. We don't have time to dwell on an awkward kiss and its aftermath, however, and the door in the ceiling is probably standard practice, some sort of emergency exit in case a courtesan changes their mind mid-appointment.

Right. *Focus.*

We're here to search the rooms of the deceased, to find clues that might point to her killer. Letters, sketches, perhaps out-of-place mementos like the silver cross. I try to think like Jean Luc or Reid or even Frederic, try to inspect the scene through their eyes, but it's difficult. The air *does* smell like lavender. A lovely bouquet of it hangs near the fireplace to dry, and my eyelids feel suddenly, wonderfully heavy. I don't think I've ever stepped foot in a room so enchanting. Beside the spiral staircase, books trail haphazardly across a low table between two floral armchairs, along with a steaming cup of tea. The porcelain even has an endearing little chip near the handle.

Instinctively, I move toward the floral armchairs. Not to *sleep*, of course, just to rest my head for a while.

"Wait."

Voice low, Michal touches the small of my back, and I turn, half dreading what he might say. But he isn't looking at me at all. No. His black eyes have narrowed on the table, on the steam curling from the chipped teacup, and he frowns. A distant part of my mind realizes the tea is still hot. And—my eyes drift back to the fireplace, to its merrily crackling flames and the lavender beside it. Evangeline used to steep lavender in my tea when I couldn't sleep at night. Unease creeps through me at the memory. Come to think of it, this doesn't at all look like the home of a deceased person, and—

I pinch my arm, hard. The sharp pain clears my head, and before it can cloud again, I snatch the lavender from the wall and pitch it into the fire, where it blackens and crumbles to ash. "Someone tended the fire recently." I wipe my hands hastily on my skirt. My palms sting where they touched the sprigs, and the lingering notes of lavender cannot hide the unmistakable scent of blood magic. "Pennelope?"

Michal shakes his head. "I can hear her with Jermaine next door."

"Is anyone else here?"

"I can't hear them if so."

"Then who—?" My gaze catches on the stack of books beside the teacup, the smallest of which lies open and apart from the rest. The pages have yellowed slightly from age, curling around the edges, and some of the inked words have faded almost past recognition. A peculiar sensation tugs at my stomach as I look at it. Because this book—it looks almost familiar, and it *feels* even more so. "Michal." I bend to examine it closer in the firelight, loath to touch it for some reason. Surely I imagine the faint whispers emanating from the pages, but I most certainly *don't* imagine the ancient handwriting scrawled across the open one.

A SPELL TO RESURREKT THE DEAD

And below it a single ingredient, written in the same hand:

Blood of Death

"Look at this." A tendril of fear cracks open in my chest at the additions made to the page; it climbs into my voice, my breath, as I stare at the words. "Michal." I say his name sharper now, my hands shaking as I gesture to the book. The black cover appears like it's been made from some sort of . . . *skin.* "Look what's written below it." I feel rather than see him crouch beside me, his chest cool and solid against my shoulder, because I cannot tear my gaze away from the page. From the fresh question mark inked after *Blood of Death.*

"What is it?"

"La Voisin's grimoire." The response comes instinctively, my subconscious recognizing the evil little book before my mind can catch up. Coco pulled it from her aunt's body after the Battle of Cesarine, and even then, the grimoire had filled me with a strange sense of dread. She must've given it to the Chasseurs to aid in their investigation. "I last saw it in Saint-Cécile with Father Achille. He hid it behind his back on his way to a meeting with Jean Luc and the others about the . . . the killer."

"Lutin. Melusine." Michal reads the list in a wary voice beside my ear. Like the question mark, the ink used to write it is darker, blacker than the original spell. New. Each creature has been scratched out with a thick, angry line. "Dame Blanche, dragon, Dame Rouge. Loup garou. Éternel." His voice hardens at the last, and he reaches past me to seize the book. The last addition is a single name, circled with the same heavy stroke.

Michal swears viciously. "Célie Tremblay."

And so it is.

He needs your blood, Célie.

I stare at the letters, at the ink strokes that form my name, before reaching for the grimoire. I flip through the pages numbly—*for Invisibility, for Precognition, for the Full Moon*—until my fingers still on a page marked *for Lust of the Blood*. I slam the book shut quickly. "Do you think Father Achille brought—?"

"No." Lip curling, Michal stares at the grimoire as if he too feels the unpleasant, tugging sensation behind his navel. "I don't."

"Then how did it come here? Could he have given it to—to Pennelope or another courtesan?" My thoughts whir wildly to fill in the blanks, to make sense of it all. His predecessor had a clandestine relationship with Morgane le Blanc; perhaps Father Achille frequented Les Abysses and gave it to a lover for safekeeping? Even as I think the words, however, I know they aren't true. Father Achille isn't the type to take a lover, and even if he was— why would he bring such a book here? Surely it would be better protected by the hundreds of huntsmen who live within Chasseur Tower. And why—my fingers tighten on the grimoire's spine— why would he ink in a list of magical creatures, only to scratch each out as if proceeding through them one by one? And why on *that* page?

In response, the title of the spell rises in my mind's eye.

A Spell to Resurrekt the Dead.

My entire body goes cold.

Darkness is coming for us, Célie. The rest of Mila's warning echoes in the quiet of the room. *It is coming for us all, and at its heart is a figure—a man.*

This book shouldn't be here.

There can no longer be any doubt—our killer and the man of whom Mila spoke are connected somehow, perhaps even the same person. These deaths are not the work of a simple killer at all, but of some great darkness threatening the entire kingdom. No. Threatening the realms of both the living and the dead.

"Someone must've stolen the grimoire from Father Achille." Beside me, Michal stills again, his face turned slightly toward the door in front of us. I assume it leads to Babette's bedchamber or kitchen. "Perhaps whoever stole Babette's body from the morgue? It can't just be a coincidence that both went missing around the same time."

Again, he doesn't answer.

Agitation claws through my chest, however, and I can't abide the silence. "So—so the killer stole her body *and* the grimoire, and he—what?" I gesture wildly to the crackling fireplace, to the steaming teacup. This close, I can see red lipstick upon its rim. "Holed up inside Babette's rooms and asked Pennelope to cover for him? Why *would* Pennelope cover for him? He killed her cousin!"

Michal stands slowly. "An excellent question."

"Unless he threatened her?" *That's it.* Of course it is. The killer must've threatened Pennelope, which is why she didn't tell us about him straightaway, and why she—

My eyes fall again to the red lipstick on the rim of the teacup.

And why she's taking tea with him.

"You said Pennelope has been next door with Jermaine." My

frown deepens at the realization, and I too rise to my feet. "This isn't her tea." Michal shakes his head without speaking, still watching the inner door. Instinctually, I draw closer to him. None of this makes any *sense*. "But Mila said the killer—she said all of this revolves around a *man* cloaked in darkness. Do you think he wears lipstick?"

"I think," Michal says at last, his voice softer than I've ever heard, "we've made a grave mistake." He steps between me and the door, his hands deceptively calm at his sides, and raises his voice slightly. "You can come out now, witch."

I freeze behind him as the door creaks open, and a familiar, golden-haired woman steps into the room. Horror like bile creeps up my throat. Because it isn't Pennelope who smiles at me now.

It's Babette.

CHAPTER THIRTY-SIX

A Time for Tea

She holds a silver knife in one hand, and blood already trickles from the crook of her opposite elbow, where—I swallow hard—what looks like an owl feather protrudes from the cut, its shaft shoved directly under her skin. "Hello, Célie," she says quietly. "I wondered whether you'd come calling." A pause as I stare at her. "You've always been more intelligent than your kinsmen."

The silence between us stretches and stretches. Somewhere behind Michal and me, a clock *tick, tick, tick*s until a chime rings half past seven o'clock in the morning. *Thirty minutes until daybreak.* Though my throat works to speak, my mouth seems to have forgotten how to form words. My mind just cannot comprehend what my eyes are seeing: Babette, whole and well once more, *alive*, without pallid skin or bite marks at her throat. At last, I manage to whisper, "I found you dead in the cemetery."

"You found me enchanted in the cemetery." She steps farther into the room, and my hand creeps to Michal's arm. He doesn't move, however. Doesn't breathe. Every fiber of his preternatural being fixates on Babette. Nodding to the book in my hand, she says, "One simply mixes a sprig of nightshade with the blood of a friend, and they fall into a sleep like death for twenty-four hours. It's a clever spell, really—quite rare and unprecedented. One of La Voisin's best."

A creeping numbness spreads through my limbs. That Babette stands here freely, calmly, that she admits to faking her own death as if discussing the weather, cannot be good. I swallow hard and glance surreptitiously at the door in the ceiling. We could flee back through the fireplace, of course, but courtesans lie that way—perhaps Pennelope herself. No. If we can inch around Babette somehow, we'll have a clearer path to escape. But first—

"La Voisin is dead," I say. "I watched her die in the Battle of Cesarine."

"Her work lives on."

"Did you"—I force myself to step around Michal now, clenching my limbs tight to stop their trembling—"did you kill those creatures, Babette?" My eyes fall inadvertently to the grimoire. It still whispers to me, horrible things I half recognize but don't quite understand. "To—to honor your mistress? Are you trying to bring her back?"

Babette laughs, a bright and sparkling sound that doesn't fit the circumstances. *Definitely not good.* Cloaked in black, she wears no makeup except on her crimson lips, and her scars stand out in sharp relief without powder. With her golden hair swept away from her face, her cheekbones too look more pronounced, almost gaunt. Deep shadows haunt her eyes. "I know very few witches who wish to honor our *mistress.* Most hope she still burns in Hell." Another step. I edge to the left. "And I didn't kill anyone, darling. I've always had very little interest in sullying my hands with violence. I leave that to him."

"Who?" Michal asks, his voice glacial.

Babette flicks her golden eyes to his face. "The Necromancer, of course."

At that, the grimoire actually *moves* in my hand—quivering in excitement—and I drop it with a little squeak, kicking it away. It lands noiselessly upon the carpet and flips open to *A Spell to Resurrekt the Dead.* "Oh God," I breathe as the pieces click into place. Though *Blood of Death* leers up at me, my vision tunnels on my own name, circled and circled again.

He wants your blood, Célie.

The Necromancer.

"Quite the opposite, I think," Babette says quietly, "if one believes in such things." With a wince, she pulls the feather from her flesh, dripping blood from her elbow to the floor. She twirls it between two fingers in contemplation. "From a common barn owl. It makes my movements silent, undetectable, even to vampire ears."

"Who is the Necromancer?" I ask.

"I do not know his name. I do not need to know it."

Michal shifts in front of me again, the movement subtle. *Good.* It brings us nearer to the stairs. "You want to bring your sister back," he says. "Sylvie. The one who died of blood sickness."

For a fraction of a second, Babette's face twists just like Pennelope's did. "Among others." Then, her features smoothing once more— "Blood sickness works slowly, you know. It takes its time on victims, poisoning first their body, second their mind. It steals their health, their very youth, until the air is thick in their chests and the wind feels like knives on their skin. They suffocate, and they wither. They feel the blood boiling in their veins, and they cannot stop it because there is no cure. Only death. Many take their own lives to end the torment." Her gaze fixes upon me. "Morgane le Blanc fashioned the pain she inflicted on your sister after the pain my own endured."

My hand clenches on Michal's sleeve, and I quite forget my plan to escape. "*What?*"

"Filippa was a husk after Morgane finished with her, was she not? Just like Sylvie."

My eyes widen, and I gape at her, stricken. Because she's right. Though my parents insisted on a closed casket for Filippa's funeral, no one knows more intimately than I how disfigured she'd been when they found her. Her limbs gnarled, her skin sallow and sagging. Her hair white. *A husk.*

"My sister didn't deserve to die that way," Babette continues in a strangely calm voice, almost serene. She lets the feather flutter to the floor. "Did yours?"

My throat threatens to close, and at her words, all I can see is the Filippa from my nightmares—half of her face missing, her smile wide and leering, as she plunges her skeletal fist into my chest. Her fingers close around my heart. As if I too suffer from blood sickness, I abruptly find it difficult to breathe, and when I glance down, the skin of my hand seems to shrivel.

Would you like that, sweeting? Would you like to die?

"We're going to bring them back," Babette says simply.

Michal can hear my pulse spike. I know he can. His own hand creeps around his back, and I stare at it with incomprehension for a second—at his smooth, alabaster palm facing outward—before realizing he's offering it to me. I lace my fingers through his instantly, tightly. For once, my touch feels just as cold. "And you faked your own death because . . . ?" he asks.

Babette considers him for so long I fear she won't answer. Then— "Because Jean Luc's theory about a blood witch killer made the Necromancer nervous." She bends to retrieve the grimoire from the floor and tucks it into her skirt pocket. "Because Cosette would never *believe* blood witches capable of killing their own—not even after her aunt. Because he knows all about Les Éternels and their taste for blood, and he thinks the world should know about them too." Lifting her silver knife when he moves, she says, "Because their king makes the obvious suspect. After Célie's note"—she tips her chin to me in sickening gratitude—"the Chasseurs have armed themselves to the teeth with silver. They're convinced *you* killed all those poor creatures, roi sombre, and it works out quite neatly that you're here with Célie now—almost too neatly. You left so many witnesses."

As before, there's no satisfaction in her voice. No relish. Only a quiet sense of assurance, of calm, like a priest reading scripture at the pulpit. I've heard this sort of conviction before, and it never ends well. Beads of cold sweat mat the hair at my nape. We really need to leave now. I glance again at the door in the ceiling. "Witnesses of *what?*"

She looks at me almost sadly. "I wish it didn't have to be this way, Célie. I wish it could be anyone but you. You've always been kind, and for that, I wish it could be anyone but me—but you saw the list." Though she doesn't dare reach into her pocket again, not with Michal poised like a wolf prepared to strike, she dips her head toward the grimoire there. "The spell calls for the Blood of Death, and the Necromancer tried everything in search of it. Witches are deadly enough, to be sure, but my blood didn't work within the spell. Nor did the blood of a loup garou or melusine. Even the vampire's blood—lethal though she was—proved ineffective." Here Michal snarls, and all plans of escape crash to the floor at my feet. He'll never flee now. "The Necromancer almost gave up after that. He didn't realize La Voisin had capitalized Death for a reason. *Death.*" She breathes the word with a macabre sort of reverence for someone planning to desecrate it. "As in the entity himself, the very creature who exists beyond all creed and religion, beyond all space and time, who steals life with a simple touch. How could the Necromancer have known? No one has ever seen Death. Those who have do not survive." She slants her head at me curiously. "The Necromancer came upon your blood by chance, perhaps divine intervention, and we tested it on a whim. You cannot imagine his glee when it worked."

His glee.

I force myself to breathe. To *think.* "The training yard."

Her golden eyes gleam brighter as she nods, as she takes another step toward us. "No closer," Michal growls, and for the first time since I met him, he sounds wholly inhuman. His arm inches back, curling protectively around my waist, and I still instinctively. "Or I'll tear out your throat."

"He means it, Babette," I whisper, the truth of my words a cold touch in my chest. "Whatever it is you're planning—don't. Even if you *do* manage to resurrect your sister, the spell will rip you apart. Look around!" I spread my arms wide, helpless, and beg her to understand. To *see.* "Have you not noticed? Already our realm has sickened with the Necromancer's magic, and the others—even the realms of the spirits and the dead—they're twisting too, *rotting* into something just as dark and strange as he is. Is that the world into which you want to bring your sister?"

Babette only bends again in response, this time to retrieve her chipped teacup. It no longer steams. Still, she lifts it to her lips with that same overwrought composure. "Why you, Célie?" She grimaces after swallowing the cold tea. "Can you tell me? Why does your blood complete the spell?"

I hesitate, crestfallen, but if this Necromancer already knows my blood completes the spell, the reason doesn't matter. "I'm a Bride of Death. He—touched me in my sister's casket, but he let me go. I don't know why."

She repeats the words softly. "A Bride of Death. How . . . romantic." Her hands tremble slightly as she extends her cup of tea toward me. "Would you like some?"

I frown at it. "Er—no, thank you."

She doesn't lower the cup. "I apologize for the lavender. It was a cheap trick, but I didn't have much time to prepare. When Pennelope warned me of your arrival, I had to make a quick decision. I could've fled, of course, but you would've realized my rooms have been inhabited almost instantly. And the Necromancer—he would've been furious with me. He thought he would need to wait until All Hallows' Eve to take you, Célie—surrounded by your very powerful friends—but instead, here you are with the vampire king. The circumstances . . . they're just too neat. Too perfect. I can't possibly let you go now." Silver liquid fills her overbright eyes, and they look suspiciously like tears. Swallowing hard, she blinks them away. "When they find your body drained of blood, everyone will know he killed you."

Michal's arm around me tightens, and he seems torn between lunging for Babette and whisking me out the door. "Find someone else," he says in that same dark voice. From any other creature, it might sound like a plea, but Michal has never been prey. He is the predator, even here, faced with witchcraft and silver.

Babette, however, does not cower. "There is no one else."

"Célie cannot be the only Bride of Death in this realm. Find another to resurrect your sister, or I will hunt her when she wakes. I will inflict such pain that she'll long for sickness once more, and Death will come to her in kindness. When you try to follow, I will turn you into a vampire, so you must live forever apart as an undead creature, never again to look upon your sister's face. Do you understand?"

Babette's pale skin mottles at the threat—no, the *promise*—and the regret in her eyes flashes to fury. "We both know vampires can die, mon roi. You may threaten my sister all you like, but it was silver he used on *your* sister to drain every drop of blood from her body." Michal's body shudders with the physical effort not to move. Her silver knife joins the teacup between us. Her hands no longer shake. "I have no doubt that you're faster than me. Stronger than me. In all likelihood, this knife will prove useless against you."

Michal speaks through his teeth. "Shall we find out?"

He still doesn't release me, however.

"Which is why," Babette continues with the ringing air of finality, "I broke my mother's mirror and ground the shards into powder."

It all happens very fast then.

In the same instant my eyes dart to her mantel, to the shattered mirror there, she flings the cup of tea in Michal's face. Despite her prediction, he doesn't move fast enough—he *can't* move fast enough with one arm still locked around my waist—instead half turning to brace against me. To *protect* me. The cold tea douses his entire right side. The skin of his face and throat hisses on contact, bubbling with angry red blisters, but it's so much worse than when I scratched him in the aviary. My eyes widen in horror. Babette's blood must've been in that tea too, because his flesh— it seems to be burning, *melting*, and actual flames leap from his face now, crackling with wicked laughter. Though I seize his cloak to smother them, the flames only grow higher, and he collapses against me. One of his knees hits the floor. "Célie," he groans. "Upstairs—*run*."

"Michal!" I crumple under his weight, hooking my arms beneath his shoulders. Because I can't just leave him here. I *won't*. Though I try to heave him back to his feet, Babette stalks toward us with a determined expression. My mouth goes dry at the glint of her silver blade. "No!" I seize him with frantic, clumsy hands, trying to roll, trying to rise, but there's nothing I can do except scream, "Babette, don't, *please*!"

She plunges the knife deep into his side.

"Stop it!" Half-buried beneath Michal, half sobbing now, I lunge at her, swiping at the knife, but it disappears between his ribs again, and again, and again until his breath rattles frighteningly in his chest. "Babette, *stop*!"

"I don't want to hurt you, Célie. I never wanted to hurt anyone." Dropping the knife, she draws great, shuddering breaths—in tears again herself—and kicks him away from me. His head strikes the wooden floor with a dull thud, and the flames go out at last. "I'm so sorry. I wish it could be anyone but you." Dragging a finger through the wound at her elbow, she kneels beside me and raises that finger to my lips. *No.* My mouth clamps shut in realization. A Dame Rouge's magic resides within their blood; if I ingest hers, she'll be able to control me, much like a vampire's compulsion. Under her influence, I'll leave Michal to die without a second thought, and I'll walk straight into the Necromancer's arms.

No. No no no—

Snarling, I seize her wrist and push her away with all my strength. My arms shake with the effort. My chest heaves. I've never been very strong, however, and soon I can smell the sharp tang of her blood beneath my nose. The tang of her tears. "You don't have to do this, Babette—"

"I'm sorry, Célie." Her voice actually breaks on my name, and I almost believe her now. She repeats the words until they blend together, echoing deliriously in my ears. *I'm sorry I'm sorry I'm sorry, Célie, I'm so sorry.* When she pushes harder, I fall backward, landing heavy on the carpet near Michal. His beautiful black eyes stare at me without seeing. I clench my teeth and shake my head with more bitter, hopeless tears. They trickle into my hair and blur my vision until the spiral stairs overhead bleed into the ceiling, which bleeds into the door, which bursts open unexpectedly.

Babette whirls, incredulous, as two identical faces appear in the room above.

We always notice when night children come to call, Pennelope said. *Two more just arrived upstairs.*

Dimitri and Odessa.

Though I want to cry out in hideous relief—because they're here, they're here, *they're here*—I dare not open my mouth. Above me, Babette's eyes bulge in genuine fear. "No," she breathes.

Her strength falters as Dimitri and Odessa blur forward, and I take full advantage, driving my knee into her stomach. She screams when Dimitri seizes her, nearly ripping her arm out of its socket and throwing her across the room. Still shrieking, she slams into a floral armchair, which cracks ominously beneath her.

Odessa crouches beside Michal. Her hands flutter over his injuries for half a second—her eyes shocked, wide—before she scoops him up and darts back up the staircase. Fresh relief surges through me as they disappear, as I struggle to my feet and snatch the silver knife from the floor. Tears still pour freely down my cheeks.

Odessa will help him. He's safe now.

"Are you hurt?" Dimitri asks without looking at me.

"I—I think I'm fine, but—"

"You should follow the others." His hands curl into fists as he stares at Babette's prone body. "It's almost daybreak."

I eye his back nervously, the rigid line of his neck. Babette wants to kill me, yes—she did her best to kill Michal—but— but— "She has silver in her bloodstream," I tell him quickly. "It was in the tea."

He says nothing.

"And the blood of a Dame Rouge is poison to their enemies. If you drink it, you'll—"

"I said *leave*," he snarls with surprising vitriol, jerking his head toward staircase. "*Now.*"

Though I startle slightly, stung, my feet rush to obey him, skirting past Babette and across the room. For a split second, her eyes dart after me like she wants to follow. Dimitri shadows my steps, however, waiting until I push open the door in the ceiling before murmuring, "It was very foolish to leave Michal alive. You've made a powerful enemy today."

To leave Michal alive.

My head snaps back toward him. For some reason, the words lift the hair at my neck, and his *face*—as with Michal, I've never before seen Dimitri look so *vicious*. His lip curls over his fangs, and the firelight casts deep shadows across his earnest eyes. They look hungry now. Unfamiliar. Gone is the sweet and charming boy with dimples; in his place stands a fully-fledged vampire.

With quaking arms, I hold the door open overhead and linger despite myself, watching as Babette climbs from the broken armchair. When her gaze darts from Dimitri to the door behind him—to the door that leads to Les Abysses—fresh panic spikes through me. Someone would've heard her screams. At any moment, Pennelope and the other courtesans could descend upon us. I should leave. I should follow Odessa into Paradise, and I should help her with Michal however I can. And yet—

"He was already my enemy," Babette says tremulously as Dimitri begins to circle her. My brow furrows. She fears Dimitri in a way she didn't fear Michal. She no longer holds her silver knife or silver tea, of course, but she's still a blood witch. The crook of her elbow still bleeds freely.

"Now he knows it too," Dimitri says. "After he heals, he will hunt you, and he won't stop until you're dead."

She lifts her chin. "He won't find me again."

"I can't take that chance." He stills in front of her. "Give me the book, Babette."

I exhale sharply at that—*he knows about the grimoire*—but neither seems to notice my presence. My arms ache from the weight of the door above me. "You'll never get it," she whispers desperately. "*Never.*" When Dimitri steps forward in silent threat, she squares her shoulders and inhales deeply, preparing to do the only thing she can—

She screams again. A shrill, piercing scream that cuts through walls and doors like a blade through butter. At the sound of it,

I slip and tumble down several stairs, and the door crashes shut overhead.

If no one heard her before, they certainly heard all *that*.

"Dimitri!" Throwing caution to the wind, I hurtle down the last of the stairs, skidding to a halt just shy of him. Reluctant to draw too close. I thought he wanted to drink Babette's blood, to punish a witch for harming his family, yet now—now I don't know. Clearly, he knows her otherwise, and worse, he knows about the grimoire too. Not only does he know about it, but he *wants* it, and—and—I clench her knife like a shield in front of me, unwilling to think the rest. I don't understand any of this. It doesn't make *sense*, and I should've left when I had the chance. Pennelope will be here any second, and together, she and Babette might be able to overpower Dimitri. They might chase me, catch me, and—*no*.

Dimitri is my quickest way out of here. My *only* way out of here. I jerk my knife emphatically toward the stairs. "We need to leave. Please."

He says nothing for several more seconds, his eyes boring into Babette's with violent promise. He still doesn't attack her, however, and we still don't flee. "Dimitri," I say again, pleading now. When he still doesn't move—locked in silent battle with Babette—I force myself to touch his arm. *This is Dimitri*, I think fiercely, despairingly. *He brought you cabbage and eggs, and there must be an explanation for all this.* "Please, *please*, Dima, let's go."

As if on cue, the doorknob behind us begins to turn, and Pennelope's muffled voice echoes sharply into the room. "Babette? Are you all right?"

At last, Dimitri exhales—his teeth grinding together—and closes his eyes, clears his expression. When he opens them again, the familiar sparkle has returned, but it looks different now. It looks calculating. Perhaps it's always looked that way. Perhaps I wanted a friend too badly to notice.

"My apologies, mademoiselle." Winking, he offers me his hand, and I hesitate only a second before taking it. He sweeps me into his arms just as Pennelope bursts into the room. Her eyes take in the scene instantly. Snarling, she lifts her bleeding hands, but we're already up the stairs, at the ceiling. Dimitri flashes her a charming, dimpled grin as he pushes open the door. Then he looks to Babette. "I hope you run far and run fast, chérie," he tells her, and the sight of his dimples sends a newfound chill through me. "Because if Michal doesn't find you, I will."

CHAPTER THIRTY-SEVEN

The Kiss of a Vampire

Paradise passes in a rush of silken clouds and marble floors, and I catch the last notes of the melusines' song before the entire building seems to contract—like a band snapping—and expels us through another odd door near the ceiling. Cursing, Dimitri tightens his arms around me as we go stumbling onto the roof. The door vanishes behind us like it never existed at all.

Guests can't stay in Les Abysses past daybreak.

In the next second, the first rays of sunlight break across the horizon.

They burn Dimitri's skin on contact, and he curses again—maliciously this time—ducking into the shadow of a nearby gable. "Hold on," he says, and I manage to fling my arms around his neck before he leaps to the gable of a roof next door. The glass of a narrow window there has been shattered. Dimitri ducks through it just as his skin begins to smoke.

Inside, Odessa crouches over Michal, who lies completely still on what appears to be the floor of an attic.

Half of his face remains horribly burned, blackened, and blood shines through the gashes in his leather coat. It soaks the dusty floorboards beneath him too, staining the old wood like a halo. Pale gray light diffuses the entire scene into an ethereal sort of nightmare. Even half-burned, half-broken, Michal looks like he could've just fallen from the heavens after God stripped his wings. Pushing out of Dimitri's arms—eager to get away from him—I crash to the floor beside Odessa. "Why isn't he healing?"

"Didn't you say the witch put silver in her tea?" Dimitri follows as if concerned, and his brow furrows when I scoot away from him. *Right.* He's going to pretend his conversation with Babette never happened. Indeed, he lifts his hands in a placating gesture and forces a bemused laugh. His gaze falls to the silver knife in my fist. "And that blade isn't made of candy floss, Célie."

"Mademoiselle Tremblay," I snap.

His eyes widen. "You're revoking our friendship privileges?"

"Can we not talk about this right now?"

"Well, I *did* just save your life—"

"Michal needs blood," Odessa says sharply, ignoring us both. Sunlight creeps steadily across the floor through the broken window. "This house belongs to humans—two of them. I can hear them sleeping below. Dima, bring them to us and barricade yourself in the basement." She locks eyes with him. "I'll call you when it's over."

His smile falters, and he tears his gaze from me to scowl at his sister. "I can control myself—"

"No, you can't"—Odessa shakes her head forcefully—"and we don't have time to argue. If you go into a rage and kill those people, Michal will die too. He won't last until nightfall to find fresh."

To find fresh. My stomach plunges to somewhere around my ankles. "You're going to—to give them to Michal? The people who live here?" When Odessa nods, I ask rather stupidly, "He's going to drink their blood?"

She jerks her chin toward the door. Wooden chairs have been

stacked against the walls there, along with hatboxes and trunks cloaked in cobwebs. "You may join Dimitri in the basement if you wish. This won't be for the faint of heart."

"I'm not *faint of heart.* I just— Will he kill them?"

"Most likely."

"But they're innocent." Unbidden, I imagine the people sleeping below, perhaps an elderly couple, perhaps young and in love, or perhaps not a couple at all but a mother and her child. Bile rises in my throat. I flit to the trunk in agitation, unable to sit still any longer, and wrench it open. Pillows and neatly folded blankets lie inside. Seizing one of each, I dart back across the room. "They've done nothing wrong, nothing to deserve such a—a cruel and unusual fate."

"Cruel and unusual?" Odessa asks incredulously. "We're *vampires,* Célie. Would you prefer Michal dies instead?"

"Of course not, but—"

"Do you have another suggestion, then?"

Unable to look at her, at Dimitri, at *anyone,* I stuff the blanket into the crack above the window, plunging the room into shadow once more. Into silence. I squeeze the pillow between clammy palms, and the words building in my chest burst out with a painful breath. "He can drink from me."

The Petrov twins both stare at me with identical expressions of disbelief. "Did you not hear me?" Odessa's brows climb steadily higher. "You could die."

For example, our pythoness once predicted that I would take a bride not unlike yourself.

She also predicted that I'd kill her.

I straighten my spine in resolve. "I won't let Michal kill anyone."

"Don't be stupid." Voice suddenly earnest, Dimitri darts to stand between Michal and me, blocking my path. "You won't have a choice. If Michal drinks from you, his instinct will take over, and he'll drain every drop of blood from your body. When he wakes, clutching your corpse in his arms, he'll tear out our hearts in retribution, and he'll kill the humans out of spite. Is that what you want? A house full of corpses?"

He isn't you, I want to snap, but I bite my tongue. I know nothing about Dimitri—not truly—except the many faces he wears. Perhaps this is his real one. Perhaps the blood rage isn't his fault. For all I know, it could be hereditary, which means Michal *could* lose control when he tastes my blood. "I won't let innocent people die." Lifting the silver knife, I add fiercely, "And I won't let him lose control either."

"You think you can stop him?" Dimitri pinches the bridge of his nose as if pained. "You've clearly never shared blood with a vampire. You won't *want* to stop him, Célie. You'll beg him to take it all, and when you realize you're dying—*if* you realize you're dying—it'll be too late."

"Get out of the way." Shoving past him—careful to keep the silver between us—I drop to my knees beside Michal and force the pillow under his pale head. "I've made up my mind."

Odessa seizes my wrist before I can cut open my palm. "Are you sure you want to do this, Célie?" Though her eyes are canny and dark and identical to her brother's, I force myself to meet her gaze anyway. She isn't Dimitri. She didn't leave Mila's body in the garbage, didn't demand the grimoire of a blood witch—the same witch who tried to kill Michal, who admitted to working with Mila's killer. "Dima is right. None of us will be able to stop Michal if he loses control. He *could* kill you. Are you really prepared to sacrifice yourself?"

"I won't let innocent people die," I repeat stubbornly.

Odessa stares at me for another second. Then— "Fine. But use this to make the cut, or the silver will poison your blood." She plucks a sharp golden pin from her hair and thrusts it at me before rising swiftly and towing Dimitri to the door. He digs in his heels. "I still want you to wait in the basement," she tells him in an undertone. "I'll compel the humans to leave before joining you." As if sensing my argument, she adds in exasperation, "We can't return to Requiem until nightfall, and I doubt they'll appreciate vampires crouching in their attic all day. Besides, Michal will need to rest." She rubs her temple with one hand, still dragging Dimitri along with the other. "He's hellishly lucky that we followed you two. You'd both be dead otherwise."

"Why *did* you follow us?"

"I didn't," she says frankly. "My brother did, and I followed *him* against my better judgment."

As one, we look to Dimitri, who shakes his head in bitter disappointment and stops resisting. "We're friends, Mademoiselle Tremblay, and Michal—he isn't thinking clearly." He pins me with a heavy gaze. "None of us are."

"A fact proven by Michal allowing a blood witch to overpower him." Looking disgusted, Odessa flings open the door. "If anyone on Requiem hears of this, there will be riots in the streets. I hope Michal is prepared to suffer the consequences of his actions."

My heart plummets. Though I open my mouth to tell her exactly what happened, to explain, she pushes Dimitri from the room before I can force out the words. Because—my gaze drifts back to Michal's ruined face, to the bloodstains that cradle his body—and my hand slackens upon the knife. He wouldn't have been overpowered at all if not for me. "You're an idiot," I tell him, lifting his head into my lap. "Her tea wouldn't have hurt *me.*"

Except, of course, that it could've.

She spiked it with her blood, and if Michal hadn't turned, it might've been my skin on fire instead of his. Had he smelled it? The poison? If so, why on *earth* had he shielded me? I may be a Bride, yes, and his only connection to Mila, but his sister already refused to help him—and he wouldn't have *needed* her help if he'd captured Babette instead. "An idiot," I repeat thickly, but my treacherous chest expands all the same.

Taking a deep breath, I draw the tip of the golden pin across my wrist.

Blood wells instantly in its wake, shocking and bright even in the darkness, and I wince. How many times have I seen Coco and Lou draw their own blood? Neither ever said how much it *stings.* Still, I clench my hand in a fist, willing the blood to flow thicker. Faster. Bracing myself for the flood of sensation to come. I don't think it'll hurt—Arielle hadn't moaned in *pain*—yet trepidation still tightens my throat. This is another line, and I'm about to cross it.

He won't last until nightfall.

Dropping the pin and seizing my knife, I lower my wrist to his mouth.

When he doesn't move, I force his lips apart and push the blood deeper onto his tongue. "Come on, Michal." I tighten my fist again and lean closer, pulling him farther up my lap. Searching for any sign of life. The dart of an eye beneath a lid or the twitch of a finger. Nothing happens. Could Odessa have overestimated how long he had left? Frowning, I reject the thought quickly. The vampires in the aviary—they'd sort of shriveled and aged when Michal killed them, and he remains perfect except for his injuries. I rock him slightly. "Come on, Michal. Drink the blood and wake up. Wake up, wake up, wake *up*—"

His hand seizes my wrist.

Gasping at the sudden pressure, I resist the urge to pull away, even as twin pricks of pain flare, as his teeth sink into my skin. "*Oh.*" My eyes widen when his second hand joins the first. He pulls me closer, bites down harder, and it—it definitely hurts now. "Michal." I push at his head weakly, hesitating when the burns on his face begin to heal. The blisters fading, vanishing into cool alabaster skin. "*Michal*—"

His eyes snap open then—black and empty and wholly unfamiliar—and the instant they connect with mine, the throbbing pain in my wrist dissolves into liquid warmth. *Oh God.* My knife clatters to the floor as a moan rises to my lips, and his mouth pulls harder at the sound. My muscles clench convulsively in response. My hips roll forward. In a smooth, almost languorous movement, he turns in my lap, yanking my legs straight with one arm and pressing me into the floor, climbing slowly over my body. "M-Michal—"

Breath low and uneven, he breaks his latch on my wrist to gaze down at me intently. "Célie."

My blood stains his mouth brilliant scarlet. It streams down my hand and mixes with his upon the floor. With a contented sigh, he nuzzles the crook of my shoulder, tasting my skin there too. His lips skim my frantic pulse until I crane my neck upward, until I arch against him, into him, desperate to relieve this great pulsing *need* inside of me.

If he doesn't touch me soon, *really* touch me, I think I might die.

"Michal, please, *please*—"

I scrabble at his back, unable to stop, and at the hitch in my voice, he pulls back to watch me once more, fascinated. A sob tears from my throat. Though his eyes remain depthless and strange, he brings my wrist to his mouth, kissing it gently and murmuring, "Don't cry, moje sunce. Never cry."

Even if I understood, I couldn't answer him. I can't speak. I can't even remember my own *name*.

Surging upward to kiss him, I crush his lips against mine, and his mouth is hot and cold all at once—and everywhere. He is *everywhere*. His hips push into mine, his teeth catch my bottom lip, and his hands cradle my face, my throat, my shoulders, trailing downward until I break away, writhing and gasping for breath. Something shifts in his eyes in response. With a low, possessive rumble in his chest—I feel it all the way to my toes—he buries his teeth in my throat.

CHAPTER THIRTY-EIGHT

Saint Célie

White bursts like stars in my vision. Bright. Blinding. I can no longer see anything, can no longer breathe at all. I am only sensation—hot and searing as his palm slides up the smooth skin of my thigh. The stars quickly fade with each pull of his mouth, however, and darkness spreads like a cooling balm across the edge of my vision. I sigh in relief. In contentment. Arching into him once more, I slide a hand through his silky hair before letting it fall to the ground beside me. It nudges something cold. Hard.

You think you can stop him? Though I frown at the intrusive thought, it dances away from me, replaced by one much slower and sleepier. Much easier to catch. *You won't want to stop him, Célie.*

Another moan rises to my lips in response.

Above me, Michal stiffens at the sound, and he releases my leg like I've burned him. Rearing backward—his knees locked on either side of me—he blinks rapidly. For a split second, confusion shines raw and clear in his black eyes. Disbelief. Shock. Though I smile in reassurance, my mind remains pleasantly muddled, and his gaze drops to my throat before I can think to stop him. His face contorts in revulsion.

My smile falters slightly. "Is something wrong?"

"*Wrong?*" His own throat works as if he cannot bring himself to speak. He lifts his hands as if frightened to touch me. "Did I—? Tell me I didn't force—"

Realization dawns two seconds too slow, and my smile vanishes completely as reality crashes back over my head.

"Oh my goodness, no! *No.* You didn't force me to do anything. I—I *volunteered.*" Though I clap a hand over the wound to hide it from sight, it does little to mitigate the damage, and I couldn't possibly hide all the blood anyway. It still shines slick and dark upon my dress. It stains his hands, my skin, the floor all around us, and—and the room starts to spin as I look at it all. His expression darkens as he too takes in the scene.

"How—how are *you*, though?" I ask quickly, pushing upright on my elbow. The movement sends the silver knife spinning, and I cringe as Michal tracks its path across the room. "Are you feeling better? If you don't mind me saying, you looked really bad there for a moment. But what *am* I saying? Of course you did. Babette must've stabbed you a dozen times—"

But Michal is regaining his bearings now. His eyes begin to shutter, and he struggles to regain control of his features, to force them back into that horrid, inscrutable mask. As if I haven't spoken at all, he wrenches my hand from my throat, which unfortunately reveals the bite mark on my wrist. "It's nothing," I say hastily, tugging my sleeve down over the wound. "It didn't h-hurt either. You never lost restraint."

"Excuse me?"

I recoil slightly from the glint in his eyes. "I—I said you never lost restraint. I meant it as a compliment."

"Oh. You meant it as a compliment." He leans forward now, the cords in his neck straining against his skin. Despite our proximity, his voice drops so low that I almost can't hear him. "Do you have any idea how lucky you are, Célie? Any idea how *stupid?*" He snarls the last word, and I blink at him, startled. "I could've killed you—I could've done *worse* than killed you—and you want to compliment my restraint? You think I'd never hurt you? I'm a *vampire*, and you offered yourself up like a lamb for slaughter. What if I hadn't stopped? What if I'd taken more than you wanted to give?"

At his tone, at his *expression*, my gaze darts instinctively to the knife, which now lies completely useless by a moth-eaten mannequin—not that it helped in the first place. My stomach swoops sickeningly at Dimitri's warning, at my own reckless confidence that I could overpower a vampire, let alone a vampire like Michal. *You won't want to stop him, Célie. You'll beg him to take it all.* The last of the pleasant fog in my thoughts dissipates, leaving me cold and humiliated upon this dirty attic floor. When Michal still stares at me, expectant, I mutter, "I took precautions."

"Precautions?" He rises abruptly and crosses the room with preternatural speed, seizing the knife and forcing it into my palm. When I hesitate to take it—because really, what good will it do?— he crushes my fingers around the cold silver hilt and pulls me to my feet. "And how did those *precautions* work for you?"

I force myself to lift my chin, to meet his eyes. "Like I said, you never lost restraint."

"I could've—"

"But you *didn't.*" As before, outside Babette's fireplace, we stand toe to toe, but Michal isn't smiling any longer. No—with the silver knife still clenched between us, he looks prepared to throw me over his shoulder and sail straight back to Requiem, where I imagine a dank cell with rats awaits me. Indeed, his lips pull back over his teeth at my obstinance, and his *cheeks*—usually alabaster white, they flush dark with fury and fresh blood. *My* blood. I look away quickly, determined to forget the last ten minutes—or perhaps the last ten *hours*—of my life. As far as I'm concerned, they never happened. "I expect we can find white vinegar in the pantry. If we dilute the blood before it sets, we might even be able to avoid leaving stains on this poor couple's floor."

Michal drops my wrist in disgust, stalking to the window as if eager to get away from me. "How did we escape Les Abysses?"

I quell the urge to snap back at him. "Odessa and Dimitri."

"They brought us here?"

"Yes."

"They asked you to heal me?"

"No." Fresh stars erupt in my vision as I shake my head, as I thrust the knife into my pocket with such force that I tear the fabric. "They wanted you to drink from the humans downstairs, but I wouldn't let them."

"*Why?*"

"Odessa said you might kill them"—I glare at his rigid back, refusing to feel more foolish than I already do—"and they didn't deserve to die because we walked into a trap."

With startling speed, he clenches the sheet in his fists, his arms tight with restraint. "So, *naturally*, you preferred I kill you instead."

"Of course not, but—"

"You really do have a fucking death wish."

A beat of silence. Then—

The room tilts as I charge toward him, as shock curdles with the sickening anger in my belly. He just—he *swore* at me. No one has ever sworn at me before, and—and how dare he speak to me like this? I've done nothing wrong except save his wretched skin. How dare he treat me like I've committed some heinous crime? Though I intend to seize him, to shake him, I sway precariously after only two steps, and I must seize a nearby trunk for balance instead. "Stop it," I say sharply. "If not for me, you'd be lying dead on the floor, so you could show a little more appreciation."

"I'm not appreciative," he says harshly. "If you ever do it again, I'll kill you out of spite."

"That's an empty threat, Michal Vasiliev, and we both know it. Now—if you're quite finished *sulking*—I'd be grateful if you could return the favor and heal me. I know how you feel about vampire blood, but under the circumstances—"

"Under the circumstances, you deserve more than light-headedness." He breathes deep as if trying to calm himself, but then curses again, tearing off his leather coat and hurling it over his shoulder. It lands with a wet *slap* at my feet. Fresh blood—probably mine—splatters all over my hem, and his voice is low and vicious when he says, "The people stoned Saint Stephen to death, after all, and Saint Lawrence met a hot grill. I could arrange for either when we return to Requiem, but perhaps you'd rather skip the preliminaries and go straight for crucifixion?"

My nails bite deeper into the wood. "You think I want to be a *martyr*?"

"I think it's your greatest ambition."

"You don't know a thing about me."

"Neither do you, apparently," he snarls at the window, "if you think sacrificing yourself for those humans had anything to do with them. As with your predecessors, it had everything to do with *you* and your desire to prove yourself worthy of some imaginary prize—in this case, *death*. Is that what it'll take? Will you need to die before they see you as more than just a pretty porcelain doll?"

My mouth falls open in outrage. In *shock*. "How did you—? *What* did you just say?"

"Is that not why you fled alone into Brindelle Park? To find a killer on the loose before the others?" He still refuses to face me, his hands clenched in the sheet. "If not to valiantly save your friends, why else would you sneak into vampire-infested streets to deliver a letter? Would they even mourn you otherwise?"

"Of course my friends would—"

"Are you sure?" At last, he turns, moving so quickly the sheet eddies behind him. His black eyes bore into mine. "Have you proven yourself kind enough? Selfless enough? Perhaps you should stick your head in a hungry loup garou's mouth next. The poor thing has a toothache, after all, and wouldn't that just show everyone how brave you are? How competent?"

I stumble back a step. "That isn't—"

"And if it bites you—because deep down, you knew it would— well, at least you tried to help someone in need." His voice grows louder with every word, angrier, and he stalks toward me like a storm building on the horizon. "Perhaps your friends will remember that at your funeral. Perhaps they'll cry and realize just how stupid they were to underestimate you. That's what you want, isn't it? Their approval?" Though I open my mouth to deny such a *ridiculous* claim, he speaks over me once more. "Or perhaps it's *your* approval you're so desperate to earn. Perhaps *you* are the one who sees yourself as a pretty doll, not them."

"Stop it." The trunk presses into my calves now, and my hands slide over the wood, clammy and cold, as poisonous hatred rolls through my stomach in waves. Never before have I felt like this—like a malignant creature has cracked open inside me, and if I don't attack, if I don't strike, bite, *wound*, its poison will kill me instead. "You will not treat me like this," I seethe. "Everyone treats me like this—like I'm small and stupid—but I'm not. If the choice is between my life or the life of a friend, I will always choose my friend. *Always*. But you wouldn't understand that, would you? You've never had a friend in your entire *existence* because you're too cold, too cruel, just too powerful to ever care about anyone but yourself. It's *pathetic*—and where has it gotten you? Your rule is weak, your sister is dead, and your cousin probably killed her."

He draws to a halt mere inches away, effectively trapping me against the trunk. "My cousin?"

"Yes, your *cousin*." I relish the vitriol in my voice, relish the fact that I know more about his family than he does—*me*, silly little Célie, the doll, the fool, the *martyr* whose greatest ambitions are hard stones and a hot grill. "Dimitri tried to steal the grimoire after Odessa whisked you away. He knew Babette somehow. He's involved in this—right under your arrogant nose—but you're too busy tearing out hearts to see it."

"Says the woman whose sister gave that cross to Babette," he snarls.

"For the last time, my sister didn't—"

"*Enough*, Célie. That cross belonged to your sister—"

"—we have absolutely *no* proof of that—"

"—and it somehow ended up in the hands of Babette, the blood witch who faked her own death, admitted to killing *my* sister, and tried to abduct you for a man called the Necromancer, who needs your blood to raise the dead." His hands twitch as if he suppresses the desire to physically shake me. "*FT.* Filippa Tremblay. This cross calls to you for a reason, and—as we have little chance of finding Babette again—your sister has become our next person of interest."

With all my might, I thrust out with both hands, pushing him hard in the chest, but he remains like stone. Like adamantine. He doesn't move, doesn't even shift his weight against the onslaught, as I lunge again and again and *again*, nearly screaming in frustration. "My sister is *dead.*"

He snatches my wrists when I lunge for the knife in my pocket. "As was Babette."

"Pippa's body didn't vanish from a *morgue*, Michal." Though I writhe and twist to break his grip, he refuses to let me go. Hot, bitter tears burn in my eyes at my complete and total helplessness, but I cannot—will not—wipe them away. *Let him see*, I think viciously. Let him see just how silly I am, how *stupid* for chasing after vampires and ghosts and *magic* when I am just Célie. "We buried her—*I* buried her—and I lay beside her corpse for two weeks as proof. Do you not remember why I fear the dark? Why I fear *everything?*"

Michal's brows draw together at something in my expression, and his grip relaxes slightly. "Célie—"

As with Babette, however, I seize my advantage and wrench away from him. "*Never* touch me again. Do you understand? If you do, I'll—I—" The strength of my rage chokes me, however, and I cannot finish the threat. Truthfully, I don't know what I'll do. As Michal has so succinctly proven, I have no natural weapons, no great skill or strength beyond disregard for my own life. My throat constricts to the size of a needle at the admission, and—without another word—I whirl toward the door, unable to bear his presence for another second.

To his credit, Michal does not touch me. He simply reappears between the door and me, halting my advance. "Where are you going?"

The tears now spill so thick and so fast that I cannot see his features. "Away from h-here." *Away from you.*

"You shouldn't leave the house, Célie."

"Or *what?*" I grind my palms into my eyes, desperate to unsee him somehow. Desperate to escape this situation—just for a moment—but hopelessly, tragically unable to do so. And I hate it—I *hate* it—but I hate him more for making me feel like this. Like everything anyone has ever said about me is true. "What will you do, Michal? Will you drag me back to Requiem in shackles? Will you lock me up and throw away the key? You're *despicable.*"

He doesn't speak for a long moment, and when I finally drag my hands away from my eyes—scrubbing the tears from my cheeks—he seems to have taken a step closer. His arms hang slack at his sides. "No," he says quietly.

"What do you mean *no?*"

He doesn't answer right away. He simply stares at me, his expression rather lost, and it's all the hesitation I need. I dart around him. Though he makes no move to stop me, I can feel his eyes on my back as I race through the door and down the stairs, nearly skidding into Odessa and Dimitri in the hall below. From the looks on their faces, they heard every word between Michal and me, but I can't bring myself to slow.

"Célie!" Dimitri tries to catch my arm, but Odessa drags him back as I bolt toward a second staircase. "Célie, *please*, I need to talk to you!"

"Leave it, Dima," she murmurs.

"But she needs to understand—"

I lose the rest of their conversation, however, barreling through the entry and out of sight. The front door crashes shut behind me before anyone can follow, and—for the first time in almost a fortnight—sunlight streams down from crystalline skies overhead, painting the cobblestones of the street a bright, lustrous gold. It warms my damp cheeks, my wild hair, and brings fresh, stinging tears to my eyes. I inhale painfully at the unfamiliar sight of it. *Sunlight.*

Then I crumple to my knees and sob.

CHAPTER THIRTY-NINE

Tears Like Stars

I cry on those steps for so long that my knees begin to ache, that my eyes begin to burn. When my body refuses to shed another tear—wholly spent and exhausted—I shift to sit more comfortably, peering blearily at the street around me for the first time. Though Les Abysses must lie somewhere beneath my feet, this looks like a perfectly ordinary middle-class neighborhood. Modest brick homes line either side of the cobblestones, complete with small yet tidy gardens, and the occasional cat sunbathes in a window. Down the way, a little boy in a woolen coat plays fetch with his dog, but otherwise, the villagers here have already started their day—the men to their desks, the women to their household duties. It's all very comfortable. Very quiet.

I cannot stand it.

Once upon a time, I would've imagined one of these homes as my own. I would've dreamed about owning a dog—a yappy little terrier—and a garden, where I would've planted roses that climbed around an oak front door, and my sister would've lived right next door. I would've kissed my husband every day, and together, the two of us would've done something worthwhile with our lives—perhaps owned a bakery, a gallery, or just a boat instead. We could've sailed around the world having swashbuckling adventures with our dog, or perhaps with our dozens of children. We could've been happy.

Life isn't a fairy tale, Célie.

Sniffling, I huddle against the crisp autumn wind. Though no one strolls past on their morning walk—and no reward signs flutter upon these doorsteps—I cannot remain here forever. Who knows how many people have peered through their curtains and spotted me? Perhaps they've already alerted the Chasseurs. Frankly, I wouldn't blame them; I'm not exactly inconspicuous. Indeed, I feel garish in such bright sunlight—wan and exposed and covered in blood. Like a carcass left to rot in fresh snow.

Perhaps it's your approval you're so desperate to earn.

Like a broken tooth, I bite down on Michal's words over and over again. *Perhaps you are the one who sees yourself as a pretty doll.* He spoke them with such conviction, such impatience, as if he couldn't hold them in for a second longer. As if he knew me better than I know myself—because that's what he implied, isn't it? That I don't understand my own emotions, my own desires? Shivering slightly, I thrust my stiff fingers into my pockets. Despite the sunshine, I feel colder than usual, uncomfortable in my skin.

I should go back inside. Whatever Michal said about me, I cannot return to my life in West End, and *that* I know for certain. I will never own a boat or a rose garden or an oak front door, never live beside my sister. The thought of my father's smug expression when he realizes I've failed—or my mother's tight concern—brings bile to my throat. I cannot face them. I cannot face *anyone*, least of all Michal, yet what choice do I have? Once again, he is somehow the lesser evil, and—and *how* did it become this way?

How did I come to choose the company of an arrogant and imperious *vampire* to my own flesh and blood?

Says the woman whose sister gave that cross to Babette.

Reluctant, I slide the silver cross from my pocket to examine it once more. It glows near blinding in the sunlight, brighter and clearer than ever before, and if I angle it a certain way—my stomach contracts—it *does* look like the initials could've originally read *FT.* The curves of the *B* seem fainter than the other lines. Newer. Just like the additions in La Voisin's grimoire. My thumb traces the scalloped edges of the cross without truly seeing them. Because how could my sister have owned this necklace? Had she *actually* been involved with Babette and this Necromancer, or had Babette stolen the cross from her somehow? My thumb presses harder against its edges. Impatient. Perhaps the FT who owned this necklace wasn't Filippa Tremblay at all, but someone else. Perhaps Michal doesn't have a *clue* what he's talking about, forcing him to grasp at straws like all the rest of us.

You don't know a thing about me.

Neither do you, apparently, if you think sacrificing yourself for those humans had anything to do with them.

Miserable, I move to rise, but at that precise second, my thumb catches on a scallop sharper than the rest. Right along the edge of the horizontal arm of the cross. I glance down at it absently—then gasp. Leaning closer, I stare at the ornate mechanism hidden within the whorls, convinced I must be mistaken. Because it *looks* like some sort of—some sort of *clasp*, which would mean the cross isn't a cross at all, but a locket. *A locket.* Holding my breath, I lift the cross right to my nose. Surely Michal would've realized if the cross opened; surely he would've seen it as plainly as he saw the true initials, yet . . . I tilt the cross in the sunlight once more. The clasp is very cleverly hidden, and if I hadn't felt along this precise edge, I never would've noticed it at all.

A fluttery sensation erupts in my belly.

Such a small, hidden compartment would be the perfect place to keep a secret.

Anxious now—mouth suddenly dry—I pry open the little door with my thumb, and a minuscule scrap of parchment flutters onto my lap. My breath hitches at the sight of it. Yellowed and torn, the parchment has been folded to the size of my nail, yet clearly it must've been important if the owner wore it so close to their heart. With trembling fingers, I unfold the parchment and begin to read:

My darling Filippa,
It looks like Frost tonight. Meet me under our tree at midnight, and the three of us will be together forever.

Two lines. Two simple sentences. I stare at them as if sheer concentration alone will make them untrue, rereading the words twice, three times, four. The rest of the letter has been torn away, probably discarded. My heart skips painfully every time I see her name at the top, as clear and indisputable as the sky overhead—*Filippa*.

There can be no doubt now.

This cross belonged to her.

This note—she read it too, held it in her hands, before stowing it inside this locket for safekeeping. Had her lover given her the cross as well? Had he carved her initials into the side and intended them as a promise, like Jean Luc's ring to me?

Meet me under our tree at midnight, and the three of us will be together forever.

I swallow hard against the lump in my throat. How long did he wait under that tree, I wonder, before realizing she would never come? Before realizing their dream had only ever been that—a dream? And who is this mysterious third person he mentioned? *The three of us will be together forever.* I frown at that line, the first tendrils of unease unfurling down my spine. Surely he hadn't meant Babette. Filippa would've received this note while alive, so Babette would've been too busy caring for her sickly sister to run away with anyone. And why had he capitalized the word *Frost*? Indeed, the longer I stare at the letter, the less any of it makes sense.

It looks like Frost tonight.

Frost. I wrack my brain, trying to place the word, but all I can imagine are glittering tufts of grass in the moonlight, perhaps a spire on Filippa's imaginary ice palace. Had he mentioned the frost to alert Filippa of leaving potential tracks? I snort at the thought—of my mother and father trailing her at midnight, examining her footprints on the lawn—but truthfully, nothing about this is amusing. No, I feel rather sicker than I did before finding the note, and part of me wishes I'd left well enough alone. I refold the letter with cold fingers.

Pippa didn't want me to know about this part of her life. She must've had her reasons, and I—

I didn't know her at all.

Pressing my lips tight, hunching my shoulders against the

wind, I tuck the letter back into the locket, pressing the silver door closed once more. I won't tell Michal about the note. I won't tell him anything about Filippa. He'll want to—to study her, to track her last movements, and what on earth could we possibly find? My sister didn't kill anyone, *wouldn't* kill anyone, and even with this locket as a tenuous connection to Babette and the Necromancer— how could Filippa have known them, really? How could she have worked with them? Morgane killed her before the murders in Cesarine even started. *No.* I shake my head resolutely, vehemently, and rise to my feet. *My sister wasn't involved in this.*

I almost don't hear the small *pssst* from across the street.

Halting mid-step, I turn—half convinced I misheard the sound—and startle at the sight of eyes in the hedgerow. My own eyes narrow, and I glance left and right before peering closer into the branches of the holly bushes. The eyes are large, too large to be human, and deep brown, almost familiar. They look like they belong to—well, to a *lutin.* Amandine boasts very few farms, however, and even fewer fields—the terrain is too mountainous, the soil too infertile—which means this lutin has either traveled a long way from home or is very, *very* lost.

"Hello?" I call the greeting to it softly, lifting a placating hand as I did in Farmer Marc's field so long ago. Has it really only been two weeks? It feels like lifetimes. "Excuse me? Are you . . . quite well?"

The lutin shuffles a little in the hedge, his overlarge eyes unblinking. *Mariée?*

I stiffen instinctively at the word, at the expected yet unwelcome intrusion in my mind. "I do not answer to that name."

Then—feeling I might as well do it properly—"I am Célie. Who might you be?"

You know me, Mariée, and I know you.

My frown deepens at the familiar trill. Surely it cannot be . . . "Tears Like Stars?"

He nods, gesturing for me to come closer, and the holly branches quiver all around him at the movement. *I must speak with you, Mariée. We must speak.*

"I—" Strangely reluctant to cross the street, I descend the last of the doorsteps, waiting for him to leave the shadows of the bush and approach me. When he does not, I draw to a halt at the edge of the cobblestones. "How did you find me?" I ask, unable to keep a wary note from my voice. Did he somehow catch my scent in La Fôret des Yeux and follow me to Amandine? And if so, how had Michal not noticed? I lift a delicate hand to my nose, my eyes watering anew. Even from across the street, I can tell Tears Like Stars smells rather . . . odder than before. The thick floral scent of his perfume is new, yet even it cannot quite disguise the fouler scent beneath. Indeed, he smells almost like—

Dropping my hand, I shake myself slightly and refuse to finish the thought. His scent cannot be what I think it is. Not here. Not now. Not on such a lovely autumn morning.

I need your help, Mariée. He gestures more emphatically now, and I cannot help but creep closer. He seems so agitated, his movements convulsive and strange, as if it takes conscious effort for him to use his limbs. A great, fat fly buzzes in the branches around him, loud and unnatural in the hush of the street. With a start, I realize the boy and his dog have gone back inside. *I need your help.*

"Why do you call me Bride?" Despite the cold touch of fear on my neck, I lift my chin, speaking louder, clearer in the bright morning sun. "Has something happened to you?"

Closer. Come closer.

"Not until you explain. Is something wrong?"

He thrashes his head in distress. *I need your help, Mariée. Cold like frost. He needs your help to fix us.*

I stop abruptly in the middle of the empty street, filled with equal parts revulsion and concern. "Who needs my help?" Unbidden, my hand slips into my pocket, and my fingers curl around the silver hilt of the knife. "Who is *he?*" Then, throwing caution to the wind— "Is it the Necromancer? Is he the one who needs my help? *Tell me,* Tears Like Stars!"

Tears Like Stars, however, merely jerks his head and gnashes his needle-sharp teeth, gesturing and *gesturing* for me to close the distance between us. Two more flies soon join the first. Though they buzz around his shadowed face, he does not swat them away. He does not even blink, instead rocking back and forth between the bows, clutching his knobby elbows and reciting, *Cold like frost. Wrong. We are cold like frost. Help.*

The sight of him there—his mind clearly affected—is so pitiful, so heart-wrenching, that I scowl at myself for ever being disgusted. This isn't his fault. *None* of this is his fault, and he desperately needs my help, not my condemnation. If the Necromancer has hurt him somehow, perhaps I can heal him again. At the very least, I can return him to his family in La Fôret des Yeux, and they can care for him properly. *Right.* Squaring my shoulders, I move to march straight into the holly bushes, but the door bangs open behind me at that precise second.

"Célie." Voice quiet, Michal stands in the doorway—just outside the rectangle of sunlight upon the entry floor—with his hands clasped behind his back. "Please come back inside now." On either side of him, Odessa and Dimitri stand tall and silent, watching. Though I cannot see their expressions in the gloom of the entry, if the tightness of Michal's eyes is any indication, the three have indeed been watching me. The realization curdles in my stomach. Unfortunately for them, however, they can do nothing *more* than watch—not with the sun so high and beautiful in the sky. I lift my chin higher, striving to sound calm and assertive. If he can be civil, I can be civil. "I have a friend in trouble, and I intend to help him."

Dimitri moves forward, but Michal blocks him with an arm, flexing his hand upon the threshold. "That creature is no longer your friend."

I bite down on a scathing retort—because this isn't about Michal any longer. This isn't even about me, not truly, and if we don't help Tears Like Stars soon, he might inadvertently hurt himself. "He needs our help, Michal. Something is wrong with . . ."

The rest of the words die on my tongue, however, as I turn to find Tears Like Stars no longer hiding in the hedgerow. No. He stands directly in front of me now, and that *smell*—I didn't imagine it before. My eyes instantly begin to water, and it takes every ounce of my willpower not to retreat a step. This close, he reeks undeniably of rot, of decay, but worse still—his once-swarthy skin looks unnaturally pallid in the sunlight, paper thin and sagging slightly upon his pointed face. An eerie white film covers his overlarge eyes as he stares up at me.

Now I do stumble back a step. "What—what *happened* to—?"

Before I can finish, he seizes my wrist with his long fingers. They feel like ice. *Come with me, Mariée. You must come with me.* Choking on the smell, eyes still streaming, I try to wrench myself away, but his grip only tightens, viselike, until I nearly cry out in pain. "Let me go, Tears Like Stars." Though I try to keep my voice measured and calm, a note of desperation breaks through, and Michal curses viciously from the door behind me. "Please. You don't—you don't want to hurt me. We're friends, remember? I gave you elderberry wine, *delicious* elderberry wine."

His head continues to thrash, as if he cannot hear me at all. And perhaps he can't. Perhaps he can say only what the Necromancer has told him to say, can *do* only what the Necromancer has told him to do. *My master needs help. He commands me to help him, and you to help me.*

"Who is your master?" I crouch to peer helplessly into his wretched eyes, and a *fly*—it lands directly upon the sclera of his pupil. Choking down bile, I swat it away with my free hand. "What is his name? Did he"—fresh gorge rises as the same fly flits into my hair—"did he kill you, Tears Like Stars? Did your master take your life?"

A drop is not enough. We must have it all.

"All of *what?* My blood? Does he need"—I swallow hard—"a-all of my blood to—to resurrect the dead? Is that what he did to you?"

He convulses again in response, and slowly but surely begins to tow me down the cobblestone street, muttering all the while, *Cold as frost. Something is wrong. I am wrong.*

"*Célie,*" Michal says sharply. "Your knife."

I dig in my heels, panic clawing up my throat. The knife still lies heavy in my pocket, yes, but it won't—I don't think it'll—Tears Like Stars is *dead*, and something indeed has gone very wrong. The realization rattles in my chest, too shocking and too terrible to ignore any longer. He is *dead*, yet he still holds my arm, still walks and talks among the living, still carries out his master's orders with the strength of a creature twice his size. What did Babette say in Les Abysses?

The Necromancer came upon your blood by chance, and we tested it on a whim.

Did they test that single drop of my blood on Tears Like Stars? Is this—this creature before me the result of their experimentation? Does the *real* Tears Like Stars still exist within it, or has his soul already departed this world, leaving only a shell behind? Can he still feel pain? I twist my wrist harder, abrading skin, but still he doesn't release me. "Tell me how to help you," I say desperately. "Please, I can't give you my blood, but—but I could hide you from him. Would you like that? I could take you back to your family."

My master is near. We must go to him. We must meet him.

"Where is he?" I look around wildly, half expecting the Necromancer to drop out of the neighbor's cherry tree. "*Where* is your master? *Tell me!*"

Wrong, wrong, something is wrong.

Somewhere behind us, Michal is shouting now—Dimitri and Odessa too—but I cannot hear them; I cannot heed their lethal commands. Because I am not a vampire, and this isn't Tears Like Stars's fault. I cannot hurt him, and even if I could— Gritting my teeth, I sink my nails into his hand deep enough to wound, but no blood seeps from the tiny crescent moons. No blood, and no shrieks of pain. My hysteria spikes at the realization.

Even if I *could* hurt Tears Like Stars, a simple knife won't do the trick. No, I'll need to—to—

A knife.

My thoughts catch on the silver blade in my pocket, on the blade that shone so brightly earlier it almost blinded me. *Lutins appreciate the finer things in life.* I painted twenty cages gold to attract Tears Like Stars and his kin at Monsieur Marc's farm. Perhaps I don't need to hurt him now either. Perhaps I just need to distract him.

Plunging my free hand into my pocket, I withdraw the blade and flash it in the morning sun, which blazes even brighter and higher in the sky than before. The silver gleams almost white—brilliant, dazzling—between us, and when Tears Like Stars's eyes fall upon it, they widen infinitesimally. "Do you like it?" I wave the knife above his head when he stretches out to seize it. It throws sparkling lights upon the cobblestones. "It's pretty, isn't it? You may have it if you can reach it."

At my words, he snaps his teeth and stretches up on tiptoe, but I'm much taller; he cannot even touch the handle while he still holds my wrist, which I strain to keep low at my side. "Go on," I tell him, nodding encouragingly. He stretches a bit taller, his frail arms trembling now. "You're almost there."

At last, his fingers slip—just an inch—from my wrist, but it's all the slack I need. Hurling the knife down the street, I twist away from him, turning and sprinting toward Michal and the others without looking back. His long hands do not find me again, however, as I leap into Michal's outstretched arms, as Odessa slams the door closed behind me, as Dimitri peers through the curtains into the street.

"He's gone," he says incredulously. "The little scab disappeared!"

Still breathing heavily, I disentangle myself from Michal and push Dimitri out of the way, gazing through the gap in the curtains to where Tears Like Stars just stood. Only cheery sunshine and orange maple leaves remain. Even the silver knife has gone—vanished—as if I imagined the entire scene.

CHAPTER FORTY

The Clucking Hen

We huddle at the edge of Cesarine that night, peering out at the docks from a rather damp and putrid alley. It smells of fish. Or refuse. My nose wrinkles in distaste. None of the vampires comment, however—except for Odessa, who grimaces like someone shoved pins in her eyes—so I say nothing either. If they can endure such stench, I can too.

"Hood on, I think," Michal murmurs at my ear. "They've almost finished their inspection."

He loaned me his traveling cloak before we departed Amandine. Though Dimitri offered, we both ignored him, and a silent truce passed between us in that moment—mutual distrust of Dimitri, of course, but also mutual understanding that neither would mention what transpired between us in the attic. I cannot decide if I'm grateful. Now that my anger has ebbed, only a hollow sort of shame remains, one that I cannot examine too closely.

And certainly not right now.

I pull the cloak over my hair, where it ripples in the midnight breeze along with the reward notices. Torn from wind and discolored from rain, they litter every available inch of this alley, thicker here than they'd been in Amandine. As if my father suspected that I'd return home eventually, or perhaps that I never left Cesarine at all. Unable to help it, I resume pacing, the cloak billowing around my feet in the muck and mire of the alley. Too long. Too large. I roll the sleeves up my hands irritably, feeling like some sort of reaper, an eternal harbinger of bad luck. All I need is a scythe. I take care not to glance at the docks.

"This sketch doesn't look a thing like you," Odessa muses, plucking a notice from the dirty brick and scrutinizing my face up close. "You look much too . . . regal. Like a rather crotchety dowager empress I used to know." When I snatch the notice from her gloved fingers, ripping my face in two, she arches a bemused brow and flicks her half away dispassionately. "Why, Célie, whatever is the matter? You seem upset."

"Shall I peruse *your* face from an inch away?"

"I would welcome it, darling. I have nothing to hide." With a smirk, she lifts a shoulder and turns away. "You should know, however," she says, "chronic anger twists the human body up inside—high blood pressure, heart and digestive problems, headaches, and even skin disorders." She reaches out to smooth the furrows between my eyes, her own glittering with mischief. Though she hasn't yet tried to trap me in conversation about her brother, she seems more determined to engage me than before, more determined to *like* me, but I *know* she heard my suspicions. "I studied medicine several years ago."

"You're practically a healer, then." I swat her hand away, irritated, but she merely laughs and sweeps across the alley to Dimitri, who's been trying and failing to catch my eye for the greater part of four hours. When I accidentally look at him now, he pushes forward with fervent determination.

"Célie—"

I turn away with a groan, unable to face him, and my sister's note seems to burn a hole through my bodice. I resist the urge to thrash my head and gnash my teeth as Tears Like Stars had done—because what I mean, of course, is *not ever.* Dimitri might make a better suspect than my sister, but if Filippa knew Babette—and that's a very large *if*—does that mean she knew him too? Could *he* have been her mysterious lover? Do I even want to know? "Just stop, Dimitri," I tell him wearily when he opens his mouth again. "Leave me alone."

Just stop, Célie. Leave it alone.

Undeterred, he reappears in front of me, reaching into his cloak and withdrawing a small linen sack. "I know you don't want to talk to me right now, but when is the last time you ate? I took the liberty of procuring bread on our way through the city—"

Reacting instinctively, I knock the bag out of his hand, and it crashes to the filthy street between us. I refuse to apologize. "And what *else* did you take the liberty of procuring?"

He blinks. "I don't know what you—"

"You still have blood on your collar, Monsieur Petrov."

Dimitri's face hardens for a split second before re-forming into a brilliant smile once more. He extracts a golden pear from his cloak next, waving it in front of my nose. "Don't be like that, darling. Despite what you *think* you heard in Les Abysses, I am not a murderer—er, not *that* murderer—and you must be ravenous by now. What sense is there in starving yourself?"

"Enough, cousin." Voice low, Michal leans against the mouth of the alley, watching the commotion at the docks and blending into darkness like he'd been born a shadow instead of a man. "This isn't the time or place."

"But she suspects—"

"I know what she suspects, and trust me"—he pins Dimitri with an expectant look over his shoulder—"the two of us are going to have a very long discussion when we return to Requiem. Though I don't agree that you killed Mila, I *will* hear every detail of your relationship with Babette Trousset, and I'll learn about the contents of her grimoire too, particularly the page marked FOR LUST OF THE BLOOD." A dark pause. "I assume you know of it."

Dimitri glares at him in mutinous silence.

Though I don't agree that you killed Mila . . .

I turn away quickly, trying not to curse Michal for his sudden and inconvenient levelheadedness. If he doesn't suspect Dimitri, he must suspect someone else, and if the note in Filippa's cross burned any hotter now, it would actually start to smoke.

Tucking it beneath my collar in a would-be casual gesture, I start to pace once more, my thoughts running rampant. Because this isn't the time or place to dwell on Dimitri. This isn't even the time or place to dwell on Filippa, and—and because my finest boots are now scuffed. They're now *stained* from our little adventure into Amandine, and the blood will probably never come out. I should've soaked them in white vinegar, should've scrubbed them until the leather looked shiny and new again. The elderly couple who lived in the town house kept their pantry stocked *full* of things like white vinegar and soap, and they never would've known if I'd borrowed some. I shake my head as I pace, growing more and more agitated. They never would've known if I'd lit my boots on *fire* either, or if I shed this bloody dress and ran naked and screaming into La Fôret des Yeux, never to be seen agai—

"Célie." Once more Michal turns at the mouth of the alley, his lips twisting in a wry grin. Fresh shouts sound from the docks behind him. "Your heart has started to palpitate."

I lift a hand to my flushed chest. "Has it? I don't know why."

"No?"

"*No.*"

He sighs and shakes his head, pushing off the wall to stand beside me. As always, he clasps his pale hands behind his back, and the familiar gesture brings me a strange modicum of comfort, despite the way he seems to peer down his nose at me. "You escaped an undead creature today."

I straighten my spine. "Yes, I did."

"You outwitted a blood witch only hours before that."

Odessa examines a sharp nail absently. "With help."

"Both were much cleverer than those you called brethren," he continues without acknowledging her. Though I long to glance over his shoulder at mention of the Chasseurs, I force myself to concentrate on his face instead. Something like pride glints hard and sharp in his eyes. "They will not check the caskets again, Célie. Even huntsmen fear the idea of death, and—though they'll never admit it—fear proximity to it as well. After the harbormaster has finished his inspection, we'll slip inside our inventory without notice, and my sailors will load us aboard our ship without interference. We'll be back in Requiem before daybreak."

As if in answer, the harbormaster—a thickset man with swarthy skin and sharp eyes—bangs his gnarled hand upon the last of the caskets and shouts the all clear. His crew moves on to the next cargo scheduled to disembark, leaving the vacant-eyed employees of Requiem, Ltd., to mill about until Michal compels them otherwise. Apparently, this shipment of caskets has been crafted from a rare conifer found only in La Fôret des Yeux—at least, that's what Michal tells me. It's been rather difficult to listen to the finer points of his plan when beyond him—beyond the alley, the sailors, and the caskets—Chasseurs swarm the docks, their blue coats like little flares of memory in the darkness. Bright and painful and intrusive.

A familiar voice rises sharply from among them.

I close my eyes at the sound.

"That said," Michal murmurs, "I can still arrange for you to speak with him."

Instinctively, my eyes snap open, and they dart over Michal's shoulder before I can stop them, searching desperately for the one person I do not wish to see.

They find him instantly.

There—striding through the heart of his men—Jean Luc kicks over a barrel of grain in frustration. The contents spill across the feet of an irate farmer, who shouts himself purple at the loss of inventory. Jean Luc, however, has already lunged to straighten the barrel. He hastily scoops the grain from the street with his bare hands, shaking his head and apologizing over the farmer's tirade. When Frederic kneels to help, Jean Luc curses bitterly and shoves him away.

I take a small, involuntary step forward.

Jean Luc.

My chest seems to seize at the sight of him—so near to me, so *dear* to me, yet so far away too. We were so similar once. I still remember the fierce, determined gleam in his eyes during the Battle of Cesarine. We spent the greater part of the night whisking children into the relative safety of Soleil et Lune. Despite the horror of the circumstances, I'd never felt more connected with another person. Both of us working hand in hand with a common purpose: to serve those children, yes, but also to serve each other. We'd formed a partnership that night—a true partnership—and that morning, when Jean had covertly wiped the tears from Gabrielle's cheeks, I'd known I loved him.

My heart aches at the memory.

Looking at him tonight feels like looking into a broken mirror; his reflection is somehow sharper than before. Fractured. Though his dark hair remains the same, his eyes now shine with a crazed sort of light, and deep shadows have crept beneath them, as if he hasn't slept in weeks. At his orders, Chasseurs seize luggage for impromptu search, while the constabulary have formed several blockades throughout the docks, carefully inspecting the face of each and every individual who passes. One of them snatches the arm of an unsuspecting woman with dark hair, refusing to release her until her husband—who holds a squalling baby with one hand and a shrieking toddler with the other—threatens civil action.

Across the way, Basile has accidentally let loose a flock of chickens, and dozens of men dart around the water's edge, trying to catch them before the harbormaster's dog, which barks gleefully and snaps at passersby's heels. Charles holds a crimson gown from another woman's luggage up to the torchlight while Frederic attempts to calm the seething harbormaster, who storms toward the farmer and Jean Luc with several of his crew in tow.

"You're a blundering fool!" He jabs Jean Luc hard in the chest, and those nearest him all mutter their bitter agreement. "*Fifty years* I've been running these docks, and I've never seen such a slipshod show of things—"

"*Ruined!*" Bellowing in rage, the farmer kicks his barrel of soiled grain to the street all over again. Jean Luc watches mutely as the kernels pour over his boots. "I'll be reporting this to the king, *huntsman*. Over a hundred quarts you've cost me, and mark my words, you'll pay for every couronne you've lost—"

"And where *is* old Achille, eh?" The harbormaster whirls around in search of the Archbishop while Jean Luc swallows hard and clenches his jaw, still glaring at his feet. Behind him, Reid emerges from the watching crowd, his face tight and grave as he leads the harbormaster's dog forward by a piece of rope. "Doubt he knows what you're on about, does he? You can be sure I'll be speaking to him too, and I'll be demanding some sort of recompense. Just *look* at my harbor. Backlogged, young'uns crying, chicken shit every-where—"

"And for *what?*" The farmer actually pushes Jean Luc now, and Reid and I both step forward at the same time. When Reid clasps a hand on the man's shoulder, scowling, the man laughs unpleasantly and spits at Jean Luc's feet. "Because your little whore might be hiding in my crop?" He jerks away from Reid and kicks grain toward Charles, who still holds the crimson dress in his hands. "Oh, we all heard, didn't we? We know all about her little tryst up north. My brother is friendly with one of your huntsmen, isn't he? And it's looking like she isn't dead, after all. Wasn't abducted either. It's looking like she ran off with some *creature* instead."

I expel a pained breath as Jean Luc's entire body stiffens.

"Mademoiselle Tremblay is wanted for questioning in a murder investigation," Reid says quietly, handing the dog's rope to Frederic. "She could provide much-needed evidence to identify and bring the killer to justice." Stepping to stand beside Jean Luc, Reid addresses the rest of the harbor, his voice louder now, strong and steady. "We apologize for the inconvenience, and we appreciate your cooperation in our efforts to locate Mademoiselle Tremblay, who—despite speculation—we still believe to have been abducted. She was last seen in Amandine fleeing a place called Les Abysses—"

"A brothel," the farmer snarls.

"—and could soon be boarding a ship out of Cesarine," Reid continues determinedly, ignoring the outburst of scandalized whispers. He looks to Jean Luc then, who nods tersely and squares his shoulders. Though Jean's eyes remain tight, his breath rather shallow, his voice carries a newfound note of authority as he addresses the crowd.

"If this happens," he says, "our chances of recovering Mademoiselle Tremblay vanish with the tide. We ask for your patience only a little longer as we try to protect an innocent woman from unspeakable evil."

Recover.

Protect.

The words catch in my throat as the farmer spits again, the harbormaster scoffs, and Jean Luc ignores them both, turning away abruptly to catch the nearest chicken. *Conversation finished.* With a shake of his head, Reid trails after him, and—to my horror—the chicken runs directly toward the caskets as the Chasseurs and constabulary resume their search.

Holding my breath, I try to imitate Michal and melt into the shadows, infinitely grateful for his black cloak.

"Jean Luc, wait." Reid breaks into a light jog to catch up to him, frightening the chicken—a fat little hen with a particularly shrill cluck—onto Michal's and my casket. "Talk to me."

"There's nothing to talk about." Jean Luc lunges, swiping wildly, and misses the hen completely. "That cockhead farmer said it all, didn't he? Célie is alive, and rumors place her at a magic brothel hundreds of miles from here. Not only as a patron," he adds bitterly, "but also, it seems, as a worker."

Reid approaches the hen cautiously. "We don't know why she was there."

"The witnesses' reports were pretty clear, Reid."

"Célie wouldn't do that to you, Jean."

My heart crashes to somewhere between my feet, shattering upon the cobblestones. I shouldn't be listening to this conversation. As before, these words are not meant for me, yet what can I do to escape them? Backing up as quietly as possible, I turn—determined to give them privacy, or perhaps to flee—and crash straight into Michal's chest. His hands reach out to steady my arms, and fresh humiliation, fresh *shame*, washes through me as I look into his cool expression. As I glance to where Odessa and Dimitri stand like statues in the alley behind, equally still and cold and silent. They can hear every word too. I *know* they can, and I—I think I'm going to vomit all over Michal's shoes again.

Because your little whore might be hiding in my crop?

It's looking like she ran off with some creature.

And then—on the wings of my shame—two words.

Recover.

Protect.

"Where is she, then?" At the sound of his voice, I turn once more, and Jean Luc extends his arms in helpless supplication, gesturing to the caskets, to the docks, to the city at large with increasing agitation. His face contorts. His hands begin to shake. "If she can visit a brothel in Amandine—if she can practically *disrobe* for a stranger—why can't she visit her fiancé in Chasseur Tower?"

But Reid shakes his head curtly, impatiently, as Michal's hands fall away from my arms. "We don't know anything about vampires. For all we know, she *could've* been coerced—"

"She wasn't wearing her engagement ring." The hen clucks forgotten between them, pecking at spilled grain. "Did Lou tell you that part? Every report said the same—crimson dress of a courtesan and no ring on her finger."

"That means nothing. *Nothing.* No, listen to me, Jean." Reid seizes Jean Luc's arm when he sneers and begins to stalk away. "*Listen.* The two of you fought the night of her abduction—she wasn't wearing it then either. She wasn't wearing it in Brindelle Park." Though Jean Luc snarls, Reid doesn't relinquish his grip. "The vampire himself could've taken it from her, or it could've been lost in their tussle during the abduction. There are a hundred possible explanations—"

Jean Luc does jerk away now. "And we won't know the real one until we find her."

Reid sighs heavily and watches as Jean marches right past the hen. "You're determined to think the worst."

"No, what I'm *determined* to do is find her," he snarls over his shoulder. "Find her, arrest the fucking *night creature* who took her, and never let her out of my sight again."

After another long moment, Reid follows him back into the tumult—the harbormaster and Frederic have nearly come to blows over the former's dog—leaving me to the aching silence of the alley. "Célie?" Dimitri asks quietly, but I lift a hand to silence him, unable to speak.

Recover.

Protect.

I knew those words tasted wrong, tasted acrid and resentful in my mouth. His previous condemnation weaves through them softly, strengthening their rancor. *I can hardly discharge her. Célie is delicate.*

We both know Morgane would've slit your throat if Lou hadn't been there.

Never let her out of my sight again.

Swallowing them down, I force myself to look at Michal, to meet those black eyes with my own. "No," I tell him, trying to adopt his composure, to adopt the cool, dispassionate countenance of a vampire. I can be made of stone too. I will not crack, and I will not shatter. "I don't want to speak with him."

Though Michal's mouth tightens like he wants to object, he nods curtly instead, readjusting his hood over my hair. When he steps backward, offering me his hand, his meaning is loud and clear: this time, the choice to go with him is my own.

I accept his hand without hesitation.

We don't speak as he pulls me into our casket, as Odessa and Dimitri follow in theirs, as their sailors tow us across the harbor toward our ship. Still I hold my breath, counting each heartbeat and praying nothing goes awry. Are all statues as hollow inside as I now feel? As brittle? Do they all secretly suffer this sense of dread? The harbormaster's dog has stopped howling, at least, and the children have quieted. Even the farmer has stopped cursing. Only the terse orders of the Chasseurs remain, the grumblings of the merchants and the harbormaster's crew.

I blink away tears of relief.

Just as I exhale—convinced we've made it to the gangplank—a sailor near my head lets out a panicked shout. A hen shrieks in response, and the entire casket topples, lurching sideways. Michal's arm snakes around my waist in the next second, but before I can draw another breath, we smash into the wall of the casket, plummeting to the cobblestones as the lid crashes open. Though Michal swears viciously, twisting midair to position himself beneath me, my teeth still rattle as we spill onto the ground.

As we roll right into a pair of familiar grain-speckled boots.

"Oh God," I whisper.

Oh God oh God oh God—

"Trust me." Sighing, staring up at the stars in resignation, Michal's head thuds upon the cobblestones as a horrified Jean Luc gapes down at us and absolute silence descends in the harbor. "He'll be no help at all."

CHAPTER FORTY-ONE

Our Last

I climb slowly to my feet.

Never before have so many people stared at me, stricken, but for once in my life, I don't flush beneath their attention. I don't stumble and stammer at their disbelief, their rising indignation. No, my limbs feel as if they're made of ice, and my hands tremble as I smooth my crimson dress, as I push the hair from my face and lift my chin. Because I don't know what else to do. I certainly can't look at Jean Luc, can't stand to see the raw accusation in his eyes. All the color has drained from his face, and though he opens his mouth to speak, no words come. He doesn't understand. Of course he doesn't—no one does—and helplessly, my chin begins to quiver.

This is all my fault.

Abruptly, I stoop to pick up the hen, but she squawks and hops through my fingers before darting away. Too quick to catch. I chase after her reflexively, my footsteps echoing loud and stilted in the hush of the harbor, but it doesn't matter; the hen could be hurt, and if she is, those injuries would be my fault too. I have to—to catch her somehow, perhaps bind her leg. My feet move faster, clumsier. Odessa studied medicine, so she might know how to—

The hen beelines toward Jean Luc.

Losing my head completely, I leap at her, determined to

somehow *help*, but with a shrill cry of panic, she changes directions and plows straight into Reid's shins instead. I skid to a halt a split second before following suit. Warily, he bends to pick her up with a soft, "Hello, Célie."

"Reid! How are you?" I straighten at once, still shaking like a leaf, and force a tremulous smile. Before he can answer, I add hastily, "Should we—should we check her wing? Her feathers look a bit ruffled, like she might've—might've broken it or—"

But Reid shakes his head with a pained smile. "I think the chicken is fine."

"Are you sure?" My voice climbs steadily higher. "Because—"

In that instant, however, Jean Luc seizes my wrist—right over Michal's bite—and wrenches me around to face him, his face blazing with a thousand unspoken questions. Though I try not to flinch at the bolt of pain, I can't help myself. It *hurts*. At my sharp intake of breath, Michal, Odessa, and Dimitri instantly materialize beside me, and Jean Luc's gaze darts from their otherworldly faces to my wrist and the obvious teeth marks there. To the blood now gently weeping between his fingers. His eyes widen and, almost instinctively, he tears the cloak away from my throat to reveal the deeper, darker wounds there. Jaw clenching, he wrenches the Balisarda from his belt.

"Jean—" I start quickly.

"Get behind me." Voice urgent, he tries to pull me away from Michal and the others, but I dig in my heels and shake my head, throat tightening to the point of pain. He stares at me in disbelief. "*Now*, Célie."

"N-No."

When I twist to loosen his grip and retreat into Michal—when

Michal slides a protective arm around my waist—realization slams into Jean Luc with the force of a falling guillotine. I can see the exact second it strikes—he blinks, and his expression abruptly empties. Then it contorts into something unfamiliar, something *ugly*, as he drops my wrist. "You let him— He *bit* you."

I clutch my wrist to my chest. "It doesn't mean what you think it does."

"No?" Though he tries to conceal his suspicion, a note of trepidation still creeps into his voice. "What does it mean, then? Did he—did he force—?"

"He didn't force me to do anything," I say quickly. "He was— Jean, he was hurt, and he needed my blood to heal him. He would've died without it. Blood sharing with vampires isn't always— It doesn't have to be—"

"Doesn't have to be *what?*" Jean Luc's eyes sharpen on my face, and cursing my own stupidity, I stare back at him helplessly. I can't say the word. I *can't*. Still clutching my wrist, I pray harder than I've ever prayed before—to who or what entity, I do not know, as clearly God has abandoned me. "Célie," he warns when the silence grows too long.

"It doesn't have to be . . . sexual," I finish in a small voice.

He recoils like I've slapped him. When whispers sweep throughout the crowd, his jaw tightens, and I brace, expecting the worst. "So it's true," he says coolly. "You really are a whore."

A low, menacing noise reverberates from Michal's chest. I can feel it all the way down my spine as I press against him, shaking my head again. This time in warning. I cannot allow Michal to attack Jean Luc, and I cannot allow Jean Luc to attack Michal. Because if either of them hurts the other, I don't know what I'll do, and because—because I deserve this anger from Jean Luc. I do. I deserve his hurt. And because as Lou and Coco once told me, a whore isn't the worst thing a woman can be. Still— "You don't mean that," I tell him quietly.

He scoffs and gestures bitterly to the crimson gown beneath Michal's cloak. "What else would you call it? For a *fortnight*, the entire kingdom has been searching for you—fearing the worst, *dreading* what we might find—and where have you been?" His knuckles clench tight around his Balisarda. "Entertaining the locals."

At the last, his eyes flash to Michal, who chuckles darkly. "I'm not local, Captain, and how fortunate that is for you."

Odessa elbows him sharply in the side.

Jean Luc glares between them for several seconds—disgust and unease at war on his face—before he turns to me and snarls, "Who *is* he?"

My mouth parts to answer before closing promptly once more. How in the *world* can I explain Michal without revealing his secret to not only hundreds of gawking people but also an entire contingent of Chasseurs, who—most inconveniently—wield silver swords?

Sensing my hesitation, Michal steps smoothly forward.

"As I'm standing right in front of you," he says in that cool, would-be pleasant voice, "it's rather rude not to ask me directly. Surely any fiancé of Célie's should know better. However"—Jean Luc's skin flushes at the insult—"for the sake of ending this conversation as expeditiously as possible, you already know who I am. Célie has told you." He inclines his head slightly, his black eyes cold and unblinking. "I am Michal Vasiliev, and these are my cousins, Odessa and Dimitri Petrov. We've contracted Célie's services in avenging the murder of my sister, who—I believe—is just one name on a long list of victims." Straightening, he adds, "It should come as no surprise that Célie has already located your missing body *and* your missing grimoire, both of which she found at Les Abysses while working undercover."

The silence deepens at his pronouncement, and I *feel* the eyes of everyone in the harbor fall to my crimson gown. "Michal," I whisper, blinking rapidly. No one has ever—they've never even *thought* about me in such a way, let alone voiced it for hundreds to hear. It shouldn't mean this much—he isn't saying anything untrue—yet my knees still threaten to give way beneath the crowd's curious gaze.

I will not break. I will not shatter.

"At this brothel," Michal continues impassively, clasping his hands behind his back and strolling around me, "Célie discovered Babette Trousset isn't dead at all, but alive and well. The blood witch faked her own death before stealing your precious grimoire and fleeing to the arms of her cousin Pennelope Trousset, who has harbored her in secret for days. Presumably, both women have been acting on orders from a man who calls himself the Necromancer. All of this, of course, Célie investigated while being quite *out of your sight.*"

Jean Luc, who looked momentarily stunned at the revelation, seems to return to himself at his own shameful turn of phrase. "Because you *abducted* her—"

Before either can do more than sneer, however, Reid appears between them, still clutching the resentful-looking hen in his arms. To my surprise, he addresses neither Jean Luc nor Michal, instead gazing intently at me. "Are you hurt, Célie?" His eyes fall to the blood all over my dress, my wrist, my throat. "Are you all right?"

"I'm—"

As if he can't hear me, Jean Luc thrusts the Balisarda back into its scabbard with brutal force. "What kind of question is that? Of course she isn't *all right.* She clearly isn't herself, and she hasn't *been* herself for a long time."

He delivers the words like an edict, like his perception of my well-being is truer than my own, and a tendril of flame licks up the ice in my chest. "He wasn't asking you, Jean. He was asking *me.* And for the record, it *is* rude to speak about a person indirectly when they're standing right in front of you."

He gapes at me like I've lost my mind. "Do you even hear yourself? The Célie *I* know would never agree with someone like—"

"Perhaps the Célie you know never existed. Have you ever considered that?" Instinctively, my hand clutches the cross around my neck until the edges bite sharp into my palm. Kindling that fire in my chest. "It can happen without us even realizing—we fall in love with an idea instead of a person. We give each other pieces of ourselves but never the whole thing, and without the whole thing, how can we ever truly know a person?"

And you'll never know a world without sunlight, will you? Not our darling Célie.

She never truly knew me either.

"Célie, what are you—what are you *talking* about?" This time, Jean Luc seizes my uninjured hand, squeezing it desperately for some kind of assurance. "Is this about the Chasseurs? Listen, if you no longer want to be a huntsman—hunts*woman*—you don't have to be. I— Célie, I spoke with Father Achille last month, and he agreed that I can purchase a house outside Saint-Cécile without revoking my vows. We can move *away* from Chasseur Tower." When my other hand falls away from the cross, he grasps it too, his eyes bright with emotion, or perhaps unshed tears. He steps even closer and lowers his voice. "I've already looked at a few—one right down the street from Lou and Reid, even. It has an orange tree in the back, and—and I wanted it to be a surprise for your birthday." He lifts my hands to his lips, brushing a soft kiss against my knuckles. "I want to build a *home* with you."

I stare at him for a long moment, striving to keep my composure. Then—

"What would you have me do there, Jean? Would I freshly squeeze those oranges every morning before you go to work? Teach our half-dozen children how to embroider and alphabetize the library? Is that what you want?"

He wrings my hands as if trying to shake the sense back into me. "I thought that's what *you* wanted."

"I don't *know* what I want!"

"Pick anything, then!" Tears definitely sparkle in his eyes now, and I hate the sight of them. I hate myself more. "Pick anything, and I'll make it happen—"

"I don't *want* you to make it happen, Jean." It takes every inch of my strength not to pull away now, not to flee and humiliate him in front of all these people. He doesn't deserve that. He doesn't deserve *this*, yet I don't deserve it either. "Can't you understand that? I want to make it happen for myself. I *need* to make it happen for myself—"

"Is that why you ran away with him?" Desperate again, his gaze plunges to my throat once more, and after another anguished second, he closes his eyes as if unable to bear the sight of it, exhaling raggedly. "Did you leave to punish me? To somehow—to *prove* yourself?"

The word sinks straight through my ribs and into my heart, too familiar and true to ignore. Jean Luc doesn't know what he's saying, of course. He doesn't *mean* to hurt me, but only moments ago, he spat the word *abduction* like a curse. "I didn't run away," I say through clenched teeth, "but now I wish I had." His eyes snap open. "Look at all the meetings you held, the secrets you kept— can you honestly say you regret them? Would you do anything differently if you could?"

Though I pose the question to Jean Luc, my own answer rises swift and sure between us.

This is all my fault, yes, but I cannot bring myself to regret the choices I've made. They led me here. Without them, I never would've noticed this deep unease in my chest as I gaze upon Jean Luc, upon Reid, upon Frederic and my old brethren. I never would've heard this deafening silence.

I might not know exactly what I want, but I know it's no longer here.

"Everything I did," Jean Luc says at last, "was to protect you."

Now I squeeze *his* hands, trying to pour every last ounce of my love and respect into that touch. Because that's what it is—our last.

"I'm sorry, Jean, but I don't need you to protect me. I never needed you to protect me. I needed you to love me, to trust me, to comfort me, and to push me. I needed you to confide in me when you had a poor day and laugh with me when I had a good one. I needed you to wait for me to catch those lutins in Farmer Marc's field, just as I needed you to break the rules and *kiss* me when the chaperone looked away." His face flushes again—he glances around quickly—but I'd be the filthiest sort of hypocrite to protect his feelings now. "I needed you to seek my counsel when you found the first body, even if you couldn't ask for my help. I needed you to value my insight. I needed you to tease me and prod me and stroke my hair when I cried; I needed a hundred different things from you, Jean Luc, but your protection was never one of them.

"And now . . . now I don't need anything from you at all. I've learned to survive on my own." Swallowing hard, I force myself to say the rest, to acknowledge the truth of those words. "In the last two weeks, I've crossed the veil and danced with ghosts. I've drunk the blood of a vampire, and I've lived in the dark. I'm still here." My voice grows louder at the affirmation, stronger. "I'm still *here*, and I'm so close to finding the killer now. He's after me, Jean—he wants *me*—and I know I can catch him with a little more time."

Though I try to pull away, Jean Luc's hands tighten around mine. "What do you mean by he wants *you*? What are you talking about?"

"Are you even *listening* to me? Did you hear anything else I—"

"Of course I'm listening to you! That's the problem—I'm *listening* to you, and you just said some lunatic who calls himself the *Necromancer* is after you!" He flings my hands away as if they've burned him. "Célie, you've been gone for less than two weeks, and you've somehow managed to capture the interest of a killer. Do you not see how unsafe that is? Do you not *see* how badly you need to be around people who—"

"—lock me up in Chasseur Tower?" Despite my best efforts,

hot and angry tears spring to my eyes. I can't believe this. I can't believe *him.* I thought—if I could just explain myself properly—he would understand, would perhaps even feel remorse, but clearly, Filippa isn't the only person about whom I've been wildly mistaken. *He's hurt,* I remind myself fiercely, clutching my elbows, but he isn't the only one. Taking another step backward, I add, "Tell me to be a good little huntswoman and wait in my room while the men handle things?"

His eyes flash dangerously, and he straightens his shoulders with the air of a man steeling himself to do something unpleasant. "Enough, Célie. You're coming back to Chasseur Tower with me whether you like it or not, and we can finish this conversation in private." His gaze darts from Reid to Frederic to the watching crowd before settling on Michal at last. "Don't make this uglier than it needs to be," he warns him.

Michal no longer sounds cool and impassive. "Oh, you've already done that."

"I'm not going *anywhere* with you," I snarl.

"Yes, you are." Jean Luc lunges for my arm, and I react without thinking—react faster than even the vampires behind me—darting sideways and snatching the Balisarda from his belt as he missteps to avoid charging into Michal instead. The rest happens as if in slow motion. His foot bends, sliding a little on the cobblestones, and he overcorrects, whirling to face me and losing his balance in the process.

With a degrading *thud,* he hits the ground at my feet, and snickers break out around the harbor. One person even applauds.

My heart stops at the sound.

"Oh my God." Whatever fury I felt vanishes instantly, and I

drop to my knees, shoving his Balisarda at him while also attempting to haul him to his feet, to brush the muck from his coat. "Are you all right? I'm so sorry, Jean, I didn't mean—" He pushes my hands away, however, his face colder and angrier than I've ever seen it. Seizing his Balisarda, he climbs stiffly to his feet, and I clamber after him, feeling sicker with each second. "Please, believe me, I never wanted to—"

"Go."

He speaks the word simply, irrevocably, and my outstretched hands freeze between us. Without looking at me, he takes the hen from Reid, who has gone pale and still, and returns her to the others in their cage. Over his shoulder, he says, "And don't come back."

PART IV

Quand on parle du loup, on en voit la queue.

When we talk about the wolf, we see its tail.

CHAPTER FORTY-TWO

The Invisible Princess

Truthfully, I remember very little of the journey back to Requiem. I remember even less of departing the ship, of stumbling down the gangplank after Michal and the others. He must've led us through the crowded market and toward the castle—one foot must've stepped in front of the other—but I'll never know exactly how I found my room, how I stripped off my bloodstained gown and collapsed into this squashy armchair by the fire.

Michal didn't follow.

Perhaps he sensed I needed to be alone, needed to think, and couldn't do that if he hovered—that, and I saw him steering Dimitri toward his study for their very long discussion, which means I'm wasting precious time by staring idly into these flames. I should be scouring the corridors for Dimitri's room, picking the lock, and searching for anything that connects him to my sister. Perhaps Michal can wring the whole truth from his cousin, but perhaps he also cannot, which means the time to act is *now*. Who knows when another opportunity might arise?

Unfortunately, my body refuses to move.

Odessa clicks her tongue irritably and rifles through the armoire behind the silk screen. Mist from outside still clings to her woolen cape and polished boots, and her damp parasol leans against the baluster. "You didn't need to follow me," I tell her.

"I did not *follow* you, darling. I *accompanied* you."

"You didn't need to *accompany* me, then." Rubbing away the beads of moisture on Filippa's cross, I trace its smooth edges with my thumb. When my nail catches on the secret latch, I sigh and replace the entire thing beneath my collar, feeling sick and confused and exhausted in general. I need to get up; I need to search Dimitri's room. A shiver wracks my frame instead, and my stomach rumbles. "Michal promised no harm would come to me here, and even if he didn't, I doubt anyone is keen to attack after what happened in the aviary."

"You underestimate their agitation at the moment. All Hallows' Eve is tomorrow, and Michal has effectively trapped us all here like rats in a cage—Priscille's words, not mine," she adds, thoroughly unconcerned, when I throw her a dubious look. She plucks a rose-colored satin gown from the rest. "You're also acting strange."

"Excuse me?"

"You're always a *bit* strange, of course—what with all the Bride and Necromancer nonsense—but your behavior has been stranger than usual since we left Amandine. You said less than a handful of words on our return to Cesarine, and you said even less on the ship back to Requiem—unless you count that rather horrid encounter with your fiancé in between, and I'd rather not acknowledge him at all. The man is a complete and utter ass, and I quite agree that you made the right decision in breaking the engagement."

I stare at her in disbelief. In *shock.* Disregarding the fact that *Odessa* has the nerve to call anyone strange, I never expected her to be quite so . . . so perceptive. Perhaps because she talks so much about the human eyeball and early Church, or perhaps because she usually dons such a supreme look of boredom. "He isn't an ass," I mutter defensively.

She looks anything but bored now. Peering over at me with those clever, catlike eyes, she asks, "Is that why you've been so quiet? Your rotten fiancé?"

I look away quickly. "Ex-fiancé."

"Yes. Him." When I fail to answer, she strides toward me and snaps her sharp fingers, motioning for me to stand. I comply reluctantly. "Or . . . perhaps you regret the heinous accusation you made about my brother?" She purses her plum lips before wrenching the rose-colored gown over my head. "No, that isn't it either. *Perhaps* you maintain that he murdered our cousin instead, and you're still plotting the demise of the entire vampire race. Am I getting warmer?"

"Drat. You found me out."

Scowling now, she cinches the stays of the gown extra tight. "I think you're hiding something, Célie Tremblay."

I cannot bring myself to argue, crawling back into my armchair and lifting my knees to my chest, wrapping my arms around them. Staring fixedly at the fire. "Did you kill her?" I ask instead. "Priscille?"

"And what if I did? She certainly would've killed *you*." Then— before I can press her for a true answer—she perches in the other armchair and asks, "Have you really spoken to Mila?" Though her tone remains casual, *too* casual, her eyes belie her interest as I nod, unable to muster the energy to lie or deflect either. She plucks a book from the table between us without checking its title. "And did she—did she say whether she would visit again? It isn't that I *miss* her, per se, but if I *happened* to see her—"

"The last time I spoke with Mila, she made it clear that she couldn't help us."

Odessa rolls her eyes. "Charming as always, my cousin, yet I do not *need* her help. I simply want to—well, talk to her, I suppose."

Thunder rumbles in the ensuing silence.

Ah. I rest my chin upon my knees. Though I've never given Mila's death much thought beyond Michal, he wasn't the only one who lost family that night. Of course Odessa would feel her absence too. Indeed, I haven't seen her spend time with anyone except Dimitri—she boasts no doting mother or fussy aunts, no peers with whom to banter or friends disguised as ladies-in-waiting. The realization brings an unexpected throb to my chest. To have only one's brother as a companion . . . it must be incredibly lonely. "Michal said she wouldn't be able to stay away for long," I say when the silence between us continues to stretch. An olive branch. "He said the temptation to meddle would be too great."

A reluctant grin touches her lips. "That sounds very much like both of my cousins."

"Would you like me to see if she's here?"

She returns the book to the table as she pretends to consider, desperately trying to remain indifferent. "I suppose . . . if it isn't too terribly difficult."

Sighing at her stubbornness, I close my eyes and concentrate on the hollow ache in my chest. *Longing,* I realize. More than anything, I long to know the truth about my sister, just as Odessa longs to see her cousin again. While the former lingers just out of reach—mere fingertips away—I hold the latter in my hands. I can do this for Odessa. I can do this for Mila, and I can do this for *me;*

I'm not ready to search Dimitri's room just yet, or to learn about Filippa. Perhaps I never will be. As if in response, the cold deepens around me, and pressure builds to pain in my ears. When I open my eyes once more, Odessa gasps slightly at their newfound silver light, leaning closer to study them. "Michal told me about the glow, of course, but his description doesn't quite do it justice. How *deliciously* creepy. Tell me—does it affect your sight? For example, does it cast a softer sheen over your field of vision?"

"Take off your glove." With a rueful smile, I extend my bare palm in her direction. She eyes it curiously but tugs the glove from her fingers all the same; when her skin touches mine, she gasps again, eyes wide and startled at our similar temperatures.

"*Fascinating*—" The word seems to stick in her throat, however, as she follows my gaze and catches sight of Mila, who hovers on the mezzanine, gazing down at us with a rather sheepish expression. Warmth blooms alongside the ache in my chest at the sight of her. Apparently, Odessa isn't the only one who missed her cousin.

"*Mila?*" Odessa practically drags me to the spiral staircase. "Is it really you?"

A small grin spreads across Mila's face, and she lifts an opaque hand in greeting. "Hello, Dess." Eyes flicking to me, she clears her throat with an awkward little titter. "Célie."

I cannot help my own grudging smile in return. Odessa still blinks rapidly, trying and failing to master her shock and delight. "For a moment there," I say, "I thought you passed on without saying goodbye—all that nonsense in the aviary about *refusing to haunt us* and letting go—but you've been following us this entire time, haven't you?"

Mila flips long hair over her shoulder and drifts to the lower floor to join us. "And it's a good thing, too, as Guinevere never would've followed *me* otherwise, and she proved quite useful in Les Abysses." A mischievous pause. "I hear the two of you are the very best of friends now. How incredibly special."

"Guinevere?" Odessa whips her face between us, clearly trying to piece together our conversation. "As in Guinevere de *Mimsy*, that audacious little tart who shattered the windows to my laboratory?" Before anyone can answer—as if she just can't help herself—she adds, "And ghosts cannot *pass on*, Célie. After the death of their material bodies, they must choose to either cross into the realm of the dead or remain near the realm of the living. Even you cannot reach those who choose the former, and the latter"—she glances apologetically to Mila—"remain trapped between both realms for all eternity, unable to truly exist in either."

Mila rolls her eyes toward the chandelier. "Spoken like you swallowed the whole of *How to Commune with the Dead.*"

"I might've glanced at it," Odessa sniffs, "after Michal told me he spoke with you." At the mention of Michal, however, the humor in Mila's eyes fades, and her face tightens nearly imperceptibly. Odessa still sees it. "Oh, come now. You cannot still be cross with him after all these years."

"For your information, I am not *cross* with him. I simply don't want to—"

Odessa interrupts with a scoff, shooting an exasperated look in my direction. "Michal turned Mila into a vampire when they were young, and she's never forgiven him for it." To Mila, she says sternly, "You were *sick*. What did you expect your poor brother to do? If I'd seen Dimitri wasting away like that, dying a slow and miserable death, I would've done a lot worse to save him."

My brow furrows at this new information. For the first time in my life, I can't think of a single thing to say. Because Michal never mentioned any of this to me—and why would he? I thought him a sadist until only last week, and I made no qualms about telling him so. Still . . . inexplicable warmth pricks at my collar, which I tug fruitlessly away from my throat. I shared so much about my sister in Amandine. He could've done the same. I wouldn't have begrudged him the attention.

As if sensing my discomfort, Odessa squeezes my hand but otherwise doesn't acknowledge it. "She didn't speak to Michal for years—*years*—and all because she too gave her heart to an undeserving ass like your huntsman."

Mila exhales sharply, affronted, and crosses her arms tightly against her chest. "This has nothing to do with Pyotr."

"No? He didn't try to cut off your head when you showed him your lovely new fangs?" When Mila scowls, refusing to answer, Odessa nods in black satisfaction, the epitome of an older sibling. That ache in my chest grows tenfold. "Michal hasn't turned a single creature since that day," she tells me. "In his entire existence, he has sired only his ungrateful little sister, who still punishes him for it every day."

Comprehension swoops low in my stomach, and his insistence— no, his *belligerence*—that I never drink from him or any other vampire makes sudden sense. Still . . . I frown at Odessa in confusion. "Who sired *you*, then?"

She glares pointedly at Mila, who—for all her wisdom—does look rather younger in the presence of her cousin. Her arms still crossed. Her jaw set. Just the way she behaved in the aviary with

Michal, who she seems to both defend and condemn in equal measure. "What?" she snaps at both of us. "You couldn't have seriously expected me to live for eternity with only *Michal* as company. I love my brother—I *do*—but he has as much personality as that bit of rock." She jerks her chin toward the cliff behind us. "Except that rock doesn't try to control my every move."

The warmth at my neck prickles sharper—no longer discomfort, but abrupt and startling irritation. My mouth opens before I can think better of it, before I can stop the scathing accusation from spilling forth. "It hardly seems fair to hold a grudge against Michal if you *also* turned your kin into vampires, Mila."

An incredulous sound escapes Mila's throat. "As if you'd know anything about it! Just because *you're* now infatuated doesn't mean everyone else is, and—and"—she lets out a groan of frustration, and her entire body seems to slump as mine stiffens—"and I'm *sorry*. That was a horrible thing to say, and of *course* I don't mean it. It's just—Michal is Michal, and he chose for me. He *always* chooses for me, and now I'm not even a vampire anymore. I'm *dead*. All of you have been galivanting across the world, having the most marvelous adventure, and I can't go with you. Not really. No one can even *see* me except through you, Célie, and it just—it isn't—"

Whatever *it* is, Mila can't seem to articulate, but I understand all the same: *fair*. It isn't fair. What did Michal say about his sister?

Everyone who gazed upon her loved her.

And now she's invisible.

Expression softening, Odessa draws herself to Mila's height by stepping on the bottom stair. "You know we all miss you, Mila. Even the villagers—no one begrudges you for Michal's decisions. They resent the heightened security measures around the isle, yes, but they've never once resented you."

Mila wipes furiously at her cheeks. "I know that. Of course I do. I'm just being silly."

A quiet sort of resignation settles over me. Even in death, Mila hasn't found peace with her brother—with herself—and if I don't tread carefully, the same will be said of me. Whether or not I hide from the truth, the Necromancer will still try to kill me. Nothing I find of my sister will change that, so why—exactly—am I so afraid to look? The worst has already happened; my sister is dead, and I refuse to follow her to the afterlife.

Not yet.

"As for *you*," Odessa says, tugging my hand until I join her on the stair. "You need to talk to my brother. Loath as I am to admit it, the thought of you plotting death and destruction doesn't quite suit—you just aren't the type—and Dimitri deserves the chance to defend himself."

"Perhaps you're right." Pulling Odessa from the stairs, I cross the room to where my deep green cloak hangs on its hook beside the armoire. "Where can I find him? His room?"

Odessa and Mila exchange a quick, furtive glance. "I'm not sure his room is the best place to meet," Mila says after several seconds. "Perhaps in Michal's study—"

"This is a conversation I'd rather have in private."

Odessa forces a pained smile. "Of course it is, darling, but under the circumstances—"

I fish the silver knife from Michal's traveling cloak, which Odessa must have hung beside mine. Her smile falters as I slide the weapon into my boot. "Under the circumstances, he has nothing to hide, correct? Why shouldn't we meet in his room?"

The two say nothing for a long moment. Then—when I fear I've overplayed my hand—Mila speaks at last. "His is the third door from the left in the north tower, but—try not to judge him too harshly, Célie. He needs all of the help we can give him."

CHAPTER FORTY-THREE

Dimitri's Tale

Whatever I expected to find in Dimitri's room—bodies, perhaps, or bloody manacles and jars of teeth—it isn't the bright, colorful chamber that awaits me. Indeed, when I first step through the door, I retreat almost immediately, convinced I stumbled into the wrong room. A large fireplace illuminates the entire scene. Scarves of aquamarine, magenta, and citron drape from the ceiling and shutters, while an assortment of hats perch upon his bedposts and stack precariously on his bedside table.

Out in the corridor, I shake my head to clear it and count the doors more carefully.

One. Two. Three.

I open the door to the same strange tentlike menagerie, which means Dimitri must be—well, some sort of *hoarder.* Taking a deep breath, I step over the threshold and click the door shut behind me.

Keys glitter upon the curved stone walls, along with baskets and baskets of books. *Odd* books. Warily, I creep closer and pick up the topmost one: a pocket-sized edition of the Holy Bible. Beneath it lies *Fashionable Cats and the People Who Sew Them.* I return both books with a grimace.

It'll take a miracle to find anything of Filippa's in this mess.

I move to the desk next—because if there was one letter, there must be more, and if Dimitri is the one who penned them, he surely would've kept them. *Or,* says a hopeful little voice in my head, *he didn't know Filippa at all.*

That would be the best case, of course.

And also the worst.

Without a connection between Dimitri and Filippa—and therefore Babette—I have exactly zero paths forward to finding the Necromancer.

The desk, as it turns out, rivals even the clutter of the walls: perfume bottles, buttons, and rolls of mismatched coins litter its top, and inside its drawers lie matchboxes and pocket watches, a fountain pen and even a tattered old doll. Ordinary things. Mundane things.

Hundreds of them, and not a single letter in sight.

Slamming the drawer shut in both frustration and relief, I sigh heavily and turn to face the room at large. Beyond Filippa and her secret lover—beyond Dimitri and Babette and even the Necromancer—this room makes no sense. *This* is what Odessa and Mila feared I'd see? Dimitri's collection of rubbish?

"What are you doing here?"

With a squeak, I leap away from the desk and whirl to face the door, where Dimitri stands with his arms crossed, his lips pressed flat in suspicion. "Dimitri! You're back!"

"And you're snooping in my room."

"I wasn't—if you *must* know, I wasn't snooping anywhere. I was simply waiting for *you.* The last we spoke, you wanted to have a conversation, and now—well, I'm ready to have it."

He pushes himself from the doorjamb and into the room, closing the door with a soft *click.* I try not to flinch at the sound. "No, you aren't," he says.

"What are you talking about?"

"You aren't ready to have a conversation. Just now, you were rifling through my desk, and I can smell you all over my books too." His eyes narrow as he studies me. "You've been looking for something."

We stare at each other for several seconds. Wariness seems to creep into his expression as the silence between us deepens, or rather, a sort of *tautness*, and I wonder just how poorly his very long discussion with Michal went. At last, I gesture to the bric-a-brac all around us. "What *is* all this?"

His eyes dart to the row of shoes beneath his footboard. "I didn't kill Mila, Célie."

"That isn't what I asked."

"And you don't *really* think I killed her either, or you wouldn't have risked coming in here alone. I'm not the Necromancer. I don't"—he hesitates, swallowing hard—"want your blood for some dark rite."

Something in his voice shifts with the words, however, and the hair lifts on my neck as I once again remember Michal's warning. *Dimitri is an addict. He has thought of nothing but your blood since he made your acquaintance yesterday.*

Suddenly, I feel incredibly foolish for coming here, and suddenly, I have nothing else to lose. Seizing the knife from my boot, I thrust it between us and snarl, "Did you know my sister?"

He doesn't recoil from the silver, doesn't acknowledge it at all, instead blinking at me like I've spoken in a foreign language. "Who?"

"My *sister*," I repeat through clenched teeth. "Filippa Tremblay. Morgane murdered her last year, but I want to know—I need to—you *will* tell me if you knew her."

His eyes widen slightly at whatever he sees in my expression, and he lifts conciliatory hands. "Célie, I've never seen your sister before in my life."

"You aren't exactly alive, though, are you? And I didn't ask if you'd seen her. I asked if you *knew* her."

"Is there a difference?" he asks helplessly.

My knuckles clench white around the knife as I study his face, as I search for anything—*anything*—that might reveal potential subterfuge. "You can know a person without ever seeing them—letters, for example."

"I never knew *or* wrote to your sister. The only person to whom I've ever written a letter is La Dame des Sorcières." He shrugs weakly and drops his arms. "She's a friend of yours, isn't she? Louise le Blanc? I wrote to her last month."

Now it's my turn to blink. "You wrote a letter to Lou?"

Shoulders slumping, he edges around me—I lift the knife higher as he passes—and collapses into a leather chair near his bed. A golden necklace dangles from its arm. He takes care not to disturb it as he scrubs a weary hand down his face. "You have to listen to me, Célie. I know you—you think the worst, but you couldn't be further from the truth. I'm not the Necromancer," he repeats, more forceful this time. "I'm not in league with him—I didn't kill any of those creatures—and the only thing I want from Babette is the grimoire. I *need* that grimoire."

"You've made that exceptionally clear."

"You still don't understand." With a groan of frustration, he tips his head backward, staring at the bundles of flowers near the ceiling and searching for the right words. "Michal told you about bloodlust," he says at last. Though it isn't a question, I still nod, and his mouth sets in a grim line. "Then you know I'm an addict. I may not kill in cold blood like the Necromancer, but my hands are equally stained—no, my hands are *worse*." He closes his eyes as if the words have cost him something, as if they've caused him incredible pain. "I deserve your suspicion, your hatred. Though I haven't always been this way—the affliction grows harder to control with each passing year—I've lost count of how many people I've killed. I can still see their faces, though," he adds miserably, motioning around the room. My mouth goes dry. "I can still taste their fear the instant they realize I won't stop, I *can't* stop, and that—*that* is the true addiction."

When his eyes snap open, I stumble back a step, knocking over several bottles of perfume. They shatter upon the floor. "Do you mean— Are you saying—?" I glance wildly at the clutter all around us, my stomach rising in realization. But this cannot be true. It cannot be happening. "Dimitri"—my voice drops to a horrified whisper as I lift the tattered doll—"are these *keepsakes?*"

"To remember them." A disturbing gleam enters his eyes as he stares fixedly at the doll. "Every single one."

"But there are *hundreds*—"

"You're right to fear me," he says darkly. "If not for Michal, I would've killed you the moment I walked into your room. I wouldn't have been able to help myself. You smell . . . delicious."

Something in his expression reminds me forcefully of Yannick, and I retreat another step, remembering the rest of Michal's warning.

When Dimitri feeds, he loses consciousness. Many vampires forget themselves in the hunt, but a vampire affected by bloodlust goes beyond that—he remembers nothing, feels nothing, and inevitably kills his prey in gruesome and horrific ways. Left too long, he becomes an animal like Yannick.

"Stay away from me." My voice trembles slightly as my gaze darts to the door, and Dimitri rises slowly to his feet. "Don't come any closer."

"I don't want to hurt you, Célie." His voice breaks on the last, and just as swiftly as the shadow crossed his features, it vanishes, leaving him small and alone and miserable. "I won't hurt you. I promise I won't."

"That doesn't sound like a promise you can make."

"But don't you see?" Though he wrings his hands desperately, he makes no move to close the distance between us, and I relax infinitesimally. "That's why I need the grimoire. That spell is the only thing that can cure bloodlust—without it, I'll kill again and again and again until Michal is forced to rip out my heart. And I'll deserve it. Célie, I'll *deserve* it for all the pain I've caused. When you first met me, I—the blood in the corridor—I'd just—"

"Stop." I shake my head frantically, backing into the door now. "Please, I don't want to know—"

"Mila tried to keep me in check. She was the only one who sympathized. Even Odessa never understood why I couldn't just *control* myself. She pored over her books searching for an explanation, a cure, but in the end, Mila is the one who suggested we visit La Dame des Sorcières."

My hand freezes on the doorknob. I don't know what to say, what to *think*, as my mind struggles to comprehend *vampires* seeking out Louise le Blanc for help—the same woman who totters around as the Crone, cackling and pinching Reid's backside. But perhaps it makes sense. Lou is the most powerful witch in the kingdom, and she *did* defeat the most evil woman in history. "She would've helped you," I whisper despite myself.

"I wrote to her about my affliction." Dimitri shakes his head in disgust, still carefully motionless otherwise. "Or at least, I wrote to Saint-Cécile."

"You *what?*"

"I didn't know where else to reach her, and even on Requiem, we heard of her marriage to the Chasseur."

"Michal collected every detail of my entire *life* in a single night. Surely he could've found her address? Why would you *ever* send a letter to Chasseur Tower asking for magic? They might've evolved since the Battle of Cesarine, but they aren't that evolved."

Dimitri sets his chin, a trace of stubbornness returning to his gaze. "I didn't want to involve Michal. He wouldn't have allowed us to go—and when La Dame des Sorcières wrote back with a time and place for our meeting, Mila insisted on coming along."

"That doesn't make any sense." Frowning, I gradually loosen my grip on the doorknob. "Lou moved out of Saint-Cécile last year. She wouldn't have received any letter delivered there."

"No." Cautiously, as if appeasing a wild animal, he reaches into his coat and pulls forth a folded piece of parchment. He extends it with a single hand, forcing me to cross the room to take it. "She didn't."

I snatch it hastily before retreating back to his desk.

The words themselves don't penetrate as I unfold the parchment. No. It's the handwriting. My eyes seize upon it, and my heart drops like a stone at the familiar pen strokes, masculine and altogether chilling. Because I've only seen it once before—in the love letter folded within my sister's locket. "It wasn't Louise le Blanc who met us outside Saint-Cécile that night," Dimitri continues. "A man in a hooded cloak attacked from the shadows, and I—I lost control." His eyes grow distant with the words, and I know they now see a different scene than his macabre bedroom. "I should've smelled the magic in his veins, should've recognized the man as a blood witch, but instead I just . . . reacted."

"What happened?" I whisper.

"I bit him." He cringes slightly as if reliving the exact moment, the exact taste of the Necromancer's blood. "And as you know from Les Abysses, the blood of a Dame Rouge—or in his case, a Seigneur Rouge—acts as poison to their enemies. Even vampires. I barely escaped with my life."

"And Mila?"

He shakes his head. "Babette joined the hooded man with some sort of injection. It must've been more of their blood because she dropped instantly. I couldn't do anything but watch as they worked a spell from the grimoire and drained Mila dry." His voice cracks at the last, and horrid pressure builds in my throat as I too imagine the scene—it would not have been painless or quick. "When they finished with her, they swept the alley, baiting me with their grimoire. Promising me they could bring her back, could give me the spell I needed to cure the bloodlust. I had to just—I had to leave her there, Célie. I had to leave Mila, or I would've died. They would've killed me too. The three of us fled just as the Chasseurs arrived."

My throat grows too tight to speak.

It just isn't fair.

Even in death, Mila hadn't wanted to speak the truth. And it *isn't* fair—she endured a horrible execution while seeking a cure for her cousin, and Dimitri escaped unscathed. He left her corpse in the garbage behind Saint-Cécile—he has murdered *hundreds* of innocents—yet he survives to mourn her. To mourn himself. If I had anything at all in my stomach, I would've lost it in this moment.

Carefully, I hand back his letter and murmur, "I'm sorry."

I cannot look at him. I cannot think of anything else to say.

"I loved my cousin." In the blink of an eye, Dimitri stands before me, fire blazing in his brown eyes. I jerk the knife upward instinctively. "I loved her, Célie, and I'll do whatever is necessary to avenge her death. I'll rip out the Necromancer's heart myself. I'll light the pyre for Babette." Knocking the knife aside and clutching my shoulders, he forces me to look directly into those burning eyes. To truly *see* him. "But first I need their grimoire. I need to regain control, and I need to ensure Saint-Cécile never happens again."

And his face looks so sincere, so *fierce*—the perfect marriage of the Dimitri I knew and the Dimitri I met in Les Abysses—that I know it's his true one. I know it deep in my bones. He's done awful things, yes—unforgivable things—but then again, so has everyone.

Even Filippa.

If someone doesn't help him, *truly* help him, he'll continue to kill, and his gruesome collection will continue to grow until it crushes him beneath its weight.

"I'll help you find the grimoire," I tell him.

I pray I'll live long enough to regret it.

CHAPTER FORTY-FOUR

A Butterfly of Silver

My parents never wrapped presents for Filippa and me—that task always fell to Evangeline, who had the unfortunate habit of waiting until Christmas Eve to wrap a single gift. It drove my mother mad, but for me, it became a yearly tradition: when the clock struck midnight, I would wake Pippa, and together—usually pretending to be pirates—we would sneak into my father's study to inspect the loot. I even cobbled together eye patches and a rather misshapen parrot to sit on her shoulder. She named him Fabienne and insisted on carrying him everywhere until my mother intervened, shrieking about filth and tossing him in the garbage. Filippa and I cried for a week.

Of course, as the years passed, Pippa grew more reluctant to pretend with me. Her smiles became less indulgent, disappearing altogether the year Evangeline left us. The next year, our new governess—a pinch-faced, sallow-skinned woman who loathed children—stowed our gifts in a locked closet outside her bedroom. When I still woke Pippa, determined to continue our game, she dragged the blanket over her head and turned over with a groan. "Go away, Célie."

"But everyone is asleep!"

"As you should be," she grumbled.

"Oh, come *on*, Pip. Father spied the most *beautiful* blue scarf at the market last week, and I want to see if he bought it for me. He said I look lovely in blue."

She peeked open an eye to glare blearily at me. "You look horrible in blue."

"Not as horrible as you." I poked her ribs a bit harder than strictly necessary. "Now, are you coming? If it isn't there, I'm going to purchase it as an early present to myself." I beamed at her in the light of the candle between our beds. "Reid is coming over on Christmas morning this year, and I want to match his coat."

She flung her blanket away then, eyes narrowing. "How are *you* going to purchase it? You haven't any money."

I shrugged, thoroughly unconcerned, and waltzed to our nursery door. "Father will give me some if I ask."

"You do know where he gets his money, don't you?" But I'd already slipped into the darkness of the corridor, forcing her to snatch the candle and hiss "*Célie*—*!*" before hurrying after me. "You're going to get us both into trouble, you know." She rubbed her arms against the chill. "And all for an ugly scarf. *Why* do you need to match Reid, anyway? Must he really wear his Chasseur uniform to add a Yule log to our fire?"

I turned to glare at her outside our governess's room. "Why are you so determined to hate him?"

"I don't *hate* him. I just think he's ridiculous."

Tugging the pins from my hair, I stooped to shove them into the lock on the closet door. "Well, what do *you* want for Christmas this year? A nice quill and sheaf of parchment? A bottle of ink? You've been writing an awful lot of letters—"

She crossed her arms tightly against her chest. "*That* is none of your business."

I struggled not to roll my eyes, twisting the pins deeper into the lock and blowing an errant strand of hair from my face. The book I'd read on lock-picking made it look much simpler than this—

"Oh, move *over*." Shoving the candle at me, Pippa seized the pins and crouched level with the keyhole. With a few quick, precise twists of her fingers, the mechanism clicked, and she turned the handle with ease. The door swung open. "There." She stood and gestured to the folded blue scarf on the middle shelf. "No need to grovel. You shall match your beloved huntsman on Christmas morning, and the world will continue to turn."

I stared at her in wonder. "How did you *do* that?"

"Again, not your business."

"But—"

"Célie, it isn't a Herculean task to pick a lock. Anyone can do it with a bit of patience—which, I realize now, might actually be a struggle for you. Everything you've ever wanted has been handed to you on a silver platter." I recoiled then, stung, my hand half outstretched toward my scarf, and Pippa slumped, shaking her head. "I'm sorry, ma belle. I shouldn't have said that. I— I'll teach you how to pick locks first thing in the morning."

"Why?" I sniffed. "You clearly think very little of me."

"No, *no.*" She seized my hand as it fell away from the scarf. "It's just—all this." Her eyes moved reluctantly to the closet, where satin hair bows and velvet jewelry boxes sat stacked in neat rows. Père had bought her a miniature model of the universe this year; its planets glittered slightly in the candlelight. "Our parents aren't good people, Célie, and neither is—" She stopped abruptly, dropping my hand and looking away. "Well, they just bring out the very worst in me. That doesn't mean I should take it out on you."

My cheeks felt inexplicably warm as I tore my gaze away from her, as I motioned toward the piles of presents. Filippa might've thought me spoiled—perhaps even vapid—but at least I wasn't determined to see the world half-empty. "I know our parents can be . . . difficult, Pip, but that doesn't mean they're all bad. These gifts—they're the only way they know how to show us love."

"And when the money runs out? How will they love us then?" Shaking her head, Pippa took the candle from me and turned, starting back up the corridor, and I understood her message loud and clear: *conversation over.* My chest fell slightly as I watched her go—until she glanced over her shoulder, surprising me, and said, "You can't get something for nothing, Célie. Everything in this world comes with a price—even love."

I had no way of knowing where she'd heard such an expression, then.

I only knew that it was true—because my sister had said it, and my sister would never lie to me.

I didn't wear the blue scarf that Christmas morning, and Filippa threw her model of the universe into the same bin that our mother threw Fabienne.

"I have a gift for you."

Hands clasped behind his back, Michal stands tall and strangely vulnerable in his bedchamber, his shirtsleeves rolled and his jacket discarded. I glance nervously at the small table beside him. Someone—presumably the foul-tempered servant who fetched me—has laden it with fruits, cheeses, meats, and pastries. My mouth waters instantly at what appears to be pain au chocolat, and reluctant, I descend the rest of the stairs against my better judgment. There aren't any cabbage leaves in sight.

"You shouldn't have—"

"Yes I should." Clearing his throat, he pulls one of two chairs from the table and gestures for me to sit. "And this isn't the gift. This is *food*, which you should've been receiving since you arrived on Requiem."

I sink into the seat, reflexively folding the napkin into my lap before reaching for the nearest platter—eggs with wild mushrooms and salty cheese. If Michal wants something from me, I need to be clever enough to recognize it. That means food. My stomach groans in agreement. "A scullery woman brought food occasionally. And Dimitri," I add as an afterthought. "A lovely meal of cabbage, butter, and hard-boiled eggs."

"Cabbage and butter," Michal repeats.

Nodding, I nearly moan at the first bite, and his eyes flick to the half-healed wound on my throat. Abruptly, he sits in the chair opposite me. "Odessa said you spoke with him."

"Good news *does* travel fast."

"Am I correct in assuming you believed his story? You think him innocent?"

I snatch a crepe from the top of a teetering stack. "I would hardly call him *innocent*, but yes, I no longer think Dimitri is the Necromancer."

Though my chest tightens with the admission, I refuse to acknowledge it, focusing instead on the magnificent spread of food before me, adding several slices of apple and fromage blanc to my plate. Michal tracks each movement with sharp interest. *Too* sharp. I know what he's thinking, of course. Without Dimitri as a suspect, we have only two persons of interest left to investigate: Coco and now Filippa. With the masquerade tomorrow night, Coco would certainly be the easiest bread trail to follow, yet if Coco Monvoisin knew anything about the Necromancer—*especially* after his grooming of Babette—he would already be dead.

Filippa's cross continues to tighten around my neck.

I spoon an enormous bite of strawberry jam into my mouth anyway, delaying the inevitable. Then, swallowing hard— "We should return to Les Abysses."

Michal pushes a loaf of brioche across the table before pouring coffee into a crystal goblet. This too he slides casually toward me. "Babette has gone to ground, most likely with the Necromancer himself. No one has seen or heard from her since she fled."

"But Pennelope—"

"—has vanished with the whole of Eden. The building now stands empty and abandoned, swept of everything but dust." A pause as he watches me inhale the coffee. "I knew Eponine wouldn't linger after our unfortunate encounter with Babette. Despite her threats, she fears vampires too much to risk my wrath—or that of the Necromancer. I'm sure he wasn't pleased with the proceedings either."

"Oh." I nod with a horrible sinking sensation and try not to grimace. The coffee tastes abruptly bitter in my mouth. "That—that *is* rather unfortunate."

"Indeed."

We lapse into silence except for the sound of my fork against the plate. It grows harsher with each passing moment—louder, *grating*—until I can no longer pretend to poke at my eggs in good conscience. "Finished?" Michal asks softly.

I nod without speaking, without looking at him either, and

instead stare out at the mica-flecked walls of his grotto. The tide must have retreated at some point during the night; a stone islet now sparkles in the center of the cavern, too small and too distant to see properly. "It's only visible during low tide," Michal murmurs, following my gaze. "Mila would always drag Dimitri, Odessa, and me out there for garden parties on special occasions—she'd pick bouquets of flowers and bring bottles of blood spiked with champagne. She insisted Dimitri and I wear lace cuffs."

I can hear the smile in his voice just as clearly as I can envision the scene in his memory: a quartet of ethereal vampires rowing out to sea by moonlight, each carrying a basket of roses and a bottle of blood. "That sounds . . . lovely," I say at last. And it's true. A vampire garden party sounds like a page torn straight from a fairy tale, and I—I don't know what that says about me.

I need to tell him about Filippa's note.

I need to tell him about the matching handwriting, need to form some sort of plan in case the Necromancer strikes again. Twisting my napkin in my lap, taking a deep breath, I say, "Michal—"

"Come here."

Startled, I look up to find Michal no longer sitting at the table at all, but standing still and silent beside his bed. Atop the coverlet rests an inky black garment box tied with an emerald bow. Golden letters stamped across the front wink BOUTIQUE DE VÊTE-MENTS DE M. MARC in the candlelight. I rise tentatively to my feet. "Is that my costume for All Hallows' Eve?"

"Monsieur Marc delivered it about an hour ago, along with his regards." He clears his throat again, and unless I'm much mistaken, he seems almost . . . *nervous* now. But that can't be right; this is Michal, and if the king of the vampires has ever felt even a *twinge* of uncertainty, I'll marry Guinevere. "I requested a handful of alterations to the original gown," he says, sliding his hands into his pockets. "I . . . hope you like them."

Curiosity piqued despite myself, I stride forward and pluck at the emerald ribbon. "What was wrong with the original gown? You don't like butterflies?"

"On the contrary."

"Then what did you—?" The answer, however, renders me momentarily mute as I lift the lid from the box and brush aside black tissue paper. "Oh my God," I whisper.

Instead of the emerald swallowtail gown as promised, Monsieur Marc has sewn a gown of bright, resplendent silver. Even folded within the box, the gossamer seems to ebb and flow like water, and when I pick it up—incredulous, awestruck—the skirt spills forth to reveal thousands of intricate diamonds sewn into each pleat. My heart climbs into my throat. Those diamonds will catch the light of every candle in the ballroom when I walk, and the *train*—cathedral length, at least, and divided in half to resemble two butterfly wings that attach at the wrist to sheer sleeves.

A capelet of diamonds—larger than those on the skirt but equally flawless—completes the ensemble.

It takes several attempts to form speech. "I can't— This is the most— How did he—?"

Watching me splutter, Michal's face relaxes slightly, and the corners of his mouth pull into a smile. "Un papillon." From his pocket, he extracts a silk handkerchief and carefully moves the capelet aside to reveal a half mask embroidered with delicate organza wings. He takes care not to touch anything with his bare skin. "Though I think I might've stretched the definition when I asked Monsieur Marc to create one from metal."

My hands slide longingly over the fabric as I tuck it back inside the box. I can't accept such a gift. Of course I can't. The words that leave my mouth, however, are quite different. "He sewed this with real silver? *How?*"

Michal shrugs, his smile stretching wider, and my hands fumble a bit with the lid of the box in response. I don't know if I've ever seen him smile before—at least, not like this. Openly. Artlessly. It softens his entire face, smoothing his cruel features into something almost human . . . and making him, impossibly, more beautiful because of it. "*He* would tell you that he spun straw into gold. Really, though, he owed me a favor, and he likes you enough to don gloves."

When he hands me the emerald ribbon, his fingers inadvertently brush my palm. They linger there for another second. Two. Then he slowly, deliberately, traces the lines there, and gooseflesh erupts down my legs. His voice turns wry. "He also requests a dance tomorrow night."

I raise my brows. "*Does* he?"

"It would be rude to refuse, I think."

"It would be ruder to my poor toes to accept without first asking *how* he dances."

His fingers continue to trail up, up, up. My breath hitches almost painfully as they skim over the thin skin of my wrist, sliding under the battered ribbon there. "Not half as well as Reid Diggory." His eyes glitter as I try and fail to ignore the tingling sensation in my arm. "He isn't half as tall either. Though I must say, pet—after seeing him—I think you're mistaken in your impression of Monsieur Diggory."

"You think you're taller?"

"I know I'm taller." His fingers creep beneath my sleeve, gathering it up my forearm until he reaches the soft crook of my elbow. He cradles it in his hand. "And . . . a much better dancer."

When his thumb presses down on a vein, heat bolts through my core, and this—this shouldn't be happening. He's barely even *touching* me. Voice shaking, I manage, "You—you cannot know that from simply seeing him."

"Nor can you—not unless you dance with me too."

The barest hint of fang flashes in his smile now. It doesn't frighten me anymore, however. Not after the attic. *Especially* after the attic. My wrist and throat seem to pulse like living things at the memory—aching not with pain but something else. Something sharp and needy. "I—" *Need to get my head on straight. Need to leave this room before I do something truly stupid.* "I don't know if that's a good idea, Michal."

"Why not?"

"Because—" I stare at him breathlessly. How do I answer such a question without completely humiliating myself? Because I can't think when you look at me like that? Because I'm a fool for looking back? Because it's too soon, and because my friends are coming, and because—*my friends.* The realization pierces my lungs like a knife. "Are you still planning to punish Coco for the Necromancer and Babette? I hardly think we'll have time for dancing if so."

His hand falls away from my elbow. His smile fades with it, returning him instantly to the cool and collected Michal I've always known. My muscles go weak with relief. I've witnessed his wrath, his grace, his *power*, and I've survived them all, but his charm? I don't think anyone can survive that.

"You have my word, Célie Fleur Tremblay," he says, punctuating the words with a simple bow, "that no vampire will harm your friends when they arrive tomorrow, including myself. If I thought it would help, I would cancel the masquerade altogether, but they'll come for you regardless. I doubt Hell itself could keep Louise le Blanc away from Requiem now"—a vicious flash of his eyes—"but Hell is exactly what she'll find if she attempts to take you by force."

Despite his threat, my heart seems to swell to twice its size. *He isn't going to hurt them.* Just as quickly, however, it punctures once more—because if Coco and Lou and Reid are coming to Requiem, Jean Luc will be coming too. Despite his last words, he won't miss the opportunity to investigate an isle of vampires. I wipe my palms on my skirt as inconspicuously as possible.

I can only hope he and Michal won't kill each other.

"Célie?" the latter asks.

"Lou would never do that."

He nods curtly. "Good. That makes this easier." Before I can even ask, he says, "I need you to do something for me, but if you agree, you'll be putting yourself in danger."

Filippa's words slash through the last of my euphoria. *You can't get something for nothing, Célie.* Of course Michal wants something in exchange for the food, the magnificent dress. *Everything in this world comes with a price.*

My eyes narrow at him. "What sort of danger?"

"The sort that involves the Necromancer."

"Oh." The first cold finger of understanding trails down my spine as we stare at each other. All the warmth in his expression has frozen solid once more, and his eyes glint like chips of black ice. "Is that all?"

"Your friends aren't the only ones who'll arrive when the enchantment lifts on All Hallows' Eve. The Necromancer won't be able to resist the temptation—if you choose to remain on Requiem, this could be his only opportunity to reach you until Yule. He won't want to take that risk."

"How do you know?"

"Because I wouldn't." He steps backward, away from me, and returns to the breakfast table, uncovering the only dish I didn't touch. Revealing a single goblet of blood. He drains half of it in one swallow, and I watch—torn between disgust and fascination—as his throat works and his hand clenches around the crystal. Part of me wonders what it tastes like to a vampire. Part of me loathes myself for wondering. "The Necromancer is so desperate for your blood," he says after another moment, "that he slaughtered at least six creatures in search of it—and one of them right outside Chasseur Tower. He didn't bother to hide the bodies of his victims, which tells me he is either foolish or fearless. We must assume it's the latter. He isn't going to wait another two months to seize his prize."

With a gentle *clink*, he returns the goblet to its gilded tray. He does not, however, approach me again.

"You want to use me as bait," I say finally.

Under different circumstances, it might've hurt more, but this is too important. If the Necromancer succeeds, not only will I *die*, but he'll also tear through the veil between the living and the dead. Who knows what consequences will follow? What if—once torn—the veil remains open permanently?

Michal inclines his head. "I understand if you're frightened, but—"

"It would be rather stupid not to be, wouldn't it? The man wants to harvest my blood to raise the dead—and he'll still attempt to do so whether I'm waltzing as a butterfly or cowering in my room." I pick up the garment box, clutch it to my chest like some sort of shield, or perhaps just something to do with my hands. Tomorrow suddenly looms very near. "Either way, I'll be in danger, so when he takes advantage of the lifted enchantment, we should too. We should be ready."

Michal says nothing for a long moment, instead simply staring at me. Then—his jaw flexing—"I won't allow anything to happen to you, Célie."

"Neither will I."

The words startle even me, and instinctively, I clutch the box tighter in response. But they're true—I will not go quietly when the Necromancer arrives, and if he thinks he can take me without a fight, it'll be the last mistake he ever makes. I am not a doll. I am a Bride of Death, and I will use every weapon in my arsenal against him. Every secret.

You can't get something for nothing, Célie.

If I want to defeat the Necromancer, I'll need Michal's help too.

"Michal"—I march toward him with newfound purpose—"there's something else you should know. I found a note inside my sister's cross from a secret lover. The two planned to elope, but Morgane killed her before they could do it." Pressing the garment box to his chest, I fish the cross from my collar and reveal the scrap of parchment within. A crease appears between Michal's brows as I unfold it, and he skims the words quickly. "The handwriting matches the letter Dimitri received from the Necromancer."

His eyes snap to mine. "You think he was her secret lover."

"Yes."

He looses a harsh, incredulous breath. "But that means—"

"I know." Folding the note into the cross once more, I tuck both safely away and reclaim the garment box from Michal's rigid arms. We can do nothing now but wait. "The Necromancer plans to kill me to resurrect my sister."

CHAPTER FORTY-FIVE

Masquerade Part I

Two weeks ago, I thought I would die on All Hallows' Eve. Somehow, everything has changed since then—everything, and nothing at all. Smoothing the silver bodice of my gown, readjusting the organza mask, and taking a deep breath, I step into the corridor beyond my room. Already, the faint strains of a haunting violin drift through the castle, along with the gentle murmur of voices. According to Odessa, the revelry won't truly start until midnight, but I can only pace in my room for so long.

Coco and Lou will be here soon. They'll be *here*, on Requiem, for me to talk with and see and embrace. Reid and Beau too, hopefully.

And Jean Luc.

My chest constricts in a way that has nothing to do with my corset. After how we parted in Cesarine, I can't imagine he'll be pleased to see me. *Go*, he said in that horribly empty voice, *and don't come back*. But that—that was then. I resist the urge to bite at my fingernails, which Odessa has painted with clear lacquer. Perhaps Jean will have changed his mind in the hours since I left him; perhaps, after his anger faded, he realized he doesn't hate me, after all. I lift my hands to pinch my cheeks instead. Will he want to speak to me about what happened? Will he want to change my mind too?

Worse still—my chest squeezes impossibly tighter—what did

he tell the others happened at the harbor? Will they be angry at me for leaving with Michal? He *did* threaten to kill Coco, and they have no way of knowing he changed his mind. Does it even *matter* that he changed his mind? I don't have the answer—I don't have *any* of the answers—and when the next question strikes, I think I'm going to be sick all over again.

Because what if no one comes at all?

In their eyes, perhaps I chose Michal over them, chose Requiem over Cesarine. They'll know by now that I've broken my vow to the Chasseurs. Perhaps they'll perceive my actions as unforgivable, as an irrevocable break in our friendship. Yes. I'm definitely going to be sick now. Except—

The Necromancer.

Beyond anything I've done to hurt him, Jean Luc remains captain of the Chasseurs, and he won't ignore what Michal said in the harbor. He can't afford to ignore it. If I know Jean Luc at all, he'll insist on due diligence, and an entire contingent of huntsmen will swarm the isle tonight—because if Michal told the truth, we're closer than ever to catching the Necromancer, and if *I* told the truth, the Necromancer is stalking me.

Jean Luc has worked too hard to miss the action. The glory. My heart sinks miserably.

Perhaps my friends will join him for the same reason.

Odessa follows me into the corridor, swatting my hands aside before they can stray to my hair. "The Necromancer cannot kill you if you're already dead. Touch another strand of my masterpiece, and I shall thwart him all by myself."

She spent the last two hours curling my hair with hot tongs, meticulously pinning half of them at my nape. The rest cascades down my back to join my wings, which she now bends swiftly to rearrange. Long gloves of deepest blue satin cover her hands, wrists, and arms. They match her sapphire cloak perfectly, complement the pearl diadem across her forehead and the garnet damask of her bodice—scandalously sleeveless and recklessly low-cut, more corset than anything else. Her breasts nearly spill from the top as she straightens with a satisfied nod. Without a doubt, she is the most sensual Madonna I've ever seen, and—judging from the smirk on her bloodred lips—she knows it.

"Are you *sure* he'll be able to recognize me?"

"Célie, darling," she says pleasantly, "you'll be the only human in attendance until your little friends arrive, and even then— there won't be a vampire, human, *or* necrophiliac in attendance who doesn't notice you in that gown. Now stop fretting. You'll ruin the cosmetics."

Despite my mask, Odessa spent another half hour dusting iridescent powder upon my eyelids, brow bones, and cheeks—every inch of me now sparkles in the light of the corridor candelabra. She even adhered tiny diamonds to the outer corners of my eyes. "Will he be— Will there be blood down there?" I ask nervously.

She arches a brow beneath a rather peculiar mask of her own: strands of gold weave in an open, diamond-knit pattern, so the mask isn't really a mask at all, but another piece of jewelry. "We're vampires, Célie. There will always be blood."

With that, she seizes my hand and drags me down the corridor.

Focusing on that bundle of nerves in my chest, I slip through the veil to find Mila, who drifts alongside us with an impish grin. "Anything unusual yet?" I ask her as a distraction.

"The enchantment doesn't break until midnight," she replies

sweetly. "Or did you mean my brother?"

"Oh, shut up."

"What is it?" Odessa peers back at me, eyes narrowing through her mask. "Is it Mila? Has she seen anything?"

If a ghost can skip, Mila does so now, clapping her hands and practically cackling with glee. "I've never seen Michal so agitated— he nearly bit off Pasha's head when the idiot suggested waiting outside your room. He and Ivan are going to join you in the ball-room instead. You *do* look lovely tonight, Célie," she adds, her voice a bit wistful. "Vampires tend to covet lovely things."

Warmth spreads through my cheeks at the compliment, but I push it aside. I push thoughts of *Michal* aside. "Never as lovely as you."

"The sentiment," Odessa says as Mila beams, "it chokes me."

Truthfully, both of them look almost surreal tonight—too beautiful to exist—and I feel as if I'm floating through a dream. The castle, too, seems different with music, with soft, disembod-ied voices and flickering candlelight in every corridor. No less eerie, of course, because the shadows and cobwebs and *sentience* remain, but somehow all the more mysterious. Like I might take a wrong turn and end up somewhere else entirely—dropped into La Fôret des Yeux on a snowy, moonlit night, perhaps, or trapped in a nightmare disguised as a room.

The impression only intensifies when we step into the ball-room, and I gasp, severing the connection with Mila and falling back through the veil. Vampires of every shape, size, and color crawl through the enormous room, not only on the onyx dance floor but also up the gilded walls, upon the very *ceiling.* My mouth falls open as my head falls back to stare at them. "I wouldn't do that if I were you," Odessa murmurs, closing my jaw with a gloved finger and readjusting the capelet around my throat. "No need to poke the dragon, so to speak."

I hardly hear her.

Across the room, Pasha and Ivan cut toward us through the crowd with determined expressions. A stringed quartet plays a plaintive song atop the dais behind them, and the couples overhead waltz between the chandeliers with uncanny grace and beauty. The candles cast their pallid skin in golden light. A thousand more tapers surround the dais, the musicians, the long and elegant tables along the edges of the room. Crystal-cut goblets of blood rise in pyramids upon each one. Odessa follows my gaze, her own gleaming brighter than usual. Exhilarated. "We spike them with champagne. I arranged *actual* champagne for you, however, if you'd like to partake."

I shake my head, overwhelmed. "No, thank you."

She prods me toward the tables anyway, skirting around a patch of enormous pumpkins carved with narrowed, wicked eyes. More tapers still flicker from within their depths, and what look like *real* skeletons lounge among them, some dangling from above. Someone has dressed the bones in wide velvet hats with feather plumes, in the lavish robes of priests and Pharisees. One even wears the ivory crepe gown and golden tiara of a queen. With an odd plunging sensation, I remember the skull outside of Monsieur Marc's shop.

Hello again, Father Roland. You're looking well.

I look away quickly to find Odessa perusing the goblets of blood, selecting one, and sipping delicately. "Ah . . . melusine. Even cold, their blood is my very favorite."

A trio of vampires join us at the table to choose their own

goblets. Jewels drip from their throats, and they stare balefully at me behind their glittering masks. One has dressed in the fur cloak of a loup garou—his sleeves dripping lace—while his two companions have painted themselves as sculptures. Their entire bodies gleam with golden paint.

They're also naked.

"What does blood taste like to you?" I ask Odessa abruptly. Pasha and Ivan materialize behind us, rigid and imposing, and the trio of vampires cast one more disdainful look in my direction before gliding away.

"Hmm." Odessa purses her lips, considering, and takes another sip. "I suppose it tastes the same to me as it does to you, except, of course, that the nerves in my tongue receive it differently. It nourishes my body, and thus, my body comes to crave it. The metallic taste is still there, yet it doesn't repulse me as it does you. And the salt—it becomes addictive. The blood of a melusine boasts a particular vigor, probably from their time spent in the seawater of L'Eau Melancolique." She tips the goblet in my direction. "Would you like to try it?"

"No." Repressing a shudder, I look past her toward another vampire dressed as a bleeding rose. Behind them waltzes a couple masquerading as ancient forest gods. One of them even wears the enormous stag horns of the Woodwose. "I think spiked blood might be stronger than the champagne itself, and we're supposed to be looking for the Necromancer." Despite my best efforts, the words hold a subtle rebuke.

"Actually," she corrects me in a miffed voice, "we're *supposed* to be blending in with the revelry. We can't do that if you continue gaping at everyone like a codfish."

"I do not look like a codfish."

She waves an errant hand, ignoring me. "Furthermore, we'll be able to smell him when he arrives. Blood witches possess a very distinctive scent because of their magic."

I bite my lip and glance around the room. "Forgive me, Odessa, but you mistook *me* for a blood witch when we first met. Their scent can't be *that* distinct, or I wouldn't be here at all." Above the music, the clock in the belfry booms half past eleven. When I jerk at the sound, nearly upsetting Odessa's goblet, she lifts it to her lips with a smirk. "Shouldn't Michal be here by now?" I ask defensively. "Where *is* he?"

"Michal arrives at midnight." Dimitri strolls up beside us, grinning, and a rather tall and pretty young woman clutches his arm. They've dressed as flora and fauna for the occasion; he wears the fur pelt and elongated mask of a gray wolf, while her petal-pink gown floats airily around her ankles. Real vines and flower buds adorn her mask. Though I cannot see much of her golden-brown face, she seems to be . . . human. "This is Margot Janvier," he tells me proudly, and the young woman offers a tentative smile in response. "She owns le fleuriste in the Old City." He squeezes her elbow. "Margot, this is Mademoiselle Célie Tremblay, our guest of honor for the evening."

"Bonsoir, Mademoiselle Tremblay," she says softly.

I return her smile with one of my own, trying not to betray my disbelief. *This* is Dimitri's florist? A human woman? Surely even *he* knows how irresponsible it was to bring her tonight, to fixate upon her at all. My stomach curdles at the thought of her beautiful silk mask ending up in his room. I force myself to curtsy regardless. "It's lovely to meet you, Mademoiselle Janvier. Your costume is stunning—are those viola and crocus blooms?"

"You know your botanicals." Margot's smile widens in approval, and she lifts her free hand to the delicate flowers on her face. "And please . . . call me Margot."

The song ends on a drawn-out note of yearning, and when the next piece starts, the two bid us goodbye, Dimitri leading Margot to the dance floor. I watch them go anxiously for several seconds before turning to Odessa. "Does Margot know about his blood-lust?"

To my surprise, Odessa's expression mirrors my own. "No. I've lost track of how many times I've told Dimitri to stay away from her. He won't listen," she says simply, placing her half-empty goblet on the tray of a passing attendant. Her mouth twists as if she's lost her appetite. "He says he loves her."

"Does he?"

"In his mind, perhaps." She tears her gaze away when Dimitri throws his head back and laughs at something Margot said. "Who can truly say? My brother tends to fall in love with everyone he meets."

We lapse into silence as the clock ticks on, and eventually, my thoughts stray from Dimitri and Margot to Ivan and Pasha, who still loom behind us. To the vampires all around who cast quick, cutting looks in our direction. None approach, however, and thank God for that. My nerves are stretched taut as it is, winding tighter and tighter with each song. I don't know whether I want the clock to speed up or slow down—because when Michal arrives, the enchantment around the isle will have broken, and the Necro-mancer will follow.

⇥‡⇤

I feel the exact second the enchantment breaks.

It happens a heartbeat before the clock strikes midnight—the very air seems to stir, seems to *wake*, and when the first chime clangs through the castle, it ripples outward in a wave toward the sea. I grasp Odessa's arm for balance as the ground seems to shudder, as the chandeliers clink gently overhead. The musicians stop playing abruptly, and—staring up at the crystal with an impassive expression—Odessa murmurs, "So it begins."

Michal appears on the dais as the last chime falls silent.

Though he makes no sound, every head in the room turns toward him, and the ensuing silence feels deeper than usual. Unnatural. It takes several long, unnerving seconds for me to realize why: Margot and I are the only ones in the room who need to breathe. The rest stand cold and still as statues. Even those on the ceiling look as though they've been carved into the fresco, perhaps created as part of the castle itself. Enduring and ancient and sinister. They don't even blink. Chills skitter down my spine at the thought, and I do not release Odessa's arm.

Michal's eyes find mine instantly through the crowd. They peruse my person slowly, thoroughly, as if he doesn't care in the slightest that every creature in the room waits for him to speak. No—as if he *expects* them to wait. And the vampires oblige. Not a single one interrupts as he stares at me, and I—

I can't help it. My *God*, I can't help it.

I stare at him too.

Chest bare, he wears his signature black leather everywhere else: his boots, his pants, his mask, even twin straps of it across his broad shoulders. They support the colossal wings that rise from his back, the hundreds of thousands of obsidian feathers on each one. My mouth goes dry at the sight of them. Unlike crow and raven wings, these feathers don't collect and reflect light; no, they seem to *absorb* it, casting Michal in a perverse halo of darkness. He looks almost like the— I tilt my head, then loose a slow breath in realization.

He *is* the Angel of Death.

And he can't take his eyes off me.

Heat builds in my belly the longer he looks, a sort of liquid fire that spreads across my chest and into my cheeks. The nostrils of the nearest vampires flare in response. Odessa cuts them a sharp glance, and Pasha and Ivan appear swiftly on either side of us. Ivan stands so close that I can *feel* the chill emanating from his arm; he doesn't wear a costume like the others. Even a mask could not hide the menace in his expression.

"Good evening," Michal says at last, clasping his hands behind his back. Though he speaks softly—his voice barely above a whisper—every word rings out with lethal precision. "And welcome to my home on this All Hallows' Eve. Each one of you looks magnificent." His eyes flick briefly to me before surveying the crowd once more. "I understand the revelry is different this year. I could not usher your loved ones into Requiem, and for that, I will not apologize. Never before has the threat of the outside world pressed closer, and we cannot risk our home for the sake of one blood-drunken night." A meaningful pause. "However . . . even I cannot stop the enchantment around Requiem from lifting. The magic that protects this isle is unyielding and eternal, but tonight—if your loved ones so choose—I cannot stop them from joining you."

Though the vampires remain unmoving, an undercurrent of . . . something seems to stir within them at his words. Anticipation?

No. *Defiance.* Gooseflesh creeps down my neck.

"That said," Michal continues, his voice still deceptively soft, "I would urge you to remember that I am also unyielding and eternal. I will not forgive those who endanger our home, and I will not forget them either." Unclasping his hands, he spreads his arms wide in supplication, and the muscles in his chest stretch long and powerful with the movement. An odd pang shoots through my stomach at the sight. Tensing, I drop Odessa's arm and keep my own tight to my sides. "With that, I bid you to enjoy the masquerade and invite you to stay until dawn."

He steps from the dais without another word, and the crowd parts reflexively as he strides through it.

Straight toward me.

"Oh God," I whisper as the musicians resume their song and the vampires gradually drift back to their drinking and mingling. "I owe Monsieur Marc a dance," I blurt abruptly, *loudly.* Cringing, I step backward and search desperately for any sign of candy-floss hair. *There.* On the opposite side of the room, he chats animatedly with a strapping young man and his buxom companion. He also wears the most ostentatious peacock mask I've ever seen.

Odessa doesn't follow my gaze, instead smirking at whatever she sees in my expression. "Monsieur Marc looks rather busy at the moment, doesn't he?" Then she twirls a lock of my hair around her finger and says, "Good luck."

She melts into the crowd before I can beg her to stay.

Michal appears a second later, and I have no choice but to return his slight bow with a curtsy. "Hello, Michal," I say a bit breathlessly. Up close, he looks even more unattainable—his chest somehow wider without a shirt, his body less cultured and more primitive. But of *course* it's less cultured. He isn't wearing a *shirt*, and I—I—

I shake my head, cursing my wandering eyes, as he tilts his head to study me. When his lips pull up at the corner, I clench my hands in the delicate fabric of my skirt to hide their trembling. Because why am I looking at his *lips?* We aren't here to gape at each other, and I need to focus. I need to *focus.* Because we're *here* to trap the Necromancer, to lure him into a false sense of—

"Hello, pet." Michal's grin widens, and—impossibly gentle— he coaxes one of my hands into his own before placing a kiss on my inner wrist. My knees threaten to buckle. "You seem . . . nervous this evening."

"Nervous? I'm not nervous."

"Your pulse is louder than the music."

"Stop listening to my *pulse*, then, and we won't have a problem. It's invasive, you know, to—to listen to things like that. Perhaps I imbibed several glasses of champagne before you arrived, and *that* is why my heart is racing. Did you ever think of that? Perhaps I've been dancing vigorously with Odessa—"

He chuckles, and the sound thrums against my skin until I shiver with it. "My cousin," he says, his voice low, "loathes to dance, and unless I'm much mistaken, it'll be a very long time before you imbibe again. After all, you asked *me* to dance the last time." His eyes glitter in the candlelight. "And what a shame it would be if you asked again. Who knows how I might answer?"

My traitorous gaze darts from the silver of my gown to the bare skin of his arms and torso. If—*if*—I agree to dance with him, it isn't as if we would need to . . . touch more than strictly necessary. Indeed, we *couldn't*, and that—that would be for the best, wouldn't it? After all, we can hardly blend into the revelry if we continue to stand here and stare at one another.

Right.

I straighten my spine.

"Would you like to dance, Michal?"

My breath catches slightly at the smile that splits his face in answer. When he looks at me this way, it feels rather like catching the eye of a ravenous wolf—like he longs to give chase, and at any second, he might yield to temptation and pounce. "I thought you'd never ask."

Careful not to touch my gown—our hands the only point of contact—he leads me to the dance floor just as the stringed quartet breaks into an eerie waltz. "How are you going to—?" I start to ask, but he wraps an arm around my back in answer, pulling me close. His skin burns instantly upon contact with my wings.

Craning my neck in horror, I say, "Michal, *no*—"

"Are you rescinding your offer?"

"Of course not, but you're— You shouldn't have to—" I shake my head to clear it, swiveling to face him in disbelief. "You're *burning.* Surely we can find a—a glove or a jacket—"

"Relax, Célie." If anything, his grip tightens around me, and his grin fades at whatever he sees in my expression. "I do not fear pain."

"No? What is your fear, then?"

His eyes linger for several seconds upon my hair, my mask, my cheeks.

"Philophobia," he says at last. Then— "If you could travel anywhere in the world, where would you go?"

The question takes me by surprise, and I answer without

hesitation. "Onirique." When he says nothing, waiting for me to continue, I explain hastily, "It's a village in L'Eau Melancolique—smaller than Le Présage, of course, but legendary for its eerie lights. Elvire told me it also boasts the oldest library in the world. She said they safeguard tablets from thousands of years ago." Now I do hesitate, regarding him suspiciously. "Why?"

Without answering, he whisks me across the heart of the dance floor, and his body moves so lithely, so firmly against mine, that within seconds, I forget about his question altogether. I forget about his burns. I forget about what *philophobia* could possibly mean, and I forget about our plan, about the Necromancer and balconies. Indeed, everything falls away except my hand on his shoulder—the way his muscle flexes beneath my touch, the grace with which he guides my every movement. Until— "Tell me about your mother."

I nearly stumble at the question, but his hand remains firm on my waist. "But you haven't answered my question. That—that isn't how our game works."

"Who says I'm still playing a game?"

I stare at him for a beat, eyes wide, before blurting, "Tell me about *your* mother, then."

"If you like." He lifts a shoulder, spinning me around Dimitri and Margot. "She died when I was young, so I remember very little about her—except for her voice. She was a lovely singer. Can *you* sing, mademoiselle?"

I resist a grimace. "Not if I can help it."

"And if I ask nicely?"

"I might think you have a deeply rooted psychological issue."

"Fair enough." He flashes those fangs again—sharp and

startlingly white—and a rumble of laughter rolls through his chest. "Would you rather be reincarnated as a canine or feline?"

"*Many* deeply rooted psychological issues." He dips me abruptly, bringing our faces closer together than before—too close—so I can see the deep brown in his eyes. When he lifts our hands to tuck a strand of my hair behind an ear, my head starts to spin a little. A *lot.* "Dog," I breathe, gazing up at his lips. "But I don't believe in reincarnation."

"Interesting. What breed?"

"I never learned any breeds. My mother detests animals." When he pulls me upright, I stagger into his chest, light-headed and flustered and bemused. This is the most bizarre conversation I've ever had in my life. If I didn't know any better, I might think he was trying to become better acquainted. To become *friends.* "Why all the questions, monsieur? This is hardly the time or place for such a discussion."

"Perhaps you're right. When *is* a good time?"

Despite the sardonic note in his voice, I can't muster the ire to glare at him. Indeed—I don't even *want* to glare at him, and that— that should terrify me. I hold him closer instead, lacing my fingers through his. "Do you talk as a rule while dancing?"

"Only under extraordinary circumstances."

My face flushes at that—with exertion, with *exhilaration*—and as the song reaches its crescendo, I spin backward into his chest, my own pink and feverish. He trails his nose along the crook of my neck before placing another kiss there. Then he whirls me away from him when I try to turn.

I've danced with many partners in my life: my father, my instructors, Jean Luc, even Reid, and none of them—*none* of them—can compare to dancing with Michal.

I never want to stop.

The song soon draws to a close on a hauntingly poignant note, however, and reluctantly, Michal and I release one another. "That was..." My eyes fall to the burns across his arms, his chest, impressions of my body left to linger on his skin. He'll need blood to heal them, and at the thought of him drinking from Arielle again—of him drinking from *anyone*—fire sears through my entire being. "Unexpected," I finish faintly.

He stares at me like a starving man. "Was it?"

"Michal, I—"

He shakes his head, however, and withdraws a length of silver ribbon from his pocket. His palms—already angry and red—hiss softly as he offers it to me. "What I said before," he says quietly, "about staying on Requiem . . . I meant it." He closes my fingers around the ribbon, swallowing hard. "You're welcome here for as long as you choose."

Unable to hold his gaze, I look down at the ribbon instead. The tail of it ripples slightly—once, twice—as I clasp it to my chest. Of course he meant what he said. Michal *always* means what he says, but to actually *live* on Requiem . . . I glance unbidden to the vampires around us. Though they give Michal a wide berth, their malevolent eyes still seem to follow me through the room, gleaming with hunger. With violence.

Would life even be possible here?

Sighing heavily, shaking my head, I open my mouth to thank Michal—

And the doors to the ballroom erupt in a sphere of blinding light.

CHAPTER FORTY-SIX

Masquerade Part II

Pandemonium ensues.

The vampires scatter in every direction, shrieking and hissing and ducking for cover, while Michal pushes me behind him and Dimitri tucks Margot under his arm to flee behind the dais. Odessa appears instantly beside us—shielding her face with her arms—as smoke undulates from her skin. "What is it?" she shouts, panicked. "What's happening?"

But I don't know—I can't answer her—and Michal is smoking too, faster than the others because of my gown. I try to push in front of him, to protect him from the impossible light inside the room, but even burning, his body is too strong. Impenetrable. "Michal, *move*—!"

"Stay behind me."

Through narrowed eyes, he glares at the sphere of light, which splits neatly into two as Louise le Blanc steps between them, holding each one in her palm. "Bonsoir," she calls pleasantly to the room at large, her hair rippling in the pulse of the spheres. Heat emanates from them in waves until—with a horrified gasp—I realize what they are.

Suns.

She holds miniature, fiery *suns* in each hand, and the vampires are cowering behind tables now, clinging desperately to the shadows of the dais. She strolls past them without a second glance, thoroughly unconcerned. The earthen scent of magic trails in her wake. "I am looking," she continues, "for Michal Vasiliev. A little birdie told me he wishes to speak with a dear friend of mine, but alas—he'll have to deal with me instead."

This—this is bad. This is *bad*. With those suns in her hands, Lou could do unspeakable damage, and she would never even know that he—that Michal—

I move to lunge forward, but Odessa's feet still stand upon my train, and the momentum jerks me backward instead. Stumbling, I twist to right myself—except Odessa also shifts, still shielding her face, and I lose my footing completely. *Oh God*. Pinwheeling, I fall against her arms, which wrap around me instinctively to stop us both from crashing to the floor. Her skin blisters upon contact. Though she muffles her cry of pain, we're thoroughly entangled now, and Michal—

He steps forward, spreading his arms to shield Odessa and me from view. "Welcome to my home, Louise le Blanc, and merry meet. *I* am Michal Vasiliev."

Lou slows to a halt halfway across the room, her grin widening as she inspects him. Her eyes lingering for a moment on the leather of his pants, the magnificent wings at his back. "Of course you are." She raises the spheres between them, and they flare even brighter, near blinding now. Even Michal winces. At his pained intake of breath, the last of my control shatters; pushing away from Odessa—*she'll be fine, she'll be fine, she'll be fine*—I sprint into the open space at the center of the room.

"Lou, wait! *Wait!*" Her eyes widen slightly as I skid to a halt before her, waving my arms like a lunatic and gasping for breath.

"You don't need to hurt him. He promised not to touch Coco—not to touch *any* of you." Though I glance behind for Coco or Reid or even Jean Luc, none of them stand in the corridor beyond. No one else does either. The passage remains empty except for shards of door and bits of metal. "You—you're to be treated like an honored guest," I say, my voice weaker now. *At least Lou came. At least she hasn't incinerated me on the spot.* "My honored guest. He promised. He promised he won't hurt anyone."

The suns in Lou's hands dim marginally. Her eyes narrow, and she searches my face for several seconds. "And you believe him?"

"I do."

"You *trust* him?"

Nodding furiously, I lower my arms and hold my breath. *Please. Please please please—*

Though Lou tilts her head, considering, the suns still burn hot and bright in her hands. I try not to glance behind me. I don't know how long a vampire can withstand sunlight—even the imitation of it—before bursting into flame. "And you're telling me this of your own volition? You haven't been compelled?"

I blink at her, startled. Because I never told her about compulsion. Come to think of it, I never told her about sunlight either, but—but that hardly matters now. I need to somehow *prove* that Michal is trustworthy before this entire place goes up in smoke. I look behind her again. "Did Coco come with you? Is she here somewhere?"

Lou's eyes narrow. "Why?"

"Because the blood of a Dame Rouge is poisonous to their enemies. If her blood doesn't harm him, you'll know we're telling the truth. Please, Lou," I add quietly when she still doesn't move. "Let us prove it."

"You're asking me to risk my best friend's life."

"I'm asking you to trust me."

After several long seconds, Lou nods—just a single, short dip of her chin—and Coco, Reid, Beau, and Jean Luc seem to melt from the very walls of the corridor. I gape at them in disbelief, heart lodging in my throat, and hardly register the sharp bite of blood magic. "It's up to you," Lou murmurs to Coco, but the latter has already pressed the tip of her sharp nail to her thumb. It draws a single bead of blood.

The entire room seems to inhale.

Ignoring the vampires' reaction, Coco moves to brush past me, but I catch her sleeve at the last minute, suddenly terrified. "If *you* think of him as an enemy, will it still—?"

"I don't want him to be my enemy, Célie." She eases my hand from her arm with a wary expression, yet a sympathetic one too. "You said that you trust him," she says simply.

I can do nothing but watch as she crosses the no-man's-land between us and Michal, her finger outstretched all the way. When she halts before him, expectant, his eyes flick to mine. His poor skin shines raw and pink in Lou's artificial sunlight, but if it bothers him, he does not say. Still looking directly at me, he swipes the blood from Coco's finger. His skin doesn't bubble, doesn't blister, but for good measure, he lifts her blood to his mouth next, sucking it gently while we wait with bated breath.

Nothing happens.

My entire body sags with relief because *nothing happens*, and when Coco turns to me and smiles, the miniature suns in Lou's hands wink out instantly. I blink in the sudden semidarkness, fighting back tears, as Lou saunters forward and loops her arm through my elbow. "Well, then," she says matter-of-factly. "That changes things, doesn't it?"

Yes, it does.

When she pulls me into a hug, I can't stop the first tear from falling. It trickles into her hair as she laughs and squeezes me tighter, as Coco hurries to join and wraps her arms around us both. "We've missed you, Célie," Coco whispers.

A sob builds in my throat as we hold one another. "I missed you too."

Odessa whisks Lou, Coco, Reid, Beau, and Jean Luc into an antechamber off the ballroom several moments later, and Michal does his best to appease his half-healed guests. At his orders, the musicians drain several goblets of blood before returning to their posts on the dais and striking up a lively tune. Dozens of attendants weave through the mutinous crowd with still more goblets—this blood somehow fresh, somehow *warm*—and dispense them with haste.

Within a quarter hour, every vampire in the room looks bright and shiny and new again.

Except for their eyes.

Sharp and spiteful, they track Michal as he too accepts a goblet, as he downs its contents in a single swallow. Almost instantly, the burns on his skin fade to smooth alabaster. Before I can approach him, however, Lou and Coco burst from the antechamber in their new costumes—Lou as a svelte black cat and Coco as the green fairy.

I can't help but smile as they beeline in my direction.

Monsieur Marc didn't have time to sew their costumes, of course, but he fitted them best he could based on my descriptions. Lou's black tights and gown fit her like a glove, as does the shimmering emerald number he procured for Coco. Michal suspected my friends would want to make an entrance when they arrived on Requiem, and he was right. Their entrance couldn't have been more conspicuous.

With these costumes, however, our trap hasn't gone completely awry.

If the Necromancer—*wherever* he is—witnessed their overly warm arrival, he also would've witnessed our reconciliation. To anyone watching, we'll look like estranged friends reuniting for a masquerade on All Hallows' Eve—and for most intents and purposes, we are. We're friends reuniting for a masquerade on All Hallows' Eve who just *happen* to be plotting the downfall of a sadistic killer. Instinctively, my gaze flits around the room, searching for any sign of a new and unfamiliar guest—an impossible task, unfortunately, as I would've needed to memorize every face in the room before the enchantment lifted.

"Me-ow," Lou says, circling me and examining my gown in earnest now. "And here we thought you'd been taken hostage. Are those *real* diamonds?"

My face heats as Coco leans closer to inspect my capelet. A wicked grin splits her face in two, and she feigns a wistful sigh. "To think, he could've kidnapped *me* instead."

"You're uproariously funny, Cosette." Beau—who Monsieur Marc befitted in the harlequin costume of a court jester—scowls as he storms up beside us, tugging at his too-short, spangled sleeve. Little bells jingle on his hat with each step. "Can you believe this? King of all Belterra—with a *lion* as my coat of arms—and they've stuck me in a clown suit." He jerks his chin irritably at a passing vampire, who wears the golden chain mail of a knight. "Now that—*that* is a costume for royalty. I can't *believe* this—"

Coco presses a kiss to his cheek with a laugh. "You aren't king here, Beau."

"No, you most certainly are not." Lou raises her brows in appreciation as Michal approaches. Apparently, all her reservations vanished when he drank Coco's blood and survived to tell the tale. Waggling her brows, she nudges me in the ribs and says, "Well *done*, Célie."

If possible, my cheeks flame even hotter. "I don't know what you're talking about."

"Don't you?" For all her talk, a truly delighted smile breaks across her freckled face when she spots Reid in the crowd. He follows Michal's path, wearing the mechanical mask and dark suit of a clockwork man. His sleeves and pant legs, however, have been rolled several times, as if the suit originally belonged to a giant. I narrow my eyes at Michal, who gazes back with an air of supreme satisfaction. "Shall I explain it to you?" Lou asks innocently.

Behind Reid, however, is Jean Luc.

He wears no costume at all, donning only a simple gold mask made of plaster. "I have huntsmen surrounding this entire castle," he snarls at Michal before moving to stand between Lou and Coco. He doesn't look at me. He doesn't look at anyone. Crossing his arms, he stares at the obsidian floor as if his life depends on it. My heart twists at the image of him standing there, stiff, surrounded by all our friends yet somehow still alone.

Lou coughs awkwardly in the silence that descends.

Unable to stand it, I murmur, "Hello, Jean Luc."

His lip curls slightly, the only indication he heard me at all. He discarded his Chasseur coat in the antechamber, at least; the pristine shirt beneath it glows white in the candlelight. Beside me, Michal says in a low voice, "Shall we continue?" Though he speaks the words to me, the others still hear him. Lou tilts her head in an unspoken question, while Reid's and Coco's eyebrows furrow. Beau glowers outright, nearly as foul-tempered as Jean Luc. His little bells still jingle with each of his movements.

When I nod, Michal extends a pale hand to Lou, who stares at it in fascination. "Would you honor me with a dance, ma Dame?"

After a curious glance at Reid, who nods once in affirmation, she tentatively places her hand in Michal's. "I don't know *what* the two of you are playing at, but I—for one—cannot *wait* to find out. Coco? Beau?" She catches Coco's hand as Michal leads her away, and Coco takes Beau's in turn. Together, the four of them stride onto the dance floor, joined quickly by Dimitri and Odessa. Margot has vanished—hopefully gone home—leaving Dimitri to intercept Coco and introduce himself; Odessa does the same with Beau.

I breathe a quick sigh of relief. This part of the plan, at least, has gone smoothly. I knew it would. My friends have always feared little and braved much.

Unfortunately, they've left me to stand alone with Reid and Jean Luc.

Clearing my throat, I turn cautiously to Jean. "I'm so glad you're here. We have a lot to talk about—"

"That's not why I came here, Célie."

"But you *are* here," I insist, perhaps a touch desperately. "Do you remember when I couldn't build a fire at the start of my training? We were surrounded by our brethren in La Fôret des Yeux, and I didn't want to try because I thought they'd all laugh at me. You wouldn't let me quit, though. You told me there's no time like the present—that sometimes we *have* to do things, even if we don't want to do them."

"Don't." The word catches in his throat as he lifts his head, and his gaze is the only weapon he'll need tonight. His hurt, his anger, his heartbreak—they pierce me just as swiftly as a sword ever could. "Don't pretend we know each other anymore."

Before I can say anything else, he pivots on his heel and stalks away to stand by the skeletons and pumpkins. Crestfallen, I watch him go without following, without protest. A small, secret part of me hoped for a forgiveness I haven't earned, but of course that hasn't happened. It may *never* happen. Jean Luc has never been one to forgive easily, and he doesn't ever forget.

"Did he tell them everything?" I ask Reid, unable to keep the plaintive note from my voice. "Lou and Coco and Beau? Do they know what happened at the docks?"

"Yes." Sighing heavily, Reid too watches his friend, who snaps at a passing attendant and flashes his Balisarda. "Give him time, Célie. He'll come around."

"Will he?"

"He wants to catch the Necromancer worse than anyone."

At his words, Filippa's cross seems to hang heavier at my neck, and I force myself to turn away from Jean Luc. With time, perhaps he'll realize we both deserved better, but that isn't important right now. That *can't* be important right now. Not when our plan is in motion.

"Are you going to ask me to dance?"

Reid blinks at me in surprise, a small smile playing at the corner of his mouth. "Would you like to dance, Mademoiselle Tremblay?"

"Indeed I would, Monsieur Diggory."

Accepting his hand, I allow him to guide me to the dance floor before leaning closer and whispering, "It would be a shame if we were overheard." As inconspicuously as possible, I tilt my head toward the vampires around us, positioning my free arm over his, my hand on his shoulder. "We have so much catching up to do."

Fortunately, he understands my meaning at once, his eyes going distant as he searches for a pattern. His magic behaves differently than Coco's, differently than even Lou's since she became La Dame des Sorcières. He and the rest of his kin are able to see and manipulate the patterns of the universe; that manipulation is how Dames Blanches and Seigneurs Blancs cast spells—they give up pieces of themselves in order to gain something in return. Just like Filippa said.

You can't get something for nothing, Célie.

That familiar, heavy weight settles in my chest again at the thought of my sister, and I watch Reid rather distantly as he searches for the right enchantment, his blue eyes flicking left and right. He knew Filippa too. Throughout our childhood, he knew her better than anyone except perhaps Evangeline and me. What would he think if he knew about her relationship with the Necromancer? Would he understand this deep *ache* in the pit of my stomach? Does he still grieve her too?

If I tell him about her secret, he'll no longer grieve only *her*. He'll grieve her memory too, and that—that would be incredibly selfish of me.

Wouldn't it?

"I can take away their hearing," Reid murmurs after several seconds, "but I won't be able to speak during our conversation." His eyes flash back to mine. "Do I need to speak?"

I'm supposed to explain the plan to him, just as Michal, Odessa, and Dimitri are explaining the plan to the others. It's my *job* to explain the plan. We thought it would be best, would draw less attention, to divide and conquer on the dance floor rather than congregate in a corner and whisper. And yet...

"It might be better if you don't."

He frowns at that, but without another word, he flicks his wrist at my waist. As the scent of the magic engulfs us, he nods for me to continue. Still strangely reluctant to speak at a normal volume, I open my mouth to tell him about our trap, about Beau leading me to the northern balcony, but the words that come out are entirely different. "Do you remember . . . those last few years of Filippa's life?"

Whatever Reid had been expecting me to say, clearly, this wasn't it. His frown deepens as he searches my face, but he nods regardless, his meaning clear. *Yes, I remember.*

"She was . . . distant, almost reclusive, and I caught her sneaking out of our nursery more than once, always in the dead of night. I know she treated you differently too." His hands tighten imperceptibly as they spin me away from him, then back again. Instinctively, I know he's remembering the same thing I am: the last time the two of them spoke, Filippa called him a pigheaded soldier and stormed from the house. Before I can reconsider, I blurt, "Reid, I think she was having an affair with the Necromancer."

He recoils slightly in shock, his eyes narrowing.

"She might not have known he was a necromancer at the time, of course, but the two—they were involved somehow," I say helplessly. "They—they planned to run away together, and I just can't— I don't know how to—" I take a deep, shuddering breath. "I don't understand how she could've associated with such a person. How she could've *loved* him." Then—because he cannot speak and I can, because there's nothing either of us can truly say— "You knew her too. You *knew* her. Did you ever suspect she could do something like this? Did I just—did I miss it, Reid? Did I even know her at all?"

Too many questions, I realize miserably. *He can't possibly answer them all—*

Squeezing my hand, Reid pulls me into a bone-crushing hug, and with it—incredibly—the tension in my entire body releases. I choke on a sob. It has been a . . . very long time since someone hugged me like this, not as a friend or paramour, but as family. As a sibling, a brother. As someone who knows me, truly *knows* me, and understands my pain and confusion and guilt because he feels it too.

But that isn't everything.

"You hurt my feelings, you know," I tell him quietly when we pull apart. "You all did. What I overheard in the counsel room—I didn't deserve to be treated like that, Reid. No one deserves to be treated like their thoughts and feelings and experiences don't matter, especially by their closest friends." Despite the words, my voice holds no accusation or reprimand, and to my surprise, I no longer feel anger either. Perhaps because this is no longer a confrontation. This is statement of fact. "I am not secondary."

Reid stops dancing abruptly, right there in the middle of the floor, and clasps my shoulders, bending to look directly in my eyes. *I know,* he mouths, his expression solemn and full of regret. *I'm sorry.*

Around us, the other couples continue to sway and spin, but Michal and Lou both track us from the corners of their eyes. The others have finished their discussions too, clearly waiting for Reid and me to move into the second stage of our plan. The trap itself.

Cupping Reid's cheek, I whisper, "I forgive you. Now . . . here is what we're going to do."

CHAPTER FORTY-SEVEN

The Trap

Half an hour later, Beau and I stand huddled together against the wind on the northernmost balcony off the ballroom. A quaint courtyard stretches below us, partially hidden by two ancient oak trees, just like Michal said it would be. One of them has grown up and over the stone balustrade, its branches straining toward the castle, while the other conceals the rest of the courtyard from view. The effect is almost total privacy—and thank goodness for that, as Beau seems determined to ruin our plan before it can begin.

"Let me get this straight." Beau crosses his arms against his chest. Half in spite, probably, but also to shield himself from the miserable cold. "*You* have volunteered as bait for this Necromancer character."

Rubbing my arms through my sleeves, I whisper, "He needs my blood to do the actual necromancy bit, yes, but can you keep your voice down? You're supposed to be consoling me."

"Right." Our breath puffs between us in little clouds of white as he obliges, grudgingly patting my back. "And because of this rather unfortunate decision, I have also—somehow—been volunteered as bait." As he speaks, the ever-present clouds of Requiem part to reveal a bright autumn moon, and it bathes the ridiculous spangles of his costume in muted silver light. "Me," he repeats incredulously, flicking the bell on his hat for emphasis. "The one person here without any means to contribute if the Necromancer does, in fact, reveal himself and attempt to *harvest your blood.*"

"Which is exactly why we chose you and not the others." I lean into him, anxious and shivering, and sniffle as loudly as possible. Perhaps I shouldn't have removed my mask so soon; it would've at least kept my nose warm. When Reid pretended to insult me at the end of our waltz, however, I'd needed to remove it to pretend to burst into tears, fleeing toward a mutinous Beau, who clearly didn't like our scheme one bit. "We need to lull the Necromancer into a false sense of security. He's much more likely to attack *us* than he would be if Michal or Lou or even Jean Luc had escorted me out here. *Console,* please."

"I'm flattered, truly." Wrapping a stiff arm around my shoulders, he forces my head into the crook of his neck and pats my ear instead. "There, there."

"Oh, don't be like that. You said it yourself—you're the least threatening person in the group."

"And suffering for it, apparently. How long is this going to *take?*" Louder, then— "Don't cry, Célie darling. My dear brother is *clearly* overcompensating for something."

Ignoring his scowl, I blow warm air into my palms and try valiantly to pluck an emotion from my chest. I just need one— *one* emotion deeply felt—to step through the veil and check with Mila, who probably waits for me there already. It shouldn't be difficult. Until this moment, I've been able to slip in and out of the otherworld as I please, yet tonight, my nerves have stretched to the point of snapping, and their frayed ends blow wildly in the wind. I can't focus on a single emotion. Indeed, I can't focus on *anything* except the *incessant* noise of Beau's costume as he shivers. Lifting my head from his shoulder, I hiss, "Can you stop *jingling* for a moment? I'm trying to concentrate."

"Oh, I'm sorry. Is this incredibly frustrating for you?" Rolling his eyes, he seizes his hat and flings it over the balustrade, except instead of vanishing from sight, it catches on a tree limb instead. It dangles there—chiming madly in another gust of wind—until Beau looks likely to leap from the balcony instead. "I'd like it noted," he says through gritted teeth, "this is *not* how I envisioned tonight would go."

"No?" I press my ear back to his shoulder in an effort to muffle the wretched jingling. Even now, the Necromancer could be hiding below, waiting for his opportunity to strike, to *kill*, but—no. Teeth chattering, I shake my head. I can't think like that. Michal is hiding somewhere too, and he won't let anything happen to us. We simply need to wait. "What part of the evening isn't living up to your expectations?"

"For starters"—Beau wraps the corner of his satin cape around my shoulders—"I would've liked it with a bit less reference to necrophilia. No one said anything about a necromancer when I jumped on that ship. Help you escape a vampire island? Yes, without question." A muscle in his jaw flexes. "Especially after Lou mentioned compulsion, and Jean Luc convinced us that *must* be the reason you chose to return to this wretched place." I recoil instinctively from the image he paints: Jean Luc arguing with the others, desperate to convince them I'd been compelled. Desperate to convince himself. Even admitting that I left would've cost him, and I—my mind skitters away from the rest of the thought. "Now that we've determined you're most definitely *not* being compelled, however . . ."

"You would leave me to the Necromancer?"

It makes sense, of course. Beau isn't like me; he isn't even like Reid or Jean Luc. He is royalty—the king of all Belterra—and his people will surely feel his absence while he chases down runaways and murderers.

"Of course not." Beau sighs in defeat, his shoulders slumping beneath the cape. "It's just—today was Coco's birthday. Did you know that? She was born on All Hallows' Eve."

"*What?*" My stomach plunges at the realization, and I jerk upright to gape up at him. Because of course I know Coco's birthday. How could I possibly have forgotten? Worse still—instead of celebrating, she spent the evening on a ship sailing to her possible demise, and I just might be the worst friend to have ever called herself one. "Oh no," I whisper in horror. "I didn't get her a present."

"In light of the circumstances," Beau says, his voice wry, "I think she'll forgive you. I had a rather special gift planned myself before I realized we'd be spending the majority of the night luring a murderous witch onto a subarctic balcony. It really is colder than a witch's tit out h— *Why do your eyes look like that?*"

He leaps away from me, appalled, and the temperature plummets as my regret ties each frayed nerve into a neat little bow. It weighs me down, down, *down* until I step through the veil into the otherworld, where Mila lounges upon the nearest tree branch, her skirt and hair billowing in the wind.

Grinning, she flicks the bells on Beau's hat in haphazard rhythm. "What took you so long?"

My gaze flicks from her to the hat, widening in indignation. "It wasn't the wind at all. It was *you*."

Beau stares at me like I've grown a second head before whipping his own toward the tree, where Mila grins broader and switches mid-jingle to a truly galling Christmas hymn. "Who are you talking to?" he asks, wide-eyed. "And why—why are those bells suddenly playing 'The Friendly Beasts'?"

"Stop it, Mila." I march over to the balustrade, stretching on tiptoe to snatch the hat away from her, but it dangles just out of reach. "You're scaring him."

"You're the one talking to thin air, Célie."

"Just give me the hat!"

"*What* is going on?" Beau strides forward and seizes my hand, pulling me away from the tree limb with an alarmed expression. "And who is *Mila*? Is it—is it the tree? Is the tree named Mila?"

Sighing, I wrench my hand away and glare at the ghost in question. "No, the tree is not named *Mila*," I snap. "The name belongs to Michal's dead sister, Mila Vasiliev, and if she doesn't stop jingling that hat, I might have to kill her all over again."

Beau blinks. "Excuse me?"

"You asked to whom I'm talking—her name is Mila, and the Necromancer killed her several months ago." His eyes threaten to pop out of his head now, but I ignore him, crossing my arms and giving myself a vicious mental shake. Because Mila's rendition of "The Friendly Beasts" matters even less than Beau's ridiculous hat. We're *supposed* to be acting like I needed a moment outside to compose myself, not arguing about bells and ghosts. Lowering my voice, I ask Mila, "Have you seen . . . anyone yet?"

Her grin fades, and she stops playing the bells at once. "More than one, unfortunately. I hope Michal is prepared to give his little warning teeth, because over a hundred creatures have arrived in Requiem tonight—dozens of blood witches included—and any one of them could be our necromancer."

"Are you *sure* about that?" Guinevere's horribly familiar voice precedes her from the ballroom, and together, we turn just as she drifts through the mahogany doors to join us. I endeavor not to groan. "I thought you said the Necromancer was a *male* blood witch. That narrows the candidates quite a bit, Mila darling."

Ghosts, I decide, will be the death of me.

Though I hastily open my mouth to tell her to *go away*, I change my mind at once—because who am I to turn down information? Without it, Beau and I can do nothing but sit here and wait for the worst. "Approximately how many of them have you seen, Guinevere? Are any in the castle?"

"Guinevere?" Beau asks faintly.

Her eyes light upon him then, and they spark with gleeful interest. "Hold on a moment. Who is *this*?"

Oh no.

Before I can answer, she darts forward—right into his personal space—and slants her head, studying him from the tips of his black hair to the soles of his leather boots. Even his costume doesn't deter her. If anything, it seems to add to the attraction; with a noise of appreciation, she strokes a finger down his spangled sleeve. "This," she says, "is a welcome development."

I swat her hand away as Beau recoils from the cold, invisible touch. "Don't even think about it, Guin."

Exhaling sharply, Beau backs toward the doors and drags me along with him. "Célie, darling, you seem to be feeling *much* better.

Perhaps the two of us should return to the party and—"

His hand tightens on my elbow, and in his dark eyes, I finally see the floating, pearlescent forms of Mila and Guinevere reflected back at me. "Holy fucking Hell," he breathes, pointing a shaking finger. "They're—Célie, they're—"

"Ghosts," I finish in resignation. "If it helps, you can only see them because you're touching me. The instant Guinevere oversteps"—I shoot her a pointed look—"you can let go, and you never need to see her again."

Scoffing, Guinevere floats around us in a circle. "Now why on *earth* would he want to do that?" To Beau, she purrs, "Guinevere de Mimsy, at your service. No need to ask who *you* are, of course. Even forced into a clown suit, one could never mistake those tousled waves and that chiseled jaw for anything other than nobility."

Though Beau gawks at her, incredulous, he cannot help but mutter, "Royalty."

If she could, Guinevere would surely bounce on tiptoe at the news, but her incorporeal form forces her to swell three times her size instead. "Your *Majesty*." She clutches a hand to her chest. "How *honored* I am to meet you."

With an air of impatience, Mila shoots forward, plucking a velvet box from the depths of Beau's breast pocket. I didn't notice it before, and even Beau startles slightly as she waves it under Guinevere's nose. "Do you know what this is, Guin?" She plunges on before Guinevere can answer. "*This* is all the incentive you need to leave the poor man alone." Flicking it open, she reveals a gold ring with a magnificent ruby centerpiece. It sparkles so brightly, so *beautifully*, that I gasp and seize it from her, examining it from every direction in the moonlight.

"Is this—?" I whirl to face Beau, and now it's *my* turn to bounce on tiptoe, an enormous smile splitting my face in two. "Beauregard Lyon, is this an *engagement* ring?"

He snatches it away, hastily checking for damage before tucking it into his pocket once more. Sheepish now, he says, "It might be."

"Ask him how he intended to propose. You can tell a lot about a man by how he chooses to propose." Drifting away from us, Guinevere lifts her pert nose in the air, and I realize Beau dropped my elbow in his haste to retrieve the ring. If possible, I grin even wider in realization. He planned to propose to Coco on her *birthday*, and that—that must be why he's been acting so churlish tonight. He wanted to make the evening special. He wanted to make it theirs. The whole thing is so ridiculously romantic that I might cry all over again, except I wouldn't be pretending this time. Because—

The warmth in my chest cools in an icy blast of wind.

Because he didn't get to do it. Despite his grand plans, he missed her birthday; because of *me*, he missed his chance.

"Oh." The word leaves me in a painful breath, and I clutch my elbows, shivering again in the cold. Though the rational part of my mind knows this isn't my fault—I didn't ask the Necromancer to target me—I still feel somehow responsible. "I'm so sorry, Beau."

He waves a hand without looking at me. "Don't be. Really, you—you probably saved me a great embarrassment. Coco has never been the sentimental type."

"She would've said yes," I say firmly. "She *will* say yes."

Though he shrugs, he says nothing else, and if the Necromancer *is* somewhere listening, I hope he feels like complete and utter *refuse* for wreaking such havoc on our lives.

And . . . well . . . ending several others.

Guinevere heaves a dramatic sigh in the silence. "A paramour of *mine* once proposed in the putrid alley behind a tavern, right there in the middle of his sick."

"That," Mila says, "is disgusting."

"Yes. Quite." Guinevere cuts Beau an arch look from the corner of her eye. "I left him for his brother the next morning."

Though Beau can no longer see or hear them, he seems to realize the conversation has carried on without him—and *about* him. Dragging a weary hand through his hair, he speaks in a low murmur. "Seriously, Célie, I think it's time to go back inside. If the Necromancer was going to attack, he would've done it by now, and—"

The bells on his hat jingle again.

Brows furrowing, I glance between Mila and Guin, but neither of them floats anywhere near the tree. The air, too, has fallen unnaturally still and silent. *Odd.* "Did either of you—?" I start to ask, but Mila shakes her head.

"It must've been the wind," she whispers, but the hair on my neck lifts regardless. Mila is a ghost. She has no reason to whisper, no reason to fear. No one can even hear her except for me and Guinevere, who frowns and peers below the balcony to investigate.

Her eyes fly wide. Whirling back to face me, she says, "Célie, *run*—"

But it's too late. Long fingers appear on the balustrade, and before Beau and I can do anything but stumble backward—clutching each other—a pale figure slides over the parapet and onto the balcony with lethal grace. My mouth falls open, and shock jolts through my body like an injection of hemlock, rooting me to the spot. Because it isn't the Necromancer who smiles at me now, her dove-gray gown flecked with bits of starlight.

It's Priscille.

CHAPTER FORTY-EIGHT

The King and His Court

"Bonjour, humaine," she says, smoothing her gossamer bodice. Before Beau and I can turn, can *run*, Juliet seizes me from behind, while another, unfamiliar vampire wrenches Beau's arms behind his back, drags his nose down the column of Beau's neck. Though Beau thrashes against him, his strength is nothing to that of a vampire, and this one presses his teeth against Beau's jugular until the king of Belterra stills, closing his eyes and holding his breath.

"Leave him alone—" Snarling, I strain toward them, but Juliet wraps a cold hand around my own throat.

"I wouldn't worry about your friend," she murmurs in my ear. "Not when your blood tastes sweetest."

Instinctively, I launch myself back through the veil before she notices Mila or Guinevere. Judging from the cold, crystalline glint in Priscille's eyes, these vampires are out for blood—*my* blood. Yannick's words from the aviary flit through me like tiny knives: *I will not be quick.* If either Juliet or Priscille realize I can see the dead, can communicate with them, who knows what else they'll do?

"You don't have to hurt us." Juliet's hand nearly crushes my throat as I swallow, searching for any sign of Michal. He should be here by now. My knuckles clench white around her arm, but no matter how violently I claw at her, my nails cannot pierce her skin. Abruptly, my lungs cannot draw breath. Because if Michal *could* reach me, he would, yet he isn't here. *He isn't here.* "There is still time to change your minds. You can leave, hide, never come back to this place, and pray Michal never finds you."

Priscille bares her teeth in a smile—fangs sharp, overlong—and three more vampires climb up the balcony behind her. "How fortunate that even His Majesty could not stop the enchantment around Requiem from lifting tonight," she says, mocking Michal's words with a harsh laugh. Casting a wicked, sidelong look at the vampire beside her, who shares her wild black curls, her full figure, her snarl. A brother, perhaps, or a cousin. "He could not stop our kin from joining us either, and how patiently they've waited for this moment."

I struggle uselessly against Juliet's hold, unable to reach the silver knife in my boot. I didn't prepare for this. Foolishly, *stupidly*, I didn't prepare—because it was supposed to be the Necromancer who attacked tonight, not a faction of mutinous vampires. Though I try to thrust backward, to force the silver of my gown against her chest, she holds me away from her with viselike strength. "Please," I whisper. "Michal may forgive your kin for coming to Requiem, but he won't forgive *you* if harm comes to us. Please, *please*, just let us go."

"*Michal*, she calls him," snarls Juliet, tightening her hand until the edges of my vision blur. Until I choke and gasp for breath. "He allows the human to say his name—to bring her filthy companions to our isle, our *home*—and he honors them above all others. One even wears the coat of a huntsman." When my shoulder manages to brush her arm, she snarls and tears the capelet in half, hurling the priceless garment aside. Diamonds scatter in every direction.

"A king with divided loyalties is no king at all."

The other vampires hiss their agreement.

I nearly scream in frustration. "But his loyalties *aren't* divided—"

"Would you have us plead for our king's forgiveness, humaine?"

At my helplessness, Priscille's smile grows positively lethal.

"Would you have us crawl on our knees and beg him to forget? We are *vampires*. We will not ask for permission or forgiveness from one so *weak*, and we will accept his regime no longer." Eyes blazing, chest heaving, she turns to address the others in a fit of passion. "Friends, the rule of Michal Vasiliev ends *tonight*—"

Eyes bulging, she stops abruptly, and for a split second, my mind cannot process the speed with which Michal moves to stand before her. When it does, however—when I recognize his sleek pale hair and alabaster skin—I nearly sob in relief, sagging in Juliet's arms. Though teeth marks ooze at his throat, it doesn't matter. Though one wing hangs half-torn from his back, Michal is here, unharmed, and his mere *presence* has terrified Priscille into silence.

Then I see the blood dripping from his hand, the viscera between his fingers, and realize he's ripped out her vocal cords.

Beside me, Beau gags at the sight and bends double—the vampire holding him has fled, only to be seized by Ivan, who vaults over the parapet and snaps the vampire's neck. He goes down like a sack of bricks. Choking, Priscille scrabbles at her throat and whirls, desperate to escape, to *live*, but Odessa rises to block her path. Dimitri, too, and Pasha. One by one, they debilitate the insurgent vampires in a blur of liquid movement—breaking their kneecaps, seizing their hair, dragging them toward the mahogany doors of the ballroom.

Lou, Reid, Coco, and Jean Luc climb from the limb of the oak tree several seconds later, ashen-faced and grim. None appear seriously injured—thank God—but a bruise already swells on Reid's cheek from whatever happened below; Coco bleeds from a cut on her forearm. Beau rushes toward her, and Dimitri—

His face snaps toward her too. Toward her *blood*. For just an instant, his eyes gleam feral, but Pasha snarls, shoving him through the doors and out of sight.

Leaving Juliet with her hand around my throat.

"Let her go," Michal growls.

Though he approaches slowly, carefully, to where Juliet has pulled us against the balustrade, her entire body tenses, and something seems to snap within her. With a snarl, she attempts to sink her teeth into my jugular. *Too slow.* Michal descends in an instant—eyes flashing with rage—and seizes her by the throat too, pushing me aside with his other hand. I spin wildly toward Jean Luc, who catches me against his chest. Instead of ripping out her vocal cords like he did with Priscille, however, Michal smashes through the doors to the ballroom.

He nearly flies as he ascends the dais with Juliet in tow.

We all bolt after him—Beau and me stumbling slightly—to find the entire room has gone silent.

Except for Juliet. She still writhes and kicks, hissing and spitting and tearing at his hand, which he uses to hold her aloft by the throat. Despite her struggle, he doesn't release her. He doesn't even flinch. Expression cold and cruel—eyes wholly inhuman—he addresses the room in a whisper. "There are some among you who question my strength."

Pasha, Ivan, Dimitri, and Odessa form a sort of barricade

around Juliet's debilitated companions. When one struggles to rise, his knees healing, Pasha shatters his tibia, and the vampire screams in pain. Priscille's relation still snaps his teeth at me, eyes burning with hatred, until Dimitri wrenches the fangs from his mouth by force. Blood spatters the obsidian floor, and I look away hastily, edging closer to Coco and Beau, whose stricken expression mirrors my own. Somehow, this feels so much worse than Yannick in the aviary. This feels like an exhibition, a *performance*, except the actors and actresses crawl and bleed upon the ground instead of sweeping across the stage. Unbidden, my gaze creeps back to Priscille and her torn-open throat.

This is—this is *sick*.

"Some of you believe I've grown too weak to rule this isle. You believe I've grown unfit, perhaps unable to protect you from the dangers beyond Requiem." A pause. "Is that what you think, Juliet?" Michal asks her softly. "Do you envision yourself as monarch? As queen? Do you think real power stems from preying upon those weaker than you?"

She bares her teeth at him in response.

"I see." Nodding to himself, Michal lifts her higher, and her feet scrabble upon the dais floor. "By all means . . . allow me to address your concerns." Raising his voice, he speaks to the entire room now. "Allow me to address *all* of your concerns and, at last, lay your petty fears to rest."

With the simple flick of his wrist, he parts Juliet's head from her shoulders, and her entire body shrivels, desiccating to bone, before he drops it to the floor with a muted *thud*. I stare at her corpse, unable to blink. Unable to *think*. Every thought empties from my head until only Michal remains. Standing above her, he stares at his people with an expression so foreign, so *empty*, that I cannot look at him either.

"Holy hell," Beau whispers, and I follow his gaze to the crowd.

I don't know what I expected—for the vampires to shriek, perhaps, or hiss as Priscille now hisses. Perhaps I thought they would scatter in fear at such a display of dominion, or else rush the dais to attack. They outnumber us, after all. They could do it.

Nothing, however, could've prepared me for the relish in their eyes as they gaze upon Michal now.

Murmuring eagerly, they part to form a crude sort of circle in the middle of the ballroom, and—when the imprisoned vampires begin to thrash in terror—cold dread whispers a warning down my spine. The circle they're forming—it looks like a pit. A *cage*. Incredulous, I step toward Michal, but both Beau and Coco seize the back of my gown, and Lou moves her head in a slow, nauseated shake. "This isn't meant for us, Célie."

Reid nods gravely. "We should go."

But we can't just *go*—I look between them in desperation—because the Necromancer is still out there. Despite all our careful planning, he didn't come, and I still almost died at the hands of vengeful vampires. I just—I don't understand this place. My throat constricts as the full ramifications of the evening catch up with me. *The Necromancer didn't come.* He didn't *come*, and how—how am I going to sleep tonight? My breath comes in short, painful bursts. How am I going to *live* if the Necromancer could be lurking around every corner? He could be hiding in my room even now, and if he isn't, it could be Monsieur Dupont instead. It could be Ivan or Pasha or even Dimitri. Bile rises in my throat at the thought of them—lurking in the shadows, waiting—and unbidden, I glance back toward Michal.

Juliet's blood still stains his hand.

She would've killed me. They *all* would've killed me in a brutal and gruesome fashion if Michal hadn't intervened. What else could he have done except strike back and strike true? What else could *I* have done to prevent it?

No.

Shaking my head, I back into Lou, into Reid, into Coco and Beau and even Jean Luc, and at the movement, Michal's eyes flick to mine. An unspoken question stirs within them. I cannot give him the answer he craves, however; I cannot do this any longer, cannot abide such *violence.* Does he truly think I could ever live in such a place? Does he truly think I could survive it?

Lou squeezes my hand in silent comfort, but even her presence does little to reassure me now. When Odessa appears beside us, seizing my other hand, Michal clears his throat upon the dais. "The revelry has officially ended," he says. "Leave this place, and do not return." Jerking his head toward Pasha and Ivan, he says, "Do with them as you please."

He turns on his heel and disappears through a nondescript door in the wall behind. Odessa pulls more insistently on my hand—whispering for me to hurry, *hurry*—as Pasha and Ivan haul the imprisoned vampires to their feet. As they drag their prone bodies into the center of the pit.

"Célie, *move*—"

Forceful now, Odessa whisks me onto the balcony, down the tree, and into the courtyard below—but not before I hear the screams.

CHAPTER FORTY-NINE

Spilled Tea

A large fire crackles in my room, where Lou, Coco, and I curl up in the squashy armchairs by the hearth, steaming cups of lemon tea in our hands. The clock on the mantel reads three o'clock in the morning. We changed out of our costumes immediately upon entering, and a knock followed shortly after. Ivan and Pasha stood in the corridor, scowling with the tray of tea before shoving it at us and explaining they'd be guarding our door tonight.

I stare numbly at the wall of books now. Rows upon rows of cracked spines. Beside me, Lou shares a seat with Coco, leaning her head upon her shoulder and sprawling her legs across the arm of their chair. The silver ribbon Michal gave me dangles loosely between my fingers as I read each title.

Adventures of Od, Bodrick, and Flem.

Briar and Bean.

Sister Wren.

Clearly the fairy-tale section. I almost laugh at the irony. Almost. Only hours ago, I thought vampires capable of living within the pages of one of these books, sailing to secret islets with baskets of roses and bottles of blood, but those bottles of blood must come from *somewhere*.

How very stupid I've been.

Michal's swift execution of Yannick and the others led me to

believe their deaths brought him little pleasure, but tonight—
tonight he proved differently. Tonight he was calculated, cruel,
borderline sadistic for the approval of his people. The thought
brings sharp, unexpected pain until I focus again on the titles.
On the faded golden letters. Anything to forget the memory of
Michal's scarlet-stained hand. Of Priscille's earsplitting screams.

How Doth the Little Rose.

The Winter Queen and Her Palace.

My eyes linger on the last—an ivory, cloth-covered spine
with peeling letters. I recognize this book. We owned a copy of
it ourselves, and for years, it sat in a place of pride atop Filippa's bedside table. She read it to me every night, the tale of the
ice queen Frostine, who fell in love with a prince of summer. He
would ride his sunlit carriage past her palace every year, melting
the snow and ice, and she hated him fiercely for it—until one year,
she found a stem of snowdrops placed upon her doorstep. Furious, she crushed the white petals beneath her boot. The next year,
however, she found a whole carpet of them across her garden, and
because she could not crush them all, she had no choice but to fall
in love with the prince instead.

It was a ridiculous story.

Later, Filippa would tell me so herself. But what would *she*
think of all this, I wonder? What would she do? Would she warn
me to flee far and flee fast from Requiem and its darkness, or
would she urge me to reconsider? She fell in love with the Necromancer, after all. Perhaps—to her—Juliet and the others would've
deserved their fate. My fingers curl tighter around my cup as I
search blindly for another section to read. *Any* other section to
read. Horticulture, perhaps, or human anatomy—

"This is an . . . interesting room." Lou follows my gaze to the bookshelf before turning in her chair, craning her neck to look up at the mezzanine. She tilts her cup to a portrait of a particularly severe-looking woman with withered skin and a wart on her nose. "That one looks an *awful* lot like my Crone form—or, I suppose, my great-grandmother's Crone form. I haven't posed for a portrait myself, but I'm almost positive those are the same chin hairs." When I refuse to laugh, to muster any sort of reaction at all, she adds, "Legend claims she liked them so much that she commissioned thirty-seven portraits of herself as the Crone and strung them all throughout Chateau le Blanc. Thirty-six are still there. After she died, my grandmother shoved all of them into a single room, and I accidentally stumbled into it one night." She feigns a shudder. "I had nightmares for a *week*."

When I still don't answer, Coco sighs and says, "They would've killed you, Célie."

I stare hard at *The Mythology of Plants*. "I know."

The three of us lapse into silence again—albeit a tense one—until Lou shakes her head in my periphery, setting her jaw in an obstinate line. "They *did* try to kill you, and if Michal hadn't been there, I wouldn't have hesitated either." She leans forward in her seat. "I might've chosen a different method, yes, but I would've killed them all the same."

When I continue to stare at the bookshelf, unable to respond, she hooks her foot beneath the leg of my chair and spins me toward them. "Jean Luc wasn't the only one mad with grief, you know," she says. "When you never turned up at my house, we thought you'd been killed. We thought we'd find your body in the Doleur the next morning—floating right there with all the dead fish."

Coco looks away swiftly, her eyes tight.

Glancing at her, Lou continues, "And then when we received your note—"

"How could you ask us not to come for you?" Coco asks in a low, strained voice. "How could you think we'd leave you here to die?"

I stare between their hurt expressions, stricken. "I never meant—I didn't think—"

"No, you didn't." Lou sighs and places her half-drunk cup of tea upon the table. "Look, we aren't blaming you for what happened— truly, we aren't—but do you really think so little of us?"

"Of course I don't." Leaning forward anxiously, I too place my cup upon the table, unable to articulate the incredulity rising in my chest. I—I need to fix this somehow. I need to *explain*.

"Michal—he wanted to *kill* you, and I was just trying to—"

"Protect us?" Arching a brow, Lou cuts Coco a sideways glance. "That sounds vaguely familiar, doesn't it?"

My chest tightens at the implication, and I lurch to my feet, striding past them toward the fireplace. When I reach it, however, I pivot on my heel and move toward the bookshelf instead. "That—that isn't fair. Jean Luc treats me like I'm made of glass, and when I'm with him, I start to believe it too."

"You've never been made of glass, Célie." I can feel the intensity of Lou's gaze on my back, and—unable to stand it—I turn to face her once more. "From what I can tell, you've befriended vampires and ghosts, infiltrated an enchanted brothel, and single-handedly exposed a necromancy plot since you came to Requiem. Before that, you incapacitated one of the most evil women alive, took oaths to become the first female Chasseur, and survived a horrific and impossibly violent abduction. Who cares if you cry on occasion? Who cares if you still have nightmares?" She shakes her head. "You may feel like a different person now, but that doesn't mean you were ever less. It doesn't mean you were ever weak."

Coco nods vehemently, still clutching her cup to her chest. "We all do our best with the hands we're dealt."

A pause.

"Is different . . . bad?" I ask them quietly.

To my shock, they both regard me with something that looks like pride. It isn't condescending, however, as I feared it might be. No, it's pure, and it's fierce. It's—it's *real*.

Grinning at whatever she sees in my expression, Lou pats the chair beside them once more. "Of course it isn't bad. You've changed your cards, that's all. You're the one holding the deck now, and the rest of us need to fall into suit."

"Speaking of *suits*"—Coco's mouth twitches into a smirk—"did you notice Reid's tonight? It looked like it belonged to a giant."

Lou cackles and sprawls across the seat once more. "At least it didn't have *bells*. Just wait until Yule—I'm going to have an exact replica of Beau's costume made and gift it to him in front of his mother. She'll insist he try it on for us."

Tentatively, I return to my seat, reaching for my cup of tea and inhaling deeply. *Still warm.* "Jean Luc will be fine, Célie," Coco adds after another moment, as if returning to a conversation left unfinished. "I know it seems hopeless right now, but he'll be fine. Regardless of what he says about a house with an orange tree, you didn't steal his future. He still has his position, and even if you'd moved into that house with him, even if you'd squeezed those oranges, Saint-Cécile would've always been his home. He loves it there—and he should. He's worked harder than anyone to change his own hand."

"Don't steal my metaphor," Lou says.

That familiar longing fills my chest as I watch them together, as I think of that house with the orange tree. It would've been so easy, so perfect, if I'd fit with Jean Luc. I could've lived right there alongside Lou and Reid, Coco and Beau. Though she doesn't know it, an enormous ruby will soon sparkle on Coco's finger—because even though they're different, even though their road together will be long and difficult, Coco and Beau love each other. They *choose* each other. "I can't go back to Chasseur Tower," I say softly. "I won't."

"We know." Lou's grin turns rather wistful as she hooks my chair again, pulling me closer—closer still—until our wooden legs bump together. "But you shouldn't worry about that either. You opened the door for about a dozen new initiates to follow behind you—and all of them women, by the way." Without warning, her hand shoots out and catches my wrist, pulling me into their chair and spilling tea across all of us. Cackling, she says, "One of them knocked Reid on his *ass* the other day in the training yard. It was glorious. I think her name is Brigitte."

"It was the first time Jean Luc smiled since you've been gone," Coco adds, happily dumping the rest of her tea in Lou's lap. When I yelp and shift away, she happily dumps it on mine too. "He won't be sad forever, Célie."

"You won't be sad forever either." Lou glances at the silver ribbon still clutched in my free hand. If she notices that I've removed the emerald ribbon from my wrist, she doesn't say. "That's pretty." She plucks at its tail. "Useful, too, if tonight is any indication."

"We certainly aren't in Cesarine anymore," Coco says, her smile fading. "Though this place seems about as twisted as the castle. Last week, Beau swore the shadows in our bedchamber *whispered* to us, and the evening before, the entire southern hedge maze just . . . died. Every leaf withered to ash right in front of his little sister."

"Melisandre has been acting odd too." Lou heaves a forlorn sigh. "She won't eat, and she hardly sleeps."

"Cats are guardians of the dead," I murmur. "They've been drawn to Requiem since the Necromancer's first experiment."

My gaze falls to the ribbon, and the tea on my nightgown abruptly feels colder than before. I haven't seen Michal since . . . since the execution, and I don't know what I'll say to him when I do. What *can* I say? The violence I witnessed tonight—already, I know I can never unsee it. It'll live in my memory for the rest of my life. "I don't think I can stay here either."

Lou's gaze remains sure and steady as she takes the ribbon, brushing my hair to one side before carefully tying it around the heavy strands. "Why not?"

"Because this *place*—it—how can anyone live alongside such cruelty without it changing them?"

Lou and Coco share a long, inscrutable look. It's a look I don't understand, perhaps *can't* understand, and more than anything else, it solidifies my decision. Because I never want to understand that look. I never want to know what it's like to live in a world like this one—a world where blood is currency and only the strongest survive.

"I don't know," Lou says at last. "Only one person can answer that, I think, and I get the impression you don't want to ask him.

You're welcome anytime in Cesarine, however. My house is always open."

"As is the castle," Coco says. "Beau and I would treat you like royalty."

Unable to help herself, Lou's eyes glitter with mischief. "But Chateau le Blanc *is* lovelier this time of year—"

"Have you visited Beau's summer palace in Amandine? The entire place is *covered* in roses—"

I force a laugh before the two can seize my arms and engage in a full-blown match of tug-of-war. "I do have one question, though." When they both turn to me, expectant, I ask, "How did you know sunlight harms vampires? And about compulsion? I never mentioned either in my note."

"Oh." Lou brightens, and with the flick of her wrist, the shutters on the windows of the mezzanine shudder slightly before bursting open. When a three-eyed crow swoops down from the eave, *tap, tap, tap*ping on the window, Lou opens it with another flick. The bird soars into the room and lands on her outstretched hand. "Meet my little spy, Talon. As it turns out, he followed me to Brindelle Park on the night of your abduction, and he followed *you* onto that wretched ship. He wanted to help, I think." She strokes his beak, and he closes his eyes in lazy appreciation. "A repulsive man by the name of Gaston locked him in a cage before he could fly back to me, however. When you freed him, he delivered more to us than just your note. Did you not know?" She eyes me curiously. "The three-eyed crow is a symbol of the le Blanc family line."

Setting my empty cup aside, I yawn and join Lou in stroking the bird's beak. "It's nice to meet you, Talon. And—thank you."

Above his head, I meet Lou's and Coco's eyes too. "*All* of you."

The bird pecks at my fingers before flying up to perch on the chandelier.

"You should rest." Coco also rises, gathering our cups and setting them on the mantel, stifling a yawn of her own. "If the Necromancer shows his face tonight, I will personally carve it to ribbons."

Lou waves her hand, and the window shuts once more, the shutters snapping back into place. They lock with a series of comforting clicks. Then she leaps up and pulls a carpet bag from beneath her chair, extracting a supple piece of leather from within. With a wink, she hands it to me. "Just in case."

"What . . . is it?"

"It's a thigh sheath, Célie. Everyone should have one."

Coco chuckles. "Here we go."

"I refuse to apologize. Show me a person who looks *less* attractive in a thigh sheath, and we'll talk." Settling back into her chair, she motions toward the bed. "You two go on. Talon and I will keep first watch."

Pulling the blankets over her head, Coco falls asleep almost immediately, but—despite my exhaustion—I lie awake for a long while. Long enough to watch Lou's head eventually droop, to watch the book in her hand slide to the rug. Long enough to watch the fire in the hearth burn down to embers. Talon's eyes, however, remain bright and sharp in the firelight.

They would've killed you, Célie.

I roll over to my side, restless and shivering. Each time I close my eyes, the image of Priscille's face flashes through my subconscious, and the sound of her screams echoes as the vampires tear her limb from limb. Filippa's locket presses into my throat as I turn again, burrowing deeper under the blankets. Trying to forget. Part of me wonders where the Necromancer is right this very moment, while another dreads ever leaving this room.

Dread.

That's what this is.

Rolling toward the fireplace, I slip through the veil on pure instinct, and—just as I hoped—Mila sits in the chair opposite Lou. Though I say nothing, she seems to sense my presence; eyes unusually strained, grave, she looks at me and says, "Your friends are right, you know. The vampires wouldn't have stopped until they killed you."

Unwilling to wake Lou and Coco, I nod.

"Go to sleep, Célie." With a mournful smile, Mila drifts to where Talon perches by the tea set. "You look like death."

As if waiting for permission all along, I slip into fitful sleep.

That night, I dream of roses—dozens of them covered in frost, each petal slowly turning blue. My breath, too, condenses into little clouds of snow as I swing the picnic basket from my elbow, descending the stone steps to Michal's bedroom. Inside the lovely wicker, ice creeps up the glass of two bottles. It paints their faces white, opaque, and crystallizes the scarlet liquid within. Plucking a rose from the basket, I tuck the dying flower into my hair.

I must look my best for the garden party.

A peculiar white light shines from the islet in the middle of the grotto, sparkling upon the dark water, the specks of mica in the cavern walls. At the sight of it, I feel a gentle tug behind my navel, and I cannot help but drift closer, each footstep leaving splintered ice upon the ground. Michal never mentioned witchlight in the fairy tale.

Perhaps he already waits for me there.

When something shifts behind me, I glance toward the bed in the center of the room. A pale figure twists and turns within it, his breathing short and fitful, as the muted emerald blanket tangles around his hips. I tilt my head, curious. Because I've never seen Michal sleep before. I never realized vampires *could* sleep, but of course, if they can breathe, if they can *eat*, it makes sense they can also dream. Ignoring the insistent pull in my stomach, I clutch the basket to my chest and creep closer—except the basket has vanished, and the roses, and the blood, leaving me to clutch at thin air instead. I stare down at my palms in confusion. *Odd.*

Michal soon fists the sheet in his hand, however, and rolls toward me with a muttered, "Célie."

I startle at the sound—tearing my gaze from my own hands—to find him clenching his eyes shut as if in pain. Though the bite marks at his throat have healed, smoothing into perfect alabaster, his breath remains shallow. His body tense. As earlier, he wears no shirt, baring the whole of his chest, his shoulders, his back.

And he is beautiful.

I don't know how long I stand there, staring at him, *aching* for him, yet here—in this strange dreamland—I can finally admit that I'll never look enough. I'll never drink my fill of this man, and part of me will always wonder. Part of me will always mourn.

Part of me will always miss him.

When I brush a lock of hair from his forehead, he shudders, and tiny crystals of ice appear where I touch his skin. Turning away, I sigh, and snowflakes drift upon the air. The pull in my stomach grows more insistent now, almost impatient, as I approach the shore once more. The light on the islet still sparkles innocently, and the longer I look at it, the brighter and brighter it glows. Indeed, a tendril of warmth seems to crack through the ice in the grotto, wrapping around my wrists and luring me closer—*closer*—until I float across the waves.

It takes several seconds to recognize the fluttering sensation in my chest, to hear the fervent pounding of my heart.

It smells like summer honey.

"Célie." A panicked Mila shoots up from the water to block my path, her eyes wild and her hands lifted between us. "You need to wake up now."

"Why?" Instead of gliding around her, I flow straight through her, my own eyes fixed eagerly upon the brilliant white light. Instinctively, I know it isn't witchlight. No, this is something else, something comfortable and familiar—like returning home after a long journey—and I cannot fight this *pull* in my stomach. Helpless against it, I say breathlessly, "Mila, I think it might be—"

"No, it isn't." Mila tries and fails to seize my hand, to prevent me from going any farther. "No matter how it looks, how it *feels*, this isn't your sister, Célie. This isn't her."

But I need to know. Whatever shines light upon that islet, I *need* to see it more than I've ever needed anything in my entire life. Without another word, I rush past her toward the rocky shore, and soon two glass coffins materialize within the brilliant halo of light. My mouth parts as we draw level with them. My vision narrows.

Because Mila is wrong.

One of the coffins stands empty, and one holds the half-disfigured corpse of Filippa.

CHAPTER FIFTY

The Necromancer

When my eyes snap open, I leap from the bed, panicked and disoriented, and almost lose my footing in the semidarkness. The embers of the fire still smolder gently, illuminating Lou sprawled across the same squashy armchair. Behind me, Coco fills the room with soft snores. *Thank God.* Exhaling a shaky breath, I lift a finger to my lips as Talon shifts on the mantel, blinking his beady eyes at me.

"Shhh," I whisper to him. "I just—I need to talk to Michal."

Though he clicks his beak in disapproval, I tiptoe up the stairs regardless, not pausing to don a robe and slippers. I don't want to wake Lou and Coco. This could be nothing, after all—just a nightmare—and the last thing we need is another false alarm. My heart still threatens to palpitate, however, as I push open the door and step into the corridor.

"What are you doing?" Pasha's harsh voice immediately greets me, and I whirl, clutching my chest and biting back a scream. His glare turns accusatory as he crosses his arms, as Ivan closes in behind me. Candlelight casts their faces in soft, flickering shadow. "You shouldn't be out here, casse-couille. It's almost sunrise."

I take a step backward and collide with Ivan's chest. "I n-need to see Michal. It's urgent."

He chuckles, but the sound lacks all good humor. It doesn't

even sound human. "Define urgent."

"Please—"

"Célie?" Michal himself stalks up the corridor then, seeming to materialize from the darkness, and I nearly weep with relief at the sight of his frown. His pale hair appears tousled, as does his shirt, like he pulled it over his head in a hurry. "What happened? I thought I felt—"

"*Michal.*" Ducking around Ivan, I race to meet him, wringing my hands and trying to tell him everything at once. "I think I crossed the veil in my sleep, or—or maybe not—and I saw, well— it could've just been a dream, but—"

His black eyes search mine intently, and he catches my hands in his own. "Slow down. *Breathe.*"

"Right." I nod fervently and squeeze his fingers, struggling to ground myself in the corridor. In *this* moment and *this* reality. "It started as a dream, but everything was cold—unnaturally cold, just like when I cross the veil. And I think—I think I was inviting you to a garden party, but when I came to your room, there was this *light.*"

"You were in my room?" he asks, voice sharp.

I shrug helplessly. "I don't know. I think maybe I was, but like I said, it could've been a—"

"It wasn't." Shaking his head curtly, he glances over my shoulder at Pasha and Ivan. His jaw hardens, and he leads me down the corridor and around a corner, down another set of stairs, away from their prying eyes and ears. "Or at least, it wasn't *just* a dream. I felt you there. You"—he releases a harsh, incredulous breath— "touched my face."

I stare up at him in horror as silence descends between us.

Because I *did* touch his face, and if he felt it—if he felt *me*— "But it was a garden party," I whisper. "There were roses and bottles of blood—"

"It might've started as a dream, but it didn't end there. It sounds like some sort of astral projection. Have you ever crossed the veil in your sleep before?"

"Astral projection?" I repeat faintly. "I don't—Michal, I don't know what that is—I don't know what any of *this* is—but the roses and blood vanished when I saw you. The dream became sharper somehow, and there was this *light* in the middle of the grotto."

"You must've woken up." His brow furrows, and I can practically *see* the gears turning in his mind. He doesn't understand this any more than I do. "What happened after you saw this light?"

"I followed it out to the islet. I sort of—floated across the water, and Mila was there." My hands tighten around his, and my eyes widen as the full scope of the scene returns in a wave of terror: my sister's supine body, her peaceful expression, the hands crossed gracefully upon her chest. And the stitches. Bile surges at the memory, and I choke on it, unable to accept their existence— unable to accept that the Necromancer, that he— "We have to go back to the islet." Pulling on his hands, I search desperately for any sign of his obsidian study doors, the suit of armor or the family tree. "The Necromancer is *here*, Michal. He brought my sister's corpse to Requiem, and he hid it—hid *her*—in the cavern by your bedroom. We have to go there. We have to—to help her somehow—"

Even as I say the words, I realize how ridiculous they sound. Because how can we *help* my dead sister? How can she be here at all? Her body burned in the catacombs with all the others, and even before Coco's Hellfire—there was nothing *peaceful* about Filippa's face the last time I saw her. For Christ's sake, half of it was *missing*. That her body could be here on Requiem is impossible, unthinkable, the sickest of all traps the Necromancer could've laid. And if it wasn't a dream, it most certainly *is* a trap. The same grim realization spreads through Michal's eyes as we stare at each other.

Before he even opens his mouth, despair punches through me like a knife—because of course I can't ask him to put himself at risk; I shouldn't even go *myself*, yet the thought of leaving Filippa's body in the hands of the Necromancer makes me physically ill. Already, he has desecrated her. What else does he plan to do?

Michal exhales slowly, and the force of his gaze would knock me backward if he didn't still hold my hands. "This could be dangerous," he says.

"I know."

"It could be a trap. Your sister might not be here at all. The Necromancer could have slipped into your mind somehow and altered your perception. He could do much worse with witchcraft."

"She's my sister, Michal." I choke on the words, swallowing bile and remembering Filippa's own words from so very long ago. *I'll never let the witches get you. Never.* We couldn't have known what the promise would cost us, but even then—at twelve years old—she meant it. She would've never left me to the Necromancer. Not even dead. "But if you're right—if she isn't here, and this is all an elaborate ruse—I need to make sure. I need to *know*."

"But *why*?" His eyes dart between mine in a desperate bid to understand. "Why risk it at all? Your sister is dead, Célie, and the

Necromancer can't resurrect her without your blood. If you go down there, you could be playing right into his hands. Unless"— he lowers his voice—"you *want* him to resurrect her?"

I stare at him in shock. In disbelief. Then, wrenching my hands away— "Of course I don't want him to resurrect her! How could you even *think* that?"

"I had to ask—"

"You didn't, but if you saw what I saw—if you *knew* what he's done to her body—" But of course Michal doesn't understand. I hardly understand myself. The risks should far outweigh the reward, yet the thought of the Necromancer keeping my sister's corpse, mutilating it, is just as intolerable as him resurrecting her. "He can't have her," I say with ringing finality.

"Fine." Michal speaks through his teeth with forced restraint, glancing up the stairs we just descended. For all I know, Pasha and Ivan could be listening beyond them, waiting for Michal's instruction. "Then allow *me* to go and retrieve—"

"You aren't going anywhere without me. *I* am the bait, remember? Our trap on the balcony didn't work, but *his*—we can use it to our advantage, Michal. We know where the Necromancer will be, and we know what he wants. If go together, we have a greater chance of capturing him than ever before."

"But the others—"

"Who knows what spies the Necromancer has in the castle now?" I throw my hands up in frustration—in *panic*—because he still doesn't understand. My palms have grown damp with sweat now, as cold as the stone around us. They shine pale and bright in the torchlight. "If we alert the others, he might flee. He might take my sister and vanish into thin air, and who knows when he'll next try again? Who knows what else he'll *do* to her? I refuse to wait another week, another day, another moment to stop him. After Pip and . . . and Mila . . . and . . ."

"You." Michal clamps his teeth together, flexing his jaw in thinly veiled patience. "He won't stop hunting *you* until you're dead. Do you understand that? Do you understand how this might end if we aren't clever?" When I glare at him, resolute, he catches my hand once more, stroking my fingers as if trying to collect himself. To *calm* himself. "You're determined to do this, aren't you?" When I nod, he shakes his head and says, "Do you have a weapon in that nightgown, at least?"

I hitch my skirt up without hesitation, revealing the silver knife at my thigh. "Courtesy of Louise le Blanc."

"Remind me to thank her." With a low curse, he brushes a swift, hard kiss upon my forehead. "Promise me that you'll stay close, and you'll listen to everything I say."

A frantic nod. "Of course."

"I mean it, Célie. If we do this, we do it together."

Together. Though the word itself solves nothing, it sounds inexplicably like hope, like a promise, and I squeeze his hand in response, breathless with it. "I swear."

We stare at each other for another long moment. Then—"Close your eyes," he says, and cool air rushes through my hair as I oblige.

When I open them again a moment later, we stand on the shore of the islet.

Though moonlight shines from the far end of the cavern, otherwise, the entire grotto lies dark and silent. Even the waves have fallen calm tonight, lapping gently against Michal's boots.

The peculiar white light has gone.

I stumble out of his arms, unsheathing the knife from my thigh and searching the barren piece of rock. Not only has the light gone, but also the glass coffins. They've simply—vanished. Only damp, mica-flecked stone remains where they rose from the ground like pillars less than half an hour ago. "Do you have a witchlight?" I ask Michal desperately.

Without Filippa's body, this can hardly be a trap, and if this isn't a trap, perhaps—

My stomach sinks in hideous realization.

Perhaps it really was just a dream. Perhaps the Necromancer isn't here at all, and I imagined the entire thing.

Frowning, Michal pulls the stone from his pocket. I snatch it from him before I can change my mind, thrusting it toward every corner of the islet. Nothing appears in response. My shoulders slump—my heart sinks—and crestfallen, I glance back at Michal. I felt so *sure* she would be here. So absolutely *certain* what I saw in my dream was real. Or perhaps—my chin quivers now, and I clamp my teeth shut, determined not to cry—perhaps I just wanted it to be.

Because even desecrated, even stitched together by a madman, I could've seen my sister again. Just for a moment, I could've pretended she still lived.

No. I could've pretended I kept my promise.

Slowly, I lower the witchlight to my side. Because I don't know what I want anymore. I don't even know what I'm *doing* here—or why I feel such bitter disappointment that I haven't walked into a trap. "You were right," I whisper at last. "I'm sorry. She isn't—"

"Wait." Frown deepening, Michal steps farther onto the islet.

His nostrils flare. "I smell blood magic."

Blood magic.

The words crash over me like a club to the head, and I dart forward to clutch his sleeve. *Of course.* "Are you sure?"

He nods again, his eyes narrowing as he studies the air in front of us. "I've never scented it stronger."

Warily, he stretches out a hand, and instead of passing through thin air as it should, it—it thunks against something. My mouth falls open. Hastily, I too fling out a hand, and my fingers collide with cool, smooth glass. Gasping, I drag them left and right to gauge the size, the breadth, of the invisible object before me. "It's a coffin," I breathe after several seconds, my voice tinged with disbelief. "Michal, it's a *coffin.*"

He doesn't answer, and when I pull my fingers away, they're covered in blood.

As if I've uttered a magic word, the coffin materializes on a platform before me, and inside it, Pippa lies just as cold and still as ever. My heart twists, leaps, nearly cleaves in two as I gaze down at her. Even in death, her raven hair falls exactly as I remember it. Her rose lips are just as full. If not for the gruesome stitches down one side of her face, she might only be sleeping—an enchanted maiden waiting for her prince.

My bloody fingers press harder upon the glass. They further smear the strange symbol I never noticed in my dream: an eye with a line slashing through it in blood. Pure, unadulterated hatred pounds through my veins as I realize the Necromancer must've drawn it there. He must've known I'd come. "Can you help me with the lid?" I ask Michal in a low, fierce voice. The Necromancer will not have my sister, and he will not have me either. "We need to move her body before he comes back—"

A choking sound is his only answer, and I whirl, confused. The tip of a silver blade protrudes from his chest.

It takes several seconds for the sight of it to penetrate—for my mind to understand the darkness seeping across his shirt, for my eyes to widen in horrified disbelief. Though I reach for him instinctively, he staggers backward, staring down at the knife as if he doesn't understand it either. Blood spills from his mouth.

"*Michal.*"

I rush for him now, but someone seizes my nightgown from behind, wrenching it backward until I collide with someone's chest. Though I try to whirl—stabbing wildly—Babette slams my hand against Filippa's coffin, and the silver knife slips from my fingertips. It skids across the ground and knocks into a polished boot.

"I didn't want to do that," says a horribly familiar voice. "I *hoped* you would come alone."

Wrenching his Balisarda from between Michal's shoulders, wiping the blood on the blue of his pants, Frederic steps into the glow of my witchlight, and his smile is more genial than I've ever seen.

Upon his wrist, he bears the same smeared eye as the coffin, and this—*this can't be happening.* Perhaps I'm dreaming again—or—or something else, something sinister—because *Frederic* cannot be a blood witch. Because Frederic cannot be *here*, on this islet, with the hidden corpse of my sister.

"Hello, ma belle," he says fondly. "This might come as a shock, but you have no idea how much I've wanted to meet you. Properly, this time"—lifting his Balisarda, he shakes his head with what looks like *regret*—"without all the trickery. Would you believe I consider you something of a sister too?"

With a casual thrust of his hand, he pushes Michal into the water, and I watch, frozen, as the immortal, all-powerful vampire king reels backward, as he clutches his bloody chest with a desiccating hand.

Frederic must've grazed his heart.

No.

My entire body seizes at the possibility, and I can't move, can't breathe, can't stop that deathly gray from creeping up his wrist. My mind refuses to believe it. Babette still holds me fast, however, and though I lunge toward him, her grip never falters. *No. No no no no NO*—

In the next second, Michal falls backward, slipping beneath the water without another sound.

Gone.

I press against Babette's chest, staring at the spot where he used to be.

"Truth be told, I feel like I already know you. Pip was right. You have the exact same eyes." Frederic's voice—still affable, almost *warm*—reaches me as if through a long tunnel, impossible to hear. Because the water into which Michal vanished has stopped rippling. Another wave crests upon the rock. It erases every trace of him until nothing remains at all. Not even me. "It killed me to look at them every day in Chasseur Tower."

Michal is gone.

"I'm sorry, Célie," Babette murmurs.

"As am I." Sighing, Frederic clicks his tongue in sympathy before pulling a syringe from his pocket. Vaguely, I recognize it from Chasseur Tower. The healers there once experimented with hemlock as a means of incapacitating witches, but the poison never differentiated between who used magic and who did not. I used the same injection on Morgane le Blanc. "But you never should've been with someone like that, Célie. Filippa wouldn't have approved."

My gaze snaps to his at her name. "Don't talk about my sister," I snarl.

"The same stubbornness too." His gaze drifts over my face with a sense of deep longing. It lingers on my ivory skin, my emerald eyes, before he reaches out to capture a lock of my dark hair, testing it between his fingers. When I snap at his hand—unable to shove him away—the longing in his own eyes shifts, sharpens, into something altogether more harrowing. "Your eye will be the perfect match after I've brought her back."

Sharp pain pricks in my shoulder, and the entire world goes dark.

CHAPTER FIFTY-ONE

Frostine and Her Summer Prince

When I wake, I see the world through a haze of bloody scarlet.

It tinges everything—the glass coffin above me, the cavern walls beyond, the witchlight I still clutch in my hand. Though my fingers twitch around it, they feel heavier than usual, clumsier. Just like my thoughts. It takes several muddled seconds for me to remember what happened.

Filippa.

Frederic.

Michal and Babette and her—

My heart gives a slow, painful *tha-thump*.

Her injection.

Oh God. Though the hemlock still runs thick through my veins—I can almost *feel* it congealing—I force my head to turn anyway, force myself to blink, to focus on the scene around me. My hands spasm with the effort.

Someone has changed my nightgown into an ensemble of opulent scarlet lace. The matching veil is what obscures my vision now. With tremendous effort, I lift it from my eyes, pull it off and away from my hair, but the movement costs me. Weakened, my arm falls back to my side, and I'm forced to stare—defeated—into the empty face of my sister. She still lies in the glass coffin beside mine. Beyond her, Frederic sits in a lifeboat with that same smeared eye drawn on the hull; he pores over the grimoire as the boat bobs gently with the waves. An empty bowl and wickedly sharp carving knife sit beside him, while his Chasseur coat and Balisarda lie forgotten at his feet. Discarded. My heart pounds furiously at the sight of them. They were only ever a disguise, anyway. A ruse.

Come now, he once told me. *Does it not feel like you're playing dress-up?*

Adrenaline pours through me in a great wave of humiliation and fury.

Frederic is the Necromancer.

In my wildest dreams, I never would've thought it possible—not with all his talk of *honoring the cause* and *reforming the brotherhood,* but of course—my stomach clenches viciously—a Balisarda positioned him in a way nothing else could. With it, he gained access not only to Chasseur Tower but also to information about every creature in the kingdom. He would've needed that access to begin his . . . experiments, and if his purpose was always to resurrect Filippa, what better way to start than by earning the trust of his enemies? He *was* the one who found the first body, after all. In Babette's own words, the circumstances were just too neat. Too perfect.

And I . . . I've been so oblivious.

My heart continues to pump the hemlock through my body in a treacherous, brutal rhythm, but instead of further weakening me, my limbs seem to be growing stronger. Blood rushes through my ears. He probably plans to *find* my body too, identical to the others, and present it to Jean Luc before weeping alongside him at my funeral. Closed casket, of course. Just like Filippa's.

I'll never let the witches get you. Never.

My vision tunnels on his profile, and I push against the coffin lid as quietly as possible. It doesn't budge. I try again, harder this time, but the glass remains fixed all around me, resolute. *Magic,* I realize bitterly. He used the same to lure me here, to render himself and Babette and *everything* invisible. My eyes dart to the grimoire in his hands.

"Where is Babette?"

Even to my own ears, my voice rings out surprisingly strong, and Frederic lifts his head in surprise. "Well, well," he says, clearly impressed that my body has worked through the hemlock. "The princess woke much sooner than expected. Makes this rather more difficult, but if you prefer to be awake . . ."

He shrugs, snapping the grimoire shut before lifting his sleeve. A fresh cut already glistens upon his forearm, and he dips his finger into the blood there before painting the same uncanny eye onto the grimoire's cover. When he slashes a line through it, the grimoire vanishes instantly. Invisible.

"Babette," I repeat, now clutching the witchlight so hard it almost gores my palm. "Where is she?"

"With any luck, she'll be distracting your friends. I wouldn't get your hopes up too much, though. You'll be dead before they arrive." He bends to retrieve the bowl and carving knife, glancing up briefly in between. "I hope you're comfortable. I had to work with what was already on the island." A small smile. "Pip told me you needed four pillows to even close your eyes at night. A coffin pales in comparison, I'm sure."

My eyes narrow at the bizarre nostalgia in his voice. "Now that you mention it, I *would* much rather be standing, perhaps even in my own clothes, but someone has poisoned me."

"Ah." He has the decency to look vaguely rueful then, but even so, such a reaction from a murderer brings little comfort—and it makes even less sense. Judging by the *carving knife* in his hand, he hasn't experienced a sudden change of heart. "I can assure you, at least, that *I* was not the one who changed your clothes—though I did pick out the gown."

He says the words as if this is a gift. As if every young woman dreams of wearing such a beautiful and lavish gown on her deathbed. Oblivious, he leans back down for his rucksack, extracting a whetstone from its depths and dipping it into the sea.

I watch, nonplussed, as he sharpens the edge of his carving knife, wracking my thoughts for anything that could dissuade him from this *madness*. Because this Frederic—he seems different from the Frederic I knew in Chasseur Tower. Affectionate, somehow—almost exasperated—like he truly considers himself my older brother. Perhaps I can talk him out of everything. "Babette said you only used a drop of my blood on Tears Like Stars," I say quickly. "Surely you don't need to *kill* me."

"You always did do your research. Our precious *captain* never realized just how valuable that mind of yours could be." He steps from the boat with an appreciative chuckle. "I never liked you with that asshole either. You were always too good for him."

I stare at him incredulously. If I could leap from this coffin and drive that knife into his chest, I would. "You assaulted me in the training yard."

"And I apologize for that—but really, Célie, what were you doing with the Chasseurs? Did your sister not explain how *despicable* they are?" He shakes his head, and all benevolence in his expression hardens into the Frederic I've always known. His lip curls. "Time and time again I tried to prove you didn't belong, and time and time again, you resisted. It makes sense, I suppose"—he glances at the dark cavern around us—"based on the company you now keep."

All instinct to rationalize with him withers at that. "You've killed six creatures."

"And I'd kill a dozen more—a hundred, a *thousand*—to resurrect your sister. Which is why," he says fiercely, drawing to a halt beside Filippa's coffin, "she'll receive *all* of your blood instead of a drop. As I'm sure you know from your little romp in Les Abysses, the spell calls only for *Blood of Death*. Not very specific, that, and I don't think we should take any risks. Do you?"

Cold creeps down my spine, and this time, it isn't the hemlock. The way he speaks, the way he *caresses* the glass over Filippa's face—Frederic isn't affectionate at all; Frederic is *twisted*, and no amount of reason will sway him from his course. Bile rises in my throat. He sewed someone else's *skin* onto Filippa's face, for Christ's sake, and he threatened to harvest my eye after he exsanguinates me. Crushing the witchlight in my hand, I smash it against the glass with a snarl. It doesn't break. Doesn't even *crack*. "My sister wouldn't want this," I spit at him.

"I've always found it better to ask forgiveness than permission." After lifting the lid from Filippa's coffin, he brushes his knuckles tenderly down the stitches on her cheek. When he speaks again, however, his voice holds no warmth, no devotion, instead dripping with slow-acting venom. It builds with each word. "Do you think she would've *wanted* Morgane to abduct her that night? To torture and maim her? Do you think—if she stood here now—she would choose death in order to let you live?"

Though I open my mouth to answer—to snarl at him—I close it again at once, the witchlight slipping in my hand. Because I *don't* know what Filippa would choose if she were here. Not truly. I don't know if she would give her life for mine, if such sacrifice is ever fair to ask of another. Even of a sister.

At twelve years old, she swore to protect me, but the promises of children are not the realities of adults.

Frederic glances up at me then, his dark eyes liquid with animosity. "You were never as naive as you pretended to be, ma belle. Even now, you know the answer—even now, you choose your life over hers—but it should've been you all along." His hands tighten protectively on Filippa's shoulders. "It should've been *you* who Morgane punished, *you* who Morgane killed. It was *you*, after all, who fell in love with a huntsman, and it was your beloved father who pilfered witches' wares. Filippa did nothing—*nothing*—to deserve her fate," he snarls, "and if I have to carve out your heart myself, I will reverse it. I *will* bring her back."

Even now, you choose your life over hers.

Frederic won't need a knife to carve out my heart. His words slide between my ribs, sharper than any blade, and impale me until I might bleed to death after all. My gaze darts back to her beautiful, ruined face. Did she truly blame me as Frederic does? In her final moments, did she wish I could take her place? Would she wish it now?

No.

I thrash my head against the thought. Frederic already slipped inside my mind once—more than once, if I'm honest with myself—and if I let him, he'll hack the memory of my sister into pieces. He'll sew her back together again as something gruesome and dark, just like he did to her body.

Bowing his head now, Frederic smooths Filippa's hair, adjusts the collar of her simple white dress. The silver cross gleams bright and silver and perfect around her neck once more. Pressure builds behind my eyes as I stare at it—because it should've been there all along. It should've never left. Frederic should've mourned my sister with the rest of us, and he should've buried her with it. When I speak again, my voice cuts with accusation. "You gave her necklace to Babette. You carved over her initials."

He waves a dismissive hand. "As a show of good faith and protection—Babette's leverage, if you will. It never truly belonged to her, and she never should've staged it with her body."

"Why stage her body at all? Did you *want* me to find her?"

"Of course we did." He scoffs. "Jean Luc suspected a Dame Rouge of the killings. How else could we put him and your precious brethren off our scent? A blood witch needed to die, and Babette needed to disappear in order to continue our work."

He lapses into silence then, smoothing the torso of Filippa's gown. *Preparing her,* I realize with a sickening swoop of my own stomach. I can't let him do this to her. To *us.* Gritting my teeth against a fresh wave of pain, I slip through the veil to check for Mila, for Guinevere, for anyone who could possibly help me. No ghosts linger in the grotto, however, and I fall back through the veil in blind panic, impossibly alone.

Instinctively, I reach for my throat—desperate to feel that small piece of Filippa, of family and hope—but there is only the slender weight of Michal's silver ribbon.

Michal.

Those knives in my heart slip deeper as I glance back toward the water.

A week ago, I would've prayed for a miracle. I would've prayed that somehow, someway, Frederic's Balisarda didn't actually reach Michal's heart. I would've prayed for him to leap from the water unscathed, cold and imperious once more. I stifle a whimper. Because now I cannot even pray for those things, cannot survive the disappointment when the heavens refuse to listen. Even if I survive, this fairy tale will never have a happy ending—and all because I wouldn't listen. Because I forced him to follow me into the abyss, and because I couldn't save him when he did.

I couldn't even save myself.

If Michal isn't already dead, he will be soon. And who knows if Frederic and Babette will spare the others.

This is my fault. *All* my fault.

My breath grows faster, harsher, with each thought, and darkness threatens my vision. Though tears prick at my eyes, I shake my head viciously against them. I can't succumb to panic now. I can't let it overtake me. If I do, Frederic will never get his chance— I'll die before his knife ever touches me.

No. I search blindly for something—anything—to pull me from the brink. Because there has to be hope somewhere. There is *always* hope. Lou taught me that, and Coco, and Jean Luc, and Ansel and Reid.

And Michal.

His name blisters in my chest, warming me like the first embers of a fire. It shouldn't, of course. He shouldn't make me feel this way, but—I have lived, thrived, in a vampiric king's castle for weeks. I have walked among monsters, danced with ghosts, and come to know them as so much more. *That* is the true reality of the world. Of *my* world. A ghost can be selfless, as kind and caring as any other, and a vampire can embrace you in a coffin. He can stroke your hair and whisper that *you* are worth more too. And sisters . . .

Sisters can love each other truly and eternally, even if they have their differences.

The thought lands like a blow to my abdomen.

Filippa wouldn't have chosen herself if it meant sacrificing me.

Conjuring thoughts of her, of *everyone*, I raise my hand and smash the witchlight into the glass. It still refuses to crack, but something shifts in the darkness far above my head, just beyond the ring of light. A flash of wing. A beady eye.

Talon.

I smile—because I know, in this moment, my strength has never been like the others'. I am not cunning or fearless like Lou, nor am I strategic or disciplined like the Chasseurs. No. I am Célie Tremblay, Bride of Death, and my strength has always and will always be in my loved ones. My *friends*.

Talon swoops dangerously low, locking eyes with me, before soaring upward once more.

My elbow threatens to buckle in relief, and I hurl the witchlight toward Frederic when he too glances up. It collides with the glass in an earsplitting shriek. If he realizes Lou is on her way, he'll kill me even faster. That cannot happen. Picking up the witchlight, I smash it against the glass again—and again, and again, until Frederic exhales slowly, forcing another smile. "I allowed you to keep that witchlight as a kindness," he says with obvious effort to return to civility. "Don't make me regret it."

"Pippa knew you were a witch?" I ask, desperate to hold his attention.

"She learned in time. Magic fascinated her."

With one last, fervent look at his beloved, he collects his bowl and knife, rounding her coffin with purpose now. Clearly, the time for talk is over, but if I let this conversation die, all signs point to me dying with it—especially with that knife in his hand. It glints crooked and sinister in the witchlight, goading me into speech. Because I refuse to go quietly. I refuse to let my friends die as collateral damage. "You asked her to run away with you."

"Of course I did." Though it isn't a question, he answers it regardless. And he'll *keep* answering me, I realize, if we keep talking about Filippa. With that horrible, avid light in his eyes, he seems unable to help himself. I just need to stall. I just need to distract him until Lou arrives. "And she agreed. If not for you and your father, much could've been different today. Who knows? Perhaps we would even now be lighting a candle and preparing for Mass on All Saints' Day, hand in hand with Filippa and Reid." He draws to a halt between our two coffins. "It no longer matters what could've been, however. Soon, all will be as it was before." Motioning toward Filippa's stitched face, he says, "As you can see, even Morgane's damage has been undone, and in mere moments, Pippa will wake. She'll breathe and walk and live again, and the three of us will be together once more."

Three?

Unbidden, my gaze flashes to my other side, where I expect to see Babette's little sister, Sylvie, in a third glass coffin. Nothing is there, however. Just empty air and dark sea. Perhaps he still cloaks her in invisibility. *Her* body wasn't necessary to lure me here, after all, yet if Frederic is about to start the ritual, shouldn't someone prepare her body too? Babette risked everything to help him.

"Don't you mean the four of us?" I ask. "Where *is* Sylvie, anyway?"

The water ripples slightly behind him. "I couldn't care less about Babette and her sister. Meeting her was a boon, yes—and sharing a common purpose—but as I said before, the spell doesn't clarify how much of your blood Filippa will need. She gets every drop."

"But Sylvie—"

"—is not my wife or child, and therefore not my responsibility."

The words—spoken so simply—are more paralyzing than any injection of hemlock. I blink, convinced I misheard, before my eyes dart past him to Filippa. Though the plane of her belly still stretches flat and smooth, her hands lie clasped gently upon it, like she cradles a—a— "Oh my God."

Though my mind instantly rejects the possibility, horror grows claws in my own belly, shrieking and scrabbling up my chest, my throat, leaving cruel understanding in its wake. The rendezvous, the note, the elopement—

The three of us will be together forever.

The *three* of us.

Frederic, Filippa, and—

"Frostine," Frederic says in a strained voice, reaching out to graze Filippa's fingertips. The knife in his hand reflects her pale face. "It's a horrid name for a little girl, but I could never deny your sister. Though I suggested Snow as an alternative, she'd already set her heart on little Frost."

It looks like Frost tonight.

"She—she would've told me. If Pip was having a baby, I would have known."

"She wouldn't have left you for any other reason." He entwines his fingers with hers then, as if they aren't cold and limp in his grasp. His mouth twists into a sad smile. "But Frost quickly became our entire world. She meant everything to us. The day your sister found out, she—she walked a mile in the snow to tell me." His grip tightens, and Pippa's fingers crack and bend within it. Gnarled now. "We were going to be a family."

The word rattles through my mind like the tail of a cornered and angry serpent. Family, family, *family.*

They were going to be a family.

And my sister . . . she was going to be a mother.

Pressure builds behind my eyes at the revelation. Inside my heart. When shouts erupt from the shore of Michal's room—when a raven shrieks—the sounds echo as if through a long tunnel, and all I can see is Filippa and her clasped hands. She never told Frederic about her ice palace. Perhaps she tried to forget it as the years passed, as her circumstances changed and her resentment grew, but she could never quite crush the white petals beneath her boot. A tear trickles into my hair. She finally found her summer prince, but instead of dancing in a snowdrop garden, she and her child were buried in it. Another tear falls.

"If it helps"—Frederic tracks the tear down my cheek, transfixed, and he somehow reaches *through* the glass to wipe it away—"I can tell her of your sacrifice. She might even mourn you."

From across the cavern, Lou's fierce voice rises above the rest, and the strange moment between us shatters.

Frederic's wistful expression vanishes at the sound, and I flinch, crying out, as he jerks the knife upward, cutting the ribbon from my throat. "Perhaps we'll even give our daughter yours as a middle name," he says fervently. "It has a certain ring to it, doesn't it? Frostine Célie?"

Though I seize the witchlight and swing it wildly toward his face, he captures my wrist and twists. Just like Filippa's, my fingers crack and break in a fiery explosion of pain. He pries the stone from my hand with ease. It falls to the ground with a clatter—spinning in all directions, disorienting, *blinding*—and skitters toward the water's edge, where—where—

My eyes widen.

Where an alabaster hand thrusts through the waves and crashes upon the shore.

A bloody and broken Michal follows.

He climbs from the sea with straining limbs, and my heart swells, stutters in disbelief at the sight of him. Even the sea cannot cleanse the blood still streaming from his chest. It sluices down his front in a macabre torrent of scarlet, staining his shirt, the rock, the witchlight itself. He shouldn't be alive. He *can't* be alive, yet he still drags himself forward with a guttural, "Célie—"

Above me, Frederic hesitates with his carving knife raised. I seize his wrist with newfound strength, newfound *hope*, and his face twists in shock as he turns and spots Michal. "What the—?"

With both hands, I push against him with all my might, and he relinquishes an inch or two, distracted before whirling back to face me. He bares his teeth. I have been around vampires too long, however, to cower at the sight of him now. Though my arms tremble with the effort, I hold him at bay. Filippa wouldn't have stopped fighting, and neither will I. Until my dying breath, I will *fight*, and even after that too—

In the next second, the scent of magic explodes through the cavern.

The water behind us retreats in response, parting like the Red Sea for Moses to reveal Lou on the opposite shore. Her own arms strain with the effort to hold the waves at a distance. With a roar of fury, Jean Luc sprints toward us along the path on the seafloor, followed by Reid and Coco and Beau. Behind them, Dimitri has cornered Babette, and Odessa pulls on his arm in urgency.

They're here.

I think the words even as Frederic seizes my hair, as a detached part of my mind realizes the distance between us is too great. When he wrenches my head upright and forces it over the bowl, I still thrash and claw at his wrist, however. I still buck and kick and thrust upward with both knees.

Though I shriek Michal's name, he doesn't answer. He *cannot* answer because he is dying too.

Just like the training yard, I think desperately, twisting my body, arching it, my heels slipping frantically against the glass. I refuse to give up. I refuse to cease fighting, and I refuse to allow Frederic to win. *Eyes, ears, nose, and groin.*

I repeat the words like a mantra in my head. Each second I say them is a second I live.

Eyes ears nose groin eyes ears nose—

This isn't the training yard, however, and when my knee finally connects with Frederic's stomach, he smashes my head into the side of the coffin. Pain explodes through my skull in a blinding wave, and hot, sickening blood trickles from my ear. It mutes the sounds of my friends' shouts, of Michal's gasp as Frederic kicks him away, until all I can hear is high-pitched ringing. The edges of my vision blur. Though I scrabble to right myself, I can't find purchase, and Frederic—

A flash of silver. A searing pain. Though I try to cry out, darkness descends as I choke on something thick and wet, and the ringing in my ears reaches a pinnacle, growing louder and louder until I can no longer think, no longer *breathe*—

And everything ends in white.

CHAPTER FIFTY-TWO

A Golden Light

As a child, I liked summer least of all the seasons. I never particularly enjoyed the heat, but sometimes—very early in the morning—I would climb into the tree outside my nursery window to watch the sunrise. I would lift my cheeks to that golden light, and I would bask in its gentle warmth. I would watch my neighbors open their windows, hear their first laughter of the day, and know a profound sense of peace.

Deep in the cavern, golden light breaks across the water.

Instinctively, I sense this isn't the same as my childhood memory. This isn't the sun, and I no longer sit in the tree outside my nursery. This is something different. Something . . . better. The longer I look at this golden light, the brighter it seems to glow, but I cannot quite name the feeling that emanates from within it. I cannot quite feel anything at all.

Though my breath mists as I drift in this nameless place, I no longer feel the cold. *Odd.* I no longer feel any pain either, and the ringing in my ears has fallen silent. Frowning, I peer down at my fingers, examining the dark liquid there. It paints my palms. It ruins the sleeves of my scarlet gown and stains the beautiful lacework black.

"Célie."

Startled, I turn to find Mila watching me with a forlorn

expression. I must've inadvertently slipped through the veil some-how, but that doesn't explain the inexplicable tears in her eyes. "I'm so sorry," she whispers. "This wasn't supposed to happen. When the Necromancer attacked, I—I couldn't help you, so I raced to warn the bird instead. Animals can sometimes sense spirits, even if we can't truly communicate."

"What are you talking about?"

Her gaze drifts below us, and I follow it to the barren islet that rises from the sea—smaller now with the tide, but no less familiar. Frederic leans over one of two glass coffins in the center. With one hand, he lifts the dark head of a pale young woman. In the other, he holds a large stone bowl, and even as we watch, it fills to the very brim with blood.

When he straightens, hurrying toward the second cof-fin, toward *Filippa*, my stomach twists with a profound sense of perversion—because my body still lies in that first coffin. *I* still lie in that first coffin, and blood bathes my hands and throat until I cannot tell where it ends and my gown begins. Though breath still rattles in my chest, my eyes stare upward without seeing.

They stare straight at me.

I drift closer, unnerved, and lift a tentative hand to my throat, fingers gliding with sickening ease across wet skin. Still no pain comes, however, even as I trace the jagged line where my flesh parts. Frederic wasn't neat in his attack. He wasn't clean. With one hand, he now lifts my sister's head, and with the other, he tips my blood into her mouth. "Mila," I breathe, unable to tear my gaze away, "why isn't it cold here any longer?"

She slips her arm around my shoulders, and a creeping sense of dread lifts the hair at my neck. Her arm feels solid. *Warm.* "You don't need to watch this. You need to prepare."

"Prepare for *what?*"

"Death," she says sadly, nodding toward my broken body.

In my periphery, the golden light continues to shine, and if I strain, I can just make out gentle laughter. Except I don't hear it. I *feel* it. It settles within my very skin, but I ignore it, staring at Mila incredulously.

"But I can't— I'm not— *No.*" Wrenching away from her, shaking my head, I dart toward the islet and my body, toward Frederic and Filippa and Michal, who struggles to rise to his knees. "I can't be *dead.* I'm *right there.*" I whirl to face her when she joins me, jabbing a finger at my chest. The blood at my throat spurts in gruesome time with my pulse. "Look—I'm still breathing. I'm not *dying.*"

She brushes the hair from my body's face with heartbreaking affection. A tear trickles down her nose. "I'm sorry, Célie. It's too late. You wouldn't be here otherwise, and you won't be able to stay long—not unless you choose to stay forever."

Not unless you choose to stay forever.

At her words, the golden light seems to dim slightly.

Forever.

"No." I repeat the word over and over again, refusing to hear any more. Refusing to acknowledge that *wretched* golden light. My friends have almost reached the islet now, and they—they'll fix this. Lou and Coco will fix everything, and Jean Luc and Reid will deal with Frederic. Michal or Odessa will give their blood to heal me, and—and everything will be fine again. *Everything will be fine.*

"It might not be so bad," Mila says tentatively, "if you do choose to stay. I'm here, after all—Guinevere is here—and your friends are all human. They would join us soon enough."

Determined, I thrust myself back toward the veil, but I can no longer feel it there. The pressure in my head has vanished, so I fling myself upon my body instead, slipping into it and searching for purchase. I find none. Despair rises through me like the tide around the islet, and I try again, and again, nearly screaming in frustration now. *I cannot be dying. I cannot be dead.* I burst upward in a rush of tears as the golden light grows weaker. "I can't stay here, Mila. *Please*, I can't leave my friends, my *sister*—"

Odessa hurtles past us in a blur then, stealing my plea and knocking the half-empty bowl from Frederic's hands. My blood splatters in each direction as she seizes his shoulders, launches him through the air. He lands hard upon the ground, but Odessa descends just as swiftly, clamping her fingers around his throat. His eyes bulge.

For one glorious second, it looks like she might end this. Like she might kill him before he can hurt anyone else.

Before she can snap his neck, however, Dimitri tackles her to the ground.

Oh God. I dart toward them, frantic, because my blood—it's everywhere, and it's fresh. It sprays the stone scarlet, coats the side of Frederic's body, even runs in rivulets toward the sea. *Oh God oh God oh God.*

For anyone else, this scene would be straight from a nightmare. For Dimitri, this scene is straight from Hell.

"What are you doing?" Hissing, Odessa grapples with him, but her brother's eyes have shifted into something feral and wild. "Dimitri! Stop it! Please, *stop*, and let me go—"

"He still has the grimoire," Dimitri snarls, beyond reason.

I watch them struggle with maddening helplessness. I never would've anticipated this—that Dimitri could attack his own sibling, his own *twin*, but bloodlust proves stronger than even family, it seems. Without hesitation, he flings his sister into the sea, where she hits the water with a tremendous crash.

"*Odessa!*"

Though she can't hear my cry, I still wring my hands and streak after her—then turn abruptly to streak toward Frederic instead. Because I need to do something. I need to *help* somehow, but when I leap at him, my body passes straight through his.

Like I no longer exist at all.

Hopeless now, I look back to my body, which grows paler with every second. As if in emphasis, the golden light dims in unison with my failing heartbeat. *I'm running out of time.* Worse still—I can do nothing to stop it. Nothing to slow it down, nothing to heal the wound at my throat, and nothing to stanch its bleeding. Nothing to save my friends.

"If you kill me"—Frederic bares his teeth at Dimitri, who lifts him into the air by his collar—"you'll never find it."

The grimoire.

If not for that evil little book, none of this would have happened. If only I'd snatched it from Father Achille when I had the chance, if only I hadn't dropped it in Les Abysses—

"Where is it, Célie?" Mila asks urgently. "Where did he hide it?"

"I don't know!" I wring my hands again, stifling tears. "He—he used his blood to turn it invisible, but I didn't see where he—"

My eyes widen in horror, however, as Jean Luc reaches the isle at last.

Like Odessa, he doesn't hesitate, unsheathing his Balisarda and diving straight for Frederic. Snarling again, Dimitri blocks him, but Reid sprints forward with a silver knife of his own. And Odessa—she rises from the water like a vengeful spirit, her eyes narrowing when Jean Luc and Reid attack her brother.

Before either can even move, she hurls Reid into Filippa's coffin, which topples over with Filippa still inside. My sister's body rolls across the stone, her limbs sickeningly limp—end over end—before coming to a halt near the water. Frederic lunges after her with a curse.

"We have to do something!" Even as I shriek the words, however, the golden light continues to fade, hardly a light at all now. My heart lodges in my throat. Because how can I possibly leave them? How can I *leave*? My gaze darts wildly between their faces.

Jean Luc lands a blow against Odessa, and her skin sizzles as she tries to evade him, to protect her brother's back. Reid has vaulted to his feet and now circles Dimitri, searching for an opening to Frederic, who clutches Filippa in his arms.

And Michal—Michal pulls himself to my coffin just as Coco and Beau arrive.

"You need to *decide*, Célie." Without warning, Mila seizes my shoulders and shakes me in earnest, distracting me from my friends. "You can't help them now, and your time is almost up. Do you understand me?" She shakes me harder when I struggle to move past her, to find a way to *help*. "If you don't choose now, you'll lose your chance forever. There's nothing you can *do*—"

But events have spiraled dangerously out of control. Everywhere I look, my friends attack each other. Beau swings wildly at Dimitri, but the vampire knocks the sword from his hand like a child with a tin soldier. Eyes wide, frenzied, he then yanks Beau toward him, sinking his teeth into the soft flesh of Beau's throat. Coco and Odessa scream in unison, and both launch themselves at Dimitri at the same time. Odessa reaches him first.

With another inhuman snarl, he flings Beau aside and snaps his sister's neck.

Even Mila shrieks now, releasing my shoulders and flying forward—determined to stop him—as Coco catches Beau and the two roll into the water. The golden light flickers once, twice, but Odessa—*I can't leave her.* Though I drop to my knees, Mila shoves me toward the last of the golden light. "*Go,* Célie! Odessa will heal!"

"I can't—"

"GO *NOW!*"

When I shoot into the air, however, the two walls of water that Lou held at bay crash together in a cataclysmic wave. Water floods the islet, and Jean Luc slips in the current, seizing Dimitri's legs as the sea bears them both away. Reid clings to Filippa's coffin as Lou steps onto the last bit of stone. Her eyes blaze with fury at the scene before her: Coco towing Beau to shore, Odessa lying prone, Michal clinging to my coffin, and Frederic and Filippa—

Gone.

With a hollow, sinking sensation, I realize they've taken the last of the golden light with them. My chest gives one last, shuddering breath before falling silent too. No one notices, however.

No one except Michal.

He leans over my body, his beautiful, ashen face crumpling at the exact second my heart fails. He can hear it. He knows.

His forehead collapses against mine in defeat, and I cannot help it—I shift closer, rapt, as his lips begin to move. "Please stay," he breathes.

With the last of his strength, he drags a hand through the blood on his chest and presses it to my lips.

EPILOGUE

It is a curious thing, the scent of memory. It takes only a little to send us back in time—a trace of orange juice on my fingers, a hint of faded parchment under my bed. Each reminds me of childhood in its own strange way. I would sneak into the garden at midnight to pick the oranges, peeling them in the moonlight and eating them fresh. On the parchment, I would write my own fairy tales and keep them secret from my sister, tucking them into the shadows beneath my bed. Hiding them there.

She wouldn't have understood their meaning. How could she? I hardly understood those stories myself—tales of swans and magic mirrors, yes, but also of betrayal and death. In some, my heroines would triumph, conquering great evil and dragging their prince back from Hell. In others, the prince himself would be great evil, and he and my heroine would rule Hell together, hand in hand and side by side.

Those stories were always my favorite.

When I wake that morning, the first thing I see is snow. It falls thickly, silently, from an overcast sky, and it kisses my cheeks in a gentle caress. It softens the sound of waves. Calloused fingers brush the hair from my face as I sit up, glancing around the boat. "How do you feel?" a deep, familiar voice asks.

The sound of that voice should set my heart racing. I never thought I would hear it again.

My heart, however, remains quiet. It remains still, and if I listen hard enough, I might think it doesn't beat at all.

"Hungry," I say, accepting the gilt mirror in his hand.

Though he tucks the blanket tighter beneath my legs, concerned, I do not feel it. In truth, I do not feel anything—not the cold, nor the warmth, nor even the heady rush of his touch. It set me aflame once. It dragged me down to Hell.

Lifting the mirror now, I gaze upon my reflection in the snow. I trace the row of dark stitches, examine the pale skin that is not my own—the slightly lighter brow and the emerald eye—and I smile.

Perhaps we can rule it together.

ACKNOWLEDGMENTS

As always, I owe a tremendous debt to many people for the creation of this book, and—as always—I extend much of that debt to *you*. The reader. Spin-off series like this one don't happen without you. They don't happen without the devotion you've given to not only me, but also to my characters. Though Célie takes center stage in *The Scarlet Veil*, I never would've been able to tell her story if not for the outpouring of love you gave Lou, Reid, Coco, Beau, and Ansel. We're all in your eternal debt.

RJ, Beau, James, Rose, and Wren, you somehow manage my deadlines better than I do, but I still want you to know—I cherish each secret knock on my office door. Never stop interrupting me. Never stop bringing me cheese and crackers or making me Tupperware snow globes. You're the brightest part of my life, and I love you all more than you'll ever know.

Mom and Dad, your kitchen table is a sanctuary; there will never come a day when I turn down lunch with the two of you. Thanks for listening to me, for supporting me, and for advising me. Most of all, however, thanks for loving me for who I am, not what I do.

To my lovely family and friends, both near and far, thank you for all the game nights, for all the Catan fights, for all the coffee dates and charcuterie boards. Thank you for every text or phone call to check in—I appreciate each one of them, just as I love and appreciate each one of you.

Pete, I am forever appreciative of your guidance and forever awestruck at your keen understanding of the publishing industry. My situation has been trickier than most, but you didn't hesitate to step into my corner anyway. That meant and continues to mean everything to me. Thank you.

Erica, after six years together, I can confidently say I trust no one more with my work—and no one has been more patient with it either. Thank you for being kind. Thank you for understanding when I need more time. Thank you for loving Lou and Célie, and thank you for helping me write this absolute brick of a book. If your bookshelf collapses under its weight, it'll make an excellent doorstop.

Alexandra, Alison, Audrey, Jessie, Kristen, Sara, Lauren, Michael, and the rest of my incomparable team at HarperTeen, thank you, thank you, *thank* you for the care you've given this book. Your creativity and skill have been imperative to bringing *The Scarlet Veil* to life. I think a trip to NYC to meet (or reunite with!) everyone in person is long past due.

And last but never least, Jordan Gray . . . I often attribute Beau's wit and charm to you, but I never could've written a character like Célie—who is unapologetically soft, feminine, and vulnerable—without your guidance. I still remember sitting down to write *Gods & Monsters* and hesitating when you asked, "What about Célie?" Though I'm ashamed to admit it, I'd already dismissed her as the jealous ex-girlfriend. You challenged me to see her differently—as a flawed character, yes, but also as a sheltered, grief-stricken young woman with a spine of steel. She became an homage to strength because of you . . . and isn't that fitting? You inspire me daily. I love you always. Thank you for being my sister.

Can love triumph over death?
Célie and Michal's flame burns on in

THE SHADOW BRIDE